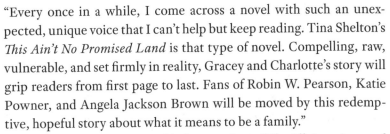

"Every once in a while, I come across a novel with such an unexpected, unique voice that I can't help but keep reading. Tina Shelton's *This Ain't No Promised Land* is that type of novel. Compelling, raw, vulnerable, and set firmly in reality, Gracey and Charlotte's story will grip readers from first page to last. Fans of Robin W. Pearson, Katie Powner, and Angela Jackson Brown will be moved by this redemptive, hopeful story about what it means to be a family."

—Susie Finkbeiner, author of *The All-American* and *The Nature of Small Birds*

"In *This Ain't No Promised Land*, Tina Shelton delivers a fresh voice, examining how wounds can get in the way of relationships. With stellar storytelling skills, she reminds us that love isn't always enough to erase the hurts, but it's the only way to survive them. A powerful read!"

—Julie Cantrell, *New York Times* & *USA Today* best-selling author of *Perennials*

"Tina Shelton's *This Ain't No Promised Land* is a powerful story about family—especially mothers and their daughters. How we are hurt, how we unwittingly pass on that hurt, and how we can heal too. It's gritty and unafraid to ask hard questions, all while being nestled in a vibrant 1980s South Side Chicago setting."

—Janyre Tromp, best-selling author of *Shadows in the Mind's Eye*

"*This Ain't No Promised Land* captures several sweet yet gritty coming-of-age stories. Some take me back to my childhood and others give me a glimpse into other teens' lives as they wrestle with life and family issues. Tina Shelton has creatively woven together these stories to create an excellent novel that invoked several emotions. A job well done!"

—Katara Patton, author of *Navigating the Blues*

"This book tells a story of the rich textures of family, unraveling, and finding redemption. Told through the experiences of three generations of Black women, *This Ain't No Promised Land* evokes the unique challenges and wells of resilience that sustain them and their families. Deeply evocative of *The Women of Brewster Place*, Shelton's storytelling masterfully draws us into the landscapes of place and heart, demonstrating that the thread of love is what finally saves us, even if we don't know why. A wonderful read."

—Dr. Stephen G. Ray Jr., former president of the Society for the Study of Black Religion and coauthor of *Black Church Studies: An Introduction*

This Ain't No Promised Land

A Novel

This Ain't No Promised Land

TINA SHELTON

KREGEL
PUBLICATIONS

This Ain't No Promised Land: A Novel
© 2024 by Tina Shelton

Published by Kregel Publications, a division of Kregel Inc., 2450 Oak Industrial Dr. NE, Grand Rapids, MI 49505. www.kregel.com.

The author is represented by MacGregor & Luedeke.

The persons and events portrayed in this work are the creations of the author, and any resemblance to persons living or dead is purely coincidental.

Library of Congress Cataloging-in-Publication Data
Names: Shelton, Tina, 1973– author.
Title: This ain't no promised land: a novel / Tina Shelton.
Description: Grand Rapids, MI: Kregel Publications, 2024.
Identifiers: LCCN 2023034689 (print) | LCCN 2023034690 (ebook)
Subjects: LCGFT: Christian fiction. | Novels.
Classification: LCC PS3619.H4535 A73 2024 (print) | LCC PS3619.H4535 (ebook) | DDC 813/.6—dc23/eng/20230919
LC record available at https://lccn.loc.gov/2023034689
LC ebook record available at https://lccn.loc.gov/2023034690

ISBN 978-0-8254-4851-5, print
ISBN 978-0-8254-7167-4, epub
ISBN 978-0-8254-7166-7, Kindle

Printed in the United States of America
24 25 26 27 28 29 30 31 32 33 / 5 4 3 2 1

To Lessere and Millard Sudduth
You'll never know how much you taught us about love.

CHAPTER 1

Gracey
September 1987

MY MOM WAS THE OPPOSITE of Clair Huxtable. Whenever Mrs. Huxtable talked to her children in that lovey-dovey tone on *The Cosby Show*, I thought, *Why can't I have a mom like that?*

Clair's voice was smooth and confident. Mom's was soft and unsure: "Honey, how about you put on your coat before going out?" Clair would have said, "Gracey, put your coat on before you open that door!" If I came home in a funk because my kind-of sort-of not really not-at-all boyfriend, Sebastian, rejected me like he does whenever he gets a new girlfriend, Clair would have gotten me a warm cup of milk, a slice of cake, put her hand on my shoulder, and said, "Sit down, honey. Tell me what that silly old boy Sebastian did today."

My mom would take one look at me, draw a deep breath, and look around awkwardly like she was trying to find the right words between the flowers on the blue-and-green wallpaper. She'd eventually ask me how my day was. I'd say fine, and she wouldn't press any further. I mean, dang, "Are you okay?" would have worked.

But at least she'd been there.

After all, she was peaceful. And she didn't yell like Grandma did, and she was pretty. And she baked. Chocolate chip anything was good for me. Francine liked snickerdoodles, which we all know she got from watching a cooking show on WTTW, 'cause I never seen Black people around here serve them as an afternoon snack except Mom, and that was because Francine was forever asking for them. She knew how to use her position as the youngest to get what she wanted. Joanna liked lemon cookies, but Mom hardly ever made those. She considered sugar cookies a nice compromise. I've heard people say the oldest kids never get what they want, and yeah, from what I've seen of Joanna's life, that was kind of true.

Sometimes the way Mom looked at us let us know she loved us, but her real thoughts were trapped inside her body and, in order to know what was really going on, we had to read, pick apart, and divvy up whatever her soul offered. We had to listen to her breathe, like the way she sighed deep at night with a sliver of a high-pitched hum. That let us know she was tired of trying to figure out whatever it was she was forever trying to figure out, but she was gonna stick with it anyway.

We had to watch her eyes, the way they lit up when she saw us walk through the door after school. We had to soak in the way she traced our hairline with her fingers when we were waking out of sleep; the touch of her thumb to our cool cheeks when we were crying. We had to watch which piece of baked chicken she'd give us at dinner and compare the sizes of our cake for dessert. We watched for her reaction to us when we stood next to her on the porch and watched the sun go down. If she smiled, she loved us; if she sighed and looked down the street, we were a nuisance. Having Mom around was like watching the sky in the spring. When she was okay, the sun shined and she made the world a happier place to live in, but when she wasn't, it was overcast. But even with all that quietness of her soul and our gray days, we knew we were better off with her home than not.

Who knew emptiness could fill every nook in a space with such thick silence? My eyes opened in the blue of dawn, and there it was—a thick, silent presence that flowed in and out of my body. The smell of polished wooden floors became the scent of barrenness; and the faint smell of greens and ham hocks lingering in the walls released chatter from early summer when we were all here. It was so quiet after Mom left that I welcomed the sound of cars passing by and crackheads fussing outside our window on their way to the main street.

So when Sebastian, with his olive skin and wavy hair, tall and fine, and with them sprouting muscles and little peach-fuzzed mustache, came out with that joke—"Yo' mama so stupid, I taught her to do the running man and she didn't come back"—I snapped. I pounced on him like a panther.

'Course everyone was doing the running man dance at parties, so the whole class busted out laughing, but it felt like they knew my business and were making fun of me. The truth of it made my soul ache. Now I wished I hadn't gone off 'cause I broke my own rule about staying out of trouble so me and my sisters could remain invisible. If nobody saw us, nobody could snoop in our business, and we could stay in our empty old house. I was starting to hate our hollow home, but it was still the only place in the world that kept us sane. And we didn't want anybody from school butting in, especially not my eighth-grade teacher. She'd be trying to fix everything and all the while blowing up our world.

When I got out of my fourth day of detention for doing the panther thing, Sebastian was waiting for me as he had all the other days. Mad as I was at him, seeing him always made me happy. I could hardly camouflage my smile. Soon as I turned the corner, he was in step with my rhythm. "So how was it?"

"Fine," I said, clutching the straps of my backpack and never making eye contact. Secretly, I wanted to bury my head in his chest and tell him everything that was going on and shed a few tears but we—me and the crew inside my head—knew that wasn't gonna happen, so I sucked it up and kept quiet. It was nice enough that he walked with me.

"You still salty about the yo' mama joke?"

"You ask me that every day, Bastian." I rolled my eyes. "I already told you I'm done with it."

"Alright, alright, it just seems like something's, you know, standin' between me and you being cool, so I've been trying to figure it out."

I shook my head like an Etch A Sketch to erase the conversation and change the subject. "Ever wonder what it's like to be an orphan?"

I could hear our steps like beats between my words. "Nobody to watch over you, nobody to answer to. You're like some dandelion fuzz bouncing from thing to thing wherever the wind blows."

"Why are we talking about orphans, Gracey? What's that got to do with anything?"

"Just wonderin'." I shrugged. "I couldn't sleep the other night, and got to thinking about *Little Orphan Annie*. You know, the comic strip in the funny papers?"

"You shoulda gone to bed."

"Yeah, maybe," I said.

Chicago's WGCI was playing after-work jams, and all the cars on the main street were bumping the same song. We stopped at the crosswalk in front of the rib joint with the barber shop next door and did a little bounce with our hands in the air while we waited for the walking man to light up. It was me, Bastian, and the music in our awesome bubble. Folks were bobbin' heads in their cars and giving us a thumbs-up. The moment was surreal, like the street was an extension of the comfort I was used to at home.

We finally walked across. "You think you can grow up to be a good person without parents?" I asked.

"Well, I don't have a dad, and I'ma grow up to be dope!"

"I don't have a dad anymore either."

"Yeah." Sebastian paused and nodded at his friend walking in the opposite direction. "I heard it's super hard for girls. They get all mixed up and start looking for love in whack places. Then it's a downward spiral of kids, brokenness, and heartache."

I pushed him with my elbow. "You're such a jerk."

"You know I'm kidding," he said, then laughed at his own joke. "We're both gonna be fine. You're not an orphan and neither am I. But even if we were"—he pointed up to the sky—"the Big Man upstairs would take care of us."

I looked to the sky as well. Maybe that was what Mom was doing on the porch back in the day, praying to the Big Man upstairs.

"Whatever."

I I I

Of course, my sisters and I didn't want to be classified as orphans, but it was how we felt. We were livin' in the fallout. Learned that word in history class. After a bomb, there was the fallout, and that was just as dangerous 'cause bricks could break loose and fall outta nowhere. Mom had only been gone a couple of weeks, but we were lost. We spent the first couple of days watching TV on the couch. We ate Twinkies and Zingers and cereal instead of dinner. We didn't go to bed or turn the lights off. We didn't take baths at night; we took short showers in the morning instead, which always made us a few minutes late to class.

We combed each other's hair but were afraid of washing it because it was too thick to detangle. Before, it took Grandma to comb through our waves with her thick afro comb. She parted our hair into jigsaw pieces and braided them, letting our hair air-dry overnight. It was the only time we got to go to bed without a scarf, and she always turned up the space heater in our room so we wouldn't catch cold. Then Mom would straighten our hair in the morning with a hot comb. The best we had as a replacement was Joanna, and she didn't have the patience to do anything but bunch our hair into one ponytail in the back of our heads. She pressed our bangs to make us look presentable, but that was it.

We didn't hardly do any homework. Not 'cause we didn't care. We just didn't have anyone to help us when we got stuck. Plus, we didn't have the energy to push past much of anything 'cause mostly all we could think about was where's Mom and why'd she leave after everything that happened over the summer and what were we gonna eat. And none of us got any of that deep, sound sleep we had when everyone was in the house—Mom, Dad, and even Grandma. A couple weeks in, and we were like house cats sitting on the windowsill, waiting for Mom to come home and take us back to normal.

"Y'all, how long are we going to live like this?" Francine stood in the doorway in her footie pajamas, hands on her hips. She was good at living like a twelve-year-old. Other kids in our neighborhood were eons beyond her. They knew all the bad words, they knew about sex, and they could do the fast-girl dances. But Francine was like them kids on *Sesame Street* and *3-2-1 Contact*—her mind was curious and her heart seemed weightless as a kite, like heaviness never lived in our home. Until now.

"I'm starving," she whined. "If we don't eat a decent meal soon, I'll turn into a toothpick."

Francine was also the most lost. She never respected the fact that Mom and Grandma didn't get along. She didn't understand why Mom only gave us a fraction of her love. And she didn't understand that when Dad walked through the door and lightened the mood with his grin and booming voice, he was actually pretty drained from work. There was never anything in Francine that made her want to shrink back and protect herself from anybody in the house. She'd climb all over Dad like he was a growing tree in the back yard. She hugged Mom too, even when Mom could barely hug her back, and she kissed Grandma on the cheek on her most ornery days.

Don't get me wrong, Francine would snap at you in a second if what you said hit her the wrong way. But for the most part, she loved and forgave freely without a second thought. It was only now that she was starting to feel the sting of absence with all our adults gone.

"Shut up, Frankie," Joanna said. Not sure when she donned herself queen of the house at sixteen. "You're such a baby. Grow up!"

"Why would I want to do that? Growing up is a slow process done gradually over time. Besides, you grown enough for all of us."

I rolled my eyes and Joanna huffed, but Francine wasn't done.

"I'm serious, you guys. I want real food. I can't be expected to take care of myself." She began walking the back of the couch like a tightrope. "Whoa," she said, almost falling. Pippi Longstocking flashed through my imagination. She'd never fall.

"Frankie, get down before you hurt yourself!" I yelled.

"That's a very grown-up thing to say," Francine announced, folding her arms over her chest. "I elect you to be our new mom, Gracey." She jumped down and sat on the couch properly. "So what's for dinner?"

"What?" Joanna gaped like a fish. "She can't be our new mom. I'm older than her."

"Yeah, but you don't act like a mom," Francine said. "You don't care what I do. All you care about is that I don't get on your nerves."

Joanna shrugged. "Ain't that how most moms are? Think about it—the grocery store, on the bus, at church. Moms act like you ain't there and then the second you start cuttin' up, they yell with that twisted, ugly face."

"Our mom didn't do that." Francine tilted her head to the side. "Her face was always soft and sad. Sad and soft."

Joanna shrugged again and walked a couple of steps to sit on the piano bench. Quietly she turned and played one random out-of-tune key at a time. The Methodist church on the corner was giving it away to make room for a new one, so Dad and his boys brought it in. We never got it tuned, but it made us look classy to the neighbors. None of us took lessons, but we could plunk out the melody of a song or two.

Joanna was a normal moody teenager like the rest of her friends. She knew all the latest songs and her wall was covered with posters of the latest actors and singers with their shirts off showing sweaty muscles, like it was a hundred degrees during the photo shoot. New Edition, Force MDs, Al B. Sure!, and Chico DeBarge—they surrounded her bed as she went to sleep. She liked to gossip with her friends and get all caught up in high school drama. She talked about her friends behind their backs and then got upset when it boomeranged back to her. Then she'd shut out the whole world and be mean to me and Francine. Of course, we'd take it 'cause we were pretty used to the women in our house being upset. Dad's the one who was always loving us forever like a big teddy bear, even when the bickering was nonstop.

I blew out a big breath. "Come on, Frankie. Let's go see what we can find to make for dinner."

"Yes, let's go, Mother!" Giggling, she squeezed my hand as we walked through the swinging door to the kitchen. We felt victorious for some reason, as if we were making progress in taking care of ourselves.

When the door finally stopped swinging, we heard a clashing bang on the piano keys, and then footsteps stomped up the stairs. On the real tip, Joanna had the same temperament as Grandma, though none of us would ever say it out loud.

Joanna wanted everybody to act the way they were supposed to. Mothers were supposed to mother, fathers were supposed to father, and grandmothers were supposed to be loving and supportive. It was like she had all these pent-up feelings because her friends were off and on, and only Daddy ever lived up to what he was supposed to . . . and then he died. And she couldn't say jack to us now about roles 'cause she just broke hers as older sister by refusing to take care of us.

"Don't mind her." Francine nudged my shoulder. "She's mad because she can't be the mom."

I yanked open the freezer and stared blankly. Everything was frozen, but I remembered Mom running meat under hot water for a long time to defrost it enough to cook. Grandma always complained that Mom didn't plan ahead enough, but she could pull a meal together no matter how late it was.

"We're not playing house, Frankie," I sighed.

"Oh yes we are," Francine said, her voice coated with attitude.

Jesus, how long?

CHAPTER 2

Gracey
May 1987

ONE NIGHT, LIKE MOST EVERY night, my whole family watched sit-coms and laughed. Joanna sat on the shag carpet, Grandma was in her old rocking chair, Dad was in his cushy leather easy chair, and me and Frankie were next to Mom on the sunken red velvet couch that Dad found in an alley behind Miss Nelda's complex. Miss Nelda was our neighbor across the street who felt like extended family. She was Mom and Dad's go-to when they had a date night and Grandma had bridge with her old-lady friends.

Francine had her legs all stretched out on me, and Mom was sitting next to the edge with her legs crossed. Twenty minutes into the last show, there was a shift in the room like always. There were only a couple of minutes left, and me and my sisters knew that soon we'd have to get ready for bed and finish up whatever homework we hadn't done before TV time. Normally we'd either become really quiet so the adults would forget we were in the room and roll through the commercials into the next show, or we'd cause a distraction to get Daddy to go upstairs with us. That night I chose distraction.

"Frankie," I scolded. "Why you always gotta put your feet on me?"

"'Cause you're comfortable." She squealed and stretched out even more.

"I don't care." I pushed her feet down grumpily.

"Ow," she whined. "Why are you so mean? I wasn't hurting you."

"I don't care . . . keep your feet off me. You're not a stupid cat."

"Meow."

Daddy broke in with his deep, soothing voice. "Alright, alright, you all go upstairs. I'll be up shortly to check on you."

"But, Daddy, wait! I'm not sleepy," Francine said.

"Me neither. Can't we watch one more show before going upstairs?" I begged.

"They have school tomorrow, Moses," Mom said, uncrossing her legs. "And they haven't even finished their homework. You all should go to bed now."

"I'll never understand why I have to go to bed at the same time as them," Joanna complained. "I'm two years older than Gracey and four years older than Frankie. Now, does that make sense to you?"

"Yep." Grandma always had something to say. "Don't nobody want to see no kids all night after they done worked hard all day. Now get your behinds upstairs and get to bed."

We all rolled our eyes and kissed our teeth.

"Besides, Joanna," Dad said, "you don't have to go to sleep. Just chill in your room. You could read, catch up on homework, talk on the phone, dream up a plan of how you're going to be successful when you grow up—"

"But, Dad," Joanna protested. "Every other teenager in this world has full freedom in their house until well after midnight, and y'all in here acting like this is some private VIP room after nine o'clock."

"Maybe it is," Grandma said. "I got some steamy movies I been waitin' to see."

"Iona, that's enough outta you." Dad looked up toward us on the stairs. "You all don't mind your grandma; she gets more bitter the older she gets."

Thirty minutes after we had gotten into our pajamas, Dad came up and turned on our night-lights.

"All right, girls. Tell me one good thing about your day."

"Hmm . . ." Francine said. "I can't think of one."

"Nothing?" Dad questioned. "Nobody brought in cupcakes for their birthday?"

"Come on, Dad. We're too old for *Romper Room*. Oh, wait!"—she interrupted herself excitedly—"I know what happened! My teacher liked my paper so much, she read a paragraph to the whole class."

"Really? And how'd that make my baby girl feel?"

Francine paused and then shrugged. "Smart."

He tucked her in. "Well, that's because you are." Francine melted in his smile.

"Gracey, what happened in your day?" Dad asked, shifting his body toward me.

"Nothing."

"Nothing?"

"Nope, nothing."

"Who'd you walk home with?"

I covered my head with my blanket. "Daaaddd!"

"What? What's wrong?" Dad asked innocently while giggles bounced about from Francine's side of the room.

"Did somebody special walk you home or something?"

I knew Dad was smiling with those dimples that made my heart warm. From the dark of my covers, I answered, "Sebastian."

"Who?"

"Sebastian," I said louder.

"Ooooh, Sebastian." Dad pulled the cover from over my head and tickled me. Francine laughed to high heavens that night.

He even made Joanna laugh with a pillow fight. We could hear the flops as they popped one another with the pillows. Their laughter made us envious, but me and Francine knew not to barge in because this time was meant for the two of them. Besides, for some reason, I think we both wanted to make our time with him linger in our room. The faint smell of Dad's cologne was still in the air, and it helped us sleep.

We didn't open our eyes again until we heard Mom scream at four in the morning. We ran into the bedroom, and there was Dad, flat on the floor like he'd collapsed on his way back to bed from the bathroom. But why? Mom was pumping his heart, and Grandma was breathing into his mouth, but he wasn't moving. Finally, the sound of sirens roared down the street, and big men with clanky equipment you only see in hospitals stormed into our little house.

They moved us all out of the way, then bent over Dad. They had electrical pads that they rubbed together and placed on his bare chest after yelling "Clear!" His body jerked upward and then dropped to the ground just as lifeless as it was before. A couple more rounds and then finally, they called it. That meant that was when they called him gone. I looked at him on the floor, and he looked like an empty house. Nobody was home. No light to be seen nowhere, no sign of hope that maybe somebody was making their way to the door.

We all stood there waiting, holding our breath, ignoring the big people. Just waiting. Mom waited with her head on his heart as her tears dripped on his chest. Eventually, we realized he wasn't going to return.

I couldn't believe the sun had the nerve to still come up as if it didn't care about what just took place, as if my dad's life was so insignificant that the rest of the world could go on like normal. Folks around us still went to work that day, and children still ran down the street to make the school bus, and mean dogs still barked when the mailwoman passed by—and there we were, frozen in time, unable to move. Why should we move? How could we?

The fact that we were still breathing when he wasn't seemed unfair.

By the afternoon, though, our house was filled with food and flowers. Our phone was ringing off the hook, and people kept stopping by to sit with us. They had more questions than we had answers, so after a while, we were all exhausted. You can only say, "I don't know," so many times. And Grandma wasn't letting nobody cry more than we were in our living room.

To one woman, she said, "Honey, why don't you go home and get some rest. All that crying won't bring Moses back. Just stop it and go on home." So the lady left with a handkerchief to her nose and the apple Grandma put in her purse.

We had the funeral five days later, and afterward, everyone came to our house again. My sisters and me, we sat on the stairs and watched a sea of black move steadily around the living room, talking to one another and eating whatever sweet and soulful foods people set on the table. Mom was surprisingly present and spoke in soothing tones to all who came to console her. She reminded me of Diahann Carroll from *Dynasty*. And that was weird.

Even Joanna noticed. "Mom looks really intelligent right now," she said. "I mean, not that I think she's dumb. It's just that she looks like she's . . ."

"Awake," I said flatly. It was the only word that came to mind.

"Yeah," Joanna responded, as if I'd nailed it.

"I was gonna say 3-D," Francine said.

"Frankie, what?" Joanna's face was squinched around her glasses, which she only wore when she was willing to risk her vanity to see clearly.

"Well, 'cause that's what we're learning in class. There's flat shapes and 3-D shapes, and Mom looks 3-D."

"Whatever," I said. "Awake, 3-D—she's different."

"Yeah, but why?" Joanna cocked her head to the side as if it would help her better analyze the situation.

"I don't know," I said.

"Maybe 'cause she has to be. Look at all these people!" Francine sounded frustrated, and I felt the same.

Miss Nelda passed by on her way out. She looked at each of us individually with her teary red-veined eyes and warm smile. "Y'all need anything, just come on over. I'm almost always home unless it's Easter or Mother's Day, and then I'm at the church. I go to the post office and Dunkin' Donuts 'bout once a week, but that's only in the mornings, you know." We half smiled back and cleared her path.

We sat in silence the rest of the time, watching the black waves continue to wash in and out. We all knew if Dad were here, he'd have made a beeline straight for us, scooped us up, and taken us to McDonald's for ice cream and then a movie. When we came back, everyone would have been gone and we could have our home back. But he was dead, and it would take us a long time to understand what that really meant—that there wasn't a single person in the room who cared for us as much as he had.

School ended a week later, and we all spent the summer adjusting. Grief was like an unwanted weight in our house that made our shoulders slouch more than we cared to notice. Sometimes we couldn't sleep at night, so we'd catch the sun on the way up and ride it into the day with a game of Double Dutch.

Francine would call from across the room, "Gracey, you awake?"

"Yup, let's go."

Then we'd tap on Joanna's door, and she'd come out in her cotton pajama pantsuit, wire-rimmed glasses, and the long white cable rolled up in her hand. Our goal in the morning was to jump as fast as we could for as long as we could. The first neighbor to leave for work left at 6:14, so we'd stop at 6:05 according to Francine's stopwatch and go inside. Once we showered and got dressed, we'd go back to bed for another couple of hours.

It was easier to sleep in the day than it was in the night. The sun brought us comfort that the night couldn't afford.

CHAPTER 3

Gracey
June 1987

THE FIRST DAY OF WARM weather in June was when the plastic film around our windows came down. Anything earlier had Grandma thinking there was a ghost in the house because of the cool breeze that seeped through the cracks. For me, it was probably one of the best days of the year. We all had to spring-clean with our aprons on and our bandannas tied around our heads as scarves.

Daddy used to put the word *beautiful* in front of our names to combat our complaints of feeling ugly. We had trouble understanding what qualified as ugly. All we knew was that if we went to school looking the way we looked with our hair hanging out of our scarves, we'd be called ugly. But when we looked in the mirror, we didn't really see ugly. And the girls they called ugly at school were beautiful to me and my sisters. They called kids ugly for the glasses they wore, the pimples they had, their dark skin, or their thickness. Only brown-skinned Barbies were safe from ugly. But Daddy made it so anyone could be beautiful. He defined that word so everybody was in. No matter how messy our hair was or how many blemishes were on our faces, even on our most pitiful, sickliest, sourest days, he still looked at us with that twinkle in his eye. And we kind of believed him.

So this year when the warm day came and Dad wasn't here, in honor of him, we tied the scarves around each other's heads and pulled at the plastic until the staples popped out.

"Beautiful Frankie, get that side." I tugged the edge of the loosened plastic sheet.

"Okay, Beautiful Gracey!" She ran and pulled her side out. And on we went until Joanna was ready to fold.

"Beautiful Joanna, here you go." The plastic dropped to the floor, and she began to fold in the same manner of clean fitted sheets.

"Oof, this plastic smells awful when it gets old. Why do we have to save it year after year?" Joanna griped. "Daddy was so cheap, bless him."

"Yeah, always ready to save a dollar by getting the black-and-white brand on the shelf."

"Generic food sucks," Francine muttered.

"Tell me about it. Copycat food without the magic that makes it taste like the name brand."

"Shhh." Joanna interrupted our conversation. "You hear that? Sounds like Mom and Grandma are having an argument again." We opened the window and held our breath so we could catch every word.

"What's this about, Mama?" Mom was tugging on Grandma's suitcase, trying to pull it from her hands. "Why you leavin' like this?"

"'Cause it's too cold here," Grandma said, frowning. "I always did plan to move back to Miss'sippi. This is as good a time as any, before the winter hits."

"The winter? Summer hasn't even set in good, and you're talking about leaving before the winter? Try again, Mama. Why now? Why today?"

"Because it's Monday."

"So what?"

Grandma froze like she was trying to come up with something clever. "So Monday is the best day to start afresh. And Moses was our buffer. Without him, we're like bad knees, bone on bone."

"Mama, what about these girls? Our family. Don't we mean anything to you?"

"Yeah," Francine whispered low enough for only us to hear. "Don't we mean anything?"

"Charlotte, you're a grown woman. You better get in that house and take care of your family. I can't do it for you."

"Is this about Micah, Mama? You know I tried to tell Moses. I ran out of time. I didn't know—"

"Who's Micah?" I whispered. Shoulders shrugged.

"Ain't got nothin' to do with Micah. That's between you and God now."

Grandma's taxi driver honked the horn, urging her to hurry. Mom grabbed her arm. People peeped through their curtains, and some boldly stood on their lawns to listen.

"Then you're leaving because Moses is gone, and you think we don't have enough money to take care of you. I told you not to worry about that, Mama."

"Charlotte, I'm leaving 'cause I got to go." The taxi driver loaded Grandma's suitcase in the trunk and opened the door for her.

"Ain't you gonna say goodbye to the girls?"

"I already said my goodbyes, Charlotte—last night while you was still sleepin' in the bed at five o'clock in the evening."

"I just lost my husband a month ago, Mama!" Mom screamed. "What do you want me to do—turn cartwheels up and down the street?"

Grandma pointed to the house.

Mom whirled around and saw us looking out the living room window. She stood there, trying to read us, and we tried to read her. We could see the word *sorry* in her startled eyes. She didn't mean for us to see or hear any of this. We wanted to tell her to get out the street and come inside. We knew not to go outside and make things worse. The neighborhood had already had enough drama for the day.

"Fine. Goodbye, Mama," was all our mom said as she turned back around and closed the taxi door. She chose our peace over her own. After the car drove away, Mom pulled the lapels of her housecoat toward each other and tugged the tie tighter around her waist. We could tell she was hurt even if we couldn't grasp all the reasons, so we went upstairs to me and Frankie's room.

"Who's the Micah dude?" I asked again, scratching my head. "Did Mom cheat on Dad?"

Francine hummed while deep in thought. "I don't think so. She's not good with flirting."

"Yeah," Joanna said. "That's the last thing she would do. Forget all that—when did Grandma come to say goodbye to us?"

"She didn't." I plopped down, cross-legged, on my bed. "She was obviously lying."

"Yeah, but for real." Francine sat on the floor in front of her bed, using her pillow to cushion against the metal frame. "We did watch a movie together, and we had popcorn, and she let us stay up as long as we wanted."

"And when it was time to say good night, she said . . ." Joanna paused.

And then we said in unison, "I love you."

CHAPTER 4

Gracey
September 1987

ME AND MY SISTERS DIDN'T find out Mom was gone till we got home from school. We came in, threw our backpacks on the ground, and went straight to the kitchen for our afternoon snack.

"Mom, can we have pork chops for dinner?" Francine asked. No one answered.

"Mom?" Francine called. "Mom!" She went upstairs, and we could hear her sneakers thumping on the floorboards. "Mom? Where are you?"

She came down the stairs. "You guys, where's Mom? She feels gone."

Joanna shrugged. "She's probably at the store or running an errand for Grand—I mean somebody, whoever."

Francine was right, the house did feel weird. We were becoming familiar with the eerie silence of an empty house, but this was different. Then my little sister reached into the cookie jar and pulled out a letter instead of a Nestlé Toll House cookie. She read it silently to herself, the paper close to her eyes. Her face took on sadness like the start of rain.

"What?" I asked.

"What is it?" Joanna stopped moving.

Francine said nothing.

We lunged forward and snatched the letter out of her hand. And then our kitchen felt like it was hit with a monsoon.

"You made Mom run away!" Francine yelled at Joanna. "If you weren't so mean to her, she would have stayed."

"What are you talking about?" Joanna shouted back.

Francine, not taking the time to explain, pushed her to the ground and unloaded with punches and slaps.

"Frankie, stop!" I yelled, as I ducked her flailing arms and pulled her small frame off Joanna.

"I hate you," Francine yelled through tears and gasps for air. "What are we going to do now? Huh? We have no family." She collapsed on the stairs and wailed, "What did we do to deserve this? Why is this happening? Where's God?"

I sat on the stairs next to her, hugging my knees but having nothing to say. I knew God was with us, but I didn't know how to explain that to Francine. God was holding us, that was all I knew. Even in our aloneness, we were still being held. We were warm; we could think; we still had each other.

I was confused too, though. I thought we were finally starting to break into Mom's space. We could ease into her silence, and she wouldn't casually move to cover her womb as if we might try to burst from her all over again. She wasn't breathing to brace herself so much, and she never seemed bothered by the shade of brown that covered our growing, curving bodies like those mothers who were afraid society couldn't handle our Blackness. So why would she leave when we were finally starting to get comfortable around each other?

"I bet she left 'cause we didn't do our chores when she told us to," Francine whispered.

"What? Frankie, that's stupid," Joanna quipped from the velvet couch. "Don't nobody leave 'cause their children don't clean up. What kind of love is that?"

Francine shrugged. "I don't know. It could happen, I think."

"Nah." I shook my head. It had to be more than that. "I think she left 'cause she was scared of something."

Joanna's palm flipped up. "Like what?"

Francine gasped and put her hand over her mouth. "Was she afraid of us?"

"Nah, something deeper, like—"

"The dark!" Francine belted out.

"Yeah, like being alone in the dark," I said.

"I'd be afraid if I had to sleep alone in the dark," Francine said. "I forgive her. No, actually I don't. That's a stupid reason. All she had to do was come sleep with us."

"I'll never forgive her," Joanna said.

Then it dawned on me. My heart sank. "She had to sleep in the same bed, in the same room where Daddy died."

"That is kind of awful," Joanna said as if deep in thought. She rubbed the soft fuzz of baby hair around her edges, then stopped suddenly. "You guys are so immature," she snapped. "People don't leave because they're afraid of the dark. They leave 'cause they don't wanna be responsible for other people."

"So what are you saying?" Francine stood up with a balled fist.

Joanna stood up to meet her. "What d'you think I'm sayin'?"

"That *your* mama didn't want *you*." Francine stepped closer to challenge her big sister. "But you can't say she didn't want me, 'cause I'm the one who helped her cook and we look 'the split of each other,' like Grandma says."

"Come on, you guys. It doesn't matter why she left." My arms were out like a referee. "She's gone and we don't know where. Nothing we do to fix whatever we did wrong can bring her back."

"Look, I am too young to be grown, so y'all better figure something out," Francine said with a twang in her voice.

"We need a plan." I took my fluffy ponytail down and put it back up again to help me think. "If the cops find out, they'll split us up and put us in foster care."

"We're not going to foster care," Joanna said.

"Fragglerock!" Francine exclaimed. "I can't be away from you guys. I promise you, I wouldn't be able to breathe. I'm already having trouble catching my breath just thinking about it. It's too much. *No más. ¡No más!"*

Daddy had loved watching old matches and explaining them to us. I remember all of us staring at Sugar Ray Leonard's opponent saying those words when he lost the boxing match. I never thought we'd see ourselves as anything other than Sugar Ray champs, shaking up the world like Muhammad Ali, yet here we were, like Roberto Duran, saying "no more."

CHAPTER 5

Charlotte
August 1963

THEM WARM DAYS DIDN'T STOP in Mississippi, and cool breezes got to be caught during the sunrise so they could be fondly remembered in the afternoon. Weren't nothin' to do but take care of your own and be in everybody else's business for entertainment. That was way more interesting than TV. Men didn't come home till the evening, and when they did, they sat on the porch with their pipes hanging out the side of their mouths and drank moonshine, raising a hand when the cars honked as they drove by.

Seemed like nothing made a Black man happier than seeing another Black man on the same dusty red road. And it weren't like they was lazy; they weren't. Or no good; they were good. Or unintelligent. No, these men were geniuses, if you ask me. Any man that can make a railroad hold a train or a farm sing God's glory or a house stand on its own with plumbing and electricity—he gotta be more than a moonshining, porch-swinging baby maker. Their main problem was, with the world on their shoulders, they couldn't see their way round to better, and they were so tired of tryin', they settled, one smoldering day at a time. Most of my aunts, they knew that about their men, that they'd had the try beaten out of them. And when the try was gone, the anger set in like layers of packed soil.

Aunt Flora, for instance—she always came to my folks' house with her bag packed to stay for a while. Always the same: She walked lopsided in her thick shoes made for nurses. One shoe had a heel thicker than the other to help with the unevenness.

31

I remember one time, Daddy watching her come up the hill. "There come Flora Jean with that big old bag," he said.

"You gonna let her stay the night, Travis?" Mama asked.

"Iona, you know we got too many mouths to feed to be taking on one more. 'Specially a grown woman like that."

Daddy got up, raised a hello hand, and went into the house before Aunt Flora made it to the steps.

"Flora, what you doin' with that bag?"

"In case Travis let me move in with y'all, I'm ready. Girl, I got my toothbrush, my housecoat, and everything all ready. I can go anywhere and take root."

Mama shook her head and continued shelling her peas. "You never know, might be me coming to your house one day with my bag. You gonna let me in?"

Aunt Flora flew her head back and hollered, "Girl! Shoot, yeah, I'll let all y'all in. We'll figure somethin' out." Then she lowered her voice. "What, you and Travis having trouble?"

Mama raised her voice so Daddy could hear. "Me and Travis is fine, thank you, Flora. One day, you gonna come over here and Travis gonna let you stay a spell, I'm sure of it."

"Uh-huh," Aunt Flora sang from the melody deep in her chest. We all knew it really meant, "Girl, I know you just talkin'. Ain't nothin' round here ever gonna change."

Aunt Flora looked my way, gave me a once-over, and said, "Miss Charlotte, what you know, girl? You been keepin' up in school?"

"Yes, ma'am."

"Good, 'cause education is what'll get you out the South. Either that or a man, and I can tell you right now, you better off with th'education."

And then she and Mama went back to talking about their pitiful marriages.

Mama and Daddy weren't fine. It was hush-hush, but we all knew Daddy had two sets of families. We were legit with rings and certificates and titles, but the other family's the one he loved. The word traveling through the trees was that in the next town over, we had siblings that look just like us. I remember asking my brother, Julian, about it one day. He was out fishing by the river. I brought him a cola I got from town and two fried bologna sandwiches wrapped in a red-and-white checkered tea cloth. He was a quiet brother. Didn't say much, but I knew inside his head was an entire world movin' and groovin'. But when he fished, he blended right in with nature. The water made the sunrays glimmer as the mallard ducks rested along the bank, and he was a peaceful addition to the tree he leaned against.

We sat quietly, and I watched him eat for a while, then I asked, "You ever want to meet them?"

"No."

"Why not?"

"'Cause Daddy's gonna leave one day to go live with them. And if we ain't enough to keep him here, then he should go."

His words hit my gut. I turned my face toward the wind to hide the quiver in my voice.

"Why?" The ache in my throat barely let me speak. "Why would he choose them over us?"

"I ain't figured that out yet, and I'm not sure I care enough to try."

With a deep breath, I shifted my body back toward the water. I could see my brother's outline against the sun—same as our father's but with gentler edges.

"So far as I can tell"—his voice rode on the sound of the slow-rolling waves—"the only difference is their skin is lighter than ours. That's what people tell me anyway. And the mom is way thinner than ours."

I turned my head ever so slightly to catch his facial expression from the side of my eye. I was afraid he'd shut down and flutter away like a bothered bird. I pushed anyway. "When did you see them?"

There was a tug on Julian's line, and he reeled in a small catfish. He finagled it off the line and dropped the whiskered critter into his bucket.

"I was working at the county fair over in Olive Branch on the Fourth of July, and there they were. A whole happy family—two girls, one boy, and a beautiful mom with long curls and an hourglass body. Daddy kept his arm around her the whole time."

"Did he see you?" Facing Julian now, I could read every inch of his face. I looked hard, trying to find some sign of foolishness, but nothing.

"Did he see me?" His voice had a bitter note I didn't recognize. "Came right up to my booth and won his baby a teddy bear. Looked me dead in the eyes, tilted his hat, and said, 'Thank you, son.'"

We sat for a while, our thoughts moving to the pace of the river, undercurrents carrying pain to the depths we didn't know we had.

"Well, he must care some about us. He still lives in our home."

"Yeah, but, see . . ." Julian began to theorize. "We live in the house he built with his bare hands. I reckon they live in the house he bought."

"So?"

Julian finally turned to me. "So how would you feel if I stole one of them Popsicle-stick houses you always building?"

"This ain't the same, Julian."

"How would you feel?"

I relented. "Mad as ever."

"Why?"

"You know why. 'Cause I built it."

"Exactly. Same with Daddy. If he leaves, he knows this house is ours and he can't have it back. The whole town would stand behind us too 'cause Dad's a deacon in the church and he should know better than to act like God ain't watchin'."

"So then maybe he'll stay."

"No, he won't. He's too weak, and that lady's got him wrapped around her finger. She thinks she's going to win him over for good someday, but he won't be faithful to her either." Julian tapped his temple. "He's the kind of man that'll go from family to family pretending to be a man. But when things get rough, he'll find another woman who thinks he's great and stay with her until she finds out the truth and starts to make him feel bad about himself."

"How you know that, Julian?"

He leaned back on his elbows. "I listen to the barbers at the shop. The ones who been there thirty, forty years. They respect real men and tolerate the no-good ones. It's a difference, you know? And when the no-good ones leave, they forecast what's gonna happen if they don't fix up."

"You heard them talking about Daddy?"

"No. But my buddy did."

"What'd they say about him?"

"Same thing I said."

I kissed my teeth. "Poor Mama."

"Good riddance."

I was sure Aunt Flora knew all about Mama's problems with her husband. But she wouldn't bring it up in the light of day with the winds alive and flowing free. No, she'd wait until the midnight oil was burning on the porch and every child was sighing peacefully in their bed. Last time I saw her, she waited till she thought Daddy was passed out drunk, laying across his bed, and there she came up the road with her bag.

"Let me sleep on the porch, Iona." She pulled out a small decorative pillow and a thin blanket. "Ain't nobody gotta know. I'll leave come daybreak. My jaw still healing from the last time. I can't take much more. Just need time to get some sleep."

"Go on ahead, Flora," Mama said. "You ain't gonna get no fuss outta me tonight."

Flora made her little pad and let her body rest. With her eyes shut, me watching from the window, and Mama looking out into the night, she summoned strength from the heavens just by laying dead still and slowly filling her lungs with air and letting it go. Maybe it was my imagination, but seemed like embers from fires near and far made their way down to her body and sank into her golden skin. All the while, Mama kept on rocking in the swing, like she'd seen this a thousand times before. Like she knew that, in desperate times, the body prays what words cannot say, and God answers in ways well beyond what magic can do.

Finally, Aunt Flora turned on her side and said, "You know you better off without him."

Mama lowered her head. "Yeah, I know."

"You got two strong boys. They'll take care of the farm."

"They need to be in school."

Aunt Flora sat up on her elbows. "And y'all need to eat."

Mama took a deep breath, then let her words out. "They'll hate me for it."

"What you supposed to do, Iona? Ain't no other way."

"What you gonna do, Flora?"

Aunt Flora took the shift. "Chile, I don't know. I'll either leave or fade away. Leaving is hard; ain't nobody willing to take me in."

Just then a breeze picked up, and the sound of my daddy's snoring interrupted the cicadas' sustained tones.

Mama's voice went softer, and I had to stick my head out the window to hear.

"Go on, Flora. Leave this town and go as far as God'll take you. When the Lord say stop, then stop and start your life over again."

"I don't know, Iona. Might be better off if I just die."

"That's the devil, girl. Ain't none of us better off dead. Long as there's a God in heaven, we got reason to run on and see what the end's gonna be." Mama pulled a roll of money bound by a rubber band from her bosom and gave it to Aunt Flora.

"Here, li'l sister. Now is as good a time as any. Nice night." Mama swayed easy in her swing. "Stars are shining bright, so the sky is clear. Crickets are chirping and the dogs ain't barking. Just enough peace to hide you till you get to Olive Branch."

Aunt Flora took the money and put it in a small pocket of her bag. "Thank you, Ona."

"Do me one favor, though, Flora."

"What's that?" Auntie said, standing up now.

"Don't, uh . . ." Mama sounded like she was holding back a cry. In the moonlight, she wiped a tear with the handkerchief she kept folded neatly in a rectangle. "Don't look back, you hear? Just . . . just keep going."

When Aunt Flora got to the bottom of the porch, I bolted down the stairs and ran after her. I hugged her with all my strength and pressed my cheek against hers until my skin warmed.

"Don't cry, baby girl," she said. "I'll see you again someday. Even if—" She stopped and patted my cheek. "I'll see you again."

That was the first time somebody close to me walked out of my life and didn't return.

CHAPTER 6

Charlotte
July 1964

JULIAN WAS RIGHT ABOUT OUR father. He had another family. And he loved them more. One night when we had all finished eating, I got up to clear the table, and he told me to sit down. Then Mama got up to do it instead, and he stopped her too. Then he said, "Everybody, let's sit down for a minute. I got something to say."

Me and my brothers looked at Mama's face to see how she'd react. Everything depended on the look in her eyes, whether my brothers would beat his selfish behind or let him walk out of the house in one piece.

"Go on, Travis." Mama sat down slowly.

"I, uh." He suddenly looked nervous, like it just hit him what he was doing was wrong but it was too late to back out. "I have to leave. I, uh . . ." His eyes lowered from embarrassment. Then he took a deep breath as if mustering up the courage to say it, but something wouldn't let him. "I, uh . . . have . . ."

Julian spoke very slowly as if to help him formulate his thoughts. "You got to go and take care of your other family that is younger than ours."

"Yes," Daddy said with a sigh of relief as if he'd spoken the words himself.

Mama showed no emotion, save a small frown that kind of looked like she thought he was such a pitiful man. "Well," she said to our father. "You pack your things and go on then. We keepin' the house.

And you gonna continue to pay the bills, 'cause we might not be young but we was here first, and that ought to count for something."

I remember that day. Mama put on a brave face as he packed his suitcases and walked out the door. The boys were nowhere to be found, but me and Mama stood there and watched. We didn't hug or say any words. He lifted his hand as he got into the car. Then I sat on the uneven cement steps and watched him drive down the road, but Mama went inside. I heard dishes crashing to the ground, along with quick bursts of screams as she thrust them through the air. And for some reason, I felt a warm presence, as if Jesus come to sit down for a spell. When my brothers got home, we sat outside and listened to Mama weep until there was silence. We didn't clean nothin' up till nightfall.

That was the second time somebody walked out of my life and didn't return.

CHAPTER 7

Gracey
September 1987

THREE MONTHS HAD GONE BY between Grandma's parting and Mom's. At least she'd waited until school started and our minds were busy . . . most of the time anyway. One night things were kicking up in the house. We watched *A Nightmare on Elm Street* and fell asleep right where we were sitting. Popcorn was scattered on the coffee table, and our mugs, still half-full of hot chocolate, were sitting on their coasters. Our bowls of instant oatmeal had dried solid.

We'd never slept in the living room until recently, but with all the adults gone, going upstairs to get ready for bed seemed too much like right and we wanted to spite them, even though they'd never know. We did what we wanted when we wanted. A house of anarchy, it was. And we dared anyone to call us on it. But that night, I heard the door creak, as if somebody was trying to enter the room quietly and the hinges told the tale. We were used to the noises in the house, the sound of water spitting from the pipes when the heat came on; the way the toilet ran longer than normal after flushing. We knew the sounds—when, where, and why. But this creak was different.

"Y'all hear that?" I nudged Francine's feet off me.

"What?" she asked, pulling her knees to her chest and rubbing her eye with the base of her hand. "Do you think it's Freddy Krueger?"

"Y'all, dude is not in this house. It's just a movie." Joanna didn't even bother to open her eyes. "Go back to sleep."

We would have listened to her, but then we heard an even louder creak, one that was undeniable. Francine screamed, and Joanna's feet hit the ground and she sat at attention, listening hard. I grabbed a broom from the kitchen and was making my way up the stairs, but Francine put on her fluffy house shoes and grabbed her pullover from the hook by the door.

"I'm going to Miss Nelda's." She said this matter-of-factly, as if it wasn't up for discussion.

Joanna got up and scooted into her flip-flops. "Wait for me," she said. "I'm coming too."

I felt kind of foolish standing there by myself. And with them gone, the house felt all the more intimidating, like the walls were inching toward me. I knew if I stayed any longer, some otherworldly hand would reach out and grab me. And there was no way I could beat him down. I dropped my broom, grabbed the keys, and ran out the house too.

Joanna and Francine were standing outside Miss Nelda's door, shivering.

"Why isn't she opening up?" Joanna asked.

"She could be 'sleep," Francine said.

I tapped on the window inside the iron gate, where everybody else did when they wanted her attention. We could see her shuffling toward the door, using the wall to support her here and there.

She stopped by the closet to put on her blue-tinted wig. She must've just put her dentures back in, 'cause she was still trying to find the good fit. I don't know why she did so much to answer the door. It was only us.

We listened to several locks unclick before we saw her face clearly. "What y'all doin' out here this time of night?"

"Freddy Krueger's in our house," Francine blurted.

Joanna took a deep breath as if she was never scared. "No, that's not true, Miss Nelda. We heard some questionable noises and thought—"

"What?" Miss Nelda said. "You think there's a burglar in the house?" She turned to walk toward the phone on the wall. I quickly looked around at her pictures. She had one with Martin Luther King Jr. and another with Jesse Jackson Jr. There was also a certificate on her wall for helping to make good bread in a basket.

"No, not a burglar," I said. "Well, maybe. Or maybe a ghost or something. It sounds silly now . . . but it was kind of scary when it happened."

"Well, I could call my nephew to go check it out. He's a policeman."

"Oh no, ma'am!" We all said it, right at the same time.

Then Francine said more. "It was probably the wind blowing the door open."

"Yeah." Joanna crossed her arms and held her elbow. "Or maybe a tree outside hitting the window."

We all laughed till I thought of something else. "Or you know what? It coulda been a cat that snuck in from the tree. It walked around and scared us, but now it's gone. I bet it's gone now."

"Yeah, probably is." Francine nodded awkwardly. "We better head back now."

We were making our way out the door when Miss Nelda stopped us. She was looking Francine up and down. "This chile done peed her pants. You mean to tell me you want to go back by yourselves?" She shook her head. "Oh no, I'm going with you, and I'ma take my pistol. It's already in the pocket of my duster."

Me and my sisters exchanged looks. Our quick glances said, *Why did we come here? We shoulda just went upstairs with the broom and checked it out ourselves.*

At the house, Miss Nelda stood still in the center of the living room. She got real quiet and told us to hush. I could see her chest rising and falling as she took in air and let it out through her nostrils. Finally, she relaxed.

"Nah," she said. "Ain't another living soul in this house. Ain't no ghost here, neither, 'cept what the walls remember."

Joanna looked at Miss Nelda sideways. "How you know that, Miss Nelda?"

Miss Nelda smiled and went to sit down on the couch. "You live long enough, you start feeling things and knowing things about the space around you. You can sense when others are with you. And can't nobody teach you neither. You got to live into it. But these walls"—she threw her hand toward them—"Lord, they can talk, can't they? Make you think you seein' and hearin' things. Take you right back to the moment stuff happened. Make every li'l sound remind you of a moment when folks were really here. I bet you hear your daddy laughing sometimes; probably hear him snoring too."

She was getting worked up a little bit, I could tell. Her eyes were larger than usual and before she spoke, her chest swelled, rising like the sea. And yeah, those things did happen, I heard Daddy in my sleep mostly—his deep laughter that ended in a chuckle, his loud snoring from the bedroom, the way his feet pounded the wood and took on the stairs when he was late for work. I even heard his keys in the door, too many times to count.

A while back, I taught my heart to stay calm no matter what I heard or imagined. Sometimes, though, I thought it misunderstood me, 'cause I didn't feel much of anything, good or bad, anymore. Except this night, and maybe that was 'cause everyone else did. We had a shooting in the night a couple of days ago. Sounded like firecrackers far away, a *bap* instead of a *pop*. We knew they happened, but we couldn't put our thoughts behind them. Daddy always taught us not to let shootings stop us from being free, so we didn't. We took on every day and night like a game of dodgeball—keep moving and don't get hit. Not that the shootings were balls we had to dodge, no. It was the grown-ups, always finding questions to ask and take us down.

"Y'all know what you should do when you get scared?" Miss Nelda asked.

"What?"

Miss Nelda sniffed the air. "Francine, take them pants off and go take a bath."

"But, Miss Nelda, what about Freddy Krueger?" Francine whined.

"When y'all get scared, you got to sing or something. It'll make the air feel better."

"Sing? Like what?" Joanna sat down at the out-of-tune piano.

"Like 'What a Friend We Have in Jesus.' Remember that from Sunday school?" She sang a few bars, and Joanna one-fingered the melody on the piano. We sang after her, kind of guessing the words as we went.

Finally, with a shake of her head, Miss Nelda told us to stop. "Now, Francine," she said, "you sing that song out loud all the while you upstairs and take your bath. You'll be fine. Go on."

And off Francine went, yell-singing with every step she took. We could even hear her singing as the iron tub filled with hot water and bubble bath.

Miss Nelda made her way to the kitchen while me and Joanna stayed in the living room. We could hear her humming and cleaning in there. Before long the smell of coffee brewing filtered in. It'd been a long time since the aroma of bitter beans filled the air. Both me and Joanna sniffed it and smiled. Neither of us liked the taste, but coffee smelled like comfort to us, like a house full of adults pitching in to keep our lives together.

Minutes later, we heard Miss Nelda as she sat down hard at the kitchen table, her chair scraping the floor. She groaned and said, "Lord, have mercy."

I went in quick-like to see about her. The ceramic teddy bear cookie jar was open, and Miss Nelda was holding Mom's letter that we kept stored inside it.

She began to read it out loud the way Grandma did when she got mail that excited her.

Dear Francine, Gracey, and Joanna,
I had to go. And it's not because of you; it's because of me. I'm
sorry. This was the hardest decision I've ever had to make in
my life. But I feel like the Lord's left me with a challenge that
I can't meet. Who am I to try to raise three girls by myself? If
you all turned out good by my hands, that'd be a miracle. But

I know it wouldn't happen because God don't do miracles in my life. I've done too much wrong in the past, and it's catching up with me. Your daddy dying was the worst thing that could have happened to us.

To be honest, I've been looking over my shoulder for years waiting for the shoe to drop. I just didn't know how hard it would drop or when. Everybody says God takes care of fools and babies. More like God gives grace to the fools who think they can raise babies.

I figure you all have a better chance of turning out all right if I take myself out the picture. You're still innocent. Make sure you stay that way. Clean hands open big hearts. That's just something I've noticed in life.

Joanna, you're sixteen now, you're responsible. If you feel something's wrong in your heart, don't do it, and don't let the girls do it neither. I'm sorry for some of the things I said and done. Girl, every time I look at you, I feel guilty. There's something about your brown eyes that causes me to feel things I don't have time to deal with.

And Gracey, you're that magical age of fourteen, when life changes all around you and you're on the cusp of growing up. When you was a little girl, old folks used to look at you and say, "She been here before." That means you're wise. You've always been wiser than your age. Slow to react but quick to love. From what I hear, that's what grace is all about.

Miss Francine, you may not believe me, but you are special. My beautiful baby. You got strength inside you you don't even know about. I seen it. Make sure you protect that heart of yours. God's ability to read our hearts is the only hope some of us will ever have.

I don't know what else to say, really. This is something I have to do. You probably won't understand it now, but maybe later you will.

Girls, love each other and keep the house clean just like I left it. You never know who's watching over you.
  Love,
  Your Mom . . . Charlotte

Miss Nelda put the letter down and looked at me. Her eyes were full of tears. "Honey, I'm sorry this happened to you . . ." She shook the letter in the air toward God. "Lord, have mercy. This don't make no sense. These girls done lost so much already, and now Charlotte?" She patted the table as if she was hitting heaven's door to open up. "Mercy, Lord."

The whole time she was reading the letter, I felt nothing, not sad or angry. My whole soul was still within me. But when I saw the tears and the thin, red veins like rivers spreading in her eyes, I got confused. Inside, I felt conflicted, like maybe I should be feeling what she felt. But why would I feel that way? We weren't important enough for anybody to cry over us. We weren't here like everybody else was.

Here people were cared for and had loving families like the Cosbys. People who are really *here* lead normal lives. We weren't nothing like normal.

I frowned. "Miss Nelda, calm down." I rubbed her shoulder the way people on TV do when a person can't control their emotions. "We're fine. There's no need to worry or even feel sorry for us."

The more she patted the table and said the word *mercy*, the more I felt a stirring inside. If I was a well, my waters were filling and I didn't know how to control the spill. Whether it was right or not, or good or bad, I draped my arms around Miss Nelda and cried into the back of her shoulder.

"I'm sorry," I said. "I'm sorry for crying."

Her head leaned toward mine and her hand reached up to squeeze my shoulder. "It's all right, baby," she said. "Don't you be sorry. You got every right in this world to cry."

CHAPTER 8

Charlotte
September 1987

I WAS SCARED THE DAY I left my children. I didn't experience any joy in leaving, save seeing the girls' faces as they came down the stairs that morning. Joanna came jogging down in a black spandex miniskirt and what looked like two torn exercise tops layered on top of one another. Her pimpled skin was covered in makeup and her eyes came alive with black liner. Her lips were shiny with chocolate mint lip gloss. With Moses buried and Mama gone back to Mississippi, she had gotten so bold.

"Mornin', Mom," Joanna said as she prepared her milk and cereal.

"Mornin'." I gave her a full-body once-over. "You wearin' that to school today?"

"Yep, it's what all the girls are wearin'." Joanna posed like a model to accentuate her outfit. "No big deal."

I kept my eyes low and took a sip of coffee before speaking again. "You might want to—"

"But I don't want to, Mom, okay? So leave it."

Gracey was next to run down with her backpack hanging open and her papers leaving a trail behind her. "Hey, Mom, I'm almost done with my homework. Can you help me with this one problem?"

I cringed at the sight of her homework, a constant reminder of what I didn't know. "You all know this ain't my—"

"I know, but Daddy's usually the one who helps me and he's—"

"Dead," Joanna said flatly.

Gracey whirled around. "You need to stop trippin'. I didn't ask you for all that!"

These children made my head hurt. Moses was Mr. Mom, Mr. Fix-It, Mr. Kiss-It-and-Make-It-All-Better. He could unravel every planet in the universe and spin it together again if you gave him time. All I could do was push a seed in the ground and water it, like the average farmer. I missed him too. He was a nice living partner. More than a roommate, less than a lover.

Joanna sniffed. "Just stating the facts. He's dead and he's never coming back. Nobody to help you with your homework now."

"You're so mean." Gracey narrowed her eyes. "How could you talk like that about Daddy? And you talkin' about Mom like she ain't even here."

Since the funeral, everything I did upset Joanna.

"Girls, please." I clapped my hands. "Gracey, I'm sure one of the teachers at school could help you with your work."

Joanna flattened her lips. "See."

I turned on the radio to lighten the mood—a daily tradition we had. WGCI's morning show was all jokes and the latest music. A little Whitney Houston, and the girls were singing away instead of arguing.

Finally, Francine rumbled down the stairs in a flowered under-shirt, jeans, and one shoe. She was holding a purple blouse with marble buttons.

"Mom, my thingy fell off, can you sew it back on?"

"She don't know how to sew," Joanna jumped in.

"Yes, she does. Grandma taught her," Francine tossed back. "You know how to sew, don't you, Mom?"

"Yes, of course I can sew, Frankie. But I don't have enough time to do it before school. Go get another blouse."

"See." Joanna flicked her hand dismissively.

Francine put the blouse down and stomped up the stairs.

"You angry with me about something, young lady?" I'd had enough out of Joanna.

"Yeah," Gracey chimed in. "What's the deal?"

"I'm not angry." Joanna finished her cereal and washed her bowl. "I just like to keep it real. You don't know how to take care of us. And you haven't worked in years. Face it, all you know how to do is keep a house clean."

Gracey jumped to her feet. "If Grandma were here, she'd steal on you like Dominique did Alexis on *Dynasty*." In a flash I replayed the Diahann Carroll slap to Joan Collins on the show. She never saw it coming.

"And if Daddy were here"—Joanna's eyes were still on me—"he'd ground me for a week. But neither of them are here, so . . . whatever."

Joanna bothered me of course, but her little daggers weren't enough to make me scold her before the leave. I looked each one of my girls straight in the eyes that morning, told them I loved them, and sent them out the door with a tight squeeze.

But the second the door closed, I felt like a rope being pulled in opposite directions. I had taken my time all morning long—bathed, cleaned the house, made some cookies. Finally, I had a chance to write my letter. I could have sworn the peace in that house was begging me to stay. I hadn't factored in how nice life could be without Mama looking over my shoulder all the time, reminding me of all the bad I'd done. Even in my mind, there was peace.

For a second I thought maybe I was just panicking and, really, if I stayed, I'd lean into motherhood like plants lean into the sun. Maybe I could stay and love my girls and they'd love me back and we'd be a normal dysfunctional family that sticks together like the rest of the nation. I could almost envision them needing me and relying on me instead of their grandmother or their father. We could do this. We could be a family, just the four of us . . . but sooner or later I'd have to tell them the truth, and what would they think of me then? Everything would have been okay, but truth was sure to knock me out the game.

So I left fast, before they or anybody else could catch me, before their eyes could talk me into staying. I wasn't going to be responsible for any more bad happening to the people I cared so much about.

Might be hard at first, but I knew they'd make a home between the three of them. Gracey wouldn't let them fall too far before she put a cushion between them and the world.

I thought about stopping off and talking to Nelda. I wanted to ask her to watch over my girls. But the more I considered it, the more ridiculous a request it seemed. What woman goes to another woman and says, "I'm leaving my children. Please keep an eye on them for me"? Miss Nelda probably would have bolted the door, put her pistol on the table, and said, "Don't make me hurt you, darlin'. Go on back to your children and grow them up like a good girl." The way Mama talked, our neighbor was a sour old woman with a few loose screws, known for carrying her gun in her housecoat. But I have my suspicions that Mama was just pulling tricks to keep Miss Nelda away. Even so, before I walked out, I stood still until I could fabricate some low tides of peace, and then I asked God to somehow tell Miss Nelda to look after my girls.

❙ ❙ ❙

Took me a few days to make my way south on Amtrak. I didn't know when or where I'd wind up, but Savannah, Georgia, had a sweet ring, like it would be kind to a woman like me, nonjudgmental, believing me to be innocent from hello. So that was where I stepped off the train and thought, *This'll do for now.* I ended up working at the first B and B I stayed in. They had a sign at the front desk: "Help Wanted. Cleaning lady with Southern hospitality needed to work at Claremont's, the best Bed and Breakfast in town." Mind you, I applied after my money was too scarce for comfort. I needed a few days for my thoughts to settle and peace to be still.

Georgia was a good place for me. It was just like being home in Mississippi, except all the familiar faces were gone, and I didn't have to hesitate every time I turned a corner or went into a store. The air was clean and warm and everything grew. It wasn't like Chicago, where the trees were few and far between and their tops were trimmed at right angles to accommodate the trucks and buses that passed by. In Georgia, the trees stood like towers, and yet they were knobbly like elderly folks, as if each had its own amazing story, like climbing onto the limbs would impart some type of wisdom from conversations spoken hundreds of years ago.

I used to have a friend named Sheila May who was terrified of living next to trees.

"What's wrong with livin' next to trees?" I asked her.

"Don't you know, Charlotte? They near suck the life out of you."

"Nah, Sheila May," I told her. "You got that wrong. Trees give life."

"Nah, girl, I'm tellin' you, I know. Like all them hangings we had last summer—you think them trees don't remember? Slaves used to hide in these woods, tryin' to blend in so well the dogs couldn't smell 'em. The second they was caught, the pain of the whippings, the sounds of vicious dogs, the vile yelling, the name-calling. All that evil had to go somewhere. You think them tree trunks didn't soak it in? Of course they did. Like the rings that tell their age, they soak in the atmosphere. Then half a century later, we come walking through the woods, and we can't figure out how come we feel like we walking through a ghost land. And they call this the promised land, please. This ain't no promised land. You got to till the land for your own promises in this life and pray God give you time to take root long enough to make something of yourself. You couldn't pay me a million dollars to live next to trees, unless the Lord take a bucket, a brush, and some Joy, and wash 'em all through and through."

"Maybe that's why God sends the rain and then the sun come cutting through."

"Huh." Sheila coughed. "That might work in the daytime, but come nighttime, them memories come to life."

I didn't have a comeback. Nothing would change her mind, and she was kind of right. Even if the woods weren't full of yesterday's ghosts, they were dangerous. When I was a kid in Mississippi, moonshiners brewed their liquor back in those woods. Bloodhounds were tied to trees back there, herbalist and root doctors were back there, speakeasies were back there, and wasn't much room for quiet folks trying to live quiet lives.

But I tell you what, them trees carried our songs as well. They could hear our church hymns from miles away, and if you sang any one of 'em while walking through the woods, the winds would change and the Spirit would come and rest on the branches.

I used to love going to church back in the day. The whole South felt easy on Sunday. Honest to God, it was the thing to do. It didn't matter how much sinning you did during the week, as long as you came to church on Sunday, everything was gonna be all right. You could walk home feeling like fresh linen. But say you fell off the wagon and went wild with sinning and stopped going to church? Well, then, you were a heathen for sure and not worth the two-second glance it took to say hello and nod. I don't know what happened with me and church. More and more I felt edged out like I didn't belong, like everybody was looking at me and whispering. Got to the point where I couldn't even get to God for all the people between us.

Looking back now, I think that was where everything—all my problems, all my pain—began. In the church . . . when Micah Richards walked into my Sunday school class.

I was proud as a peacock, being the youngest Sunday school teacher at the age of twelve. Everybody else my age was in the junior class throwing spitballs and giggling over their Bibles. But Ms. Jenkins said I was such a mature Christian, I needed to be teaching. All the other teachers were fifteen and sixteen, and they never took the time to prepare their lessons. Like Sheena. She was always running after me on the way to church trying to find out what Scripture the lesson was taken from.

So when Micah Richards walked in, looking all confident and nonchalant, I told him he'd have to go to the junior class, since he seemed to be about my age.

"Uh, no," he said with a sweet smirk on his face. "Ms. Jenkins sent me in here to help you teach." He pointed in my direction.

I looked at the children and smiled, and then I sized up this Micah kid. He was thick-boned and had a fullness like satisfaction. And his eyes were so alive I had to look away. That was when I noticed the dimple that dug into his earlobe like needle-pricked dough. He had on a nice suit like it was Easter, and his shoes were shiny with a squared-off point at the top. A showboat.

I didn't care what he looked like, he wasn't going to teach a class with me.

"Uh, you must have misunderstood Ms. Jenkins. You see, you have to be a mature Christian to teach Sunday school, and I don't think you fit the qua-li-fi-ca-tions." I said the word slow to stress the meaning.

The kids started whispering and giggling. "Charlotte and Micah sittin' in a tree, kissing—"

I turned and stomped my foot. "Y'all, shut up."

They sang louder. "First comes love, then comes marriage . . ."

One of the snaggle-toothed girls was singing so loud, Ms. Jenkins came walking over.

The children hurried to finish. "Then comes thebabyinthebabycarriage." They were all laughing so loud they had to hold their hands over their mouths.

"What in the world is going on over here?" Ms. Jenkins had her hands on her hips and was looking down at us over her bifocal glasses.

"Ms. Jenkins, I don't need nobody in here helpin' me 'cause I'm mature. You said so yourself, remember?"

"Obviously not as mature as I thought you were, Miss Charlotte. This boy is my nephew. His father is my brother-in-law who happens to be the bishop over the eighth district of the AME church. He's living with me for a while till his mama and daddy get some things straightened out."

By now, everybody from all the classes was looking at us, and I was feeling real small.

Ms. Jenkins was still talking. "Now, I'm the one who told him to come and help you. If you have a problem with that, then you can march yourself right up to the service and sit next to yo' mama in that hotbox of a choir stand. Is that what you want?"

I lowered my head and looked to the floor. "No, ma'am." Sitting in that choir loft was like sitting in an oven with the smell of chalky talcum powder and sour perfume.

I looked at Micah and rolled my eyes. He just walked to the table and sat down, looking at the Bible lesson in the book. From then on, I made him do little things like pass out the pencils and crayons and help the kids color in their pictures. Whenever he even fixed his mouth to talk, I gave him a look so mean he just swallowed his breath. We taught together for the next six months, and I never even said so much as two words to him outside of the Sunday school.

One day I saw him at the church picnic in a pair of jeans and a paisley, button-up shirt tucked neatly into his pants. He even had on a pair of them cute suede Hush Puppies shoes everybody raved about. He was talking to his friends by the drinks table, and when I walked past, he smiled and nodded his head. I gave him a quick half smile and looked away. I had on my yellow-and-pink summer dress with the straps that crisscrossed in the back and my almost-new white leather sandals that my mother bought soon as the heat hit the season. And thank goodness Mama had finally gotten around to pressing my hair so I could put it in a long, curly ponytail with white and yellow ribbons tied around the rubber band.

There wasn't much to do at the church picnic 'cept listen to the choir sing and eat and maybe gossip if you had somebody to gossip with. Sheila May was 'bout the only girl I talked to in the church, and she wasn't coming to the picnic 'cause she had to go on vacation with her family to Florida to visit her uncle. That day I was just hoping that Mama wouldn't want to stay too long.

I sat in a chair and leaned over to admire my sandals. Ants were forming a line in the dirt on the ground. And while they carried little pieces of food, I kicked up a sandstorm on some of them to mess up their organization, but they kept coming back to line.

"Do you always stare at the ants when you go to a picnic?" It was Micah.

I quickly sat up and tucked my feet under my chair. "Only when I'm bored. I usually talk to Sheila May, but she's not here."

"Well, why don't you talk to me?"

"'Cause I don't like you."

"Why not?" Micah had his hands out in question. "'Cause I'm not *mature enough* for you?"

He looked at me as if he were waiting for me to laugh. I rolled my eyes and turned my chair away from him. "You make me sick. You think just 'cause yo' daddy's a bishop, that makes you mature."

"Well, don't it?" He leaned over and looked at me straight on, licking his lips as he waited for my reply.

And I felt a funny tingling I had never felt before.

"No. Being mature has nothing to do with who your daddy is. It has everything to do with how well you know God."

"So now you think I don't know God."

"I didn't say that."

"No, but you meant it. Why do you think I don't know God?"

"'Cause whenever the kids ask you a question, you say, 'Ask Charlotte.' And whenever I tell you to pray, you get all shaky and whatnot, like you ain't never prayed in yo' life."

"Alright, alright, so maybe I don't know God like I should, but I go to church. I'm in Sunday school. Can't shoot a guy for tryin', can you?"

"No, I guess not." I gathered a piece of hair from around my ear and twisted it.

"Come on, let's go for a walk."

My heart started beating real fast then, and I thought about Ms. Jenkins. She'd told us big kids to stay away from boys 'cause it was real easy to get sick. "Girls who go off into the woods with boys get swole bellies like in Africa," she said.

"No, I ain't going for no walk with you, Micah. It ain't right. Ms. Jenkins said so."

"Ms. Jenkins—you mean my auntie? Aw, please! If it was up to her, we'd all be walking around like sticks never having any fun."

"I'm staying right here. I'm going to eat my hamburger and po- tato chips and finish watching these ants." With my pretty sandals, I pointed my toes in the direction of the ant line.

Micah looked at the ants and followed my legs up to me. "Suit yourself, Charlotte. But if you get bored, come on over. I just wanted to take a walk with Miss Sunday School, nothing else."

Right, and the moon ain't jealous of the sun.

If the tall trees could tell the story of my walks with Micah, they'd say we was a perfect match, but they would also tell stories of all the folks far and wide who said we weren't meant to be.

CHAPTER 9

Gracey
October 1987

HALLOWEEN WAS MY FAVORITE TIME of year after summer. I liked the heat in the summer, and the fact that the days reached into the night, but Halloween was all about the costume and trick-or-treating. Dad would always dress up in some 1970s getup with bell-bottoms and a wild-colored polyester shirt, and me and my sisters were whoever was hot that year. Last year, Joanna was Janet Jackson with her black shirt hanging off her shoulder, tight black jeans, and her hair crimped, I was a ballerina in combat boots, and Francine was Tinker Bell. She chose her costume from the grocery store because she said being creative was too stressful. She'd rather put a mask on and lift it up when she started sweating. We'd go trick-or-treating in the neighborhood to all the houses with their porch lights on and decorations around their windows. Everyone opened the door to see Dad's cheesy outfit, and then they'd look down at us and pretend to be blown away by our costumes. It was a time when our whole block felt like one big family, and we were going from room to room to visit people. While Dad did the schmoozing, I was checking out people's homes. We all pretty much had the same taste in normal, uninteresting furniture, different colors, of course.

School was the bomb too. Our teachers treated Halloween like a free day. We had a costume contest and all the classrooms had mini Snickers and Twix and those little Smarties that you had to untwist to open. Ohh, I could eat those all day.

Not gonna lie, though, this year, Halloween kind of sucked. I didn't have the motivation to get into costume. I just wanted to chill and read my book. Miss Mabel had created a cozy nook for us in her classroom, and I loved sitting on the giant beanbag chairs. Sometimes, sleep would sneak up on me there, and I'd slide off the big yellow puffball onto the orange shag carpet and drift away right in front of the bookshelf.

So anyway, that was where I was instead of at the Halloween party, and I was just beginning to doze off when Miss Mabel came back from her break.

"Oh,"—she startled—"hey, Gracey. I didn't know you were in here."

Miss Mabel was my favorite teacher. First day of school, I brought her an orange and told her I was going to be her best student. She smiled back and said, "Every student is my best student, Gracey, you're already there." That took a load off. I had spent the day before trying to imagine all the ways I could impress her with extra homework and cleaning up after class. She saw students in a different way than other teachers. All the kids loved her. It didn't matter where we were, whenever she stopped to talk to us, she made us feel like we belonged. There was this straight up surety with her, like there was no question in her mind of our success. I knew if I stayed in the shade of her shadow, me and my sisters would be okay.

The coolest classmates were in my eighth-grade homeroom. Sebastian, the soccer star and my best friend; Mitch, class clown and hands down the number-one beatboxer in the entire school; and Kendall, who was known as a fast girl but she kept us slow-blooming girls up-to-date with fashion and makeup. Slow girls only tried makeup at home, in the bathroom with the door locked.

Our class had cliques like all the others. Everybody came in and settled in where they belonged. There were the hard-core Salt-N-Pepa girls who were mean and ready to stomp you if you looked at them the wrong way. I always froze when they walked by as if that suddenly made me invisible. And they were thick enough to be in every classroom, so it made no difference to switch out. There were the fast girls—all they talked about was kissing and tongues and other weird things that made them cry after the boys went bragging. You could tell them by their pink lip gloss, miniskirts, and cleavage. And then there were the plain kids. We liked our sitcoms and our pop magazines, and we just wanted to blend in, so we didn't get called out for a fight and we didn't get bullied for reading or trying to solve the Rubik's Cube. The less we made waves by being different, the more peace we had in our day.

One rule we all had in common with complete solidarity—never, *ever* talk about the struggles in your home. You could brag all day about the cool stuff, but never come in dumping on your classmates about family drama. Keep that stuff buried in your chest, work it out at gym time, or put your Walkman on and listen to music, kiss somebody, or join a yo' mama session, but do not air your dirty laundry. When we walked into Muhammad Ali Middle School, we were safe from home and our only worry was surviving each other, which was usually the more welcomed challenge of the day.

"Hey, Miss Mabel." I stretched and yawned at the same time with my book in hand.

"What are you reading?" She leaned on the bookshelf, using her elbows to support her.

"*Bridge to Terabithia.*"

"Oh," she said, as if she knew all about it. "That's kind of deep."

"Well, yeah, I mean, I overheard a bunch of white girls from another school talking about it on our field trip to the science museum. They said it made them cry, and I thought what kind of book would make them cry?"

"You mean, you don't think white girls cry?" She crinkled her brow.

"I dunno. I think white girls don't have a reason to cry."

"Oh, why? 'Cause you think their lives are—"

"I don't know what I think, Miss Mabel." Dang, why was she sticking on this? "I wanted to read the book 'cause I wanted to know what would make a white girl cry, but I forgot about them soon as I started reading. It made me think about my own life and whatnot. I didn't know ol' girl was gonna die. I thought maybe one of them would move away or something. This is some real grown people stuff happening in this book."

Miss Mabel wanted to ask more questions, I could tell. Her silence felt like water behind a dam about to burst through. One relaxed move, and she'd feel the freedom to flow into her next question. I tensed up and lowered my head into my book.

"So what do you like about it?" she blurted out, as if she was taking an illegal chance.

Flipping the book closed around my finger, I said, "I'm not sure I do like it. It feels like . . . comfort, like the sadness in this book puts its arms around my sadness. Two best friends living their lives and then one of them is gone. It's so unfair when the one person in this world who truly gets you and still loves you in spite of your weirdness suddenly disappears and you never get to see them again."

Hopefully that was enough, but I could feel her thinking in her silence. She had another question to get past the dam. "You miss your dad." It was more like a statement than a question.

I forced a dimple into my right cheek. I didn't just miss my dad. I missed everybody. I missed the layers of love that used to cover me every day from start to finish. I didn't have no emotion to give Miss Mabel. Home was home and school was school—the boundaries weren't s'posed to be crossed. Ever.

Miss Mabel took a breath, as if all the waters were broken open. "You know, I've been trying to get in touch with your mom to remind her to sign up for conferences, but every time I call, it goes to your answering machine and she doesn't call me back."

But the waters weren't open. "She's picked up a part-time job. I forget doing what," I said.

Just then the bell rang, and students flooded the classroom.

Mitch busted into the room wearing a fat afro wig, bell-bottoms, and alligator shoes with soles that lifted him six inches off the ground. "What's up, what's up!" He strutted in with a limp, the cool kind that said his life was on purpose. The usual crew followed behind him with Sebastian sliding in backward doing the moonwalk. Kendall, dressed up like Lieutenant Uhura on *Star Trek* with her red jumpsuit lined in black, came in looking CCC—calm, cool, and collected—even though she was as anxious as the rest of us. Her girls followed behind her in their own costumes; one was the oldest sister, Denise, from *The Cosby Show*, and the other was Mae Jemison, the Black astronaut.

Mitch stopped and looked at me, examining my hair with his head cocked to the side. "What's up with you?" He spoke around a toothpick hanging out of his mouth. "Who you supposed to be, Raggedy Ann?" I had managed to put on my red sneakers and a skirt with some overalls I borrowed from Daddy's drawer. Dorothy from *The Wizard of Oz* was on my mind, but I thought if I explained myself, everyone would laugh at me. It might have worked if I said I was Diana Ross from *The Wiz*, but I didn't have the energy to go there.

Crap. Why'd I have to be the one he picked on first? I didn't have a mind to back down and be passive. I was already on edge after talking to Miss Mabel. I shoved it right back to him. "No, that's yo' mama, Mitch! You better leave me alone before I tell her you been dippin' in yo' Daddy's closet again."

"Ooohh!" the crew wailed. "She told you."

"Check it," Mitch yelled. "My little sister can comb hair better than that, Gracey." Oh, he was talking about my hair. I felt the fuzz above my right ponytail holder. The waves near my roots assured me that I was beautiful but I knew they'd never see it that way. He pointed at me with his thumb, talking to the class. "Man, her hair is jacked up."

"Shut up, Mitch!" I yelled, my fists balled.

He looked me up and down, unfazed. "Only reason yo' mama let you out the house like that is 'cause it's Halloween."

"Mitch, why you gotta be so cold?" Kendall whined. Now the girls were in it, echoing her words. "Yeah, Mitch, why?"

"Chill, Kendall. I was just messin' with Raggedy Ann here. No biggie."

My heart skipped a beat when Sebastian spoke out of nowhere. "Alright, alright!" He put his arm around me. "Y'all got to leave my friend alone. She didn't comb her hair 'cause she goin' to my mom's shop after school. We got it all set up for three-thirty. Ain't that right, Raggedy Ann? I mean, Gracey."

I gave him a playful punch before answering. "Yeah, it's true."

Miss Mabel got the class started after that. I was miffed at her for letting Mitch go on so long, but whatever. She had her reasons. Maybe she wanted to see if I'd lose it and start crying. Nope. Last thing I wanted was help from a teacher. They talked too much, and they were always in our beeswax, asking questions.

When the last bell rang, me and Sebastian walked to the beauty shop his mom owned.

"Thanks for what you did in class," I said, turning toward him and then quickly away.

"No big deal." He did a quick spit to the side of the road. Part of me wondered if he thought girls found spitting cool. The other part *did* find it kind of cool. It was the way he did it, like a grown-up who knew how to handle the world, like a cowboy who could take a rope and lasso a calf. "Once Mitch gets started, it's hard to get him to back down and you don't need that right now. I know I wouldn't want to deal with it if I was going through what you're going through."

"What do you mean?"

His mouth parted as he said, "Uh . . ." He searched my eyes and then said, "You know, with your dad passin' and all."

"Oh." I sighed at having to be reminded. It felt like we were eons from his death already, but it had only been five months. "Yeah." Probably wasn't normal, but other things were more pressing nowadays.

At the beauty shop, there was some of everybody. Sebastian's Mom, Rosa, was good people. She was from the Dominican Republic, so she had different sounds in her shop. The music had beats we didn't hear on WGCI—it made your hips want to twist different and your chest rock from side to side instead of up and down. Accents like syncopated clapping filled the air and made us wonder what magical things went on in that world. I could hear accents from Haiti, Nigeria, Ghana, and Trinidad.

But most of us were plain ol' Black people whose families had migrated from the South. That was all I ever saw on the South Side—Black people who were full of love and passion and at the same time tired of the struggle of making ends meet, like pushing a boulder up a hill. Most of the adults from my world were from Mississippi, Alabama, or Georgia. And many of our parents still had Southern accents that were fine in the house but caused them trouble in public. Soon as people heard them speak, they put them in a category that wasn't good—like "I can charge you more and pay you less" not good; "call you names and you won't be bothered 'cause you're used to it" not good; or "treat you like you're invisible and look right past you" not good.

Mom's accent was lovely. Even still she would practice her words as she stood over the stove, cooking. The words that we say without a second thought were hard for her, like *bread, beautician,* and *escalator.* Sometimes getting that second and third syllable to work in step with the tongue was a shared pain we all inhaled and never let go. She listened to us and mumbled to herself, echoing our words. Her voice was soft and her pronunciation was just as lyrical as French or Spanish or Italian. She fit right in at the beauty shop. All the accents reminded me of Pentecost, Mom's favorite service of the year where the color red is everywhere and we talk about fire on the head and speaking in different languages. It probably sounded just like the cacophony of sounds in this little room, and I was having fun imagining it . . . until I had to go under the dryer and then Miss Mabel walked in.

My whole heart nearly fell into my stomach. What was she doing here outside of school? She felt like a hound dog, hot on my trail. I could see her leaning on the counter talking to Rosa. They were speaking discreetly, and every once in while they'd glance at me. Miss Mabel's eyes got big, and her mouth dropped open. And then it was obvious Rosa was trying to get her to calm down. She put her finger to her mouth and turned to see if anyone was listening. Miss Mabel wrote something down on a piece of paper and slid it across the counter. Then she turned and waved at me before walking out. I smiled and put my hand up and then went back to my *Essence* magazine with Naomi Campbell on the cover. I was looking for an article on *The Color Purple.* The trailer gave me goose bumps and it felt too rich, like something I should watch with adults. But the little I saw made me feel like we're all like those big old trees whose roots connect underneath the ground, and share waters when one's brook dries up, trading secrets when a tree is close to falling about how to survive another hundred years. I was looking for wisdom from that grown-up world to tell me how to survive my childhood.

Forty-five minutes later, I was out from under the dryer and Rosa had finished my hair. She spun me around to look in the mirror. I immediately wondered if anyone could see the queen inside of me as well as I could. Long curls fell past my shoulders, and my edges were flat to my skin. I could feel moist silk on my hand when I touched the sides of my hair, and the word *pretty* circled round in my head. I wondered what Sebastian would say if he saw me. Would he like me enough to want to kiss me? I stared into the mirror until I knew the person staring back at me believed that I could actually be happy and successful one day, whether my mom returned or not. "Thank you, Rosa," I said.

"You're welcome, *mija*," she said. "Bring your sisters by too, anytime. S'on the house."

"All right, bet," I said on my way out. "I'll do that."

CHAPTER 10

Charlotte
October 1987

GEORGIA WAS NOTHING LIKE CHICAGO. It was softer, without the edge; there was space to breathe. That water was fine as they say, and the invitation to come on in was always there. Felt like I was in a pool and just learned how to float with nothing holding me up—no life jacket, no flotation device. Just drifting on my own. And as I stretched out my arms and began to kick, I moved. Maybe not forward, but I moved.

Only way I could make progress was by letting go of everything that ever held me back. I knew I had children. Three girls. Named Joanna, Gracey, and Francine. And in the perfect world, I should have been there, I really should have. But it was like I was trapped in a field of opium poppies, and the more I tried to make myself fit that role in Chicago, the more I just wanted to float in the pool of nothing.

But it was a funny kind of freedom I felt, like a prisoner on the run. Like my days were numbered, and I'd better use them wisely. Like I knew God was watching me and would only let me go so far.

And anyway, if I was honest, it was only my skin that felt free. My heart was haunted by the presence of my little women, and sometimes, even though I knew they weren't with me, I could feel them where they were. The nights I fell asleep praying, I'd hear Frankie giggle or Gracey sigh. Now and then, I could hear Joanna groan like she did when she had to do her homework. Those days I'd take a blanket over my head and imagine hiding in the little pocket of God's heart that I knew belonged to me. In that place, everything felt okay if only for a few minutes.

When I wasn't thinking about my girls, Micah Richards took up residency in my mind as a squatter. Thoughts of him brought me back to my cleaning job at the B and B and made me snap the sheets and beat the bed to smooth out the quilts.

Candi Goodin was my closest friend in Savannah. We'd only known each other for a few weeks, but she always pushed my clouds away with her smile.

"Uh-oh," she said now as she stood in the doorway of the room I was cleaning. "You're beating beds again. That must mean you're stuck on rewind."

"No, not really." She knew it was a lie as well as I did but let me shift anyway. "How's Mr. Goodin?"

"Stubborn, bitter, mean-hearted—"

"Candi," I said, trying to figure things out. "How can you sit up there and talk about your husband like that? Y'all been married what, ten years, you said?"

"Yes, ten long years." Candi laughed wryly. "And in that time, I've aged twenty years, what with him always going after my sister behind my back."

Candi was what I called healthy. She was the kind of overweight that went perfectly with the joyful way about her. She was born to be heavyset, and I don't think there was a doctor out there that would tell her to lose the jolly that made her cheeks doughy and her arms pudgy.

Her husband, Mr. Goodin, was always trying to make her skinny like her sister, Ebony. His latest scheme was to save up a hundred dollars so he could buy her a fancy girdle that sucked her in like Marilyn Monroe. Only problem was, he didn't have a job, so Candi had to take her own money and put it to the side for him.

"I don't understand why you put up with him." I moved the old-fashioned porcelain knickknacks of perfected animals to the top of the dresser to polish the wood.

"Because I took a vow." Candi punched a pillow. "And I don't want to break my promise to God."

"Really, Candi, I think God would understand." Her life was so simple compared to mine. It seemed easy to fix. She was the breadwinner, and the house they lived in was hers. All she had to do was get a divorce, keep her house, and go on with her life.

Candi sat on the bed I had just made and turned the conversation to me. "What was it like being married to a man who was really into you?"

My hand stopped moving in its circular motion. I had returned the knickknacks and moved on to the end tables by the bed. I sprayed the counter, inhaled the pine scent, and started up again. Of all the people in the world to talk about, my husband was the last one I wanted to put my mouth to. Moses was an aspect of my life I couldn't unpack on my own. I didn't even know how to go about describing him. He was just there, like a nice piece of furniture, like that grandfather clock in white folks' living rooms.

I was supposed to be floating, but more and more, the waters were pulling me down until I felt fully submerged with no resurrection to help catch my breath.

Clearing my throat, I closed my eyes. "My husband, Moses, was more divine than handsome. Tall and dark, muscular arms like thick branches." I opened my eyes. Candi hung on to my words as if she needed them to live. I forced myself to continue. "He had a way with people—made everybody feel important, like he really loved and cherished them."

"Oh my days." Candi rubbed her hands together. "If he did all that for everybody else, what'd he do for you? Breakfast in bed? Flowers after work?"

I wish I had some way to signal Candi that this wasn't the road I wanted to go down. Couldn't she sense my hesitancy? Didn't she know what boundaries were? Maybe boundaries were my responsibility to lay down. That had always been a weak spot in my life. But she was the only friend I had, so I went ahead and answered. "He tried all that stuff. But somewhere down the line, things changed and our rhythm, it just got off."

"What do you mean, your rhythm got off?" Candi rose from the bed and pulled the quilt tight around the edges before shifting to the chair in front of the vanity desk. "Did he forget your birthday?"

Good Lord, I prayed. *Help me out of this one.* I stopped. Folding my arms across my chest, I turned my back on her. "It's complicated, Candi. And Moses never forgot my birthday long as we were married."

"I hear that, honey." Candi stood up and straightened her skirt. "At least y'all didn't have no kids."

I looked at my watch. "Almost eleven o'clock. I need to get back to work."

The next room I cleaned was already tidy. No one was staying in it. Only had to touch up lightly here and there to maintain the look of perfection. This room had a great view of the river, and I could see families walking by on their way to go sightseeing.

My hand was still trembling from the conversation with Candi. Had I just lied? If God was technical, then I was safe. I never said I didn't have children. But if God wasn't, then my omission was a sin, and I had to add it to the long list of others.

The questions Candi asked were the same ones I got at Moses's funeral. People wanted me to tell stories about him and talk about how wonderful he was, but I couldn't. Silence rose up and took my words from me before I could get them out. I listened and responded with care. I supported everyone there, but I shared no stories of my own.

Moses was the perfect man for somebody, for a lot of women. But not me. To this day, I still don't understand why he chose me. He treated me with the utmost respect and he loved me beyond a shadow of a doubt. I knew this. But I always wondered, if he knew who I really was and all the things that happened in the past, would he have still loved me? I'd lived the lives of two different women—who I was, and who Moses imagined me to be. And the more I couldn't live up to

Moses's imagination, the more we drifted apart. None of this was fair and I was beginning to think that maybe I was the one who put myself in this prison before ever hearing God's thoughts on the situation, as if I assumed I was guilty before proven innocent.

I was thankful for the gifts Moses bought me—the little diamond, the thin gold-plated watch, the flowers—but I didn't gasp with the big thank-you and hug that he deserved. I simply deposited the jewelry in a drawer, dropped the flowers in water, and went on with my dishes. And when he took me to dinner, he'd tell me to order whatever I wanted, but always, always I chose the chicken Caesar salad and only had a plain scoop of vanilla ice cream for dessert.

One night, I remember him leaning across the table and putting his hand on mine. "Tell me, baby, what's wrong? Why are you so afraid to live? Don't I make you happy?"

I took a sip of my wine before answering. The restaurant was of the fancy kind with white tablecloths and tall glasses and polyester cloth napkins. "Moses, please, don't go there. You know I love you. You're so good to me and our kids. This is just the way I am."

Moses shook his head, brushing away my excuses with the sweep of his hand. "No, no it isn't. You used to laugh. You used to go to the carnival and ride the rides, used to go on picnics and run through the fields. That's not who you are now. Every year you crawl deeper and deeper into yourself. It makes no sense. Everywhere I go, people are happy to see me, they open up, tell me their problems—and then I come home to you, and you shut down. I have to be honest, sometimes what I'm getting out there is better than what I'm gettin' in here." He moved his finger between me and him.

That night was the closest I ever came to telling him the truth. He had every right to know. But my insides closed me up, leaving him out.

So many people at the funeral testified of how great Moses was. He'd done so much for the people in the community. I'd had no idea he was so well-known. Over eight hundred people showed up. Folks

I hadn't seen in years and still others I'd never met. Several women came to me to shake my hand and say, "So Moses really did have a wife." They smiled with their perfectly manicured nails and puckered, glossy lips. "We didn't believe him for the longest time and then he brought us pictures of you two together. You had an amazing husband. I hope you enjoyed every minute with him."

"Thank you" was all I could muster up before turning to the next person.

My daughters knew just about everyone there. Folks hugged on them, pinched their cheeks, cupped their faces in their hands, and poured words into them, watering their parched souls. I didn't understand it all, but I wondered if I'd missed out on life. I listened to every story told, hugged every tear-stained face, and held the hands of many who wanted to be closer to him through me.

Mama had stayed fixed to me like a parasite, talking about everyone. "Did you see those women that came up to you? Look like models for a brothel. I bet you Moses had a good time with them," she muttered. "He may have been a good man, but he was still a man."

"Shut up, Mama," I snapped. "I've heard enough out of you."

"Oh, chile, calm down. Wouldn't even be an issue if you'd'a just told the man the truth."

"Mama, please." I massaged my head just above my brow. "Go get a drink or something."

I looked at my life, and I couldn't figure out how I could have handled things any other way. My mother's words had pushed me to the edge of myself.

Anger rose up again as I vacuumed the rug like a lawn mower in tall grass. I was so stupid to fall for Micah.

He had grown finer and finer as the years went by. Rumor had it that his mama and the bishop split up, and they wasn't never comin' to get him. With his daddy traveling all the time and his mama taking extravagant trips to Europe, neither of them had had the time to take care of their little country boy.

Boy. He really wasn't a boy anymore by the time we got to high school. Micah was a man, and he looked like a man. The kind of man that could give you a hug and make you feel like you'd never have another problem in the world. The kind that seemed to squeeze all the tears out of you so you'd never have to cry again. Of course, that was a lie. Ain't no man out there that could take all your problems away. Even if he's rich, some other problems will come along and make you cry. But Micah had that way about him that just made me feel like we were two matching puzzle pieces sitting on a counter. Only problem was, there was no puzzle to place us in. We didn't fit anywhere.

In high school, I couldn't hardly concentrate while teaching Sunday school for staring at him all the time; he was so smooth. He liked to kneel down and look the kids right in the eye when he was working with them, but he always had this way of turning his head and smiling my way whenever he felt me staring. Then I'd look away at the Noah's ark poster behind him, trying to make it seem like I wasn't thinking about him.

"Micah, I got a question." One of the kids waved his hand back and forth in the air. They loved to ask him questions he didn't know anything about.

"Yes, Gerald."

"My daddy said that Jesus was a Black man, but I don't believe him. You think it's true?"

Micah looked at me, and I turned my head. He could answer for himself by now.

"Well, I guess, Gerald, he could be a Black man, but we don't really know 'cause nobody's ever seen him. I mean, I guess white folks made him look white because they're white. But really, we don't know what kind of skin he had."

"That ain't true, Micah. My daddy said it's in the Bible, he got bronze skin. That mean he Black, don't it, Miss Charlotte?"

I came and put my hand on his shoulder. "Well, Gerald, let's not worry about what color the Lord is. The point is, we saved 'cause of him. Ain't that right, class?"

"Yes, Miss Charlotte."

I looked at Micah as if I'd won a victory, and he smiled and winked as if the world were beneath his feet.

After church that day, I was walking home, singing to myself, when Micah came running up behind me.

"Where you going in such a hurry, Miss Charlotte?"

"I'm going home. I gotta get the table ready for Sunday dinner. Don't y'all have Sunday dinner at your aunt's house?"

"Yes, but I don't have to do anything 'cept show up and eat." He put one hand in his pocket and steadied the sack he was carrying on his shoulder with the other. "I figured I'd walk you home. Is that all right with you?"

"I suppose so," I said, focusing on the horizon ahead, watching the sun hide behind the wispy clouds.

"Good, 'cause I didn't feel like being embarrassed today."

I smiled to myself as we walked in silence for a while.

The dirt roads were red with tire grooves leading the way home. On each side were ditches deep enough to catch the water if a flood ever came about. Unlike the roads in the city, our country roads had walls, like the engineers had plowed right through a hill. Kind of made me think of Moses and the splitting of the Red Sea. Only instead of fish and whales swimming in the water beside me, tree roots wove through the layers of sedimentary rock that took hundreds of years to take shape. And between all of that was insects sticking halfway out the dirt.

"Miss Charlotte, Miss Charlotte, I gots a question." Micah raised his hand and jumped up and down like the kids in class.

If there was one thing Micah could do, he could make me laugh.

"Yes, Micah?"

"Um, I was just wondering if you know'd how much cotton candy it takes to fill a teddy bear."

"Well, I guess it depends on the size of the bear. And I hope it isn't really filled with cotton candy, 'cause then, soon as that child takes the bear outside, the ants will go marchin' in."

"Did I say cotton candy? I meant cotton. You're just so sweet, candy must have escaped out of my mouth." He stopped and pulled a teddy bear from his bag. He never took his eyes off mine as he slipped the bear into my arms.

It was the only nice thing a boy had ever given me, save maybe some dandelions in elementary school.

"Oh, Micah, where'd you get this? It's so cute and cuddly." I put it to my face and looked at him. "Thank you."

I reached out to give him a hug, and he took me in his arms and held me tight enough to feel his chest rise and fall. I swear, I wanted that moment to last forever. When I pulled away, my cheek brushed his jawline, and as Grandma says, I liked to fainted. His skin was so warm and smooth, I could have sworn I smelled chocolate. I quickly licked my lips just in case he was going to kiss me, but he didn't. He just held my hand the rest of the way until he had to pivot back toward his aunt's house in the opposite direction.

As I turned into the walkway, my mama was standing in the screen door with her paisley apron on; I saw her as soon as I raised my chin toward the sky. I was glad I had told Micah to go long before we reached my house.

"Girl, where you been? Get in here and set this table. Yo' brothers is waitin' on you."

"Sorry, Mama, I was . . . I was helping Ms. Baker. She couldn't quite gather all her kids up to get them home."

"That heffa know she got too many kids. You tell her next time, you ain't got time to be helping her with her kids, you got to help your own mama."

"Yes, ma'am."

"That woman know she somethin' else. How many kids she got, twenty-two?"

"Nah, Mama, she got sixteen."

"Sixteen kids, and ain't a one of 'em got a lick of sense. I ought to tell her about herself."

"Oh no, Mama. I won't help her no more, I promise."

"You better not. That woman made her bed, and now she got to lie in it. It's a wonder she still in her right mind."

She looked at the bear. "Where you get this bear from?"

"Oh, one of the kids asked me to babysit it for her. Said she needed a break from watching all her stuffed animals."

"Now I know you lyin'. Them kids ain't got no toys. They too poor. They hardly got clothes to wear on their backs, and you tellin' me that one them little girls has got so many stuffed animals she had to send one away to get a break? Chile, please. I ain't no fool. Now, I'ma ask you one more time, where'd you get that teddy bear from?"

"My friend gave it to me."

She raised her hand like she was going to slap me down. "Girl!"

"Mama, little Gerald gave it to her." My brother had come and put his arm around my shoulder. "He showed it to me before Sunday school, said he saved up for it so he could give it to his favorite teacher. Ain't that right, Char?"

"Yes, Johnny." I was crying now, scared to death of what might come next.

"Is that who gave you the bear, Charlotte?"

"Yes, ma'am."

She relaxed and put a smile on her face. "My God, Charlotte, you don't have to lie about a six-year-old boy. I'm not that strict."

"Sorry, Mama."

"Go on to the kitchen."

"Yes, ma'am."

"But I tell ya, girl, you get knocked up before you get married, I ain't got nothing to do with you."

"Yes, ma'am." I went into the kitchen and started setting the table. The silverware was heavy and curved with a point to the side of the handle. Other homes had lighter, shorter silverware, but ours was different, passed down from our grandmother whose slave mistress gave her the silverware unboxed, wrapped in a tablecloth before her husband could lose everything they owned at the races. She never asked for it back.

Johnny came into the kitchen and stood beside me. He put the glasses to the right of all the plates.

"Thanks, Johnny."

"Yeah, you welcome."

"If you hadn't come in . . ."

"Mama would have knocked you to the moon."

"Yeah."

"Listen, I seen the way you and Micah look at each other in church. Y'all better be careful. Don't do nothin' stupid. You deserve the good life, Charlotte. That's all Mama wants for you too."

"Oh, please, I ain't about to let that boy get near me like that. I got big dreams, you know. I'm going to live in the city, have my own boutique, and buy one of them brownstones with the grand piano in the front room."

"Just don't mess up."

"Fine."

Johnny sat down and started reading a book at the table, adjusting one of the chairs to rest his feet. He knew I had to set the table.

"Move, boy!" I swatted his shoulder.

"Ain't no law says I got to."

My heart went out. "Mama lettin' y'all go to school next semester?"

Johnny frowned. "Nah, she say the crops came in and she need us at home for the harvest. Dreams deferred."

"Langston Hughes." His poem was right. We don't really know what happens when dreams are delayed for God knows how long— whether they spoil like old fruit or fade over time. Johnny's chair screeched across the floor and fell to the ground as he left the room. I knew he wasn't mad at me. He was mad at the situation. All he ever wanted to be was a professor.

I yanked the cord on the vacuum out the way, popping the bubble of my memories. The bedroom was finished. I quickly put my foot on the power button and pressed the release button to suck in the cord. "Oh, Mama," I exhaled. "If only you knew how much you hurt. My life could have turned out better if only you'd been kind."

CHAPTER 11

Gracey
November 1987

MY HAIR WAS LAID WHEN I went to school the next Monday. Now instead of making fun of my hair, they wanted to feel it and turn me into one of those head dolls that you can practice styles on. All the boys were flicking my ponytail, and the girls were like, "Let me take your hair down and French braid it into two." And I was all like, "Boy, go somewhere and leave me alone." And to the girls, I was like, "Nah, that's okay. I'm good." I mean the attention was nice, but they didn't like me too tough when my hair was messy, so why start now. Besides, a press and curl only lasts for two weeks, and I didn't want to live the Cinderella life. My pumpkin was my hair, and I knew it. A little rain or moisture in the air and they'd be calling me Raggedy Ann again.

Miss Mabel was up to her antics again, trying to get in my head. She made it so we had to write in these doggone journals. They were really just spiral notebooks, but she said we could decorate them to make them our own. I kind of liked that idea. I opened the notebook and felt the cool of the page with my hand. The empty lines were begging to be filled, calling me to write like Sunday dinner called from the kitchen.

Mitch was the first to react. He threw his on the floor. "Man, this is whack! What's this got to do with school?"

"It has everything to do with school," Miss Mabel said. "Now pick up your notebook before I send you to the principal's office." With one hand, he snatched his book up and slammed it on his desk.

Sebastian raised his hand. "Miss Mabel, what are we s'posed to write about?"

"I'm glad you asked, Sebastian." She walked to the board with her chalk. "Every day I'll write the first line of a sentence and I want you to finish it with a paragraph. That's three to five sentences for those that don't know." She turned to the class to make sure we were following. "And if you want to write more, then feel free."

A boy named Brian raised his right hand while using his other hand to smooth his waves with a brush. "So what we writin' about today?"

"Good question, Brian." She turned to the blackboard and wrote as she spoke. "Today's topic is, 'Every morning I wake up and I feel like . . .'"

Everybody moaned and slid down in their seats.

Kendall smiled and looked up as if she were saying hi. "A'ight, bet. Miss Mabel, I don't even have to write it down. Every morning I wake up and I'm like, 'Dang, I gotta go to school again?'"

"Yup, yup, me too, Miss Mabel." Their voices landed like raindrops. "I be thinking the exact same thing."

Sebastian stood up. "Wait y'all," he said. "Hold up, hold up. I ain't like you. I wake up every morning and I'm like, 'I wonder if I'm gonna get that honey's seven digits today?'"

This time the boys cheered while the girls threw wadded paper at Sebastian.

Miss Mabel cut in. "You're not listening to me. I said"—and she pointed to the board—"'Every morning I wake up and I *feel* like.' I want to know how you all *feel* in the morning."

Mitch raised his hand. "We feel fine. What you mean?" Both his hands went into the air in question.

She took a deep breath. Obviously, this wasn't going the way she expected. But I had already started writing. I started with one sentence and then another thought came and another and then I couldn't stop until I heard my name from out of nowhere. I had no idea when all the chatter had stopped.

"Gracey, are you working on your assignment already?"

I sat up and looked her way. "Yes, ma'am."

The class sucked their teeth and moaned "teacher's pet" to one another.

"Do you want to share any of it with the class?"

"Whatever." I shrugged and stood up to read. Don't ask me why. It felt like an out-of-body experience. Was this me and my voice speaking with power? "Every morning I wake up and I feel like somebody's playing me like a game. Like I have no say, no control over nothing. I'm still young, barely a teenager, and already I feel like my life is shrinking. I feel like it's falling through some kind of hourglass, and I can't break in to catch the sand. And that's not fair. It's crazy. I watch *The Cosby Show* and wish I had Vanessa's life, like all I have to worry about is a paper I accidentally left in the refrigerator or a boyfriend who likes some other girl. Ain't nobody in her family ever going to leave her. Her house, all that money they have is dope—only way Vanessa's life could get messed up is if she messed it up herself. How come I don't get choices like that? So there, every day I wake up and I feel like my life, it ain't even my own."

"Whoa, that's deep, yo'," Sebastian said. "I feel ya, right there." He knocked on his chest with his right fist and pointed toward me.

I looked around the room, and everybody was nodding or saying "Word."

Miss Mabel looked moved. "Thank you, Gracey. That's exactly what I'm talking about."

The bell rang, and everybody gathered their stuff to shuffle out the classroom. "Don't forget to write in your journals," our teacher shouted over us.

Who was Miss Mabel anyway? Why did she care so much about us? About me? I always had the feeling she was lonely. Like she didn't have kids but wanted them. And everyone knew she didn't have a husband 'cause she was a little too free with the men. Plus, she didn't have a ring. That pretty much summed it up.

But she also didn't have that way about her that was surrounded by love. She reminded me of a garden snake you'd find in the back yard while minding your business and planting tomatoes. Out of nowhere, she'd give a startle. Maybe she was one of those people who felt like her students were her children and she didn't need a man to make her happy. But those were the same women who had two cats and a million plants in their homes. They needed a channel for their love. She liked her music too. Always playing annoying '70s music, same stuff my dad played—Earth, Wind & Fire, the O'Jays, Miles Davis, and all that jazz. I think she thought it helped us concentrate, but it didn't. It only made us daydream and pass notes because we couldn't focus. There was always too much emotion in the music. We would have been better off working to our own beats and sounds, pencils tapping, humming, and quietly beatboxing. Let us go long enough we could create our own musical sounds and still get our work done. The music in our head always filled the silence. We didn't need anything clashing with it, creating chaos.

It was a few weeks before Miss Mabel collected our journals. The best day was when she asked what we really wanted to be when we grew up. Turns out Mitch really wanted to be a businessman, and Kendall really wanted to be the first in her family to go to college and stay on campus. Another good one was, If the impossible were possible, what would you do? Everyone said cool stuff but then ended with the word *but*, and their dreams washed away like sandcastles made too close to the water. "I want to be an airplane pilot, but there's no way for me to take flying lessons 'cause we can't afford it."

I didn't write nothing 'bout what Miss Mabel asked us to write. I ignored her and wrote whatever I wanted. What was she going to do? At least I was writing. Fact is, I wrote more than anybody else in the class. And my stuff was fly, worth reading. I knew she liked it because she always gave me a check plus, which was the same as excellent. And I didn't play around with my handwriting, trying to bubble my letters or use hearts to dot my *i*'s. My pen didn't have a fuzzy cutie pie at the end neither. I always used a blue erasable pen, and I kept three extras in my backpack, but I never told anybody 'cause I knew if I did I'd never see them again. This journal was my friend, and I treated it with the respect it deserved. I even glued gift wrap paper on the cover and stuck some classy puffy stickers on it. I needed my journal to know that it was okay to love me back.

November 18, 1987
Winter is no joke in Chicago. You have to be like the squirrels and stock up before the cold air hits. I started looking in September at the Salvation Army for warm coats that didn't belong to any decade, so we could wear them as long as we need to and not feel bunk. Then, when the first autumn winds came through, I got us some scarves and gloves and hats from the big sale baskets at Walgreens. I went to the secondhand shops in Evanston and Glencoe for our school clothes 'cause Grandma taught me that white people throw away good clothes just because they're out of style. Francine and Joanna didn't care where I got 'em, just as long as they weren't worn out. For some reason, they knew not to ask.
Our house is getting colder by the minute, and no matter how high we turn up the heat, it gets out through the cracks around the windows and the gaps under the doors. I hated to do it because it was so much work, but I had to pull out the old smelly plastic that Daddy used to staple around the windows. We rolled up bath towels and put them under the doors, and in the morning we warm up the kitchen by turning on the oven. At night we fill the humidifier with water and watch for the mist to blow out. The only good thing about winter is that the summer's ants are gone.

The day I wrote that entry, I wasn't feeling too well. It was that time of the month. I had cramps, but probably had a fever too because I had the chills. What sucked was not having anyone to complain to. Before, I'd go home early when it was that time. But now, Grandma wouldn't be there to tell me to stop being a baby as she let me lean on her shoulder long enough to get a quick nap in while she watched her stories. And Mom wasn't there to warm up the teakettle for the hot water bottle to hold over my belly.

It was the loneliest day of my life. I remember walking down the hall thinking I couldn't go another step, and then I woke up in the nurse's office. Mr. Tutti, my history teacher, was standing over me. "Cotton, you okay?" He liked to call me Cotton because that's what he thought of my hair before it was pressed. He asked to touch it one time, and I said yes, but I should have said no. White teachers had so much curiosity about brown people, and none of us knew what to do with it. We knew everything about them because our parents schooled us. They wanted to make sure we knew how to stay on their good side. Mr. Tutti always smiled with his tobacco-stained teeth. His chin carried salt-and-pepper hair that he liked to finesse, and his mustache was always longer than his upper lip. One thing's for sure, though—he cared way more than the other teachers, enough for us to let him in even when we didn't fully trust him. But there was rule number one: never ever share your business with folks that could use it against you later down the line.

I pretended to be sleeping a little while longer so I could hear their conversation. "Oh dear." Miss Mabel was there too. "Maybe her mom's at work or something. We don't have a work number listed."

"Nah, I heard she doesn't have a job."

"Well, maybe she went to the store or something."

I focused on the smell of the air in the office to keep quiet; cough syrup, Band-Aids, and disinfectant. What did they know about my mom?

"Poor thing, I think she's just exhausted." The nurse had two fingers on my wrist checking my pulse. "Trouble is," she continued, "we can't let her go until we get in touch with her mother."

"Do you mind if I try?" Miss Mabel casually asked. "She might be back from an errand by now."

"Suit yourself." The other woman slapped a hand against her thigh.

Miss Mabel picked up the receiver, and I heard buttons being pushed.

"Oh, hello. Is this Mrs. Downing . . . it is? Oh great!" She sounded excited. "Well, we have Gracey here in the nurse's office, and it seems she passed out in the hallway . . . Ummm, yes. I don't know what she's been doing, but she's near exhaustion . . . the nurse wants to send her home. Can you come pick her up?"

There was a pause, then she said, "No, we can't allow a taxi." Another pause. "I tell you what, how about we have one of our bus drivers bring her home? And then the nurse says she should probably rest for, what, two days?"

The nurse walked over to Miss Mabel. "Give me the phone. I need to talk to her."

"Um, sure. Here's Ms. Martha, our nurse."

"Hello, Mrs. Downing? Hello, hello?" Martha clicked the receiver. "Hello? She hung up!" Attitude rose in her tone. "I'm finna call that heffa back."

"Come on, Martha, you know how these mothers can be." Miss Mabel's voice was calming. "Just send the child home and leave it. Matter of fact, I can get one of the assistants to cover my class. I'll take her home myself."

"Would you do that for real?"

"No problem."

I slowly opened my eyes and sat on the edge of the metal bed with my feet dangling.

"Come on, Cotton," Miss Mabel said, poking fun. "Let's go."

Something in my spirit wouldn't let me get excited, even though my mind was racing with the possibility of my mom being home. The rest of me, my heart, my soul, was unmoved. The okey-dokey ball wasn't hitting me.

I I I

The drive home wasn't so bad. Miss Mabel turned on the radio, and I listened to jams while looking out the window. Even though school was in, there were still a lot of kids outside, drinking from soda cans and carrying big greasy paper bags full of french fries. They laughed and laughed as if today had nothing to do with tomorrow. It reminded me of a haunting poem, "We Real Cool" by Gwendolyn Brooks, about ditching school. Hearing it was enough for me to never play hooky.

"You all right, sweetie?" Miss Mabel asked. I hated being called sweetie. We were odd outside of school.

"I'm fine." I pulled my journal from my backpack and started writing.

> *I saw this shriveled-up old Black man sitting on the corner with a bottle of liquor wrapped in a slim paper bag. Red eyes so haunted, I bet he can't sleep five minutes without Father Time trying to steal his soul. I saw a young mother pushing a stroller with young kids in their costumes walking and skipping around her. They were swinging their empty plastic pumpkin baskets by the handle, no doubt excited about the candy they were about to get. I saw fast walking women who wore heels and carried briefcases and looked at their watches and never stopped to notice me or anyone else who might cause them to have to look down. I saw barbers taking a break with a cigarette, folks reading the paper while waiting for the bus. Today I saw people, all kinds of people, who all seem to believe that life isn't about living, it's about surviving.*
>
> *My only question is: if life is just about surviving and it has nothing to do with living, then why did God put us here? I mean, if I was in heaven, you know, playing the Life game, and God said to me, "Okay, Gracey, it's your turn now. Go see how long you can survive," then I would have said, "No, God. I don't want to go. I don't want to be born. I don't want to lose."*

I was looking for something out there, looking for someone. In every face, in every eye, I was looking for a familiar smile, a nice conversation. I was looking for peace, for a quiet soul or a brush with love. I was looking for fire, a yell, a scream, a screech that could burn me worse than my pain. Something that could give me a good reason to go back into my house again. But I didn't find anything.

"You know, Gracey"—Miss Mabel cleared her throat—"sometimes when you're writing, you make me think of Gordon Parks."

"The photographer? My dad loved him. But how do I remind you of him?"

"I don't know, it's the way you see life. You take photographs with your words."

We pulled up in front of the house and I took a deep breath. I had to beat my disappointment to the punch. "That wasn't really my mom on the phone, was it?"

Miss Mabel looked down at her steering wheel and traced the Chevy sign etched in the material.

"No, it was your sister."

I bit my bottom lip and put one leg out the car. "That's big, what you did today."

"Honey, it's nothing compared to what you do every day."

"Was it Rosa who told you?" I asked, looking into the car.

"By way of a neighbor who lives next to Miss Nelda who puts meals on your doorstep from time to time . . . and then there's your journal." She shrugged.

"Oh." I wondered how many people in the neighborhood knew.

"Whatever happens, Gracey, we're on your side."

Just as I slammed the door, an older teenager I didn't know walked out of my house pulling on his puffy jacket and positioning his jeans.

Joanna stood at the top of the stairs with an oversized sweater hanging below her waist. "Bye, Chill," she yelled after him. "Call me!"

He didn't say a word. I was able to catch his eye as he passed by. He nodded before he shoved his hands in his pockets and walked on.

Miss Mabel honked her horn and rolled the window down. "Gracey, don't forget to rest, you hear?"

"Yes, ma'am," I hollered back, then stepped past Joanna into the house.

She closed the door, and I turned to face her. "Who was that?" I asked. "You know we ain't allowed to have boys in the house."

"Well, look around." Joanna showcased our house with her hand. "There's no adults here. Besides, he's just a friend and we were hanging out."

"What about school?"

Joanna shrugged. "What about it?"

CHAPTER 12

Gracey
November 1987

POTPIES WERE OUR FAVORITE TV dinners. We loved the flaky crust with the aftertaste of baking soda and the fact that we got our meat and vegetables all rolled into one. With potpies, we were pretty sure we'd done our due diligence in acting grown. I was feeling better after passing out earlier at school, and my sisters pampered me with cut up slices of apple and peanut butter for dessert, two things we found inside the brown grocery bag someone left on our doorstep. That night, the second we finished everything and tossed our aluminum foil containers in the garbage, Miss Nelda came knocking.

"Open this door, y'all," she called. We thought she was in danger, so we ran to undo the locks. Miss Nelda pushed past me with a "move" and stood in front of Joanna with a scowl on her face.

Joanna looked horrified. "Miss Nelda, what's wrong?"

"Don't you try to smooth-talk me, you little tramp." Miss Nelda looked her up and down in disgust. "What I want to know is why at one o'clock in the daytime both of you were at home. And why was there some nappy-headed boy leavin' here, pullin' up his nasty little pants?"

Joanna looked embarrassed, and I was dumbfounded. Who knew she was watching? I wanted to hug her on the spot. Knowing Miss Nelda was looking after us took a load off; she instantly became the new grandma in our family.

Then she doubled down. "What in God's name is going on in this house?"

"Miss Nelda, please calm down." Joanna spoke softly.

"Calm down? Calm down!" she yelled, her voice breaking. "Don't you know it's my responsibility to take care of you? If they find some mess is going on, they goin' take you away from me again."

"Wait, what do you mean 'again'?" I asked. It was like Miss Nelda was speaking to us from a whole 'nother realm or dimension.

"Just like they did in 1979. Wasn't nothing wrong. We was handlin' things just fine, and then come the authorities and they took you away. You and Phoebe, just like that, you was gone."

"Great!" Joanna threw up her hands. "Now she's gone senile."

Now was not the time. "Shut up, Jo!"

"Don't you test me, Phoebe." Miss Nelda made a lunge for Joanna while holding on to her walker.

Francine looked startled and amused. "Are we in *The Twilight Zone*?" Then she started to hum the show's siren-like theme song and flipped through the channels on the TV.

"Frankie, stay in the living room and watch whatever you want. Find some sitcoms or something."

"Cool, I didn't want to hear your conversation anyway. Too much drama for my young ears."

Joanna and I led Miss Nelda to the kitchen where we made her a cup of hot coffee with skim milk and one heaping teaspoon of sugar, just the way she liked it.

When all was calm, she looked around and realized she was at the table where all of our serious conversations went down. "What happened?" The evening had ushered in a quiet like a thick cloud. She rested her hands around her coffee mug as she smiled with satisfaction. "How y'all keeping?"

"I sort of passed out in school."

"You what, chile?" Miss Nelda sat back in her chair and let her arms flop to her sides.

"I sort of passed out in school, Miss Nelda." I twiddled with my fingers.

"Now, how did that come to be?" She spoke in breathy words from high pitched to low, just like the parents from the South at school.

"I think maybe I was working too hard, ma'am." I looked up at the lights. "We still gotta pay the bills and all, keep the gas going. I've been raking leaves and ironing, painting people's rooms, whatever I can. And it's that time of the month."

I didn't mind doing those things for us, but I never talked about it much because that was what Dad taught me to do—always do what you gotta do to keep things rolling. I didn't know why my sisters didn't learn that. Maybe they were too cool for school. But thinking about it too much gave room for bitterness so I always shut it down and got on with it. Joanna and Francine were good with making sure we had some form of dinner and dessert on the table, so that was good enough. Plus they liked to clean more than me.

"Uh-huh," Miss Nelda grunted. "And what about you?" She looked over to Joanna who busied herself wiping the counter. "You can put the dish towel down. The counter is clean. You the only one old enough to be working in this house. What're you doin' to help?"

I shook my head. "It's okay, Miss Nelda. It doesn't really matter."

"I keep the house clean," Joanna said, leaning her hip against the steel sink. "I wash the clothes, clean the bathrooms, sweep, vacuum—you name it, I do it. And then I go to school to top it all off."

I didn't think she really did all that much, but whatever. She could have the excuse.

"Evidently school isn't too important, you spending your days with boys while ain't nobody else home."

Joanna stretched out her arm as if she were offended. "We were studying for exams, Miss Nelda." She pointed to a nearby counter. "My chemistry book is right over there."

Miss Nelda and I looked to the counter where the thick hardback book sat closed. In bold orange letters, the word *Chemistry* posed as truth. "You don't take time off school to study. And you wasn't studying no chemistry. If anything, you was studying anatomy. I ain't no fool."

She struggled to get up from the table, and I went to support her arm until she was able to stand strong enough to make it to her walker.

"You know"—her cup seemed filled with so much disappointment—"it's some places in my life I don't ever want to visit again. Some scenes, I don't ever want to live through again. And I'm not going to." Miss Nelda pointed her index finger at Joanna even though she couldn't get it to stop shaking. She stepped closer and peered at my sister.

"I ain't gonna do it, you hear? Social services came over to the house after the girls had run away and been found in the club. I remember how them officials looked—Black women with thick pale stockings made for white people, navy blue suits that came down past the knee. Their hair was pressed so straight it shined and the curls so tight you could still see where the rollers had just been taken out and sprayed to hold. The looks on their faces as they sat on my couch—disapproval and judgment, as if I had done something wrong. I wanted to throw my coffee in their faces.

"I had two foster girls, Phoebe and Rachel. Bad to the bone. When they messed up, I told them right from wrong. But they still ran away. Got so's I couldn't keep up with 'em. Them ladies were sitting in my living room—one was doing all the talking and the other one was writing. The more I said, the more they wrote, and nothing I said was good enough for me to keep them. Next thing I know they said, 'Miss Nelda, we have reason to believe that you're not equipped to handle girls with extreme behavior issues such as these.'"

"What you mean I'm not equipped?" Miss Nelda was in the moment again. I felt like I was watching her in the theater acting out a role. "Who is? What does being equipped look like?"

"'We've come to take the girls away.'" Miss Nelda mocked their voices. "I couldn't see no love in their souls. I couldn't see no family. How could they care for children and be so cold? I told them"—Miss Nelda looked at us to make sure we were still with her—"listen, I told them to go on ahead. Maybe, you know, I'm not the one to raise them. God knows I tried everything, and if they want out so bad, then maybe they should go." She leaned into the table. "'Just tell me,' I asked them, 'tell me what happened to them when they were little to make them like that, make 'em so hard and unruly?'

"That's when that maroon-lipped woman closed her file and said, 'They watched their home burn down when they were just three and four years old. And they watched as police tried to rescue their mother, but the whole place exploded before they could get to her.'

"If I'da known what they went through, I coulda helped them. They just told me there was a tragedy in the home," Miss Nelda said, pointing again. "You understand?"

"Yes, Miss Nelda," me and Joanna answered in unison.

"I can't help you if I don't know what's going on. Now tell me, Jo." Miss Nelda focused on her. "What's your issue? Is it 'cause your mama gone? Your daddy dead? You sick of this house? Why is it that you losin' it, and your sisters ain't?"

"It's nothin', Miss Nelda." But then Joanna took a deep breath and looked up as if she wanted everything to stop, as if she couldn't keep the tears from falling. "I just want to know that somebody loves me." She wiped her face and took a seat. "And I don't want to hear it, I want to feel it. I don't want to have to wonder in my heart, you know? I shouldn't have to wonder if my mother loves me or if she *ever* loved me."

Miss Nelda made her way back over to the chair and sat down at the table. There was silence in the room for some time as we sat and listened to the clock tick above the sink and the steam pushing through to heat our home. The light above us hummed as if it were about to go out, and Joanna sniffled, using the palm of her hand to wipe her nose. Every once in a while we could hear Francine giggling at whatever reruns she'd found to watch. Miss Nelda looked more tired than she'd probably care to admit. She wore old age like a burden she could hardly stand, having to lug it around everywhere she went.

A siren set off outside. As it faded, I said, "Joanna, I remember you used to pray more than all of us. Me and Francine would wake up sometimes, open your door, and you'd be on your knees by the side of the bed, praying. Hands folded, talking to God. You used to say things like, 'Seems like God is saying this' or 'I bet you this is a sign from God.' And then we stopped seeing you pray. It's like you let God escape from the cage of your heart. What happened?"

Joanna wiped the sweat from her brow. "All that praying didn't do a thing. Daddy died, Grandma's gone, Mom left . . . We're all messed up and spread out."

Silence rolled in again, save the giggles from the other room.

"You're right. I failed big-time," Joanna confessed. "I ain't prayed since the first time Miss Nelda came over and we thought we had a prowler. Haven't talked to God, nothin'. I have nothing to say. There's nothing in me that wants to pray."

I looked at Joanna, wanting to give her a hug. I kind of knew how she felt. Maybe not so much, but—

"So you just stopped tryin' and decided to fill your empty spaces with some boy that don't care nothing about you." Miss Nelda looked to have some strength rising up.

"Well, no. I mean . . . yes. Maybe." Joanna twirled her hair.

"I'ma tell you somethin'." Miss Nelda straightened up and squared her shoulders best she could. "Gracey, give me a li'l bit of water . . . thank you." She drank as if the caffeine had dried her out, then put the cup down. "Now listen here. I ain't no God expert, but it don't seem like God would expect you to save your whole family with prayers. You ain't no Mother Teresa."

"I know that, Miss Nelda, but I thought prayer would keep us from—"

"Here's what I think God thinks of prayer." She stretched her arms out as if an announcement were being made. "I think God wants us to love our families no matter what they do. We ain't supposed to give up or stop showing love."

"But, Miss Nelda, that's not prayer," I said.

"Come on, y'all," Miss Nelda hollered. "It's been a long time since I been to church, but I know you can pray with a hug and you can pray with a smile. If you got a warm heart toward your family, you can reach God with a quickness. Ain't got nothing to do with words." She was getting worked up again and began to wheeze. "Now, what you got to say to that, huh? I'm eighty somethin' years old. What you got to say to me? I'm saying it ain't yo' fault things are the way they are, and sometimes prayers are too little too late. Better off praying God help you to love better in the situation you in."

Joanna shrugged.

"So you think . . ." I stopped to figure it out. "You think maybe God looks down on us showing love to each other and being nice and whatnot and then—"

"And then God says, 'Look at this family, all the love they got.'" Miss Nelda pretended she was God, pulling the small salt and pepper shakers together like a married couple. I'm going to bless them real good." Her voice got soft.

"Soo . . ." I still didn't understand. "Sounds like you're saying we're in this mess because there wasn't enough love in our home?"

Miss Nelda deflated, looking on the verge of offense. "Okay, well . . . like I said, I'm old, Gracey. And I don't know God like I should. I can't speak for what I don't know. I guess what I'm trying to say is, best thing we can ever do is love each other and walk with God no matter what comes—ups, downs, whatever. Prayer ain't about all that knees and folded hands stuff. Shoot, most of us can't even make it to the ground let alone get up again." She motioned the up and downs with her hand and then let it go.

"Joanna, you need to learn to love yo'self before you have another mouth to feed."

My big sister looked small as she stared at Miss Nelda and wrapped her arms around her own small frame.

CHAPTER 13

Charlotte
November 1987

CANDI WAS OUTSIDE SPLASHING YELLOW and red paint on a canvas when I started my shift. Our manager allowed Candi to paint outside the premises because he thought it gave the place an "aesthetic" look. Today the plush green world around us made her painting look like a patch of petunias there by chance.

"And take that, you pathetic piece of marmalade pie." Candi took her brush, dipped it in red paint, and flicked it through the air. "And I hope all your cakes and pies fall." She dug her hand deep in the yellow paint and smeared it all over the red on the canvas with a vengeance.

I lifted up the window and called to her quietly. "Candi."

She didn't answer.

"Candi!" I gave up stealth. "*Candi!*"

She stopped and looked up, wiping paint onto her smock and clearing the hair strands from her forehead with the back of her hand. "What?"

"What's wrong? What's this all about?"

"It's my sister." The woman sounded like a whining child. "I came home last night and found her snuggled up next to him."

"Hold on." I tucked my cleaning cloth in my cart. "Be there in a second." I ran down the stairs, grabbing a couple of oranges from the kitchen on my way out. The air still carried that kind of morning majesty that made me step lightly as I walked across the yard. I took off my shoes and let the dew-endowed blades of grass caress my feet.

Candi came over, and we plunked down on the bench. She sat

with her back straight and her hands out so she wouldn't get paint on anything.

"Now just relax and tell me what happened." I wiped her tears with my thumb because I didn't have anything else and set to peeling the orange.

"After work, I got off the bus and walked home. And they're snuggled up watching television together like an old married couple." She sniffed. "And my heart dropped like somebody had invaded the privacy of its beating for the umpteenth time. 'Can't you just leave me alone?' I asked her. 'Can't you just stay out of my life?' And that Mr. Goodin, he sat there watchin' the both of us. Wasn't stickin' up for nobody. That man, he brings me so much misery, I can't tell it all. And my sister . . . *Lord!* She think she's supposed to have some of everything I got."

I tore off half the orange and handed it to her with paint on her hands. "So what are you going to do now?"

"Well, ain't much I can do." She tore off a single segment of orange and bit in. I twisted my face, thinking about the paint she was ingesting with the orange, but didn't interrupt. "Mr. Goodin done ran off with her. Say she a better pick and he feel sorry for her being so skinny and all. He even said she makes a better cake than me."

"Oh, Candi, if he can go that easy, he didn't really love you. And you don't want nobody that don't really love you."

"Uh-uh, that's where you're wrong. Mr. Goodin does love me, he just never had a chance to show it. My sister been workin' on him so many years. He must have got like Samson and couldn't take Delilah's nagging anymore. That's all, he just couldn't take it anymore. I mean, really, you put me around chocolate too long, I'm gonna eat it." She pressed a slice of orange into her mouth, red paint prints and all. "No, see, I forgive him, but I can't forgive my sister. That's why I had to throw paint—'cause I can't stand having bitter layers in me. Makes me want to throw up, it does, if I hold things too long."

"Well, I don't know what to say to make you feel better." Candi

confused me. She was so wise when it came to my problems, but—
Lord, forgive me for saying this—so stupid when it came to her own
mess.

"Oh, honey, I don't need you to say nothin'. You being here is good
enough for me." She smiled and patted my hand, dabbing orange
paint on my skin. Candi shook her head and looked to the clouds.
"You know, when we was little, my sister always used to get jealous
'cause everybody called me *sweetie* but they called her *twiggy*. And I
always laughed."

I couldn't help but crack a smile at that.

"I almost wish she'd drowned all them years ago."

I sobered quickly. "What?"

"Yeah, I said it. We were at the beach one day. Ebony was playing way out in the water and then she started bobbing up and down
and waving for help. I remember standing there frozen, staring at her
while she was lookin' for me to come and save her."

"So why didn't you?"

"I don't know. I couldn't move. Maybe I was afraid I'd drown too?"

"So what happened?"

"The lifeguard jumped in and pulled her to shore. I stood there
while they worked on her, giving her mouth to mouth and pumping
her chest. She eventually came to. She coughed up water, her body
jerking. Then she turned and looked at me like I'd done something
wrong. I took off running. I have no idea why. Seems like we been
enemies since that day."

She rubbed her chin, leaving a little paint behind. "Looking back,
I wonder if maybe I really had it in for her."

"Or"—I interrupted—"maybe in that moment you stood still 'cause
you couldn't imagine life without her and you knew that if you made
any sudden moves and broke her gaze, she might not make it out
alive. And maybe you ran because the thought of losing her scared
the life out of you, and you knew she was safe and you never wanted
to have the responsibility of keeping someone alive again."

She blinked at me for a minute. "Charlotte, girl, that's deep. And it feels right."

"I might hate you too if I were Ebony. Sounds like you're Jacob and she's Esau."

"What?" Candi sounded outraged. "She's the one that's stealing from me."

"Yeah, but I bet you stole some stuff from her in your childhood. Things like confidence, peace, joy . . . love. Right? It's just the stupid game we play when we're young."

"Still don't give her no right to steal my man. Don't go apple picking on my land."

I held my breath to keep from laughing as long as I could and then a giggle escaped. Candi leaned on my shoulder and elbowed me to be quiet.

We stayed outside a good twenty minutes more, talking about life and crazy kinfolks, and eventually we got around to talking about the seagulls and the swallows and the possum, and I knew our conversation was over.

Candi went back to her painting and hollered over her shoulder, "Girl, you need to come to Sunday dinner one day and meet my whole family. They crazy as a bucket of crabs. You'll see, I'm the only sane one in the house."

"I'll see," I hollered back. I didn't want to admit it out loud, but I knew a thing or two about letting go and holding on. And there were some things in my past that I didn't think I'd ever be able to let go of. Or forgive the people involved.

Candi had one thing right. Chocolate candy was irresistible. Put it around me long enough, and I'd eat it too. Micah was my chocolate candy, and as much as I had tried to ignore that boy, I couldn't do it. If I wasn't dreaming about him at night, I was thinking about him while I was walking down the road or sitting in class. I thought about him all while I was eating, and while I was doing my schoolwork. I even thought about him while I was praying to God. Oh my goodness, I was pitiful. It got so bad I would trip over my words when he walked into the room, and he didn't help me neither, winking at me every time he passed me by. I tell you, I got on my own nerves over that boy.

l l l

December 1969

I was sixteen the first and last time my mama let me go to the Christmas dance. There wasn't no snow, but inside the gym the garland looping across the ceiling with twinkling lights peeking out and The Drifters' "White Christmas" pumping through the sound system were enough to make us feel the Christmas love that spreads throughout the heathens and the holy folks alike. In a way, Christmas was like drinking red wine—it gave you the courage to do the things you wouldn't normally do. It was the only time of year a homeless man could look up from his weathered hat, stick out his hand and say, "Merry Christmas," and expect a gold-watch-wedding-band-wearing, strong arm to return the shake with a twenty-dollar bill and a "Thanks, man, same to you." It was a time when we understood that we were all equal under God, if only for a limited season.

I was so happy that Christmas, I could have twirled and twirled in my new pleated red dress. But I drank my punch and contained myself as best I could. Sheila May swore I'd been drinking, but I told her plenty times I was sober. It was the season that made me giddy.

When I saw Micah walk through the door, I ran and gave him a big hug. He hugged me back, and I held him long enough to feel his breathing change.

Uh-oh, I thought. *I went too far.*

When he finished, he moistened his lips and looked as though he were soaking me in with his eyes. "You been drinking?"

"No," I said. "I'm just happy."

Micah smiled and relaxed, and then he excused himself and passed me by to join some of his friends in their usual shake, pull, and snap hand thing.

I shuffled back to Sheila May, who seemed happy to welcome the castoff.

"So how do you feel? Stupid, embarrassed, like a fast girl from the wrong side of the neighborhood?"

"Are you kidding, girl? I feel great." I took a sip of my punch, trying to hide my disappointment. "Okay, maybe I do feel a little bit embarrassed."

"I can't believe you did that. You acted like one of them white cheerleading girls at Thompson High."

"I was just . . . I felt so free, I couldn't contain myself. Oh, Lord, have mercy, now what am I going to do? He'll never talk to me again."

"Nah. It's easy to fix." Sheila May put down her punch and started playing with my hair. "For the rest of the night, don't say another word to him. Totally ignore him, like you don't even notice he's here. And when you talk to anybody, just act like you havin' a really good time. If he really likes you, he'll be watching and wondering why you aren't paying him any attention. I guarantee by the time the night's over, he'll come walking your way."

"What makes you so sure?"

"Trust me. Go on. Mingle." She turned me around and gave me a push.

And I did it. I worked that room. I talked to everyone I knew and even started conversations with folks I didn't know. I sang Christmas carols with a group at the piano, helped my teachers refill the refreshments, and danced with the boys who asked me. By the end of the evening, I was exhausted. Every once in a while, I felt Micah's eyes on me, but I never returned his looks. I ended up sitting in a chair next to Sheila May, watching everyone else work the room.

Micah came my way as I was gleaning dancing tips from others, checking my watch, and wondering if it would ever snow in Mississippi.

"He's coming this way, don't turn around," Sheila May said out of the side of her mouth. "Look my way and pretend to tell me something you just remembered."

I took a deep breath and turned toward her. "Oh yeah, I forgot to tell you—"

"Hey, Charlotte." Micah was standing over me with his hands in his pockets.

"Oh, hi, Micah. You enjoying the party?" I crossed my legs and looked up at him. Nat King Cole was crooning in the background.

"Yeah, it's been pretty nice. It sure looks like you been having a good time."

"Well, like I said, I love the Christmas season."

"Well, I was just wondering if I could have this last dance."

"I'd love to."

He took my hand like I was a princess and guided me up. I had just enough time to flash a thank-you smile to Sheila May when he turned his head.

We started out at a proper distance, my left hand on his shoulder, his hand around my waist, our other hands intertwined. But he kept looking into my eyes without saying anything. I was so light-headed, I didn't dare return the gaze. If I did, I might've passed out. He must have read my heart, because then he pulled me close and I rested my head on his shoulder. His cologne wrapped around me, something manly, something spicy and fresh. I breathed in his air and closed my eyes.

The only way I knew the song had ended was because Micah slowly pulled away. I scrambled for composure before I met his eyes again.

"So how about I walk you home?" he asked.

Sheila May came running up behind me. "Hi, Micah. Charlotte, we got to go now. You know we both got curfew."

I looked at Sheila and then at Micah. "Well, I was thinking about walking home with Micah."

Sheila May looked at Micah and said, "Excuse us." Then she dragged me by the arm to the punch table. "Are you crazy? I saw the way y'all were dancing. You got what you wanted. You got his attention, y'all danced, now leave it be."

"He's just going to walk me home."

"Charlotte, you know that boy want to do more than just walk you home. Don't be no fool."

"I ain't no fool, Sheila May. I can take care of myself."

"If he walking you home, I'm walking with y'all. And I ain't taking no for an answer. Whatever y'all do after you walk me home is yo' business."

"All right, then, fine."

There we were, all of us walking down the dirt road together. Weren't no lights, just the moon and the bright dots in the sky. Occasional headlights passed by. None of us had much to say, we just kind of kicked rocks down the road and talked about what we usually got for Christmas—a record, or a book, or maybe one special thing like a dress or a suit for church.

Sheila May's house came up too soon. I imagined we'd be walking for ages and then Micah and I would only walk a few steps alone before I was home. But it was the other way round. As Sheila May opened the gate to her front yard, she looked at me and said, "Remember what I told you." Then she turned and ran to the door.

Yeah, I remembered. But somehow the desire in me had grown larger than my conscience. Micah was an uncontrollable urge I had to act on. I was tired of daydreaming and doodling and hugging my pillow at night to quench my urges. I had to hold him, kiss him, if only for just a little bit. Just a little bit more of him was all I needed, and then I could walk away fine as Christmas Day.

As Sheila May let her door close, Micah grabbed my hand and held it. For a long time we didn't say anything. Little squeezes to my palm let me know that we were communicating, saying stuff that only our souls could understand. And then he broke the peace.

"You know, we've been friends a long while now."

"Yeah, it's been, what? Four or five years?"

"Yeah, a long time. And we've never kissed."

I tripped over a rock that wasn't there when I looked behind me.

"Excuse me, Mr. Micah? What do you mean we've never kissed? What in the world makes you think I want to kiss you?"

He stopped right before we got to the barn on the side of my house, and he took me into his arms.

"So you're telling me, Miss Charlotte, you don't want to kiss me."

"Well, no . . . I mean yes, but . . ."

And then he planted his soft, sweet lips right on top of mine, and like wilting flowers in the rain, the inner me came alive. We kissed until my lips went numb, and my cheeks were sore. Wasn't until his hands had worked their way under my dress that I opened my eyes and yelled, "No, stop!"

I peeked around the corner and saw the porch light come on.

"Charlotte?"

And there was my mama walking through the grass in her long flannel nightgown, rollers, and house shoes . . . carrying a shotgun.

"Charlotte, is that you? Girl, if that's you, you better come out here, 'cause I'm about to start shootin'. You hear me?"

My heart was beating so fast, I could hardly breathe. "Go! My mama ain't playin'. She liable to kill somebody."

Micah took off running while I straightened out my panties and smoothed my hair as best I could.

I came out from the side of the barn with my hands up. "It's me, Mama, don't shoot. It's me."

"Charlotte?" Mama was squinting her eyes to see me in the dark. "Girl, you look a mess. You been back there makin' out with some boy, ain't you? That Micah child. I'm callin' his auntie tonight. Get yo' butt in the house before I make this shotgun go off by accident."

My brothers were still at the dance, so I knew I was in real trouble this time with nobody to stick up for me. I tried to explain myself all the way to the door.

"Mama, I'm sorry. Please don't call his auntie. Don't call her, Mama. We didn't do nothin'. We was just talkin', and then he kissed me. It was just a little kiss. Mama, please."

She raised the back of her hand and swung it down across my cheek. "Don't you stand there and lie to me, child. I can look at you and see y'all was sharin' more than a kiss on the cheek!" She put the shotgun on the table and stood there with her arms folded. "Git upstairs," she said.

"What? Mama, why?"

She slammed her hand on the table and yelled, "Do it!"

I ran upstairs in tears and balled myself up at the head of the bed, the drops from my eyes darkening the red in my dress. That was so stupid, I thought to myself. It was stupid to go that far. Maybe I *was* fast, like the girls that never went to church. But was I the only one with these feelings inside me? Wasn't anyone else fighting the way I was? Maybe nobody else had fallen in love like I had. I knew I would marry Micah one day. I was sure my mama never had real love like that.

Footsteps came up the stairs, and I straightened myself out on the bed and spread out my dress. Mama walked in. A long, wide leather belt was wrapped around her hand with just the tail sticking out.

"I'm sorry I got to do this, Charlotte. But I can't trust you no more. Don't know when you lyin' or when you tellin' the truth."

"Mama, no. Please don't." I crawled away from her on the bed, but it didn't work. I felt the heat of her belt coming toward me, slicing through my skin, causing it to rise up and redden in revolt. For a second, I thought I'd be stuck screaming in pain forever. *This must be what hell is like.* Sustained pain between whips, like the vibrations from a tolling church bell.

And then she stopped and stared at me, watching me heave as if she was trying to gauge whether or not she'd caused me enough pain. "Maybe you'll remember this next time you even think of allowin' somebody 'tween your legs."

The door slammed as she left, and I folded into my body, skin burning like it was set on fire. The words of an old deacon came back to me as I tried to gather my soul back into the cup of my body. He'd been sweeping up before church, still tall for a ninety-two-year-old, still agile in his movements. Mama had just tore into me for going to the bathroom during the prayer. He paused, leaning long on his broom.

"Darlin'," he said. "My mother once told me love comes wrapped in ugly packages, and it didn't have nothin' to do with looks. She told me how hard it was to love during slavery. Say some women carried their babies on their hip, taught them everything good they knew, poured the light of life into their souls. And when them children was sold to other plantations, the mothers went places in their minds they couldn't return from. So they had to find ways to stay sane. Mother say one girl made the same quilt over and over with her baby's clothes, pickin' the stitches apart and putting them back together again. Other women, she say, just waxed hard, keepin' a distance from their children, never huggin' or kissin' them. That way when master come to take them children away, they wasn't so hurt, they could stay in their right mind.

"And then there's those like yo' mama, mean 'cause they scared. She wants you to turn out good so bad, she gonna make you more 'fraid of her than anybody else. She thinks if you can make it under her roof, you'll be invisible to the white folks long enough to make somethin' of yourself.

"My own mama loved me recklessly. She didn't care nothin' 'bout what other people thought and losing me wasn't a good enough reason to hold back.

"When I look at some of these women today, I can't sweep their pain away. Ain't no reason to treat their children so bad. Slavery's over, I want to tell 'em. It's over, pull your babies close now . . ."

I didn't like the way he talked about women as if he had us all figured out and needed to let us know we'd been emancipated. I would have told him so if he weren't ninety-two. Yet I found myself praying, *God, send me somebody that will pull me close.*

I I I

Sunday wasn't any easier. Everyone stared at me when I walked to my class and whispered as I walked by. When I got to the room, there was already a girl there teaching the kids. She was twelve years old. I went to Ms. Jenkins, who was sitting at her desk.

"Ms. Jenkins, what's going on?"

"I've decided to give you a break and let you go learn with the children your own age. You've been teaching so long, you never get a chance to just sit and learn."

"But, Ms. Jenkins, I like teachin'. I learn by teachin'."

"Things have changed. This is the way it's going to be. Your class is upstairs in the counseling room."

I looked for Micah but couldn't find him. "Is Micah going to class too, or are you going to let him keep on teaching?"

Ms. Jenkins cleared her throat and took off her glasses. She came and sat on the edge of her desk right in front of me.

"Micah had to go home. It seems he's been getting into things he didn't have no business gettin' into. When his father found out, he sent for him. Left this morning on the Greyhound bus."

"You mean he's gone?"

"Yes, dear, he's gone. To be honest, chile, you ought to be happy." Ms. Jenkins gave me a slow look with her head turned to the side and then went back to her normal voice. She patted my back. "Go on, Charlotte. They're expecting you."

I didn't allow tears to drop on my way to class. I caught them all with my fingers as they tried to escape the bank of my eyes. The door was already open when I reached the room, and the backs of ten teens were facing me. Didn't nobody say nothin' to me, just lowered their heads. My face burned on the outside, and I patted my cheeks and wiped my forehead to stay calm.

The teacher waved her hand for me to come closer. "Come on in. We've been expecting you. Have a seat over there." She pointed to the front row.

Payback, I thought to myself, *is horrible*. Everybody looked so shamed, like I had uncovered them instead of myself. I almost couldn't understand it, 'cept there was something 'bout the way they looked at me from the corner of their eyes let me know it could have just as easily been them. *Humph*. I sat down to a sharp pain and eased up for comfort. Somebody sighed, and I raised my head while planting myself deeper into my seat, this time swallowing the sting.

"Today we're talking about Mary, a teenager who was blessed and highly favored because she was still a virgin . . ."

The rest of the lesson was one long high-pitched note in my ears as I imagined myself in my home, in Micah's arms, him holding me and telling me not to worry because he would take care of everything.

I I I

"How was church today?" Mama met me on her way to the choir room, a knowing smile on her face.

I was yelling at her in my head. *You evil woman, I wish I could hear the sound of you tearing into a thousand pieces!*

"It was right nice, thank you." I stood with my back straight and my face solid.

"Good."

And we never said another word about it.

But my soul was drafty. I missed Micah, and I never got a chance to say goodbye. For the first few days, I could hardly get up. I even slept through Christmas morning. When I was little, I used to hear about how in the olden days, folks would just lie down from a broken heart and never get up again. I tried that, but I kept waking up every morning, and Mama kept sucking her teeth and cussing me when she passed by my room.

So I figured, since the Lord wasn't going to let me die, I'd better get on with my life. Besides, now that I thought about it, the Lord was right to let me live. Micah wasn't worth dying for. He wasn't even half the man I thought he was. And time, I learned, had its own way of unfolding the truth.

Some men can't hear you when you scream, and Micah was one of them.

CHAPTER 14

Gracey
November 1987

FRANCINE GOT HER PERIOD a few days ago in math class. Right on time for her age. I only got mine a year ago at thirteen. Apparently, she was walking down the hallway with a big ol' stain on the back of her jeans. At first, I was like, no way. But then my source was pretty reliable—Rosa from the hairdresser's. Usually, her gossip is for real. I went upstairs and checked the dirty clothes hamper in the bathroom. Holding my breath, I lifted the lid and turned the plastic box upside down and emptied out the clothes. Underneath a bunch of stinky underwear and dirty tops was a pair of wet jeans, balled up and matted down. I stretched them out, and sure enough there was the outline of a blood stain spread across the seams.

Oh boy.

It looked like Francine had tried to wash the blood out, but she didn't know how, so she just stuffed the jeans in the bottom of the hamper. Inside the pants was a pair of panties even more stained, like a bad tie-dye job.

What would Mom have done in this situation? Probably she wouldn't even touch it. She stayed away from any problems that were too personal, like we had the plague or something.

I tried to think about what Dad would say, but I knew he wasn't comfortable with girly subjects. When I first got my period, I screamed, and he came running in. When he saw me on the toilet and looked at my underwear, he did a one-eighty and was like, "I'll go get Joanna."

She came in with some thick maxi pads and taught me how to peel off the film and stick them in my panties. She told me that it was just the way a girl's body was made and that I shouldn't have sex because I could get pregnant if I did. The rest I learned in sex education. Women are like flowers. Men are like bees.

I put my head down and sat on the closed toilet in silence. I supposed I could tell Joanna and ask her to talk to Francine. I hated to do that, but I knew it was the best thing.

She answered my knock, annoyed.

"I need to show you something," I said in defense.

She followed me down the hall to the bathroom, where I pulled out Francine's jeans and lifted them up for Joanna to see.

She put her hands over her mouth. "Ugh, that's gross!"

"Will you go talk to her, please?"

"Oh, poor baby," Joanna said. "I'm going now."

I started to follow her down to the living room, but she tossed back, "I don't need any help. You stay here and wash out those pants."

I stopped midstride. "Great."

After about a minute of scrubbing with gold Dial soap, I put the pants and underwear on the heater to dry. Then I washed my hands with scalding water. I tiptoed to the top of the stairs, careful not to step on the floorboards that squeaked, and sat down to listen.

"Now the whole world knows," Francine was saying. "I'm a freak."

"Hel-loo, we all get periods," Joanna replied. "Does that mean we're all freaks?"

"No, but you all know how to keep it inside."

"Well, I can teach you that."

"I already know now. The nurse told me what to do."

"Yeah, but did she teach you everything? Like did she tell you Coca-Cola, ice cream, and french fries make cramps worse? And hot chocolate makes you super heavy?"

"That sucks."

"I know! It's the only time of the month I don't eat chocolate chip cookies."

"It'd be nice if Mom coulda taught me that. Why I got to get private information from public people."

"Let's not keep secrets, Francine. Next time, just talk to us when something's going on. It's the only way we're going to make it."

When I thought the conversation was over, I made my way down the stairs. "Are we all good now?" I asked.

"Yeah," Francine said. She still looked down about having to go through this. I wished I could make it all better, but I almost had a fit too when I realized I had to go through this every month for the next forty years. Neither of us had the heart to tell that part to Francine. She'd find out soon enough.

"Group hug!" I lunged for both my sisters on the couch, and we squeezed each other until we toppled onto the ground.

⎮ ⎮ ⎮

Back at school, I was learning how to flirt. I'd watched Kendall and her girls enough to pick up a few tricks here and there. I thought I'd try them on Sebastian and see if he'd think of me as one of the cool girls worth dating. He was walking with his boys down the hall when I interrupted him.

"Have you been shaving, Bastian?" I asked.

He smiled, rubbed his chin. "Yeah, can you tell?"

"Only by the pieces of toilet paper stuck to your chin." Why'd I have to point that out?

He sucked his teeth with a frozen smile. Then he spoke as if he were coming out of a pop lock, quick and sharp with his words in syncopation. "Aw, that's bogus. You know I got some peach fuzz coming in." His hand lightly rubbed the top of his chin.

"Whatever." I closed my locker and walked away. I stunk at flirting. I had way too much pride.

"Nah, wait, Gracey," Bastian shouted after me. "Come back." He walked up to me and stuck his chin out. "Feel."

I touched his skin, then quickly pulled my hand away and put it behind my back. His fuzz felt like the fur of a newborn puppy. It gave me goose bumps. "I don't feel jack."

"Aw, you ain't right, Gracey!" Bastian went and found another girl to caress his chin and tell him what she felt. I watched with a hangdog in my soul as a cheerleader in a maroon-and-white uniform came and told him everything he wanted to hear while giggling into the fold of his neck. Then he looked at me and pointed as if to say, "Now, this is what I'm talkin' about."

"Jessica," Miss Mabel shouted. "Get your hands off that boy and go to class before I tell your mother what you're doing." The girl straightened and trotted off without looking back.

I looked at Miss Mabel, and she ducked back into her classroom. I figured I might as well go and see what she was up to.

"Miss Mabel, you okay?" I asked. "You sounded annoyed."

"Hey, sweetie. I'm good. How about you?"

"Well, yeah, I was just wondering . . ." I made something up 'cause I didn't want to talk about Sebastian but I did want to chill in the reading nook. "How come you haven't responded to any of my journal entries lately?"

"Oh, well, I . . ." she stuttered.

"Are you even reading the journals?" Was I doing this for nothing?

"Let me ask you this, Gracey. Why do you share so much when you write? And who are you talking to, me or your journal?"

I frowned big-time. "Neither. When I write, I'm talking to God." *Duh.* I might not talk *about* God, but I know somebody's watching over me and I'm sharing with that person.

"And it doesn't bother you that I'm reading it, that I know so much about what's going on in your life?"

"No."

"Why?"

"'Cause, Miss Mabel, you don't really matter. Like, you're not going to criticize me or hurt me. You're safe. Who cares what you know?"

Miss Mabel looked like I'd just called her super ugly and she believed it.

"I'm sorry if what I said is whack." I touched the desk where she sat. "It's just the way it is." I turned to go since it was too awkward now to chill in the reading corner. "Can I give you my journal to read this weekend?"

She chuckled apologetically. "Sure, Gracey."

Truth be told, I wanted her to read my latest entry. Someone we could trust needed to know we were going to need some help down the line.

November 10, 1987

I was thinking about my mom today, wondering about her past. I'll never forget watching her sunbathe at the end of August. There's a big oak tree I like to sit under not too far from the open field where everybody plays softball. Even on the cold hard ground, I like to sit there and point my face to the sun like I seen my mom do. One time, I just came and sat right next to her, hip bone to hip bone, and I asked her to tell me what she was thinking about. For a long time, she acted like she didn't even know I was there. But I kept asking and staring over at her.

Finally, without ever looking my way, she told me she was thinking about life in Mississippi when she was a girl. I asked her if she was scared of Grandma. She gave a grunt and raised her face further to the sun. She said Grandma always had a big switch in her hand and a wad of snuff in the side of her mouth. Mom looked at me and said, "Who wouldn't be scared of that?"

She said she grew so scared of that stick, she'd just stay in the fields and daydream until it was time to go home. She told me there was a time she really did try to do her farm chores, but she would always faint on her way up the hill back home. Grandma liked to beat her silly when she came to, just to toughen her up. After that, her brothers always poured some of their cotton into her bag. They said they didn't know what

God called her to do, but any perched bird could tell what she wasn't called to do.

Mom gave a little chuckle and looked at me to see my reaction. Then she cleared her throat and tightened her face again. Maybe I should have laughed with her, but I was too busy thinking about what she said. Seemed awful.

It's amazing how much Joanna acts like Mom. The two could pass for sisters, from the dainty way they move their hands to the deep breaths they release when they're sad. Joanna's got more spark than Mom—she'll never be as shy, but they both have this way of looking past the eyes and deep into your soul when they talk to you. They usually eat the same amount of food too, like birds, which is why they stay slim.

Come to think of it, Joanna's getting chubby lately. She eats all the time, and she seems stuck in her thoughts. Mom would never allow herself to get big like that. The other day, Miss Nelda went to eat with her nephew's family. She had somebody named Thelma bring us this amazing feast. Roast beef, gravy, mac and cheese, sweet potatoes. Everything we love to eat was up in there. Joanna pigged out big-time. We were like, dang, girl. And more and more, Joanna spends hours in the bathroom every morning. Me and Francine hear the shower going, but we can also hear Joanna throwing up. Then she walks out real slow like the world is spinning and she could fall over at any time. Francine asked her if she was sick, and she said no.

I hope she's not pregnant.

CHAPTER 15

Charlotte
June 1970

GOING TO CHURCH GOT TO be like walking through the fire every Sunday. If the Sunday school teacher wasn't teaching about me, the preacher was preaching about me, and everybody would turn their heads to look my way. Got to the point where I just couldn't go no more. Even Mama felt sorry for me. One Sunday, six months in, she went through all the motions of getting dressed and ready for church, humming her hymns and praising the Lord, and then she called me from the kitchen and asked if I was ready. She called again, and I didn't answer. Her heels clicked on the wooden floor as she walked to my room.

I faked a hard sleep, the kind a tornado couldn't wake up.

"Girl, you . . ." Then she stopped. I knew she was thinking as she took the time to put on her white gloves.

Then my door closed, and I heard the front screen door slam shut. She let me stay home. And she didn't ask me to go to church no more after that.

But I had no idea what to do with myself. Church was such a big part of my life. Not going felt like walking into a big empty room that used to be beautifully furnished but had been stripped down to bare floors, bare walls, and an echo to my own voice. I was retired from church.

I decided the first thing I'd do was make myself a nice breakfast—scrambled eggs and fried ham, grits and toast with butter and orange marmalade. That wasn't such a good idea because my brothers came in, expecting me to cook for them too. They'd stopped going to church a long time ago. Sleep was their staple when they went anyway, embarrassing the family. Mama had made faces at them from the choir stand, thinkin' couldn't nobody see her. Everybody could see her.

"That for us?" they asked.

"No, it's for me. You can cook for yourselves."

"Nah, we can't. Besides, you're a woman. You s'posed to cook."

That first Sunday I made breakfast for my brothers, but after that I had cereal and fruit. Sunday became my day for me. With most folks in church, there wasn't nobody trying to make me the poster girl for sinners. I'd pack a lunch and blanket and go to the meadows to have a chat with the Lord. I told him about everything I felt through the week, and then I prayed about things that seemed to be stuck to my heart, like Micah and how he was doing. I prayed for my brothers that we'd stay a family after they grew up and my mama, that she wouldn't be so mean and ornery. Every blue moon I thought about my father and his other family, how they were farin' in this world. We didn't see nor hear from him after the day he left. It was like he wanted to pretend he was never a part of our family and we didn't exist. I wondered if he regretted having us. My brothers and I didn't talk about it, but we missed him. Admitting it out loud, though, felt like a form of betrayal to ourselves and our mama so we never let his name get past our chest. We all just kept going like we were at a party and even though the music stopped, we continued to dance. I prayed over and over that God would forgive me for my sins, for being so weak and all, but I never did hear anything back.

In one of the few sermons I managed to listen to, Pastor said that if you throw away the church and keep God, you could still get into heaven. But not hearin' anything about my forgiveness made me kind of nervous. I just didn't have the stomach to go back to church right now. I told that to the Lord. I said them ladies in their big brazen hats and white gloves kept looking over their shoulders at me with their lips turned up and all the while fannin' their little perspiration before it soaked the edges of their hair.

And I told him how the boys would look me up and down like a piece of meat and pat their stomachs when I passed by. I even told him about the conversations I heard in the public bathroom while I was sitting on the toilet, and I ain't told nobody that stuff, not even Sheila May. They really thought I slept with Micah. Some of the things I heard them saying was so nasty it made my lunch push up my throat. Since when did church folks start talking that way?

I just can't do it, I told the Lord. *I can't do it.*

Nothing. God didn't say a word.

I felt the sun shining on me as a cloud moved out of its way, but I didn't really think that counted any more than a butterfly landing on your finger. I shrugged and went on to the next subject.

I   I   I

I was walking home from the meadows one day when I first met Moses.

He walked up right beside me and first thing he said was, "I hope I don't sound too fresh in sayin' this, but you're the prettiest girl I've ever seen in my whole born life."

"Thank you." I swung my picnic basket behind my back, hiding it like he didn't have eyes in his head to see it already. *Walk on*, I told myself. *Just keep walking.* But my feet were nailed to the ground. It wasn't that this boy was so fine, 'cause he wasn't. He looked plain, regular, a bit dusty. It was his voice that arrested me. It took me out of my sorrows and made me stand at attention.

"What you got there?" he asked, peering behind my back.

"This old thing? It's just my picnic basket."

"So you comin' back from a picnic?"

"Yes, you might could say that." I smiled.

"Oh." He seemed intrigued. "You was with your boyfriend. I understand, I'll leave you be . . ."

"No," I confessed. "I was just having lunch with a friend."

"Oh. Well, I'd better go." He squinted at the sky, measuring the light left in the day. "There's things I got to get done before the sun goes down."

"But it's Sunday," I protested. "Don't you know you ain't supposed to work on Sunday?"

"Seem like these days only the Lord can afford to rest on Sunday."

"You ain't from around here, that's for sure." Folks was sho'nuff superstitious in these parts. Bad luck to work on Sunday.

"Nah, I'm from Biloxi. But once I'm old enough, I'm moving to Chicago. Gonna get me a nice job, big house, and settle down with a family."

"That sounds solid," I said. "Well, it was nice meetin' you, Mr. . . ."

"Downing."

"I'll see you again, I'm sure."

We said our goodbyes, and I went on home, pulling seeds from the tall grass as I went. Chicago was a long way away. But wouldn't it be wonderful to live in such a big city, where folks could do whatever they wanted to do and wasn't nobody there to tell them they was wrong or evil or nasty? They said Chicago was full of big, tall, pointy buildings, and the wind threatened to take the breath out of you if you walked too fast. They said it was right next to the lake, and folks went sailing in the summertime with nothing but bathing suits on, and they drank champagne while they were hanging on to the rail. From what I seen on Sheila May's television, they had fancy homes with spiral staircases, marble floors, and big old chandeliers that sparkled when the sun hit 'em at just the right angle. I loved Chicago.

Soon as I got home, I threw my basket on the floor and ran to Sheila May's house. She was bound to be home from church by now. The preacher could preach long, but he knew good an' well every woman there had a roast or a ham or a chicken in the oven, and if they burned their food, somebody's husband was coming after him.

At my knock, Sheila opened the door. She'd already changed from her church clothes and was wearing a purple cotton skirt and a white blouse with ruffles on the shoulders. Flip-flops spanked her heels.

"Girl, you won't believe what happened to me." I hauled her out of the house and made her come with me to the tire swing hanging from the maple tree in the yard. I lifted myself in, and she started pushing me.

"So what happened, Charlotte? I ain't got all day."

"Well, I went on my usual picnic during church—"

"With Jesus . . ."

"Yeah. And I prayed and did a lot of thinking, and then I met this boy on the way home."

"Uh-oh." Sheila stopped pushing.

"No, Sheila, no uh-oh. I'm just telling you about this boy I met. And his voice was so manly, like he knew exactly what he wanted to do and how he wanted to do it."

"Charlotte, I don't think I want to hear this."

"No, Sheila, listen . . . Guess where he wants to move when he's grown?"

"Chicago."

"Yeah, how'd you know?"

Sheila turned around and yelled, "Charles Moses, come out here."

"What?" He came through the screen door like it was a fly in his way. Two big towels were folded in squares attached to his knees by strings, and tan dust covered him from head to toe.

"Just come here," she said.

I got out of the tire swing as quick as I could and dusted myself down.

He was frowning all the way to the tree till he saw me, and then his face softened.

"Moses, this is my best friend, Charlotte. Charlotte, this here's my cousin, Charles Moses. We just call him Moses. He's helpin' my mama out while Daddy's off working on the railroad."

"How'd you do, Miss Charlotte?" he said, bending down and shaking my hand.

"Nice to see you again, Moses."

"Small world."

"Too small, I'm sure."

"That's all, Moses, I just wanted to introduce you two. You better get back in there before Mama come lookin' for you. She wants that floor sanded before Tuesday come."

"I know. It'll get done." He waved quickly. "I'll be seein' ya again."

"Bye." I raised my right hand and put it down quickly as I watched him run back to the house.

Sheila put herself in the swing, and I pushed her from the front so I could see her face.

"Tell me everything you know. And don't leave nothin' out."

"Girl, what's there to tell? He's a boy. I only see him every couple of years on Thanksgiving or Christmas or something, and even then we don't hardly talk. All I know is that he's always been a hard worker, always had these dreams of going to Chicago, and everybody likes him wherever he goes. He could walk downtown and not know a soul, but after a couple of hours, it's like he's always been there. But nobody gets everything right, so must be a downfall in him somewhere."

CHAPTER 16

Gracey
November 1987

TONIGHT SHOULD BE EXCITING. SEBASTIAN'S mom, Rosa, invited me and my sisters to Thanksgiving dinner. It was going to be off the chain, for sure. I couldn't wait to see what Sebastian's house looked like, especially his room. I had to make sure to go to the bathroom and sneak a peek into his bedroom to see where he slept. We invited Miss Nelda too, 'cause we didn't want her to be alone. We knew she had a nephew, but he didn't seem too active in her life. And she didn't talk about him like people talk about close family. Sebastian, such a gentleman, came by as our escort. He even helped us get Miss Nelda into the taxi and made sure all of our seat belts were clicked into place.

"Seventy-Ninth and Loomis," he said, then tapped the taxi for it to go.

"Hey, wait! Stop!" I yelled, rolling down the window. "Ain't you coming? It's your mother's house."

"Nah." Sebastian looked around him. "I'm on my way to eat at a friend's house."

"What? You're not even going to spend time—I mean, I thought we could hang out?" I didn't want to be at his mother's house without him. How weird was that? I'd rather we all go home and eat peanut butter and jelly sandwiches and potato chips. Who cared about Thanksgiving anyway? It was a stupid holiday for people with families. And no one could give two cents if you didn't have a family.

Sebastian got a serious look on his face and glanced in the direction of his house. "Right now, I can't even stand to be in the same room with my mom."

His words didn't make sense to me. It was like he was speaking in code. "Aww, Bastian, why you got to be like that? Come on, it'll be fun. Whatever's going on between you and your mom, put it aside for one day, shoot, a couple of hours."

Miss Nelda tugged on my jacket. "Come on, honey. Sit down now and close the window. It's cold."

Bastian grabbed my arm. "Listen, I want you to know I had nothing to do with this."

Now he was annoying me. I was so angry at him, I pulled my arm back. "What are you talking about, boy? You're hurting me."

Sebastian looked at his grip and let go. "Man, just forget it." He stepped back and hit the taxi again.

"I don't know what's wrong with him," I apologized to everyone. "He's usually so cool. And tonight he's acting all whack."

"Dump him," Francine said flatly.

I shook my head like one of Fat Albert's friends. "We don't go together, doofus."

"Whatever."

Miss Nelda looked at Joanna, who seemed oblivious to the conversation. "A penny for your thoughts, young lady." She touched her knee, displaying the plain gold wedding band on her ring finger.

Joanna faced her. "Nothing, Miss Nelda."

"Nothing?" she repeated.

"I feel kind of funny is all. Nervous, I guess." Joanna looked at her boots and crushed snow into the carpet at the base of their seat.

"Well, shouldn't be nothing but eating and talking so—"

"Yeah, true." Joanna went back to her thoughts while me and Francine exchanged looks. We all gave it a rest until we arrived.

Rosa answered her door with a nervous look on her face. "Hola, hi, girls." She looked around us. "Miss Nelda, how are you?"

"Rosa, is everything all right?" I interrupted. "You did invite us to dinner, right?" I was still trying to make sense of it all.

"Yes, I just, um . . ." She rubbed her hands together and then stretched out her arms. "Come on in. We have a few guests here. I don't know if Bastian told you."

"Nah," Gracey said. "He didn't say much at all tonight. In fact, he looked annoyed."

"Oh," Rosa said. "Don't mind him. Boys can be moody, no?"

I smiled showing no teeth. My way of politely disagreeing.

Sebastian's house was smaller than I expected for someone whose mom was a business owner. From hanging out with Dad and his DIY projects, I could tell Rosa remodeled a lot of her home herself. It wasn't quite professional. Everybody round here did their own remodeling 'cause it was the most affordable way to go, and you could get the fake brand and make it look kind of like the top of the line. People understood the concept: not wood floors but laminate; not porcelain but fiberglass; not wallpaper, just bright-colored walls.

In Rosa's house, the floors were still unlevel, some of the electric sockets were uncovered, and the paint on the walls had patches where the original pink color shined through. Surely she would make her way to adding another coat sooner or later. Pictures of Sebastian were scattered all over the place, from when he was a baby till now. I felt special to be allowed to look at the pictures. I didn't realize I was gushing until Rosa touched my shoulders lightly as she passed by as if she knew we shared the same love.

Miss Nelda lifted her shaky finger and began to point. "All these people look like a bunch of teachers," she said. "Y'all know them? If you do, you might not like this."

I pulled myself out of Sebastian's world and looked around. There were many familiar faces. Why would Rosa invite teachers and the principals to Thanksgiving dinner?

"You ain't never lied, Miss Nelda," Gracey answered. "I'm starting to see what Bastian was talking about, straight up."

"Mm-hmm. Who's that tall white man over there?"

Ugh, Mr. Tutti was here. He was sitting on the opposite three-seater couch with his legs crossed and one arm stretched over the back. Then I looked and saw Miss Mabel. She was sitting across from a few teachers at Francine's part of the school, and Joanna pointed out her principal, Dr. Campbell, wearing a tight navy blue suit and glasses. And then there was a white woman none of us knew, and she had a clipboard in her hand.

"Excuse me, Rosa." Miss Nelda raised her chin so her voice could be heard throughout the room. "What's all this about? I thought we were invited to dinner, just me and the girls. Why are all these people from the school here?"

Rosa cleared her throat. "Miss Nelda, one minute, please. Before we talk about what's going on, let's eat."

"How about you just tell us now?" I didn't mean to be disrespectful, but I was starting to panic. This was obviously some kind of intervention, and it wasn't going well.

Miss Mabel looked at me and spoke softly but in a stern voice. "Everything's fine, Gracey. Go on in and sit down."

Miss Nelda led the way behind Rosa as we all slowly followed. At the table there was all kinds of food. I noticed the white-people food first: scallop potatoes, spinach quiche, rhubarb casserole. Then I saw the soul food: turkey, stuffing, candy yams, mac and cheese. There were other foods too, typical of what I had heard Sebastian talk about for the Dominican culture: rice, beans, plantains, fried fish, and stew with "every meat you could think of." When Francine's eyes landed on the sweet potato pie, she let out a *yes*, and Miss Nelda patted her leg under the table to hush her.

"Miss Mabel, why don't you lead us in prayer before we eat?" Rosa asked.

"Okay," she said and bowed her head. "Lord, guide us as we eat this food. When we break bread, I pray that you are with us just as you were with the disciples at the Last Supper."

"The Last Supper?" Miss Nelda interrupted. "What kind of prayer is that? Why you talkin' about the Last Supper?" She looked at the door. "What? Jesus goin' walk into the room and take us all away?"

Me and Joanna loudly shushed her, and Miss Mabel ended her

prayer with a calm and collected, "We need to hear from you, God. Bless us tonight as we try to do your will, in Jesus's name, amen."

"Amen," said the chorus of people.

Mr. Tutti rose to carve the turkey and handed out the sliced pieces with the three-pronged fork. I picked up Miss Nelda's plate and scooped up everything she pointed out. Then me and my sisters filled our own plates with the Southern foods we loved so much, leaving the unfamiliar untouched.

It seemed like ages went by before anybody spoke up. Little by little, people began asking us questions about our lives and how we were doing and what our home life was like. All the while, the clipboard lady was taking notes.

Miss Nelda stared her down like she was up to no good. Finally, she spoke. "Don't I know you?" Her finger twitched beneath her chin.

"No," the lady answered. "I don't believe you do."

"Yeah." Miss Nelda nodded. "Yeah, I do. Your color may be different, but you feel the same. You one of them people that take children away from their homes." Her eyes widened. "That's who you are, ain't it? You took my Phoebe and Rachel away. That's how come I know you."

"Ma'am?" The lady shifted. "I don't know any Phoebe or Rachel, and my job isn't to take children from their homes. It's to help them find a home."

"Liar." Miss Nelda shook her head and tried to get up from her chair. "She lyin', girls. She's lyin'. Let's go."

"Wait, we haven't had dessert yet." Rosa quickly took away all the main dishes and brought out the pretty ones: lemon meringue pie, apple crumble, red velvet cupcakes, and ice cream.

Joanna's principal, Dr. Campbell, tapped her glass lightly with her fork over Miss Nelda's grumbling. "Girls." Her voice carried authority that caused a quiet to come over the room. Miss Nelda sat down and looked attentive. "It has come to our attention that the three of you are living unsupervised in your house. Is that right?"

I answered no, Joanna answered no, and Francine said yes. We all looked at each other, unable to read what answer we'd all give in unison.

"Well, which is it, yes or no?" Dr. Campbell asked.

This time Francine said no, and me and Joanna said yes.

"That's unacceptable." Dr. Campbell drummed her fingers on the table.

"Where did your mother go, girls?" Miss Mabel asked.

Francine spilled first. "Well, after Daddy died, we came home from school one day and all she had left us was a note, some cookies, and some money."

"And what did the note say?"

"It said how much she loved us and that we should be good and take care of ourselves," Francine answered innocently. I was upset at first with Francine spilling all the beans. But then I felt guilty leaving her in the hot seat like that. She should not be our spokesperson.

"And how did that make you girls feel?" asked the lady with the clipboard.

"Well, of course, it hurt." I took over. "But we got over it. And now we take care of ourselves just fine, don't we?" I looked around to my sisters.

"Yeah, we're fine," Joanna chimed in.

"I don't think it's right that three teenagers should be living at home alone. How do you pay your bills?" Mr. Tutti asked.

"Well, the house is paid for. We just pay taxes and utilities and food, and I . . . I mean me and Joanna do that with our part-time jobs. I found Mom's checkbooks, so I mail bills off like clockwork. And lots of times people give us money through the mailbox and sometimes someone sends us money from Savannah, but we don't know who."

"Do you think it's your mother?" Those in the background nodded in tune to Miss Mabel's question.

"No," I answered confidently. "She'd go back to Mississippi if she went anywhere, not Savannah. She doesn't know anybody there, and she's not the type to just pick up and start fresh."

"How do you know?" asked Miss Mabel. I felt like I was on trial.

"I don't, that's just what I think." I never disliked Miss Mabel so much. She was ugly.

"Girls, I think what everyone is trying to say here is that it's dangerous for you to be home alone. All of us would feel awful if something happened to you." Mr. Tutti crossed his legs and shook his dangling foot.

One of Francine's teachers spoke. "Don't you have any relatives or somebody who could watch you? Francine, I remember you had a grandmother who used to drop you off every once in a while. Where is she?"

"She moved away, back to Mississippi," Francine said. "And I'm glad. She was a mean old battle-ax, and nobody liked her. I mean, I kind of liked her on good days."

"She's not willing to take them in anyway," said Dr. Campbell. "We contacted her, and she, uh . . . she wasn't too friendly."

"Well, what about on their father's side? Aren't there any aunts or uncles?" Mr. Tutti asked.

"We tried everyone we could find, and nobody was willing to take on three adolescent girls," said Dr. Campbell. "People, we've gone over this multiple times, before the girls ever got here. What is the problem?"

Miss Mabel put her hands out apologetically. "I guess we just wanted to hear it from the girls."

"Doesn't matter. They hate us. We know that," Francine said. She stuffed her mouth with sweet potato pie and put her elbow on the table in defiance.

"No, Francine," Miss Mabel said. "They just don't have the money."

Sweat gathered around my temples. "Look, we've been on our own now for almost three months. Some of you knew we were on our own, you were helping us. Now suddenly you want to do something about it? Why? What happened?"

Dr. Campbell spoke up. "I think I can speak for everyone here when I say we were all rooting for you girls and trying our best to keep our eyes on you, trying to buy time until your mother came back. But we must have slipped up somewhere, because one of you has gotten into trouble."

I dropped my head. How in the world did they find out?

"What are you talking about," Francine protested. "None of us is in any type of trouble. We're all fine."

"No, Francine, you're not all fine. Joanna is pregnant," Dr. Campbell answered.

Francine gaped at Joanna. "Jo, is that true?"

"Yeah . . . I'm about two months now." Joanna swiped the tears from her face with the palm of her hand. "How did you know?" she asked Dr. Campbell.

"One of the ladies at the salon works at the clinic. She said you cried so hard when you found out, and she just wished you had someone to talk to," Rosa answered, her hand rubbing Joanna's back.

"I didn't need anyone to talk to. I'm fine by myself. We're fine."

Francine looked at Joanna, confused. "You said there was no secrets between us. We were all in this together." She whined as if she'd just woken up. "What happened, Jo?"

"I was going to tell you—" She kept her head down.

"When? When you were in the hospital screaming your head off? Or maybe you was gonna be nice and tell me the truth when I asked you why you were walking around with my basketball under your shirt?" Francine crossed her arms over her chest. "No wonder you're always throwing up."

"Girls," Mr. Tutti said.

"No, I was going to tell you"—Joanna turned toward Francine in what seemed like a very private moment we were all eavesdropping on—"I just needed to think things through first."

Francine turned to me. "Did you know, Gracey? Why didn't you tell me?"

"I just wanted to protect you. I didn't know how to explain it." I didn't even want to believe it was true. It was hard enough taking care of the three of us—I couldn't imagine how we would care for a baby. I was wanting to check out a dozen books from the library to read up on it, but I knew it would raise flags.

"Girls," Mr. Tutti said again. "You're not helping your situation."

"Did you ever think of not having it?" Francine said sideways.

"Yes, all the time," Joanna said solemnly.

"At least then we could have stayed together," Francine said.

All the adults sighed as they looked to one another to gauge their level of acceptable outrage.

"Frankie, shut up!" I wanted to smack her. "You have no idea what you're talking about."

"I'm not stupid," Francine said. "She put us all in danger. If she doesn't have the baby, we can all go back to being a happy family."

"We weren't happy," Joanna said matter-of-factly.

"Doesn't matter," Dr. Campbell said. "Now that we officially know, we still have to hand you over to DCFS."

"So what happens now?" I asked.

"Well, your case will be referred to social services. This woman here, Ms. Hearken, will turn in your file, and the state will decide how to move forward. But let me be honest and say that it's . . . unlikely that you will all get placed in the same home."

"So basically, my mistake has torn apart whatever little family we had left." Joanna covered her head with her hands.

"Joanna, please," Miss Mabel said. "This is the best thing for you girls and the baby. There's no way you all could handle the stress of taking care of a baby on your own."

"What happens if we say no?"

Ms. Hearken spoke up. "You're underage. You don't have a say about your life until you turn eighteen. And Joanna, if you decide to play hardball with us, then we have every right to say you aren't a fit mother and take the baby away from you."

"What kind of dinner is this?" I protested. "You invited us over to eat, relax, and tear us away from each other? This is jacked up."

Rosa looked over to Dr. Campbell and Mr. Tutti. "I knew we

shouldn't have done this. My son was right. What kind of people do this over Thanksgiving dinner? You should all be home with your own families."

Dr. Campbell spoke like a tall person towering over small people. "Rosa, we agreed that the atmosphere was conducive to this type of intervention. The fact that we are here today shows how dedicated we are to the welfare of these girls."

"Either that or it shows how much you want to be the next council-member in our ward," Miss Nelda muttered.

"Ladies, please, this has nothing to do with moving up the political ladder," Mr. Tutti said. "Dr. Campbell just wants to make sure these three girls get the most life has to offer. And I myself am all for that. I mean, I love seeing my little Cotton in the hallways, but I hate to see her hurting."

Miss Nelda was leaning on the top of her fist, looking amazed. This time she turned her finger on its side. "What—you some kind of Freedom Fighter? Did you march with King or something? I bet all your best friends are Black, and you think you ain't racist."

"I'm far from racist." Mr. Tutti uncrossed his legs and leaned forward. "And I didn't march with King, but I was there at the March on Washington. It was amazing, so many people. So much harmony and love. We were one with God and each other."

"You full of bull—"

"You know what, that's it." Rosa threw her hands in the air. "I want everybody out of my house. Girls, you stay, but everybody else, get out. *Vamos*, go. Please." She shot up from her seat and started picking up dishes and putting them in people's hands, uncovered. "This is wrong."

"But, Rosa, we haven't solved the issue yet," Dr. Campbell said.

"Don't matter. You got to go. Adios. Get out of my house."

"It's okay," Ms. Hearken said, writing down her last bit and getting up. "We have enough to take to the state. Girls, we'll be in touch soon. Miss Williams has agreed to let you stay at her place until we make a decision. She's a licensed foster parent."

Miss Nelda stood up, trembling. "Now you wait a minute. Wait one sixty-second minute. What you sayin'? I don't understand."

Ms. Hearken paused and pursed her lips. "Miss Nelda. The State of Illinois cannot allow minors to live alone. Therefore, until we can find a suitable guardian, we have awarded Mabel Williams guardianship—just until we can thoroughly search out options for relatives."

Miss Nelda got behind her walker and moved as close to the woman as possible. Staring up into her eyes, she looked to examine her. "On the inside, you look just like the women who took my girls away."

"Miss Nelda, I promise you—"

"Don't promise me nothing. You're the same. Cold-blooded. You don't care. You're just doing your job. You don't care 'bout how we all come together to help—praying for them, putting money to the side to give to them, doing their hair, having folks in the grocery stores givin' them discounts, making sure they got somebody to talk to when they scared at night. We care, Ms. Clipboard Lady. You don't know nothin' about carin'. Now you want to waltz in here and split them up, take them away from me? Have you thought about what they mean to me? Huh?" Miss Nelda's voice was straining as she ran short of breath. "You thought any about how much it might hurt—to have these little women walk outta my life just like that—after we been together all these months, me watching them and them watching me?"

A stillness came over everyone in the room. Miss Nelda was waiting for an answer and wasn't moving until she got one.

Ms. Hearken looked around for help, but no one, not even Dr. Campbell looked up to meet her eyes. Finally, she released the air that puffed her up. "Miss Nelda, I'm sorry. I didn't know that you'd done so much. You're right. I don't know these girls or how they've managed, so I'm not as close as you are. But I want you to think about it. Do you honestly believe they can continue to live without an adult in the house with a newborn baby? Do you think you have the strength, the wherewithal to get them through all that? Really?"

"'Course I can't do it on my own, but all of us together, we can. At least until—"

"Until what, Miss Nelda?" Dr. Campbell asked.

"Well, until their mama come back."

"And what makes you think she's coming back?" Dr. Campbell blurted, then quickly clenched her lips.

"Why, it's just a feeling. Like how you know it's going to rain, or that a train is on its way. She's coming back."

There was a common groan in the room like a truth had been spoken that resonated with their souls so deeply it pulled a sound from their bellies.

"Well"—Dr. Campbell shook off the silence—"until she does, Miss Nelda, I'm sorry. We don't have time to wait. While that woman is out there trying to get her life together, time is moving on and those storm clouds are rolling in as fast as these girls are growing up."

Miss Mabel pulled her jacket from the hall tree by the front door. "Come on, girls. I'll take you back home to pick up a few things, and then we'll head on over to my place."

Francine rose quickly and brushed past Joanna and me, like trying to walk through a narrow tunnel without touching the walls.

Rosa stood at the door, her eyes sad and watery. She reached out to hug us. "I'm so sorry."

"None of this would have happened if you'd just kept your promise," I reminded her. Everything happened so fast. That whole conversation went over like a waterfall and there was nothing I could do to control it.

"Oh, Gracey, this isn't 'don't tell my mommy I stole the cookies.' This is your life! You girls have been abandoned, and you need help. I can't take the responsibility of looking after you all the time. It's too much. I haven't slept for weeks worrying about you three . . . four."

"So this is about you? If it was too much, then you should have left us alone." I knew I shouldn't have trusted this woman. She was like everybody else, only looking out for herself. "Did we ever ask you for anything, ever? Money, food, my hair . . . you offered!"

"Mind your elders, young lady." Miss Nelda's finger went wagging.

"No, you didn't ask me for anything." Rosa stayed focused. "But the second your mama left you, she demanded everything from all of us, whether we liked it or not."

"You act like she's some kind of criminal."

"She is," Mr. Tutti answered sadly.

"She is not, Mr. Tutti, you time-warped hippie!" I screamed. "And don't you ever call me Cotton again."

"That's enough." Miss Mabel raised her voice over everyone's. "It's time to go, girls. Say goodbye to Miss Nelda."

Miss Nelda didn't seem to want to say much. She was smiling as if she was proud of me for snapping like that. But her eyes were also filled to the brim with tears. We each hugged her but she kept her arms to her side.

Joanna gave her a soft, light kiss on the cheek and said, "Thank you."

Francine hugged her tight and sobbed into her sunken bosom. "I'm going to miss you, Miss Nelda."

I took Miss Nelda's trembling hand and put it on my cheek. The palm of her hand was silky and wrinkled, her fingertips lacking prints from touching hot pots and skillets without cloths. "Miss Nelda," I said, "we grew a mile in your hands."

"Ah, honey . . ." She sniffed. "Whenever you get a chance, go to church. And when they sing that song—can't think of the name . . . oh yeah." Her voice went weak and quivered as she moved her head to the melody. "*What a friend we have in Jesus.*" She smiled. "You remember ghosts and things fade away when you have faith."   '

CHAPTER 17

Charlotte
November 1987

FINDING CANDI'S PLACE WAS NO easy task; it took three buses and a twenty-minute walk, but when I got there, I knew it was hers. A tan frame house with bright orange shutters stood as the biggest one in the neighborhood. Candi had a wraparound porch with pink pillars and green ivy growing up the side of the railing. I let out a big laugh as I walked up the sidewalk. The wrapping fit Candi perfectly. I couldn't wait to see the inside—had to be bright and beautiful in there.

Roasted turkey was the first thing I smelled from outside, then greens with ham hocks, and then some kind of pie crust just out the oven.

Candi answered the door with a ready hug. "Girl, what took you so long, we been holdin' dinner for you. Come on in and meet my people."

The floor had a worn runner over it to keep the carpet clean, but the wood beneath it was unstable, begging for padding. Inside the dining room was a long table, almost the size of the room, covered with every dish you saw on television, including my favorite, peach cobbler. That was what I smelled. I set my corn muffins down next to the biscuits and the skillet corn bread.

"Sweet caramel apples, I ain't never seen so much food in my life. What you tryin' to do, Candi, plump us up before the slaughter?"

"No, girl, this the way we do it every Sunday. Then family can take it home and have food to eat through the week."

Every chair at the table was filled with what Mama referred to as boulder pushers, folks that put all their strength into a job that don't have much payoff. Makes 'em old before their time.

Candi introduced me to her two uncles and their wives, her cousins, her mama, her pastor, and finally her husband and her sister, "the new couple." I was shocked as ever to see them there. And it must have shown on my face, 'cause Candi quickly added, "Mama has to have all her family with her on Sunday, don't you, Mama?"

"Yes, I do. Wouldn't have it no other way. Ain't nothing going on at this table the Lord can't handle. Now come on, Charlotte, and have a seat," Candi's mama said.

The pastor cleared his throat. "Shall we bow our heads?"

We all obliged.

"Lord, bless this food, and bless the fellowship, amen." The pastor had his spoon in the macaroni and cheese before he got his amen out.

"Amen," everyone said and quickly dug in.

Candi and her sister Ebony may have been opposites, but their sound was similar, as if their vocal cords had wear and tear from secondhand smoke and talking too much.

"Candi ever tell you about me?" Ebony leaned around the cheating husband to take a gander at me. "It's hard to believe we sisters, ain't it? 'Cause we don't look nothin' alike."

It was the first time I had really looked at Ebony since I'd been there. And she was right, she didn't look anything like her sister. Candi was shaped like a pear, and Ebony was shaped like an asparagus, Lord help her. Candi smiled happy with her whole body. Ebony gave half-hearted smiles, and she sat bent over like she was trying to protect her soul. Candi didn't have much of nothin' to hide.

I caught myself, though. I hadn't realized how much Candi's talking about her sister had made me bitter toward her. I wanted to tell her about herself, how she needed to get her own man. But I knew better. Didn't make sense to make things worse for Candi.

"You right, y'all don't look alike, but that's good. It means you each have your own lives, and folks can't get y'all mixed up. Right?" I raised an eyebrow.

"What? What she tell you? You been telling her about me, Candi?"

"No, Ebony. I ain't told her nothin'. Now shut up and eat." Candi was shaking salt onto her turkey.

Oh boy. I was tryin' my best not to say nothing stupid, and what was the first thing come out my mouth? Stupid. Candi bugged her eyes at me, and I bit my lip.

I closed my mouth and let everyone else do the talking while I excused myself and went to the bathroom. Candi's house was like a cozy art museum. Her paintings were in every room, mostly red, yellow, and orange arrangements. In her living room, there was a canvas over the fireplace of a fire-red sun sitting in a yellow sky. The land, of course, was orange, with thin strokes of green trees and faint wisps of birds flying toward the trees. Her curtains were a paisley tangerine, and she had beige couches made pretty with peach and orange pillows. A glazed tree-trunk coffee table sat on top of a polar bear throw rug, and pictures of the family in black and white hung in little rhythms around the house—sets of three, sets of two, and then three again.

Going up the stairs, there were thick oil paintings of angels with big wings mimicking people as they sat on benches and read the paper, played chess on the street, or walked into a building. The one with the angel standing next to a girl as she kissed a boy made my brow sweat and my heart pound. I touched the pearls on my necklace and quickly walked straight into the bathroom, shutting myself in.

It was adorable, that room. Old-time Black figurines sat on the sill. The window was open, with a lace curtain blowing in the breeze. As I sat down, there was a painting of a child taking a bath and reading the Bible; at the bottom it read, "Wash your soul and be made clean." I finished up, washed my hands, and was making my way downstairs when I stopped at a little picture frame in a nook in the stairway that said, "Believe in Miracles." Her home was over-the-top Christian, so different from the Candi I knew. Like she was using this stuff as a form of protection.

I wasn't sure that I did believe in them at all. Miracles. Candi's house looked like a televangelist's home, and yet her life was an absolute mess. And me? I didn't even know what I thought about God lately, but I knew part of me thought Christianity was a big fairy tale story that people desperately wanted to be true. The other part of me thought somebody was watching over me. It had to be God.

"Charlotte," Candi called from downstairs. "Charlotte, you all right? I got some Pepto-Bismol if you need it."

I met her on the stairs. "Oh no, Candi, I'm fine. I was just, um, taking care of a little female business. You know how it is."

"The friend who never checks your social calendar before dropping by. Yep, I know."

We laughed and went back to the dining room together.

Candi's cousin was looking at me like I did something wrong. "Dang, girl, you all right? You need a match?"

"All right, Barlow, no need to get nasty."

I flattened my lips and sat down. It was going to be a long night.

Somebody had finished making my plate for me while I was upstairs. It was spilling over with food.

"Wow, this is a mighty big plate y'all made me. Thank you," I said.

"Uh-huh" flowed easily from the women at the table, their way of saying *You're welcome.*

"Reverend." One of Candi's uncles spoke up. "What they doing down at the church for Christmas this year? I hear tell they gonna have a big gospel concert with all kinds of famous singers coming through."

"Really, Pastor, like who?" Candi's mama asked.

The pastor took a deep breath and stuck out his chest. "Well, we got Yolanda Canning comin' from the next county over. You know she sang to a crowd of almost five hundred people last year. And we got Peter Bailey coming; I believe he's from Alabama somewhere, but his third cousin removed is Shirley Caesar, so you know that boy can sing. And then we got good old Candi from right here in our hometown singing with us." He turned and shined on her with all his teeth.

"Candi, you didn't tell me you could sing too," I said, forgetting about my code of silence.

"Girl, I been singing a long time. It ain't nothin' I do seriously. I just sing."

"Pastor, how come you don't never ask me to sing? You know I can." Ebony was speaking in a whiny tone, the same one that Candi used when she was crying the other day.

"'Cause you cain't sing. How many times I got to tell you? You just cain't sing . . . My dog sound better than you."

Ebony's fork stopped midway to her mouth. "Pastor, what you say to me? What you say?"

"Now, Pastor, please." Candi's mama put her fork down, the veins in her hands heightened, pumping at full force as if her fist had been clenched for years. "Ain't you caused enough trouble between my girls, always paying favor to one and not the other?"

"All right, y'all, that's enough. It's no big deal." Candi waved.

"So, Miss Charlotte." Another of Candi's uncles tapped on the table to draw attention away from the argument. "Tell us about yourself. Where are you from?" He acted proud, like he had more education than everybody else. He enunciated even though he didn't have to, as if perfect diction was his nature.

"I'm originally from Mississippi. Then I moved to Chicago and lived there for about twenty years, and now I'm here," I said, thinking that should be enough.

"And what brings you to Georgia?"

"Charlotte came here to get some work." Candi smiled like she knew exactly what her uncle was doing and why I was evading all the same. "And she found a job with me at the bed-and-breakfast. She's a real good friend to me. She's like a sister, she is."

"Oh, right, 'cause your real sister ain't good enough. Right, Candi?" Ebony fired back while adding an extra piece of corn bread to Mr. Goodin's plate.

Candi sucked her teeth. "Lord have mercy, Ebony, this ain't about you. I'm just talking about my friend."

The faucet dripping in the kitchen could be heard from the dining room. What I wouldn't give to be the water going down the drain right now.

"Uh . . ." Candi's mama started, obviously searching for a topic. "How d'you like workin' at the B and B, Charlotte? You live there?"

"Oh yes, I love it. It's nice and quiet."

"Uh-huh, and what makes this stranger so good?" Ebony interrupted, still holding the matter.

"She's been there for me when I needed her."

"And I ain't?" Ebony looked to be trying to pout, but her piercing eyes gave her anger away.

"Well, no, Ebony. All you've ever done was try to wreck my life."

"That ain't true. You've always had the best life. I'm just trying to have some good too."

I grabbed my napkin and started patting my forehead. It was hot.

"Anyway, you know what, I bet you this little Charlotte friend of yours, I bet you she ain't so great. Anyone can look at her and tell she hidin' somethin'. What you hidin', Charlotte?"

My heart beat like an African drum, and the air wouldn't flow through my body right.

"She ain't got nothin' to hide, Ebony. Why don't you leave her alone?"

"Nah, I'm looking at her. I can see something ain't right. Can't y'all see this goody-two-shoes Candi brought home ain't no good?" She stared at me as if she were trying to see through me. "You ever kill anybody?"

"No."

"You been to jail?"

"No."

"What you hidin', girl?"

"None of your business."

"There it is!" Ebony pointed like she was a fox hound. "There it is. She said it's none of my business, which means it is something, just none of my business, see?"

"Ebony," the pastor said, all exasperated. "Leave the woman alone now. She came here for a nice Sunday dinner, and you over there giving her the end of your broomstick."

"Well, she deserves it. Why ain't she with her own family? You supposed to spend Sunday with your own family. Where's your family, Charlotte? What happened, they kick you out?"

"No, they didn't kick me out," I said. I stood up and pulled my purse from the side of my chair.

"Ebony, stop it!" Candi yelled. "Her husband's dead." But Ebony just ignored her and kept me on the stand.

"They didn't kick you out? What that mean, you left? Why'd you leave, Charlotte? You do something wrong? What'd you do, cheat on your man? You went a ho-in', didn't you? Then your husband came home an' knocked the stew out of you, right? Then your man knocked him in the head with a lamp base and he died. Now you here in Georgia trying to make a living 'cause don't nobody want you at home. See, Candi, there's your friend unraveled and undone. Pass the mac and cheese, somebody."

I started shaking, and my legs trembled until they buckled back into the chair. The room went black as the sounds of arguing faded into silence. And that was the last I remembered of Candi's Sunday dinner.

CHAPTER 18

Charlotte
November 1987

WHEN I OPENED MY EYES, a wet towel rested on my forehead, and I was laid out on a flowery orange sofa. Candi sat in the chair next to me, humming softly. Her voice made me think of change, like autumn leaves lightly blown about on a patio. The last time I'd heard singing like that I had fallen asleep in the meadow. I dreamed of angels covering me with their wings and singing over me in words I couldn't catch hold of. Waves washed over and through me until I was in a weightless state where nothing was heavy and nothing was too hard. When I woke up again, the loud hum of cicadas eased in and out of cadence.

"Gracious God," Candi prayed. "Please help my sister Charlotte. I don't know all that's going on or what your answer to her problem is, but I pray that you would lead her and guide her just like you did Ruth and Esther and Mary. Whatever happened, Lord, that was so wrong or simply not right, I know that you still love her, just like you did Mary Magdalene, the free loving spirit that she was. You know we ain't mad at her. Show Charlotte how much you love her. Fix this mess as only you can."

I opened my eyes, and Candi reached over to hug me. She finished her prayer with a big smile and a confident "Amen."

Embarrassed, I laid there not knowing what to say. The mahogany grandfather clock in front of me looked stately and wise with its classic round face. It reminded me of Moses. He always presumed me better than I was. He gave me strength to tell my story.

"I have three girls, Candi. After my husband died and my mother left, I–I left the girls at home by themselves. For some reason, it didn't occur to me that they would miss me or even need me. I was pretty useless as a mother anyway, everyone always said so. I had to get out of there because I couldn't cope with everything, not with all I'd done. It was either I leave them, or I break. I didn't want to break."

"So you left."

"Yes."

"But why, Charlotte? What happened?"

A boulder fell on me, that was what happened.

"After my husband and I had our first child, Joanna, my mama called from Mississippi and said she couldn't keep up with all the work on the farm. She wanted me and Moses to come down and help her sell the farm and then take her back to live with us in Chicago. We did that, you know, went back, sold the farm, got her all packed up.

"And then one morning while we were down there, the phone rang. I answered it. It was Micah, the only other man I'd ever loved, back when I was young, you know? Back then he'd gotten us into a lot of trouble. His father was some kind of bishop, but Micah—he was far from holy and I knew it, but I didn't care. In fact, I think it made me love him more. Anyway, the adults split us up, sent him back home. I had to deal with so many rumors, I left the church altogether.

"When he called, he said he knew I was married now, but he just wanted to get together to say hi and catch up on old times. He wanted to meet in the meadows down by my house. And girl, I don't know what came over me. As soon as he asked, I didn't even think about it, I said yes. I was so happy, I mean in the wrong sort of way—my heart was racing, my insides were melting, and my mind was back in high school feeling scared and excited; free yet guarded. What would Moses say, would he understand, would he think I was going to cheat on him? What if he said I couldn't go?

"Wasn't no doubt I had to go. I had to see Micah. I, uh, I didn't have with Moses what I had with Micah, that passion, that desire, the heat. And I figured if I just got one kiss and one little hug, it would all go away. My thirst would be satisfied, and I could live the rest of my life with Moses in peace. So I didn't tell my husband."

Candi let out a little sigh.

"Just before noon, I left Joanna with Moses and told him I had some business to take care of. Then I went to see Micah in the fields. I had on my yellow sundress and matching sun hat, and I brought a picnic basket full of muffins and little cakes and cookies I'd gotten from the bakery because I was planning on a sweet afternoon.

"Micah was leaning on an old oak tree. When he saw me, he started walking toward me. He had aged well and grown beyond his adolescent frame. His skin was smooth and even toned. His cheekbones were more defined; his eyes had deepened. Anyway, he hugged me, and we sat down to catch up. He told me how he went to college, got his degree, and became a teacher. How he almost married but couldn't go through with it.

"And then he told me how much he loved me. He said he would do anything to spend his life with me. And I told him I cared for him too and that there was a time when I'd loved him, but I loved Moses now. He said he was sorry to hear that and that he knew if my mother hadn't told his auntie on him, we'd be married right now. 'Maybe,' I said, 'but life takes its own path sometimes, and God chose this one for me.'

"Then he asked me for a kiss and took it before I could answer yes. And I thought, this is okay, our final goodbye, that's what I wanted. I leaned into his kiss, and we kept on kissing, and kept on. But then my heart started gettin' that sinking feeling, you know? I heard this *snap* behind my ear, and I thought it must have been an angel or something warning me. I knew I'd gone too far.

"I tried to stop him, but he put his arms around my waist and pulled me in close, and inside I was like, yes please. And I thought, okay maybe a little more because it felt so good, and then he went up under my dress and thrust me down, and I was right there with him until I heard a *snap* again in my ear. This time I yelled. 'No, stop!' I screamed. 'Stop! Get off!' And I hit and punched . . . But it was too late, he was already . . . he was so heavy, and he just kept going until . . ."

Candi was rubbing my back.

"And . . . and when I turned over to get up, my mama was standing not ten feet away, shaking her head, with Joanna in her arms. Mama had her head turned, but she fought to look at me, disheveled, my hair all over my head. Soon as we locked eyes, me and Joanna, she reached out for me, crying. Mama turned around and blazed through the tall grass, holding my child as secure as she could."

"Have mercy." Candi sighed.

"I put my sandals on, and I kicked Micah as he was still all sprawled out there on the ground. I just kept kicking him and kicking him until he curled his arms and legs into a ball. I called him every kind of disgusting animal I could think of, and then I told him I hated him. Then I ran away to find Mama. She was at home in the kitchen packing the last of her glasses in newspaper. I stood right next to her and begged her not to tell Moses, but she ignored me.

"'Mama, please speak to me,' I begged her. Nothing. Finally, I turned toward the stairs to go take a shower. Then she raised her head and said, 'I hope you had a good time, 'cause that sin's going to follow you for the rest of your life.'

"And I tell you, Candi, she almost killed me with that one sentence. I have no idea how I got through the next couple of days, except that I think I pushed everything so far down inside that it couldn't touch me. I thought the only thing that could help was to make love to Moses. I cried the whole way through, and you know what he said? He said, 'You're so beautiful.'"

I looked at Candi, and she caught my eyes.

"If he only knew." I looked away again.

"Nine months later I had another baby girl, Gracey, and I thought maybe this baby is Moses's, but when I saw the dimple on the side of her ear, I knew. She was Micah's child. And Mama knew too. Right in front of him, she said, 'Ain't she something, Moses. Wonder where she got that cute little dimple from?'

"And Moses said, 'Must be in the genes from way back.' And Mama just looked at me.

"I never could get up the nerve to tell him, Candi. I never could. And then I thought, maybe I could live my life like that and just suffer. But as the years went on, I felt like I was drifting further and further away from my family. I thought if I gave Moses another baby, it would make up for the one in the middle. But it didn't. The whole thing, it just wouldn't go away.

"And then . . . and then Moses died. He died, and he didn't know a thing. He'd been so good to me all those years, and he didn't know how bad I been to him."

Candi went to the dresser where she had hot water sitting in a teapot. She returned with an orange-colored teacup with a gold trim full of chamomile tea and a cinnamon stick tilted to the side. "Drink this, honey. It will make you feel better."

"Thank you."

"I'm so sorry that happened to you."

We rested in the silence of the moment.

"I think you know what you have to do, don't you?" Candi spoke softly.

I took a sip and answered. "I have to go back home. I have to face my girls, and I have to tell them the truth. I have to tell Gracey who her real father is. I don't even care anymore if they hate me, at least they'll know the truth."

"Oh, Charlotte, they won't hate you. Life happens and if they didn't know it before, they know it now. And you know what? You ain't done nothin' that the Lord can't fix. Shoot, honey. You didn't do any wrong. And this was not your fault. It was Micah's for not respecting you enough to listen to you. The second you said stop, he should have put his stuff away. He raped you. Shoot, if I was your mama, I woulda took off both my shoes and threw 'em at him. Picked 'em up and threw 'em again. Shame on her for just watching you suffer like that."

I blinked. I shook my head, tryin' to make sense of what she'd said.

But I didn't have time to process that, so I brought Candi round to my biggest concern. "What if they won't take me back? What if they never talk to me again? I'm telling you, I couldn't take it. I couldn't handle it." Again with the tears.

"But, Charlotte, what if they do take you back, and you take your place as their mother? What if they get to spend their last years in the house with their mother hugging them before they go to sleep every night, kissing them goodbye as they go off to school, and doing special things like going to games or recitals? What if you allowed yourself to be the mother you've always wanted to be? The mother every child needs."

I took another sip of tea and thought for a moment. "That would be a miracle," I said.

"Then you better start believing."

I I I

I wasn't really in a state to catch all those buses home, so I stayed the night at Candi's. She made a place for me in one of the spare rooms, but I wasn't comfortable in any of them, so I took my blanket and pillow and went to the room I woke up in earlier and stretched out on the couch. Before, I didn't notice the cassette player, but this time, it seemed to be sitting there on an end table calling for me to press Play. I hit Play expecting to hear gospel music or maybe some '80s contemporary love songs and was surprised to hear chimes and blended voices. I pressed Stop and took out the tape. Written in pen was "Taizé cuts for sleepless nights." They took me to a world where my problems didn't exist.

I left early the next morning, but the B and B looked different to me when I returned. Everything was smaller—the furniture, the walls, even the ceiling seemed lower. Outside, the garden looked well-maintained with trimmed edges against the sidewalk. A mother picked up her child and tossed him in the air. His laughter was priceless, echoing through the different-colored rosebushes. Same old place but different.

Then came a knock at the door. It was Candi. She went to tell me something but stopped herself. "How are you? You okay after the weekend and all?"

"Yeah, I'm good," I said, knowing she needed to get that out the way first. "What's going on?" I sat down on my bed.

"My sister tried to take her life last night. They found her unconscious in the bathroom with an empty bottle of pills."

"Why in the world . . . What happened? Is she still alive?" I'd just seen her.

"She's still alive, but barely. We found a note on the floor in her bathroom. It said that she'd felt really good breaking you down last night, and she enjoyed seeing you cry and making me mad at her. But then she realized all the things we been saying about her must be true, that she's evil and crazy and bitter and twisted. She said for a second she was outside her body watching herself laugh, and she was so disgusted she wanted to put an end to it all."

Candi folded her arms as she sat down and rocked like low waves, back and forth. "She said for years all she thought about was making my life worse than hers, but I kept on risin' anyhow. Every time she tried to set up a raccoon trap, seem like she the one ended up walkin' into it. And she figured that must be the Lord telling her she's no good. At the end she said, 'I love you. I just ain't too good at showin' it.'"

"Oh, that's so sad." I reached out to hug her drooping shoulders.

"Doctor said it's amazing she still alive. If the neighbor who found her had brought her in just a little bit later, she might not be here."

"Why would she think taking her life would make everything okay? It wouldn't make up for what she did, that's for sure. Don't she know that's why we have Jesus? We could never make up for all the mistakes we make, that's what the whole Jesus thing is about."

Candi pulled away from me. "Shut up, talking that ying-yang to me. Look who's talking. She chose to take her life; you chose to separate from your family. Other folk choose to drown their lives in drugs or alcohol. The way I see it, Charlotte, you ain't got no right to judge my sister."

"What? I didn't leave my family to punish myself," I said.

"Yes, you did!" Candi yelled. "Stop lying to yourself!"

I covered my ears and shut my eyes. It was too much. "I can't talk about this right now. I just . . . I'm sorry, okay? Let's just leave it." I rubbed at the stitches in the quilt on my bed. "What happens next with your sister?"

Candi clenched her jaw a bit, seeming to decide to let me off the hook. "She'll be in the hospital for a while. And she'll get counseling. Mama's gonna stay with her for a bit when she gets out."

"Are you going to see her?"

"I'm sure she doesn't want to see me. Or maybe I'm just scared I'll make things worse."

"Maybe you could write her a letter or send a card and tell her that you love her."

"Maybe," Candi said, staring miles away. "Maybe if I go stand outside her room . . . I just want to lay eyes on her. Even if she won't see me, I want to know for myself that she's okay."

We sat with our own thoughts for some time.

"Is there anything I can do?"

"Get on with your life. That'll make me happy."

"Candi, aren't you . . .?" I didn't want to come right out and say it, but . . . "I mean, don't you think this is a blessing in disguise? Maybe Ebony's life will change now. Maybe she'll treat you better."

She heaved a big, disappointed sigh. "This isn't about me. I don't care about me. I care about my sister living. Once again, when she needed me, I wasn't there to help her."

"Candi, I am so sorry. I never should have come for dinner."

"Humph . . . I'm glad you did. Apparently enough was enough for the both of you. I love my sister no matter what she does to me. All I ever wanted her to do was love me. I wanted someone to share my secrets with and to go to the movies with, someone to help me eat a piece of cake when I couldn't eat the whole thing. But instead, we're sisters with no moments to cherish, no inside jokes that only we understand. We just always fighting. The worst part of it is, no matter how much I talk to her about God, she won't listen. Whenever I bring up the subject, she just says there's no point. She thinks God loves me more than he loves her. I've tried to tell her Jesus isn't like that, that he loves us all the same, but she ain't havin' it. And why should she? What proof does she have?"

I took her hand as we sat. Then I hugged my friend until she wrapped her arms around me and hugged me back.

CHAPTER 19

Gracey
December 1987

MISS MABEL SAID IT WAS Dr. Campbell, Joanna's principal, who sold us out to social services. Apparently, we were the talk of the neighborhood at the hairdresser's and when Dr. Campbell went to get her hair done, the customers urged her to do something. They even knew Francine took M&Ms to class on her birthday instead of cupcakes like all the other kids.

This whole deal lately had my life turned upside down. For the first time in all these months, I felt homeless. So now, not only had we lost three stable people in our lives, now we were losin' our home, the one thing we were trying to keep. That first night, I kept waking up wondering where I was, hoping everything was a dream—the dinner, the move. We wanted to go home to our beds and our red velvet couch. We wanted to be able to go into our closets and pick our outfits for the day; go into the kitchen and hope to find an ant scouting around for crumbs. But instead we were in a strange house, in a weird situation, and nothing made sense.

On my way to the bathroom, I peeked into Miss Mabel's room. She was knocked out with her scarf neatly tied around her head to keep her hair. On her nightstand was a picture of her with friends at a restaurant I'd never seen. Something about it made me step closer. And then my mouth fell open. My dad was in the picture, smiling, with his arm around her. I looked at Miss Mabel sleeping soundly, the picture, then her. I tiptoed out the room.

Another thing that didn't make sense, and at this point, I didn't want to know. I'd had enough.

The next day at school, everything was copacetic, and I didn't miss a beat. It was Sebastian who was different. He scooted his desk next to mine in class and tried to speak in low tones. I was too stuck in my funk to feel excited about him being so close to me.

"Hey."

I ignored him so he spoke louder.

"Hey, I heard about what happened. Are you okay?"

"Yeah, I'm fine. No big deal. I've left the only place I've ever called home to stay with someone who hardly knows me and my sisters. Of course I'm fine. Just as happy as I can be."

"Okay, I get your point, my bittersweet. But I thought maybe you wanted to talk or something. 'Cause, you know, if you do . . . I'm here."

"Until a squirrel catches your attention."

"Huh?"

"Nothing."

"No, really. Jokes aside, Gracey. I'm here."

"Thanks. I may take you up on that." And then I turned toward the blackboard.

"Meet you by the tree after school?" he asked, touching my hand with the eraser of his pencil.

I looked at our hands but not at him. "Yeah, I'll be there." It was a little late for him to be getting a guilty conscience.

After school Sebastian met me under the oak tree. The branches were bare and lined with snow. We both had our scarves wrapped around our necks and mittens on because everyone knew they were better than gloves.

"So that night." I moved the dried leaves on the ground with my feet. "You knew what was going to happen, didn't you?"

"Yeah, pretty much."

"That's why you stayed away."

"For sure, yeah," Sebastian said. "But now I'm sorry I didn't go. I should have been there for you."

"S'ok." I touched his peach fuzz. "You were a scaredy-cat. I get it."

Sebastian rolled his eyes. "I wouldn't go that far. I just didn't want to see you hurt like that."

"You mean you care about me, like that?"

"As a friend, yeah." Then he looked out toward the cars passing on the street. "Sometimes more."

"Sometimes more what?" I needed clarification, otherwise I'd be thinking about it nonstop for the next two months. "More than a friend?"

"Yes, Gracey," he said, moving closer to me. "Whatever you are to me, which I can't define and don't know what to call it, I care."

I touched his face and played with his curly hair, and he leaned in to kiss me. At first it was a bird's peck, and then it was real. I was convinced our full lips were made for each other. We broke away just as someone threw a ball at Sebastian's shoulder.

"Man, stop messing with that girl and let's get to practice."

Sebastian trotted backward and pointed to me. "Hold that thought, Gracey." He turned to run toward his friend. "I'll catch you later, I hope."

"Yeah," I shouted. "I'll be around a little bit longer, I guess."

I went inside and checked to see if Miss Mabel was in her classroom. She wasn't, so I sat in the reading corner and put some Miles Davis on her record player. I sat still for a few minutes, fully allowing myself to soak in what just happened between me and Sebastian. Over and over, I replayed the words he said, trying to make sense of them. We are undefined but more than friends. Finally, I was able to write in my journal.

Gracey Downing is my name. I am the daughter of people I can no longer see. I am here with my sisters on this earth, but we are alone, before our time. We are floating in space without a line to keep us tied. We are free; I am free. I been free for a long time now. I don't like it, 'cause I don't remember September, November, or December, or the year before last, or what it's like to do things with the family, like, go to Great America and ride on the waterslide or have family birthday parties and cool gifts for Christmas. I am free to be me, but I don't like it so much because I'm not sure I can say that I know me. But I am learning I don't like people who lie and break promises. I don't like people who promise without crossing their heart. I don't like people who know you and act like they don't know.

I'm also beginning to understand how love can make you do stupid things like kiss your friend when you know you'll never be anything more than someone to confide in. But you'll secretly hold on to that kiss for the rest of your life, and if you imagine long enough, you can re-create it over and over again and feel the same brush with love. I understand, but I don't like it. So, whatever, thanks for loving me and my sisters and whatnot.

PS: Bad words flowing.

I put my journal on her desk and left.

At Miss Mabel's house, me and Francine shared a room while Joanna had her own. It was the same setup as home, but it wasn't home. Friday, late into the evening, me and Joanna were still up trying to right our world like crickets in the dark.

"Are you guys still talking about us?" Francine sounded like she'd just woken up from dozing.

"We were just talking about what we're going to do," I answered, forcing myself to stay awake until we had answers.

"Should we all try to run away? Should we try to find Grandma or something? Or maybe we can ask Miss Mabel to adopt us. Or maybe—"

"I told you, just forget it. I don't have the energy to plan anything," Joanna answered. Then she changed the subject. "What'd you guys think of that prayer with those ladies?" She was reclining on her bed, rubbing her belly like a person trying to move the gas around. But really I knew she was imagining how it would feel as the baby grew.

She was referring to what happened with Miss Mabel's sisters, who met us when we walked through her door Thanksgiving night. They were all different versions of Miss Mabel, either a shorter or taller her, her as an older or younger person, thinner or more heavyset, long hair or short afro. The genes ran strong in that family. Even their voices were similar, like a radio personality playing smooth jazz.

Apparently she couldn't prepare the house on her own, so they had come to help. It didn't make sense to me—put some clean sheets on the bed, a comforter, and a few pillows and call it a day—but there was more to it than that. All the towels matched and were neatly folded a mile high in the bathroom and new battery-operated toothbrushes for us rested in the toothbrush holder. We had brand-new soft, fluffy face towels and washcloths. We had slippers that hugged our heels and tickled our toes when we wiggled them. We even had housecoats that kept us warm as if we were wrapped in teddy bears.

In our rooms, we each had our own hair oil and body lotions— homemade concoctions of vanilla, shea, and cocoa butter. We had fancy soaps and shower gels that smelled like flowers, deodorant, pink razors, and maxi pads. We had new socks, loads of panties with cool prints, and padded bras to protect from embarrassing moments. We even had nail polish and cotton balls and nail polish remover. We had all the things we so desperately needed but we never realized. We'd thought we were fine in our ash and dryness. We thought nothing of the jokes in gym class about how hairy we were. It really was nothing. We had more important things to think about. That night, we said thank you in hugs and tears and smiles. And their smiles back were the most beautiful we'd ever seen, as if they thought we were precious and worth all of that and a bag of chips.

"Sorry we couldn't get you more," one of them said. "I hope this is a good start."

"We're good," Francine answered. "All of this is dope. We've never had—"

"Uh," I broke in. "What she means is, we usually have to order from the Sears catalog and sometimes—"

"Sometimes they get our orders all wrong, and it's too much to send it back. You know how it goes," Joanna finished.

A shorter sister answered with a hearty laugh. "Oh sure, we know all too well, don't we, sisters?" She clasped her hands and held them to her face as she grinned toward us.

The taller, more serious sister said, "Let's pray."

"Oh yes, let's do that," the giggly one answered.

Together they joined hands in a circle with us in the middle and began to pray at the same time in low tones. I never experienced prayer like that before. It felt like rain on my head and shoulders. Words like *guidance, protection, peace, health,* and *strength* dropped from the sky and floated by on sound waves. It was so good I bounced to the beats that accompanied them in my head. I could hear a rap bubbling up from deep down, "We're loved, we're beautiful, we got it going on, and can't nobody stop us from being the bomb diggity. Ain't no biggie what's been done, we finna rock it like we number one." When they were done praying, we all stood still, waiting, like those who wait for the spirit of a song to lift before clapping at a school recital. Maybe prayers needed to settle before we moved on to the next thing too.

"That was so cool." Francine's voice went up an octave, and her eyes went wide with the memory. "Kind of weird, little butterflies all around us." She flickered her fingers.

"A warmth came over me," Joanna added. "You know how cold melts off your body when you come in from sledding down Mt. Trashmore in Evanston? It was like that, only a hundred times better. Like, for that minute, all of our problems were on the shoulders of somebody else."

"Then why were you crying?" Francine asked.

"It'd been a long time since I felt love like that." Joanna's voice went so soft I could hardly hear. "I was crying 'cause we're not alone in this mess. We're not fighting against a great big giant with nobody to back us up." Then she turned to me. "What about you, Gracey? What was up with you bouncing and whatnot?"

"I don't know." I laughed at myself. "Man, if God is music, then last night I became part of his melody." I started dancing again. "Something in me was like, get it, girl, everything you need is in this holy moment."

"Wheeew," Francine cooed. "You sound like you're in love."

Hours later, we had sweet sleep, full-house sleep until the sun drifted higher in the sky. The heat began its journey through the pipes. The clanking and whistling got louder and louder until finally our rooms began to warm like answered prayers. It was my favorite time of morning, when sleep was cozy, and rest deep and restoring. Whether we were going to run or stay, like a thief in the night, peace drew the subject away from us.

CHAPTER 20

Gracey
December 1987

SOCIAL SERVICES CALLED WHILE WE were eating breakfast. They
told Miss Mabel our grandmother had agreed to take us in. I bet whoever said "let the chips fall where they may" never imagined they'd
just keep falling. Joanna sucked her teeth. Francine put her textbook
to her forehead and let out a short burst of a scream. And I wiped my
face as if it had mud caked on.

"Bump that, we can't go to her," I said. "She doesn't want us. I bet
the only reason she's taking us in is because they're paying her big-
time."

"Now, Gracey!" Miss Mabel sounded shocked. "What would make
you say that?"

"It's true," I answered. "Miss Nelda used to have foster kids, and
she said they paid her nice money, enough to get herself things she's
always wanted—like them hats in her closet."

"Girls, please. Social services wouldn't send you someplace they
didn't think you'd be taken care of properly."

"What are you talking about?" Francine said. "We already told you
she doesn't like us. She's a mean old woman, just like in *The Wiz*, and
all she knows how to do is put us down. Is that the kind of house you
want us going to? We'll end up hating ourselves and never having the
confidence to try anything great so we just stay stuck in some backward town doing nothing."

"Come on, Francine. Shut up," Joanna volleyed back. "You talk too
much." She turned away and shook her head.

"Now, that's enough out of you, ladies. You will be respectful while you're on my watch, d'you hear me?" Miss Mabel gave us the mean teacher look and I, recognizing it, immediately shut down.

"Yes, ma'am."

"Now, I know you girls are upset, but there's not a thing I can do about it."

"When do we leave?" Francine asked.

"Saturday, just after Christmas."

"What?" Joanna slid down in her seat until her head touched the back. "That's not enough time for anything."

"It's enough time for you to go to your house, pack your bags, and then go to school and say goodbye to all your friends and teachers."

"I guess," Joanna moaned.

"I'll tell you this much, I'm going to miss you all." Miss Mabel's bottom lip quivered a little.

"Then why don't you take us?" Francine wedged her way into the moment.

"Because, sweetie, you have to go to family first, and then if they won't take you, someone else will. But usually kids feel more comfortable around their family members. Maybe not all the time, but usually. And it was hard enough to convince them to let you come to me for the month."

After school, when we got back to Miss Mabel's house, me and Francine camped out in Joanna's room for a meeting with her.

"You scared?" I was looking for signs of queendom in her face, that invincible faith she used to carry.

"Yeah, sort of. But it's going to be all right." There it was. I took a sigh of relief. "We're on a really wild roller coaster, but as long as we hang on tight, we'll be straight." I believed the queen.

Francine sniffled. "But what if Grandma starts acting all messed up again?"

"Then we'll take a sock and stuff her mouth," Joanna said. The bedsprings squeaked as she shifted her weight to be more comfortable. "We can handle Grandma. We done it before, we'll do it again."

"Guys, I was wondering," I said. "What happens if Mom comes back and she can't find us?"

Francine's eyes got big, but Joanna just shrugged. "She ain't comin' back, but if she does, Miss Nelda'll know where we are." Out of the blue, she picked up the phone and started dialing.

"Who you calling?" I protested. "We're in the middle of a serious conversation."

"Shh," she said. "I know. I tried talking to him today, and he brushed me off. Let me just—Hello, Chill . . . Yeah, this is Joanna. I just wanted to let you know I'm moving away. And I'm going to have this baby like I said. We're moving to my grandma's in Mississippi on Saturday, so if you want to see me you better come round to the Cultural Center at five tomorrow night. I hope you're there. It's the last time you'll see me. A'ight . . . Bye."

"Were you talking to a machine, Jo?" Francine asked. "Don't you think his mom is going to have a fit?"

"Maybe, but she's always working. He'll get it before she does."

"But why are you calling him?" Francine continued to press.

"'Cause I want to talk to him."

"Why?"

"'Cause I love him."

"Does he love you?"

"He used to, before I got pregnant. Now he don't want nothing to do with me."

Francine flipped her hand like she was waving a wand to make him disappear. "I don't think he ever loved you."

"Why do you say that?"

"'Cause he never treated you like Daddy treated Mom."

"Oh, please. I know you're too young to understand this, but there ain't no men out there like Daddy. These days, you just got to take the best you can find. There's no cream of the crop."

"Then I'd rather wait for the next crop," Francine quipped.

"Me too," I said, joining Francine in a high five.

"Oh shut up, Gracey," Joanna grumped. "You should see how stupid you look drooling over Sebastian all the time. And he couldn't care less about you. That boy got more women than LL Cool J in one of his videos, and if it weren't for your droolin' and secret-sharin', we wouldn't be in the mess we're in, would we?"

"Oh, really? I thought it was 'cause of you. You shared your best secret, and now you've brought forth fruit for the whole world to see." I had one hand on my hip and the other waving in the form of the letter S.

"Don't think I won't come over there and slap you." Her neck pivoted back and forth on her shoulders.

"You know better. I'm like Muhammad Ali, 'Float like a butterfly, sting like a bee'; mess with me, girl, I'll knock you up a tree." I flexed by checking my nails instead of looking at her. She wasn't worth my energy today.

"Oh, *snap!*" Francine yelled, cupping her hand over her mouth as she laughed.

We talked until the sun set and the house got dark.

"Girls, come downstairs so you can eat," Miss Mabel called.

Downstairs, lamps were on instead of lighting from the ceiling. It wasn't as lively as our own house. And the TV news wasn't blaring from the living room. And the radio wasn't playing in the kitchen. Miss Mabel's whole world was quiet and calming. She had short, stocky vanilla-scented candles burning in frosty glass. There was fresh potpourri on the end tables, and her walls were filled with African American art like the Cosbys had, including *Funeral Procession* by Ellis Wilson with the entire congregation marching from the church to the river for baptism. Our house had mostly bare walls with a few framed photos scattered here and there. I could see why Dad may have liked her, if he did.

I I I

Christmas morning, we woke up to a decorated tree like the ones in the stores on the Magnificent Mile in downtown Chicago. We were used to our plastic tree with tinsel tackily thrown on the limbs and ornaments wrapped in yarn that didn't quite match our red velvet couch. And our lights were multicolored, which was cool, but not as classy as Miss Mabel's tree that matched the decor of her living room perfectly with white lights carefully spaced like sparkling stars. We opened our gifts, which were mostly clothes we knew her sisters had given us, and the latest gym shoes which didn't really fill us with the excitement it would have given us a year ago. We were sad, actually, because it never occurred to us to get Miss Mabel anything for Christmas—not a card or a jewelry box or anything. We all looked at each other, coming to the same realization. We sucked at thinking of others and giving.

"We didn't get you anything, Miss Mabel."

"Oh, that's okay, girls," she answered, her hands resting on her knees. "You have no idea how much of a gift it is to have you here."

"No." Francine shook her head. "We're so selfish. We should have gotten you something."

"Well . . ." Miss Mabel spoke while looking to the ceiling, thinking. "If you could have gotten me anything, what would it have been?"

"Ooh!" Francine raised her hand like she was in class. "I would have gotten you some big gold hoop earrings 'cause you wear those a lot."

Miss Mabel smiled.

"I would have made you a batch of snickerdoodle cookies and wrapped them in a pretty box with a bow," Joanna said.

"Oh." Miss Mabel touched her heart. "That would have been lovely."

And then it was my turn. "I would have gotten you your own pretty journal, so you could write at night, just like you taught us to do."

Miss Mabel dabbed her eyes around the edges. "Oh, Gracey." She sniffed. "I would have loved that so much. I feel like I've received these gifts from you girls for real. It's the thought that counts, truly."

At the table that night, we ate in silence with two dinner candles adding light to the rack of lamb and vegetables and rolls. It was our last supper together with Miss Mabel.

CHAPTER 21

Charlotte
December 1987

It took me through Christmas and a couple days more to decide to go home to Chicago. But once I'd turned in that direction, I only spent an hour getting everything together and packed. I think I threw out more than I kept—all the baggage I had collected from the past and thought I couldn't do without.

In my jewelry box, I found the friendship bracelet that Micah gave me years ago . . . I threw it out. I still had the yellow dress he took me in . . . I threw that out too. I threw out my old sandals, my old clothes, coats . . . I even threw out all my love journals where I talked about my Sundays with Micah and my Sundays without him. That pity party had gone on too long. It was finally over.

I looked at the ring on my finger. Moses and I were parted now . . . though not by choice. I took off the ring and put it on a gold chain around my neck. Most of what Moses gave me I kept. He was the one God gave to me, and I had every right to cherish him. There were still things I had to move past, though. The first place I would go when I got to Chicago was to the cemetery.

I said my goodbyes to my room. It had sheltered me so warmly, like a womb. The bed was made, the sink and tub were clean, and the windows were wide open for the fresh air to flow through. Let the other cleaners come and close them later. I looked up to heaven, waved a quiet thank-you to the Lord, and switched off the light.

In the lobby, I sat in a big plush seat usually meant for new guests as I waited for a cab to come and take me to the train station. Lord knows, I hated the train for its long rickety rides and busy, talking people, but I didn't really have a choice. My mama took the train, my mama's mama took the train. If it was good enough for them, it was good enough for me.

Candi walked in as I was waiting for the cab. I looked up from the *Town and Country* magazine I was holding.

"What airline you takin'?"

I laughed. "Airline? Girl, please, who do I look like, Zsa Zsa Gabor? I cannot afford no airplane."

Candi checked her watch and looked at me.

"Well, Ebony's stable, and Mr. Goodin's bent on taking care of her. I'm a little out of sorts these days, so I asked if I could combine my vacations if I promised to work through Christmas and New Year's. I can't concentrate on nothing noway."

She paused for an even longer moment while I did my best to push out any thought of coaxing her into doing what I thought she might be thinking of. *Don't you dare manipulate*, I scolded myself.

"I guess I could drive you to Chicago."

Yes! "Oh no, Candi. I can't let you do that."

"Nah, I think a long drive will do me good." She turned to the receptionist at the desk and said, "Tell Mr. Bridges my time starts now."

The receptionist looked at her with consoling eyes. "Sure, Candi. He'll understand. Listen, I hope things get better for you."

"Thank you, dear." Candi turned back to me and smiled sweetly. "Well?"

"Well, if you insist," I answered.

"I do. Come on, girl. Let's go." She took my suitcase and dragged it to the car while I carried my duffle bag and popped it into the trunk of her 1972 Jaguar.

"How'd you get the money to pay for this?"

"I sold one of my paintings to this rich man who came to stay at the bed-and-breakfast. He took one look at 'em and said I had painted the story of his life. The next thing you know, I'm buyin' this old Jaguar, the car of my dreams. That's how I got the down payment on my house too. A man saw one of my paintings sitting outside in the yard, and he said he'd never seen the truth in paint before. He had to have it in his home. My house was a real dump when I bought it, so obviously he didn't give me that much. It took me years to restore it, one room at a time."

"I guess there is something to doing what you love."

We stopped talking over the hood and slid into the car. After Candi picked up some things from her house, we were on our way. We let the news radio do the talking for the first part of the trip, commenting every now and again.

"So tell me something . . ." Candi said, her hands steady on the wheel.

"What?"

"Did you ever call your daughters?"

I cleared my throat and shifted in my seat. "No."

"How come?"

"I don't know. I guess I don't want to deal with the situation. I don't even know how to approach it. I have beautiful girls, beautiful. And their voices are so pretty and pure, can you imagine if I called and heard so much as a tear or a *why* in their voices? I woulda broken down. I woulda had to go home in the same mess I left in."

"Okay." Candi glanced between me and the road. "That's fine, but I guess I'm wondering after things got better, like in the last few days, do the girls know you're coming home?"

I took a deep breath. "No."

"Charlotte, why not? What's going on?"

"I don't know. I'm just scared, I guess. I mean, what if they hate me by now?"

"They can't hate you. You're their mother."

"Hmm . . . I'm not so sure that means anything."

"I could say the same for you. Does it mean anything?"

I took a breath as if I were going to answer but decided to let the question roll over me or settle. Being a mother did mean something. But I wasn't sure what it meant to me. Sheila May used to say being a mother was like constantly having the life sucked out of you and then pumped back in in overwhelmingly wonderful ways. She couldn't wait to have kids after marriage. Last I heard she tied her tubes at baby number seven and she lived in Brooklyn of all places, where the trees were sparsely placed and her husband owned a comedy club. I was always too ashamed to face her after the Micah incident. She would have been so disappointed in me.

We leaned back in our seats as the road stretched out before us. We had miles and miles to go, and a lot of ground to cover. Kenny Rogers filled the air with "You Decorated My Life," and we were lost in our own thoughts.

Before I knew it, I had drifted off to sleep. Hundreds of multi-colored butterflies were flying past me in a field. I tried waving them away so I could see where I was going, but they just kept flittering, so I dropped to the ground and started crawling. And as I looked up, I could see my girls, Frankie, Gracey, and Joanna, in the distance calling me. *Come on, Mom. Come on. Hurry!*

"So this Micah man and your husband, them the only two men you ever been with?" Candi's voice startled me awake.

I took a deep breath. My heart was thumping. Were my girls really calling me home? Did they need me? Nah, it was just a dream.

I settled down and replayed Candi's question in my mind. "Yes. I don't think I could have handled any more than that."

"Hmm . . ." Candi looked like she was in another world.

I probably should have returned the question, but it would take us places I didn't want to go right then.

I paused, and then let out a laugh. Every woman has a story.

∎ ∎ ∎

Candi and I did a whole lot of talking during that trip. We parsed our lives like flowers from weeds in a garden—pulling the crab weeds up from where they didn't belong, digging down deep to yank out the dandelion roots. We weren't exactly sure how to put everything back together, but we did our best. Candi's life was colorful and complicated. Most of her pain came from folks who erased boundaries to do what they wanted to do and never put them back 'cause they didn't know how. Flower gardens with wild things growing are never very pretty.

I was watching the wind turbines go by when I started talking again, randomly.

"It was near impossible to sleep in that room, in the same bed I'd slept with Moses in every night since our marriage. I was so lonely without him, felt like I was being sucked into a black hole. Some nights I didn't think the morning would ever come. In so many ways, Candi, I just had to get away from that house."

Candi's face tensed up. "Then you should have taken your children with you."

"I know." I closed my eyes. "I know."

There was no sympathy in her voice, no way to climb over the wall of reality. So I camped out there.

"I thought you were all right with what I'd done. I thought we agreed that I was going to right a wrong and everything would be okay. That's the miracle we're praying for, right?"

"Of course it is. But you left your girls! I forgive you, God forgave you, and I know you were in a bad way and you just couldn't take any more, but there must have been an ice patch on your heart somewhere to leave them alone just like that. I mean, girl! You and I both know that life is war, and to abandon your children in the middle of a battle is . . . it's crazy. And every time I think I understand it, I find I don't.

"I think you need to pray, Charlotte. Pray that God would teach you how to love and what it means to love and how deep love can run. When people love each other, they don't just give up and walk out. They stay and they practice and practice until they get it right. Fear starts out innocent, but if you let it sit too long, your whole life'll pass you by, just like them little candies on the conveyor belt of the *I Love Lucy* show. One thing you could say about Lucy, she never let fear stop her from trying anything."

That wall seemed to be getting taller and taller. If I'd known I was gonna get life lessons from a 1950s sitcom, I woulda taken the train.

But still. She had a point. "I can't even imagine that, love without fear," I said. "If there were such a thing, such a love, I never would have left. But that's it, isn't it? All these years, the one thing that's held me back from giving love and getting love back—" I stopped. Sat silent as light suddenly poured into my heart. When I could breathe again, I said, "It was fear."

"Yes." Candi nodded her head with a teacher's accomplished smile. She seemed content with her ability to make me have an aha moment.

"But it was more than that, right?"

She sobered her lips. "Wait, what do you mean?"

"I mean, yes, there's fear. But there's also the trial."

"What trial?"

"I dunno. I think I've always wanted God to prove me innocent. To show me I deserve the love I have—Stop the car!" I said.

"What?"

"I said stop the car!"

Candi pulled over, and I got out and started walking back and forth on the side of the road. I was thinking and battling within. The white wind turbines were turning like pinwheels, helping me think. I stood very still with breezes flowing through me until I felt one with all that is divine.

"God, I'm so confused. I feel like a bad person, but I don't believe I'm bad. I feel dirty, but I know I'm not. As soon as I think it's okay to live like I'm forgiven, something happens and I put myself right back in the loveless prison. Please speak to me. Let me know that I'm innocent, I'm free. That I was right all along to believe that he was wrong. That I may not have done everything right, but I tried to stop it and was overpowered.

"Tell me the verdict," I yelled toward heaven. "I need to know what you think of me! Am I innocent? Am I free to live and love?"

The wind picked up, and as I stretched out my arms, pieces of me, like dead petals, blew away. When the air went calm again, I lowered my head and pulled my arms in around me. Like a baby, I wept. My shoulders collapsing as I turned my back to the cars whizzing by and my body away from Candi's gaze. This moment was between me and God.

My soul felt bare, smooth, and I didn't want to move. I wanted my body and my spirit to settle into this newness, this freedom that felt so incredibly scary and completely fine at the same time. This was something I could get used to.

Candi sat in the car watching me. She had lit a cigarette and was flicking it out the window as she stared. Cars honked as they flashed by, and she waved at them to keep going.

CHAPTER 22

Gracey
December 1987

THE DAY AFTER CHRISTMAS, WE went with Joanna to say goodbye to Chill. She and I had yelled at each other about it the whole morning with Francine backing me up, until finally Joanna told us both to *tais-toi*, something she learned in French class, and slammed the door. We looked at each other and shrugged.

Of course, we followed her to the South Shore Cultural Center. We made Sebastian come too, just in case we had to go ballistic on Chill.

Joanna stood in the lobby of the building while we waited in the cut on the side, shivering in the cold, huddled up next to each other.

"I can't believe we're out here like this." Sebastian rubbed his hands on his thighs. "This is straight crazy."

"Shut up, Bastian. If it was your sister, you'd be out here with the whole basketball team behind you."

"Got that right. This dude wouldn't know which side was up. But I don't have a sister, so it ain't no thing."

"What time is it?" Francine asked.

"It's late," I said, looking at my watch. "He should have been here fifteen minutes ago."

"He ain't comin'," Bastian said. "Let's go."

"As long as Joanna's here, we're here." I gave him a light shove with my shoulder.

"Hold on, guys, be quiet. There he is." Francine pointed to a guy walking up in Adidas.

Chill's hands were shoved in his pockets and his cap was pulled over his eyes. His baggy pants and injured knee walk gave him away.

"Dang, man." Bastian shook his head. "He's such a wannabe gangsta. He's just a regular guy. You didn't see him switch up his walk when he got in front of South Shore?"

"I totally missed that," Francine said. "That explains why Joanna said he could never talk because he was studying." She shrugged and raised her voice an octave. "Maybe he really was."

We both looked at Francine, then Bastian looked at me and wagged his thumb at her. "You better watch out she don't start running after the roughnecks like her big sister."

"Please. I know what's up," Francine said. "Ain't nobody getting between these knees."

Francine was right, though. Chill was a different kind of guy. And Joanna wasn't just any girl—she was special. If she had picked Chill of all the people in the world to date and then accidentally get pregnant by, there must have been a good reason. Like, maybe he looked into her eyes and made her cry, or maybe the way he touched her gave her goose bumps, or maybe he bought her gifts she'd only ever whispered in her thoughts. There must have been something special about him.

But then again, I remembered sitting next to Grandma when she was watching *All My Children*, and Erica would claim she was so in love with some new man. Grandma would yell at the TV while chewing popcorn: "Don't you marry that man, Erica. Your heart is lyin' to you, girl. They don't tell ya that in school, but it do. Your heart is lyin' to you!"

Back then I was confused, 'cause in all the good movies when the teenager doesn't know what to do, the fairy godmother and the nanny and the good witch, they all say "follow your heart," and here was Grandma saying, "your heart lies to you."

Maybe that was what happened to Joanna. Maybe her heart lied to her, and she followed it.

"Why do you think he even came?" I asked.

"Aw, come on, the girl's carrying his child!" Bastian said. "If he has half a conscience, he'll try to figure out where she's moving to. He might not love her, but, man, having a baby . . . that connects you forever and a day, man . . . forever and a day!"

"Oh yeah?" I said. "What about your dad, Sebastian? What happened to him?"

"What's that got to do with anything?" Sebastian looked very annoyed. His nose wrinkled like he smelled something foul. "I see him, like, once a year. He'll come in with some flowers, cheesing, like it ain't nothing wrong with the way he treats us. If he's lucky, Mom lets him spend the night, and then like that"—he snaps his fingers—"he's out. Sometimes he leaves enough cash for me to go shopping with, but not much. And if he's feeling really good, he'll play me in a game of B-ball. I whipped him so bad last time, though, he hasn't brought it up since. I know for sure, if I wasn't around, my mom and dad wouldn't have nothin' to do with each other."

"That's sad. People come together and get all caught up and start making families and can't finish them," Francine said. "Michael Jackson's right in 'Wanna be Startin' Somethin''—you shouldn't make babies if you can't feed them. We shouldn't even think *maybe* if it's gonna be an issue."

We were laughing away when we saw Chill leave out the front doors. Joanna stood on the top step outside, wiping her cheeks with her mittens. She looked like an innocent schoolgirl just trying to grow up and live a decent life. We waited till he was out of sight before we gathered around her.

"Hey, Gracey." Bastian tugged on my arm to pull me away from the others. "I'm going to head out. I don't want to hear all that mushy girl stuff."

"So I guess that's it then." I glanced over his shoulder toward my sisters, half-distracted by what Joanna might be sharing.

"Yeah, I guess that's it."

"You got my new address?"

"Yup, got it."

"Not that you'll write . . ."

"I might," he said.

He won't, I thought.

He reached out and hugged me long enough for me to leave an imprint on his body, and then he walked away just like Chill, with his hands in his pockets. Maybe they weren't so different after all. But then again, Bastian was my friend, that was more than I could say for Joanna and Chill. I wondered if Bastian would miss me, or maybe he'd look through our old pictures and throw a thought my way. One thing's for sure, I was going to miss him. He was my first love.

I took a deep breath, turned to focus on Joanna, then walked back to my sisters.

By the time I caught up, Joanna and Francine had already started on their way, linked arm in arm, with Francine leaning on her big sister.

"So what happened?" I asked.

"Nothing." Joanna shrugged.

"What do you mean, nothing? He walked out without looking back, and you came out crying. That don't look like nothing to me."

"Well, it was nothing. I asked him if maybe we could get married and start a family, then I wouldn't have to leave. And he asked me if I was crazy. He said I was trying to ruin his life. And I was like, 'What do you think you've done to me?' And he said he couldn't help it if I was an easy case to crack, and he thought I was on the Pill. He said he wanted to be a lawyer someday and get out of this hole, and having a baby would mess everything up. Besides that, his mom doesn't even believe the baby's his. She wants a paternity test. And I was like 'I'm not taking a test. You're the first and only guy I've ever been with.' And he looked me dead in the eyes and said, 'Nothing's gonna stop me from getting out the hood, Joanna.' And so I asked him, 'Why'd you come, then?' and he said, 'I figure I owe you that much.'"

"What a putz." Francine kicked at a broken piece of concrete.

"Yeah . . . Wait a minute. What'd you just say?" I stopped walking. Joanna and I looked at each other. Where'd she get that from?

"I said he's a putz. Everybody calls everybody that on the cross-country team. That's what my coach calls the boys when they call us slow. I think it fits Chill pretty well."

She imitated her coach's voice, and we busted out laughing.

"What are you laughing at?" Francine continued. "Coach says, 'You're a putz. I don't think this behavior is acceptable in public. Now get ahold of yourselves and focus.'"

We giggled all the way home, making fun of other people. No sense in talking about Chill. We were through with him.

When I went to sleep that night, I had the strangest dream. I grabbed my new journal that I'd bought with my own money to write it down. Miss Mabel could have my old journal, but not my new one. She wasn't getting any more of me and my family.

December 27, 1987
12:01 a.m.
Tall green grass surrounded me as I stood in a field watching the wind blow all the daffodils and purple wild weeds in the same direction. The trees clapped their leaves, giving a loud applause, and the sun warmed my skin. Laughter rippled in the grass, so I followed the voices, but every time I got to the place, there was no one there. Then I heard groanings and moanings, kisses and sighs, and then a loud, "No."

"Mom?" I ran all through the field trying to find her. "Mom, is that you?"

"Stop it! Stop!"

I heard hitting now and screaming. My mom was screaming.

"Mom!" I yelled louder. "Mom, tell me where you are. I'll help you! Where are you? Where's Daddy?"

And then there was silence in the field, as if no human had ever crossed its path.

I closed my journal. It wasn't enough. I tiptoed to Joanna's room and found her standing in front of the window like she was trying to figure something out. She and Mom had that same way about them, like the answer might fly in with a little birdie and everything would be okay. Now that I think about it, looking at my mom over the years, she kind of reminded me of those flowers in my dream—leaning into the wind and digging deep into the soil at the same time. Holding on for dear life, refusing to be blown away. But eventually the wind got her. Was it us that made her let go? Is that why she left as soon as Daddy died?

"What's wrong?" Joanna asked, her eyes looking at my reflection.

"I had a bad dream."

She turned and sat on the bed. "'Bout what?"

"I don't know. It was silly, I guess." I slumped in the desk chair next to the lamp. "I think it was about Mom, being a flower. The wind was trying to pry her from the ground, and she screamed and screamed until there was silence. I guess the wind won."

"Hmm." Joanna shook her head. "Your dream sounds like a recurring dream I have that I lose soon as I wake up. I only remember seeing Mom's face, so upset like somebody caused her harm and then nothing."

"You think she's dead?"

Joanna pursed her lips. "Come on now. Really."

"Well, I mean we haven't heard anything. What if she's in the bottom—"

"Stop it. It's too dark, too sad." Joanna wiped her face against the moonlight. "Some thoughts you can't afford to think about."

"I guess. Kind of like I can't afford to think about what went on between Miss Mabel and Dad." I had told her about the picture the day I saw it.

"Let it go, Gracey. The longer I live, the more I understand, grown folks have messed-up lives. It's like they steal from one place to make up for an imbalance in another. And they all think their balance scale makes them right. But really, the fact that it's even doesn't mean it's just or fair."

I grunted in response. I hated it when Joanna got philosophical.

The quiet in the room was enough to put me on edge. I wouldn't ever admit it to Joanna, but I was glad to be leaving. Chicago was squeezing me out like old toothpaste from a tube. Whatever, I didn't want Chicago either. And as for Mom, after that dream, she was gone with the wind.

CHAPTER 23

Charlotte
December 1987

IT MUST HAVE BEEN CLOSE to midnight when Candi and I pulled up to the motel. I woke up not remembering a thing that had happened.

"What's going on, where am I? Am I late for work?"

"Relax, Charlotte. We're in Carbondale. I couldn't drive another mile, so we're stayin' in this motel overnight. I'll pay your half."

We went to the desk in the lobby. A couple was in there, necking in a telephone booth. Candi turned her mouth down as if she smelled something foul and dropped all her things on the floor. She reached down into her bosom and pulled out a small vial of what could only have been holy oil, 'cause she started shaking little droplets on the carpet and waving her hand and saying "the blood of Jesus, the blood of Jesus."

"Can I help you, ma'am?" The receptionist raised a skeptical eyebrow at us. "You here to evangelize, or do you want a room for the night?"

Candi put the top on the vial and stuffed it into her bosom. "It'd be downright wonderful if I could do both." She leaned on the desk and said with celebrity candor, "Do you know Jesus?"

The lady never cracked a smile. "Yeah, he's the Mexican dude that lives on the floor above me. Now, would you like a room?"

Candi just stood there like somebody had thrown pie in her face, so I stepped in.

"Yes, we'd like a room."

"Double or single?" She had fingers to be proud of, long and slender with a French manicure, a diamondless gold band on her wedding finger.

"Double."

"How long you stayin'?"

"One night."

"Name."

I looked at Candi.

"Candice Mulberry."

"Mulberry?" I said.

"Yes, I changed my name back to what it used to be."

"Riiiight," I said calmly.

We hauled our luggage to the room, and out came the vial of oil again.

"God, cleanse this room from all the sin and filth and mess that goes on in here." She sprinkled the oil on the floor, the beds, and the bathroom as if she were a priest. "Purify it, Jesus, the blood, the blood . . ." Then she fanned the air and walked around the room.

A few minutes later, she declared the room clean and sat on the bed.

It was a dingy place . . . one of those with no outside light because the window curtains opened up to a view of the indoor swimming pool.

"I'm not used to waking up without sunlight," I said, missing Georgia already.

"Don't worry about it—we'll be gone before you know it."

I was too tired to shower. I put on my nightgown and climbed into the crisp, cold sheets. But Candi was setting up her canvas and paints. I watched her whisk orange and red on the canvas until my eyes were too heavy to keep open.

Butterflies fluttered over my bed as I looked between them to the blue sky above me, but when I sat up, the few became thousands and I couldn't see anymore. I could just hear their wings. My girls were still calling me. "Come on, Mom, hurry up." And I tried to fight through, but I couldn't. There were just too many butterflies, like a plague. Then I heard Frankie saying, "Get on the ground and crawl, Mom, it's clear on the ground." So I got down, and I could see three pairs of shoes, two pairs were gym shoes and the other, black flats. And I crawled toward those feet until I got close enough to touch them, but then another pair of shoes came, high heels with fat stubby feet in stockings, and stood by my girls. I didn't mind at first, but then, one by one, they followed the heels. And I called after them. No one answered. I yelled but there was silence, just Luther Vandross crooning one of his love songs.

Luther was on the radio as I woke up, and the smell of paint hung thick in the air. A beautiful sunrise sprawled across the canvas, painted from the view of one sitting on the top of a mountain looking down. The horizon seemed to go on forever as the sun's semicircle birthed itself through the atmosphere. The colors were brilliant, reds and maroons, purples and oranges, and a golden yellow glow near the bottom.

Candi was still knocked out in the bed. She had about ten pink rollers in her hair and a mask over her eyes.

There was a knock at the door. "Housekeeping."

"Can you come back later?" I glanced at the alarm clock and bolted upright. Checkout time was minutes away. I shook Candi awake, and we threw our things together and checked out.

"How'd you sleep?" Candi asked when we got back on the road.

"I keep dreaming about butterflies and the girls calling me to hurry home. Last night scared me a bit because I saw some high-heeled shoes walk onto the scene. And whoever she was, the girls followed her. What do you think it means?"

"I think it means we need to get you home as soon as possible."

"Yeah, I was thinking the same. But I got to go to the cemetery before I see my girls. I have to make the confession."

"Oh, for Pete's sake. Don't tell me you're still going to go to the cemetery when you know your girls could be leaving any second if they haven't left already."

"I have to risk it. I have to talk to Moses and tell him the truth. Otherwise I'll feel like a liar when I walk through that door."

"You are a liar."

I gaped at Candi.

"Don't look at me like that. Yes, he was awful to force himself on you. Yes, everything that happened was by no fault of your own—remember, you fought back like you were supposed to and he ignored you. But you've still been lying to your family for almost fifteen years now, and you think a confession to some dirt is going to change things? Girl, please. You might as well be talking to the trees."

"You're unbelievable. You're like a two-faced mask, one side is for me, the other side against me. I never know who I'm talking to."

She didn't say anything further, and that set me off.

"You think you're Miss Super Christian, but you're more messed up than I am. At least I'm trying to fix my mess. What are you doing? Painting pictures and refusing to face your problems. How does that help? You let your own husband be with your sister. What kind of crazy mess is that? From the word *go*, you should have put your foot down and told your sister, 'I'm sorry I hurt your feelings and everything, but you ain't got no right to take away my husband.' But no, you let her walk all over you with a pair of high-kneed go-go boots, and now you're sorry."

I ain't never talked to anyone like that in my life. *Jesus forgive me*, I thought, *but she brought me to it.*

"Oh, now you think you know me." Her eyelids went half-mast.

"Yeah, I know you. All the time we done spent together—I know you real well."

"So easy to spew off at the mouth. You think it's easy to walk the road of escape?" She jerked the wheel left, passing some slow-moving truck.

"What? I'm not trying—"

Next thing I knew, Candi had lost control of the car and we were spinning onto the other side of the road. We both screamed and covered our heads as drivers banged on their horns and swerved around us. After a few seconds, we looked up and saw a big truck from far off coming straight toward us.

"Get this car on the right side of the road!" I screamed.

"I am! I'm trying!" Candi was shaking now. Still she got control, sped to the right side of the road, and pulled over. When she stopped the car, we both just sat there with our heads leaning on the dashboard.

She was the first to speak. "I'm sorry."

"I'm sorry too."

"You're right, you know. I act like a Super Christian, but the truth is, I don't have it all figured out. I don't know anything. And sometimes it gets really hard because I don't know what to do and God is nowhere to be found no matter how many angels and Bible verses I put in my house. And then I get so angry, you know, 'cause I'm trying to do right and follow God, but I just make a bigger mess of everything. And then I wonder if God is even real. And if God isn't, then it's all for nothing. This life, this struggle, is it all for nothing?

"It's like you pour your life out on people, trusting God to fill you back up, but if God isn't even real, then at the end of the day you're an empty pitcher with a lot more life to live and nothing to pour. And then I realize it's just the devil trying to get me to go down the doubtin' road, and I know that leads to no good, so I get back on the right road, the faith road, but I still don't hear anything. So I'm right back to where I began. Confused. Sisters are supposed to be a blessing, but this one that God gave me, she must be a curse."

"Maybe if you let her go—"

"I've let her go so many times, but she's like a boomerang. She just keeps coming back."

"A boomerang doesn't come back if you move out of its path. Sometimes even a big old town is too small for two people to live in."

"Hmm . . . maybe."

She started up the car, and we rode the rest of the way to Chicago listening to country music until the stations changed to R and B.

Lionel Richie was singing "All Night Long" on the radio as the Chicago skyline came into view. The Sears Tower, the John Hancock building, the beautiful *Ebony* magazine sign, and the lake, sittin' pretty to the east. I was overwhelmed. I rolled down the window to feel the change in the air. Everything was fast and crisp, one step ahead of time. I'd forgotten all about the pace and the fancy folks who never slowed down.

Candi pointed to all the tall buildings and couldn't stop gushing over Lake Michigan. I marveled at her inner child. She suddenly seemed real country to me. Even her accent made my ears twitch.

"Girl, roll up that window before you freeze us," she yelled over the sound of the wind.

I rolled up the window.

"Now tell me where this cemetery is."

"Just stay on Lake Shore Drive. I'll tell you when you get there. It's a far cry from the ones in Mississippi where I grew up. The cemeteries there are still segregated, and it's hard to get in to see our ancestors because the land is so overgrown."

Candi flattened her lips and shook her head. Maybe I had overshared. Mississippi was in so many different eras at one time. From town to town, folks lived in different historical decades.

There was no one at the cemetery when we arrived. The ground was hard and frosted over, and many headstones had flowers wrapped in plastic next to them. I tried my best to walk between the graves, but after a while, I couldn't tell what was what, so I walked without paying attention. It was a little eerie in the dark, so I sang to myself to scare off the ghosts.

I tucked the flowers I had bought on the way in under one arm and rubbed my hands together to get them warm. And then I saw the shiny stone standing on the ground: *Moses Downing 1945–1987, Humble and Loved.* I knelt on the grass and traced the stone and the engraved letters. Everything was so cold. At the bottom of the stone were some fresh flowers with a card on the inside. I ignored them and got straight to my business.

"Hi, Moses," I started in. "I'm sorry I ain't come to see you since everything happened, but I got some things to tell you. Some things I want you to hear straight from my mouth." I made the sign of the cross over my body and chest like the Catholics did and continued. "Of course you heard all the rumors about me and Micah back in the day. I tried my best to show you that there was nothing between us. But one day when we went back to get Mama, I met up with Micah. I just wanted to say goodbye, get some closure. You understand. And he uh . . . he took advantage of me. And I couldn't stop him. And our second child, Gracey, well . . . she ain't yours. I mean she is yours, but she belongs to Micah. I was so scared of losing you, I kept it secret. I tried to make it up to you with Francine, but it didn't make things no better 'cept we got another beautiful little girl. That's when things changed between us 'cause I couldn't forgive myself. I messed everything up. You were a wonderful husband and father, and you didn't deserve to be treated so. If I had just told the truth, maybe we could have been better together. I am so sorry. Please forgive me, Moses."

The night seemed to stand as my jury, the stars discussing my situation. Maybe they'd carry my message through the heavens till he got it. I knew Moses wasn't going to say anything back. But at least I told him. And for me that was freeing. I drew a heart in the snow with a stick and closed my eyes to soak in the moment.

I was pressing on my thighs to push myself up when I noticed the card again. I knelt back down to open it. I knew right away from the small, square-rounded letters that it was Francine's writing.

Dear Daddy,
A lot's happened since you been gone to heaven. I don't know
if they tell you things or not about what's going on down

here, but I thought you should know we're moving in with Grandma in Mississippi. So it'll be a long while before we come visit you again. If you see Jesus, could you tell him we need his help? I love you, Daddy.

Francine

I turned to run to the car in a panic, but then I was engulfed by a peace that wouldn't let me go. I was like a kite kept from falling, not by the wind but by the suspension of gravity.

I walked calmly back to the car with the note in my hand and found Candi leaning against it, smoking a cigarette.

"Never seen you smoke till recently."

She threw the cigarette down and stomped on it. "I don't smoke, hardly ever . . . 'cept when I'm in a car or in a spooky old cemetery by myself trying not to run outta here screamin'.'"

"Learn more and more about you every day." I shook my head and climbed into the car. I didn't feel like saying much of anything else.

But Candi settled into her seat, slammed the door, and turned to look at me, trying to read my face.

"So . . . how'd it go?"

"I have to go home. Francine, my youngest, wrote a letter to Moses saying they were moving in with their grandma."

"Oh, that doesn't sound good."

"No." I felt like someone had given me painkillers. All I wanted to do was breathe and sleep.

Candi must have picked up on it, 'cause she didn't talk anymore either except to get directions.

"This is it," I said an hour later. Candi pulled to a stop in front of the house.

My heart pounded again as I dug around in the bottom of my purse and found my keys. The furry little dice I'd had on the chain were long gone, probably in Savannah somewhere.

The neighborhood hadn't changed a bit. Folks still hung out on the steps even in the cold, staying in the know. Loud, thumping music occasionally vibrated the trunks of cars, and a couple of dealers hung out on the corners like they was waiting for their best buddy to come by and pick them up.

I got out of the car and made my way to the front door. I had to steady my hand so I could put the key in the hole.

I knew the house was empty from the second I walked in. The heat was on bare minimum to keep the pipes from freezing, and the lights were off. I picked up the phone; it was dead. I went to the side drawer where we keep the emergency flashlight and pulled it out. At least it still worked. The house was nice and neat just like I told the girls to keep it, everything in its right place and not a crumb to be found. They really were good girls. I walked through the whole house with my flashlight, with Candi right behind me.

"Hello, hello!" she kept yelling. "Anybody home?"

"Why do you keep calling out? I told you they weren't here."

"Look, I just want to make sure ain't nobody else here. You know what I'm sayin'?"

I breathed in the smell of the house. It felt so good to be home. Those alderwood doors and potpourri cups that sat on shelves around the house were still releasing their scents. Upstairs, the door to the girls' room was closed. I opened the door and shined my flashlight around. Their favorite teddy bears and stuffed animals were gone, but their dollies still sat on the bed. Abandoned by maturity. Inside their dresser drawers were just a few items, old underwear and bras that probably didn't fit anymore. The kitchen radio sat on the stand next to Gracey's bottom bunk. I opened the closet. Metal and plastic hangers clanged together. Nothing there but some worn-out little shoes sitting neatly on the floor together.

In and out, in and out, I breathed. "It's okay, it's okay, everything will be fine."

I closed the door back to the girls' room and walked into mine. My knees buckled as I walked through the door, but Candi caught me.

"Hang on there, girl. You all right? Maybe we should come back another time."

"No, this is a better time than any."

Moses's things were already gone. Somebody had cleaned his closet out and pushed all the hangers to the side.

"Hold this." I gave Candi the flashlight.

"Why?"

I pulled all the blankets and sheets off the bed, leaving it bare to completely air out. I held Moses's pillow to my nose and tried to find the scent of his cologne or hair moisturizer.

Candi made a face and moved the flashlight away. "Girl, come on here. Let's go. This ain't housekeeping!"

She didn't understand. I needed to loose the trapped spirits of our memories and let them go.

We were back on the porch and I was about to lock up the house again, when a young cop whooped his siren and climbed out of his car. He strode up the walk to where I was and said, "We have complaints about a disturbance at this house."

"This is my house, officer. I haven't been here in a while, and I was just—"

"Mrs. Downing." The officer squinted his eyes. "Is that you?"

"Yes." I couldn't quite tell who he was, but I'd remembered him around the neighborhood as a teenager. Now he was a cop. How long had I been gone?

The cop looked around and pulled on his holster. "Listen, you know there's a warrant out for your arrest, right? You left your kids. I'm supposed to take you in for child neglect."

"Oh, oh, please don't. Please don't do that."

Candi turned her head and started praying softly.

He looked over my shoulder at her. "What's she doing?"

"Oh, I don't know, talking to the birds. Officer, look, you don't know what I've been through the last six months."

"Yes, I do. Your husband was Moses, and he died. We were all shocked. That was a real blow to the neighborhood. And then you kind of lost it. That's what everybody says, anyway."

"Well, I guess you could say I lost it, but I got it back now. I had to leave to take care of some things, and while you might say I've been away from my girls for too long, I've really been working my way back to them the whole time. And now I've found out that they've been sent to Mississippi with my mama. If you arrest me, God knows when I'll get to see them again. I don't have any money. Please believe me— I'll never leave my girls again."

I grabbed my head to make it say the right things. "I don't have the words, I just know you gotta let me go," I pleaded. "If you don't and I go to jail, my girls' lives will be ruined forever. And they deserve the chance to live a good life. That's what I'm trying to do, that's why I'm here. I want to fix this and be happy and live happy and pour as much love as I can into my babies."

His radio blared. "Car thirty-two, come in. You at that house yet? What's going on?"

The officer looked me in the eyes as if he were trying to see my truth. I could see him thinking as his tongue clicked behind his teeth. He looked over my shoulder to Candi, who was still praying quietly, and then finally he lifted his walkie-talkie to his mouth. "It's quiet over here, Sergeant, no sign of any trouble."

My look of pleading broke into a smile as the officer put his walkie-talkie back into its place.

Candi lifted her hands in praise. "Oh, thank you, Jesus! Thank you!" She started prancing around while the neighbors peered through their rayon curtains. The officer looked at Candi again and turned his attention back to me.

"Listen, you're not out of the woods yet. You're lucky everybody knew and respected Moses. I mean, he got a lot of people out of trouble, and he even tipped the cops off on more than one occasion. His name may just carry enough weight to keep you out of trouble with some police officers, but I tell you, keep your head low and get out of town 'cause if the wrong cop sees you, there ain't no turnin' back. Do you understand? There's a whole lot of mothers in jail, wishin' they could see their children."

"Yes, sir. I understand." It was humiliating talking to this young man like that, like I was a criminal, and maybe I was, but I thank God there wasn't a talk-back bone in my body. I was just happy to be free. The nameless, kinky-headed child I used to see riding up and down the street on his minibike was now a man in authority, and I had to respect that. I looked at his name tag. *William Sanders*. Recognition hit.

"Oh! You Miss Nelda's grandnephew, ain't you?"

"Yes, ma'am, I am." He bowed his head. "She told me you'd be turnin' up sooner or later."

"Thank you."

"You're welcome." He turned to get into his car. He sat there for a while writing out some papers, and then he drove off.

"Charlotte. Can you believe it?" Candi came over and gave me a big hug.

Quickly, I took her by the arm and pulled her down the street. "Come on, we have to go somewhere."

"Girl, it's cold out here. Let's drive."

"It's quicker to walk."

We crossed the street and I knelt down, hanging on to the lamp pole outside the apartments. There in the garden window was Miss Nelda in her wheelchair, watching reruns of *The Jeffersons*.

I picked up a stick and tapped on the iron gate. Moses showed me that trick. He said it was easier to tap on the gate to get her attention than to spend fifteen minutes trying to get her to come to the door.

By the second tap, Miss Nelda peered out the window, trying to figure out who was there. I waved like a crazy woman.

"It's me, Charlotte Downing, Miss Nelda. Come and open the door."

She smiled and nodded her head. A few minutes later, the thick wooden door with cracks down the middle and sides opened up.

She was already calling me and squinting over her reading glasses. "Charlotte, Charlotte. That really you?"

"Yes, Miss Nelda. It's me. I'm back. I came to get my girls." I kissed the soft loose skin on her cheek and lightly hugged her frail body.

"Oh, honey, I always knew you'd come back. I told them you were a good girl. I was right too. Look at you standing right here in front of me."

"Yes, Miss Nelda, I'm here. And this is my friend Candi. She drove me back to Chicago."

She nodded hello, and Candi reached out and gave her a big hug. "It's so nice to meet you, Miss Nelda. You have a lovely nephew."

"Who, Billy?"

"Yes, ma'am. We met him just a minute ago. Real nice officer, he is."

Miss Nelda stopped her smiling and looked from Candi to me. "Did he take care of you, Charlotte?"

"Yes, ma'am, he did."

"His daddy raised him right."

We all smiled, and then I took a breath to speak, but she interrupted me.

"You're on your way to see your girls, I presume. You know the state awarded temporary custody to your mama."

"Oh." I sat down on the side chair. "I knew they were at Mama's, but I didn't know how they got there. How were they? Did they cry? Did they seem upset?"

"They were plenty upset. That baby girl just disappeared for a few hours, they couldn't find her nowhere. But she came back, didn't tell nobody where she went. The other two seemed all right, just sad, hanging their heads. You got strong girls, Charlotte. Some folks round here might say they took care of 'em for you. But that ain't true. Them girls took care of themselves. They was like soldiers marching in a storm; they just kept on going."

"Oh, Lord, my poor babies."

"No, they ain't babies no more, Charlotte." Miss Nelda waved her hand in weak protest. "You got little women on your hands now."

I hid my face behind my fingers and lowered them enough to reveal my eyes. "Miss Nelda," I said in a muffled voice. I was so tired, energy was seeping out of me as I spoke.

"Hmm?" She sounded so sweet and so forgiving, so soothing.

"Could I use your phone to call Mississippi? I'd like to say I'll pay you back, but I can't even make no promise like that."

"Go right ahead, honey. You know a wise woman always has a stash for emergencies."

"Oh, thank you, Miss Nelda, thank you." I walked over to her nightstand and looked at the cream-colored telephone. Then I looked at Candi, who had moved closer to Miss Nelda and started up a conversation. I looked at her, and she looked up at me and smiled.

"Fear blew away out there on that road, remember? You're innocent."

I flashed back to our time on the road. Fear wiped away. I could still hear the wind. I nodded, then with sweaty hands, I picked up the phone and dialed the number Mama gave me when she left the house.

Seven times the phone rang, with my heart beating faster and faster. Finally, someone picked up.

"Hello." It was an older, more mature Francine.

I took a deep breath. "Francine?"

"Mom?"

Warm, salty tears rolled across my lips. I couldn't even talk, let alone catch my breath.

"Mommy, is that you?"

CHAPTER 24

Gracey
December 1987

THE TRAIN RIDE WAS LONG but not so bad. It was probably the worst for Joanna, 'cause she had to keep getting up to pee and, as the doctor said, "circulate her blood." But she seemed to handle it, she didn't complain once . . . Okay, not that much. She made Francine keep saltines in her pocket just in case she had the urge to vomit. She was pretty done with that phase but didn't trust it to be over.

Honestly, though, it wasn't until our feet hit that red dirt road and we saw Grandma standing there in her pink duster with her hand on her hip looking like Mr. Roper's wife in *Three's Company*, it wasn't till then that we accepted the fact that we had gone from the mountain top to the valley low.

Grandma hadn't been happy to see us neither. Either she had her lip turned up because she smelled something foul, or she thought we looked really jacked up.

I was the first to walk through the press of people and hug her. "What's the matter, Grandma, you smell something? Are we musty?" I smelled my underarm.

"No," she said, looking us up and down.

I was right—we looked jacked up.

"I just can't get over how poorly y'all look. Like you ain't eaten in days."

"Good to see you too, Grandma," Francine and Joanna mumbled as they went to hug her next with quick pats on the back.

"Girl, look at you. You sure you got a baby in there?" Grandma frowned at Joanna. "And look how much that hair has grown, and your skin is smooth as ever. Bet you wish you kept them knees closed, though. Long hair won't take care of a baby, that's for sure."

Joanna's initial half smile drifted away with a small groan as she picked up her backpack. Francine clicked her heels three times and whispered, "There's no place like home."

A woman in a pretty pink suit sashayed by with a smile. Francine looked hopeful, like the woman might turn out to be the good witch, Glinda. But nothing happened.

"Well, come on, let's get a taxi home." Grandma picked up Joanna's bag.

"I'm sorry, Grandma, could you just give us a minute?" I put my finger up and instantly thought of Miss Nelda. In a quick flash, I wondered how she was, but she'd tell me to watch after my own, and that focused me back on my original thought. I called my sisters over into a huddle. Grandma dropped the bag and her hand went back on her hip as she tilted her head to the side.

"Listen," I said. "I don't know what life is going to be like when we step into this woman's house, but I do know that every time we've prayed, God has helped us out. So let's just do it one more time."

We held hands in a circle and bowed our heads. By this time, we couldn't care less who was watching. We didn't know any of these people, and not a one of them would ever be there for us like Jesus had been since our parents left.

Joanna started. "God, we're doing what the state says we have to do, and we don't like it. We pray that as we go to live with Grandma that you would protect our hearts from getting hurt and protect our lives from being another generation of a hot mess. Help us, Lord, to hold it together. And when it feels like we can't take any more, please shazam us with your peace. In Jesus's name. Amen."

My turn. "Dear Lord," I prayed, "I don't know if it's possible to make a mean woman like our grandma nice, but we pray, Lord, that you would please help her to love us in a nice way. Help her to see some good in us, and maybe our time together won't be so bad. Amen."

And then Francine went. "God, don't let me go off on that wench. And if I try to hit her, let your angels hold my fist back. If I go to cuss her, Lord, tie my tongue up 'cause I know you don't like it when we act ugly. And if I go to kiss her cheek like I did when I was young and naïve, please don't let her punch me in the stomach. Amen."

"Let's say that Scripture Mom taught us long time ago," Joanna said. "Psalm 23."

"I don't remember it," I said.

"Just say what you remember, then."

I closed my eyes and said, "Um . . . the Lord is my Shepherd, we're not supposed to want anything."

"Something, something, I will fear no evil," Francine said.

Joanna finished. "Surely goodness and mercy got our backs."

Now we were ready to go to Grandma's. Funny thing, as we walked toward her—it almost looked like she had a smile on her face.

I I I

The first thing Grandma made us do when we walked through the door was wash our hands so we could cook. Never mind showing us our rooms or letting us unpack. She could have let us use the bathroom to freshen up or something or maybe rest a little. But no. "Straight to the kitchen," she said.

There was a white door with six small windowpanes separating the dining room from the kitchen. We opened that door, and the warm smell of apple pie kissed our noses.

"Now," Grandma said, "I made the dessert, y'all gonna make the dinner."

She went to the refrigerator and pulled out a thawed chicken, some carrots, onions, broccoli, and cheese. Then she reached under the cabinet and pulled out some potatoes. After all that, she reached up into the cupboards and pulled out all kinds of spices—garlic powder, seasoning salt, pepper, paprika, and on and on.

We rolled up our sleeves, and she walked us through the whole process as we huddled around her. She treated that chicken like a happy baby, rubbing a spice all over its skin. Then she passed the chicken to us and gave us each a spice. Seemed to me like this was going to be one salty chicken, but maybe I was wrong. After that, she made me and Francine cut fresh broccoli and boil it. Then she had me boil the potatoes so we could mash them later. And she put Joanna to work, making macaroni and cheese.

Two and a half hours later, we sat down to a big feast that we had made ourselves.

Grandma patted our backs as she sat down and said grace. "Thanks. Amen."

We couldn't move quick enough to get all that food onto our plates. We were so hungry, we had seconds and thirds, and after Joanna sat back and waited for a while, she had a fourth plate. We hardly had room left for pie, but we managed.

Grandma didn't talk much. She just looked at us mostly and asked a few questions like, "You like them potatoes? You know if you bake 'em and put some cheese on them, they real good too. We'll try that one day." Or, "That chicken was easy to make. Tomorrow we'll try roast beef, and the next day we'll have some fried pork chops."

We just mumbled things like *yes'm* and *uh-huh*, because we couldn't see why she was being so nice to us. And we didn't want to mess up; being nice to someone who was usually mean could be like falling into a pit of snakes.

Anyway, after we ate, she made us clean up. We saw the dishwasher and went crazy just stuffing everything in.

But then Grandma said, "I don't know what y'all are doing over there—you still got to rinse them dishes with your hands before you put them in the machine. You know you can't trust no machine to clean your dishes properly. End up with dried food sticking to the plate."

"Oh brother," Francine said.

"What'd you say to me, li'l miss?" Grandma said, her frown etched in her forehead.

"Nothing."

"Nothing what?"

"Nothing, ma'am."

See, I knew her niceness wasn't anything to count on. After everything was all spick-and-span, she took us upstairs to our rooms. Joanna had her own, with a baby crib inside and a pastel knitted blanket hanging over the side. I know Joanna wanted to cry, but instead she walked over to the crib and traced the railings with her fingers—down to the mattress where the baby would lay.

"I got it with the money they gave me," Grandma said. "I figure babies don't deserve to suffer for the mistakes we make."

Joanna lowered her head. "Thank you, Grandma." We put her luggage near the window and let her tend to the wound Grandma had tossed her.

"Mm-hmm. Come on, girls, let me show you where you're sleeping."

Grandma walked slower than what I remembered. She seemed to have pain in her leg, and her ankles were really puffy; they looked like biscuits baked over the lining of her shoes.

She stopped in front of the biggest room we'd ever seen meant for us. Single beds on either side with a nightstand between the wall and the bed with a little lace lamp on the top. We each had our own dresser drawers, white with gold frosted swirls around the golden handles. I elbowed Francine, and she elbowed me back.

"I expect y'all to keep this room clean, you hear? All the time."

Then Grandma walked to the middle of the hallway and said, "Now, y'all listen to my rules. Every night you go to bed at nine o'clock, no fussin', no talking back. And you wash your own clothes. I'm too old to be takin' care of children again. I will teach you how to cook for two weeks, and then y'all will do all the cooking for a while.

"You can't talk all night on my phone. Somebody call you, you got twenty minutes and then it's time to hang up. And don't even think about bringing no boys up in here. You might as well just wait to leave and go to college, 'cause I ain't havin' no part of it. And I know in Chicago y'all took showers like they was going out of style, but in this house, you take a bath three times a week and wash up the rest of the days. Oh, and ain't nobody allowed to set foot in my room for any reason whatsoever."

And on and on she went with her rules. I almost fell asleep looking straight at her. Still, I figured if we just used good old common sense, we should be safe from Grandma's fury.

So that was how we spent the first few days at Grandma's, learning how to cook and trying to live by all her commandments. You could say we were surviving, but it was hard. We were so used to doing what we wanted, when we wanted—we did a lot of lip biting to keep our mouths shut. Frankie hated not being able to watch *Late Night with David Letterman*. When we went to bed, with the exception of Jo-anna, we weren't sleepy; we stayed up and read whatever books or magazines we could get our hands on.

Life in Mississippi was deafeningly quiet. All you ever heard was the birds, leaves rustling, and cars driving by. But with all of us in the house, I was beginning to feel the layers of love surround me like they did during our *Cosby Show* era in Chicago.

Grandma's house was the smallest in the neighborhood, but it was brand-new, like somebody made it just for her. The stairs were short, the hallway had rails for holding on, and all the lights were clap on, clap off. Even the shower in her room had a big special chair inside it so she could sit and bathe herself. The second day we were there, me and Francine turned her bedroom upside down when Grandma left, just trying to figure out what made her tick, like who she really was deep down. We didn't find anything, though, just some old black-and-white photographs in a shoebox under her bed. The people looked unhappy. There was one with Grandma not smiling, standing over three children, a girl and two boys. The girl that looked like Mom had a half smile at least. The boys looked like they hated life. We wondered if we had uncles. We put the photos back in the box and covered our tracks out the room. What was the point of taking pictures if you weren't even going to smile?

Only took us four days to agree that we didn't like Mississippi.

Everyone talked real slow with a country drawl like the characters on *The Beverly Hillbillies*. The men walked in fancy boots with heels and big old cowboy hats on their oily heads. And the women wore anything that fit on their body. They didn't care about fashion for nothin'. Where were the multicolor slick jumpsuits, the bandannas, the tight miniskirts with oversized shirts? Even the kids dressed strange, in faded T-shirts and holey jeans.

All the cars were about ten years old—Chevys, Mustangs, Impalas—and five-and-dimes were everywhere packed out. I'd never seen a store where you could get anything you wanted for a dollar. And the grocery store was a trip. Piggly Wiggly, they called it—sold things like neck bones and pig feet, chitlins, and Neapolitan coconut candy, black walnut ice cream, and spicy pork skins that people ate like potato chips. Joanna took to the pork skins like chocolate chip cookies, hooked at first bite. The coolest thing to me about Mississippi was the Coca-Cola machine that sold the cola in these cute little antique glass bottles. At least the old state had some class.

Just when we'd stopped thinking about Mom and given up hope that she'd ever come back, especially since she didn't know we left Chicago, the phone rang.

❙ ❙ ❙

December 1987

Mom called just before the new year. We hadn't been there a full week when I heard Francine say the word *mommy* into the phone. I liked to fainted. I mean out of the blue, she just called. What was up with that? What'd she want? She was too late. We were already gone.

I couldn't say whether I was straight up jealous or mad or what, but I snatched that phone out of Francine's hand and slammed it down on the receiver. And when Mom called back, I picked it up and slammed it down again.

"What'd you do that for?" Francine yelled. "Are you crazy?"

"No. We don't need her. She's been gone all this time, let her stay gone. She don't care about us."

"Yes, she does, 'cause why else would she call!" Francine went off on me. I could see her debating whether or not to get violent.

"Frankie, I swear, if you throw a punch, I will pour cold water on your face while you're 'sleep every morning for the next seven days."

Joanna stepped between us. "Stop it, you two. It's just a phone call, and you're fightin' like cats and dogs."

"It's her fault," Francine yelled. "All this time we've been waitin' for Mom to call, and when she does, she hangs up the phone on her!" She came charging at me and I jumped back.

Joanna pushed Francine back so hard she fell on the beige carpet that ran throughout the house. "Mom called?"

"Duh," Francine said. "That's what I'm trying to tell you."

"And you hung up on her?" Joanna spun on me. "Why?" She was serious.

"She been gone all this time, and now she wants to call and see how we're doing? We don't need her—we already proved that. We made it just fine without her. If she tries to come back into our lives now, she might mess everything up. Besides, what if she didn't even want to talk to us? What if she just wanted Grandma?"

"She sounded like she wanted to talk to me," Francine whined.

"What'd she say?" I needed to know.

"The second I answered the phone, she knew who I was. She said, 'Francine?' And I said, 'Mom,' and all I could hear on the phone was her breathin' and snifflin' like she was cryin'."

"Maybe she did want to talk to us," Joanna said.

"So what if she did? She don't deserve to talk to us. Look at us, we're in Sweet Tea, Mississippi, living in a country house with a thousand trinkets and a grandma who hates us."

"Oh, come on. It's obvious Grandma doesn't hate us," Joanna said.

"Whatever."

Joanna perched on the corner of the couch and placed a pillow over her belly. "What's going on, Gracey? I thought you were the one expectin' Mom to walk through the door any minute. You had more faith than all of us."

"Yeah, and look what happened! We were pushed out of our home and our city, and she never showed up to rescue us. That's like havin' faith for nothin'. You believe, believe, believe, and nothing happens. I threw my hope out the window the minute they put us on that bus. Bump her! She never loved us. She already showed us that once. She's a bad girl. First time, shame on her; second time, shame on us."

Francine and Joanna laughed at my calling Mom a bad girl, but I didn't care. I didn't want to explain myself. I meant what I said.

"Besides," I said, "why ain't she called us back yet?"

"'Cause you scared her off, you idiot. She probably thinks we hate her now." Francine popped a hip.

"Well." I folded my arms and rolled my neck.

"Oh, come on, Gracey. You don't hate her. You never know what she's been going through," Joanna coaxed.

"There's nothing she can say to me to justify what she did. Nothing."

"I don't think it's any of y'all's business why she did what she did, as long as she comes back." Grandma stood in the doorway. "Now, let me tell you something. I forgot to tell you another rule—silly me, I thought this was common sense: there'll be no hanging up on anybody as long as you're in this house. I believe in respect—hello and goodbye, good morning, and good night. These words don't belong to you to share or not when you got an attitude. Ain't no fightin' neither. Y'all wanna tear each other's hair out like a bunch of idiots, take yo' behinds out to the ranch down the way and roll with the farm animals.

"You're right that your mama had some things she needed to deal with, that much I know. But it's grown folks' business, and when she ready to tell you, she will. And if she ain't never ready, well . . ." Grandma took a deep breath. "Then God have mercy on her."

After that, there wasn't nothing to say. Grandma told us to get ready for bed because in a few days she was going to take us to our new school and she wanted us to be rested. As if that was something to look forward to.

I wondered what kind of kids lived in Mississippi. I heard someone on TV say people are the same wherever you go, but I couldn't really see the truth in that.

Francine refused to talk to me all night. I kept saying sorry, but she ignored me, so I turned over. The void in the room was so loud, I pulled comfort from my childhood and sang the itsy bitsy spider song to myself until I began to drift.

That presence of peace filled the room. I could see Francine moving her arm to wipe her face, and I turned over, grabbed the dolly on the bed, and hugged it close to my chest. "Out came the sun and dried up all the rain—"

"Shut up," Francine said.

And then her sweet voice joined mine as we finished the song. "And the itsy bitsy spider went up the spout again."

CHAPTER 25

Charlotte
January 1988

THE SUN WAS SITTING HIGH hours later, and I was still in shock. "I can't believe they really hung up on me."

I kept looking at the phone like it bit me. We were in Miss Nelda's house trying to get our bearings since nothing worked in my house. We had stayed the night since it wasn't really safe to be out and about after dark on New Year's Eve.

"Maybe they didn't know it was you," Candi said.

"They knew. I have to go there, is all . . . I have to see them."

"How you gonna get there?" Candi asked. "I wish I could drive you, but I need to get back home and tie up a few loose ends. I have work, and my sister needs me. So much has been about you lately; I've ignored my own reality too long."

"I understand, Candi. I'm not asking you to drive me. I'm thankful for all you've done. And you're right, I have taken up too much of your time."

Candi rolled her eyes and smiled as she looked away. In that one moment, I knew she'd always be my sister.

"How much it cost to get there by bus?" Miss Nelda's tired voice yelled out.

"At least fifty dollars." The words near gutted me. "But don't you worry, I don't want your money. The phone call was all I needed."

I did not want God getting on me about taking advantage of an old woman, no matter how close.

"Oh, don't worry 'bout it, chile," Miss Nelda said. "Go pull that bottom drawer all the way out there."

I pulled the drawer out and found a white envelope sitting in the base.

"How much money's in there, dear?"

I counted it. "Ten dollars."

"Hmmph. Go over to the mattress there and look in the lining by the handle."

I went to the mattress, pulled up the sheet, and looked. "There's nothing there."

"Nothing there? Darn that cleaning girl, always stealing from me!" She thought some more as Candi and I watched, then she snapped her fingers. "Go look under the rug in the hallway."

I went to the hallway and bent down to look under the runner on the wooden floor. There was a small brown envelope with one five-dollar bill inside.

"Found it," I said, coming back into the room.

"I knew she was a shoddy cleaner. Never vacuums under the rug." She clapped her hands. "All right now, how much we got, fifteen?"

"Yes, ma'am."

"Go into the kitchen and look under the sink under the contact paper where the bleach is."

"Oh, let me go," Candi said, like a little kid. When she found it, she came back with the money in her hands.

Miss Nelda took the money from Candi's hand and counted it, another thirty-five dollars. "Was that bottle of bleach full or empty, girl?"

"Oh, it was nearly full. And your kitchen could use some bleach too," Candi bravely answered.

"I ordered that stuff over six months ago. I was wondering why she hadn't asked me to order some more."

Miss Nelda turned to me and asked if that would be enough, and I told her yes. And then Candi told her she would take me to the bus station and come back and clean her home from top to bottom, no charge. Miss Nelda was so delighted she clapped her hands together and lifted her feet from the wheelchair stand.

"Oh, that would be wonderful! Look at God!"

We smiled at her glee but then a look of concern crossed her face.

"Before you go, Charlotte—" Her finger pointed with a tremor.

"Yes, ma'am?" I was hoping it wasn't no bad news.

"You may want to go see Mabel. You know, the lady who lives down the street? She was Gracey's teacher this year, before they left."

"Okay, but why would I go see her?" I supposed it wouldn't hurt to see how she did in school. But why not Francine's and Joanna's teachers too?

"Well, Mabel . . ." Miss Nelda paused like she was trying to get words right before she let them out. "She was a big help in taking care of the girls. You should stop by and say thank you, no matter."

"No matter what?" I asked. She seemed disturbed. Her head lowered, and then she stiffened up as if mustering courage.

"I'm just saying, she was good to your girls."

❙ ❙ ❙

For some reason, I didn't want to go see Mabel in the evening on the first day of the year—I never had liked how she looked at Moses, and she was the last person I wanted to know my business—but I knew it was the right thing to do. Woman to woman, I was wrong for leaving, and I had to face that. Her porch light was on so I assumed she hadn't gone to bed yet. The scent of vanilla and coffee beans rested peacefully between the screen and the wooden door.

"Charlotte, oh my goodness," she said as she opened the door. "How you doin', and what brings you here so late?" She looked beautiful, healthy, and clear. Her hair was thicker than I remembered, and she had put on some weight, at least ten pounds. I could see it in the thick of her arms and the width of her waist. And her face was more rounded, so her cheekbones were lost in translation. Thank goodness, she was human after all.

"I was just at Miss Nelda's, you know . . . trying to track down my girls and, um . . . well, she said you did a lot to watch over them."

"Oh." A blush crept up her neck. "I didn't really do that much. Close to nothing, really."

"Well, whatever you did," I said, obliging her, "a little or a lot, I just wanted to say thank you."

"You're welcome, Charlotte," she said, sounding a little confused. "It was a real pleasure for me. Your girls are"—Mabel gave a blown-away look—"amazing."

"Yes, I know." I wanted to slap her and hug her at the same time but decided to be quiet. I wanted her to invite me in and tell me all about the girls and what they went through. I wanted to know every detail of every day. I wanted to get back the time that was now settled in her bosom. "Well, I better get going," I said.

"You take care, Charlotte." Mabel raised a hand while using the other to secure the tie on her housecoat. "Thanks for stopping by."

I had turned to go when Mabel cleared her throat. "Charlotte, hang on. Wait just a minute, please." She disappeared from the doorway. When she came back, she was holding a journal, and she placed it in my hand. "I had Gracey in my class this year. She's such a thoughtful and gifted writer. I hope it gives you greater understanding of their journey since you, um, you know. Left."

I stared at the journal with Gracey's name written across the bottom in cursive letters. I couldn't believe she gave it to me.

"Thank you, Mabel," I said softly. I felt like a deer in front of a lioness. "That's very kind of you."

"It was a real pleasure, and the least I could do."

Again I turned to walk away and Mabel called.

"Yes, Mabel."

"Give your girls a tight squeeze from me when you see them."

I smiled back, thinking, *I'll probably never do that.* "Sure will."

CHAPTER 26

Charlotte
January 1988

NINE HOURS LATER, I WAS on a coach to Mississippi, trying to get some sleep. I didn't talk to anyone the whole time, just prayed and slept, prayed and slept. I figured the sooner I went to sleep, the sooner I'd wake up and we'd be almost there.

I tried really hard not to listen to other people's conversations. The man at the magazine stand gave me a free copy of *Essence*, so I did my best to keep my nose in the articles. But there was a couple in front of me talking too loud for me to focus. He kept telling her they could work it out, get a counselor, and she kept saying that it was no use because she didn't love him anymore.

"I don't care what the new counselor says, I'm still leaving you."

"But what if he says something to make you fall in love again?"

"He won't, Peter. I'm done."

The man, Peter, broke down. I could see his back heaving between the seats while his wife put her hand on top of his.

Poor guy, I thought. He needed to know there was somebody out there better for him. Somebody who would cherish waking up next to him every day for the rest of his life. I watched with my spirit frozen in my body, hoping the awkward moment would soon pass.

I was embarrassed for both of them. And hearing a man cry unsettled me. The world would tell you that men were the pillars that held everything up. And we grew up believin' it to be true. But when them muscle-bound arms crumbled under the pressure, then we'd realize they were the same as us, human. And we needed to work together.

Moses always took care of everything. I always knew the bills would be paid and food would be on the table. But I also knew when he was hurtin' or bothered. If everything was okay, he ate with a knife and fork, patient enough to put the knife down and switch the fork into the other hand. But if something was really bothering him, he'd cut the steak with the side of his fork and stuff it into his mouth. Or he might rest his two fingers on his temple while he was watching TV. That meant he wasn't really watching. He was thinking.

I remembered a time he was really bothered. He didn't even touch his knife, and he stayed in front of the TV for hours on end. For months, he was real quiet and only smiled when the kids were around. He was sweet and respectful and all, but I could tell he was a million miles away, fighting a battle on the other side of his world. I tried talking to him and massaging his back, but he would just kiss me on the hand and say, "I'm all right, sugar. Don't worry."

Then one day he was back, like nothing happened. He talked and laughed, telling jokes and pranking the kids, like putting a whoopie cushion in Francine's chair before she sat down. That was all there was to it. I went to him and gave him a big old hug, and he stopped and hugged me so tight I could have just put myself inside of him, right there.

"I love you," he'd whispered into my ear.

I had had a real man. What I wouldn't do to go back to restitch my path.

That night on the bus was easy. I didn't have to worry about getting gas or keeping the bus driver awake or being too cold or too hot. I waited until everyone had gone to sleep to read Gracey's journal, each page filled with erasable ink, front to back. Her soul was like a Monet painting, every stroke a shade of pastel adding to the big picture.

That day I left, I never could have fathomed that they would suffer so much in my absence. I left them in that house alone, when I couldn't even take it myself. How did I expect them to manage? I shoulda trusted that peace I felt that told me everything would be okay if I stayed. If only I understood then what I was beginning to understand now—it was never God's intent to punish me, and I didn't need to punish myself while waiting for what I thought was an impending judgment. Nobody ever told me how freedom felt. I still didn't know, but I was thinking maybe it was that thing I was always afraid to embrace.

It wasn't till the sun started coming up that I could feel the butterflies building in my stomach. Was like they all just gathered in a knot and wouldn't let me move. I made my way to the toilet just in time to vomit. Then I leaned over the sink and examined my face in the mirror. I thought I'd aged a bit around the eyes, and gray hair was inching its way into my edges. But other than that, I looked the same. To think I used to pray that I'd age gracefully. I rinsed my mouth, washed my face, and took my hair down. Maybe God thinks I'm beautiful. Pulling out my brush, I started taking the tangles out my hair. I put some lip balm on and puckered my lips. Turning to my side, I could definitely tell I had lost weight. My clothes hung slightly at the shoulders. So what . . . as long as I could see my girls.

When the bus stopped, it let out a big sigh. It was my station to get off. Before I left my seat, I made the sign of the cross over my chest and forehead again. I wasn't Catholic, but it seemed like the right thing to do. Maybe God would come and sit in the center of his cross.

Warm air consumed me as I eased off the bus. I'd forgotten how warm Mississippi winters could be, one step shy of spring, all the time. Seeing the Mississippi dirt made me feel welcome for some reason, like the bronze and orange in the streets were my saving-grace colors, my colors of peace. It smelled the same as I remembered too, like wet clay and old wood. I couldn't imagine what Mama's new house would look like. Our last place with the farm was a slanted frame house that seemed to tilt more and more each year.

I hailed a taxi, planning to pay for it with the little money Candi slipped me from her bosom. Driving to Mama's new house filled me with a hope I had a hard time trusting, but it was there, nonetheless.

The house was brick. Back in the day, only rich folk had brick houses, and anyone that had made it that far up the ladder had become uppity, putting other folks down for not having what they had.

I hoped Mama hadn't gotten worse. I hoped she got enough sense to be kind to her granddaughters and give them the love they deserved. I didn't want to walk into the house and see the kids full of anger and rage 'cause they ended up with the last person in the world they would ever want to stay with.

Oh, Lord, they hate me, they hate me. What must my little Francine be feeling? What if she's put a big shield around her? What if Joanna's an atheist, and Gracey is depressed? *Oh, Lord Jesus, tell me, what have I done?*

Love was an art I didn't think I'd ever master. You know who found love easy? People who ain't never been hurt, never been scarred. They the ones got all the happiness and joy. But then that couldn't be true, 'cause Candi had a heart full of joy, and her life was a right mess. She'd love again, I was sure. But I didn't think I would. Shoot, I didn't think I could. But I was gonna give it a try.

I was doin' what folks said you should never do, puttin' all my eggs in one basket. Like I had a choice anyway. If this didn't work, then this whole journey'd been nothing but a joke. It'd mean God actually brought me this far just to watch me get my punishment. You reaped what you sowed, right? Had I ever sown anything good in my life, ever? Maybe for me love was meant to be like a kite that was always out of reach or a stupid little needle I could never thread no matter how much I crossed my eyes.

As close as I got to Mama's house, when the taxi pulled up I told him to keep going. "Take me to Greater Missionary AME church down the street there."

The doors to the church were wide open when the driver pulled up. Inside, the rounded oak pew tops parted for a center aisle that led to the pulpit. A single stained-glass window shined brightly behind the podium—Jesus walking toward his sheep with a rescued lamb resting on his shoulders. There was no one there but an old man, straightening out the hymnals in the back of the pews. He reminded me of that one so many years ago who was so closely removed from slavery. But upon second look, I knew he was different.

He stopped and looked up. "You lookin' for the pastor?"

"No," I said. "I just came to sit a spell, if that's okay."

"Sure, sure, don't mind me here." He hummed an old bluesy tune and stretched his back before sitting down a few pews in front of me.

I sat there for a while, and he didn't move the whole time. Quietly I walked up to where he was. His bony knees stuck out through his brown uniform. His short-sleeved shirt revealed slight muscles that bulged like little hills on a plain. And he was asleep, his heavy chest rising and falling in rhythm.

I pulled the broom from his grip and swept every nook and cranny of the sanctuary. Every time I gathered a pile of dust and dumped it into the garbage, I felt like another part of my heart was getting cleaned up. In the choir stand, I looked out over the church congregation. Suddenly I was a little girl again and laughter of decades gone circled my ears.

"Ain't gonna forget the past by reliving it all the time."

"Oh! You're awake," I said, startled.

"Yeah, what'd you think, I'd gone and died?"

"No sir, I just—"

"Listen here, young lady," he said. "I don't know what it is you're running from, but your best bet is to face it head-on."

"Oh no, I'm not afraid. I just—" My mouth shut automatically. I didn't have the words.

"Whatever it is, you gonna be all right." He said it with a firm voice. "Now bring me my doggone broom back."

Funny thing is, I knew that. I just needed to hear it one more time.

CHAPTER 27

Gracey
January 1988

AFTER WINTER BREAK, GRANDMA CAME in with her big voice, telling us to wake up and get washed for school. Didn't matter that we hadn't even been there two weeks and still nothing was familiar. Downstairs on the counter were three backpacks filled with pens and pencils, folders, and notebooks. She told us we'd get our books when we got to class. But that wasn't all. Grandma had made us scrambled eggs, grits, bacon, and toast. And Lord knows, it smelled good. This was our new home, and it felt so much better than the cold, empty house in Chicago.

"Good morning, Grandma," we all said in unison.

"Morning." She took off her apron. "This just for the first day now, don't y'all be thinking I'm gonna cook like this every day. And I made your lunches. Hope you like what's in there, 'cause if you don't, too bad. I ain't payin' for hot lunches, 'specially since I know what ingredients they use."

We sat down and started eating.

"I arranged for the big yellow bus to come pick us up and take us to the school."

The clanging of our forks across our plates stopped as we looked at each other. "What?"

"Y'all gonna be in the same school—it goes from kindergarten to the twelfth grade. Harriet Tubman Prep School. They prepare you for college and the real world out there."

"Um, Grandma," Francine said, "do you really have to come with us on the bus?"

"Yes, I need to make sure you get to the school, take you to the classes and all. What? You got a problem with it?"

Francine squirmed in her seat. "I just think we might get teased."

"Oh, girl, please. Teasing ain't nothing but some stupid words. If anybody ought to worry about getting teased, it's Ms. Lady over there walking in pregnant. But you know what, chile? Don't you worry a thing about that. Know why? 'Cause you won't be the only one. They have lots of pregnant girls in this school. They teach them home economics. They even have classes telling you how to take care of a newborn. Don't y'all worry about a thing; it'll be all right."

When we finished our food, Grandma went to the cabinet and pulled out some Flintstone vitamins. She told Joanna they were just as good for the baby as they were for us girls.

Not too long after that, the bus showed up and honked its horn. We gathered all our stuff and walked real slow while Grandma moved swiftly, swinging her cane along to help her balance better.

"Y'all come on now, you don't want Hank to leave us."

Who the heck was Hank? That was all we wanted to know.

The driver saw us coming and pulled the lever to open the door.

Grandma was the first to hike up the stairs. "Mornin', Hank, these're my grandchildren I been telling you about." She touched us as we passed by. "This Frankie, the baby girl."

Hank nodded hello and smiled, showing a missing bottom tooth. "They say she run real fast."

"Gone give them girls a run for their money at the school, huh?"

They both laughed.

I was next.

"This here is Gracey. Ain't she pretty—got that pretty smile and coarse hair. Them girls gone be jealous, ain't they?"

"She better be careful, Miss Iona, they likely to try and cut it off." They laughed a hearty laugh again, and then Hank stopped and stretched out his hand. "You must be Joanna."

"Yes, sir," Joanna said.

"Nice to meet ya. You gone have a right nice day today, you

hear?" He smiled sweetly. Like the way a grandad would act, if we had one.

"Yes, sir."

"She's the oldest. She the one, you know. 'Member I was telling you?"

"Yes, Iona, I remember. Now sit down so we can go."

Grandma sat up next to Hank and chatted while we sat near the back where there were two open seats, one for Joanna and one for me and Francine.

All the kids stared at us. Then this rusty kid with ringworm spots on his head turned around and said, "I can't believe you brought your granny to school with you."

"I can't believe you goin' to school with a nasty, crusty, checkered head." Francine sniffed at the boy. "Now turn around and mind your business before I smash your nose." She waited till he turned back around before leaning into me and whispering, "We got to start out hard so they know not to mess with us, and they spread the word quick around the schoolyard that we're tough."

Pretty soon all the kids on the bus were whispering and staring at us.

"Yo," said a coffee-skinned girl with Jheri curl juice staining the back of her collar and shirt. "Is it true y'all from the ghetto in Chicago?"

"No." I took this one. "We're from Chicago, but not the ghetto."

"What's it like up there?" Another kid from a few rows up said. "Y'all got the Serious Tower and all them tall buildings. I bet you it's cold up there, ain't it?" He had on a Run DMC T-shirt that said "Walk This Way."

"Yes," I said. "But it's the *Sears* Tower."

"Colder than here?" a girl from behind me yelled.

I yelled back. "Yes."

"And y'all got snow up there?" Another boy turned his body around and leaned into the aisle.

"Yeah. We got snow."

"Aw, man, that's so cool," Jheri Curl said. "I bet y'all be having snowball fights and makin' snowmen and all."

"Yeah, we used to do that. Not too much, though, 'cause the snow makes your hands cold, and then it melts through your clothes."

"Why don't y'all wear snowsuits, like what they got on TV?" Run DMC asked.

"You could do that if you're a baby," the girl behind me said.

The whole bus started cracking up, 'cause by now everyone was turned around listening to us field questions. I think I was the only one who saw this white girl get up and waddle down the aisle. She made her seat next to Joanna, and the two of them started talking.

"My name's Jean," the girl said.

"I'm Joanna."

Jean cleared her throat. "Your grandma told me in confidence. I won't tell nobody, promise. I'm six months, how 'bout you?"

"I don't know . . ." Joanna put up four fingers.

I didn't get to hear much more before some other kid started in on Francine.

"Hey, I heard your granny say you was fast." She looked long and lanky and had a fake ponytail clipped around her rubber band, her edges barely in check. "You ain't faster than me, that's for sure. I'm the fastest in the whole school. Won all the contests for two years now. Ran the fifty-yard dash in 6.9."

"Really? I ran it in 6.7, broke the record in my school." Francine blew on her nails and buffed them on her jacket.

"Why don't we have a race after school? I'll leave you standin' in the dust, take away all your braggin' rights."

Francine's eyes narrowed and her lips pursed, a lioness ready to pounce. "Let's do it. Oh, and don't forget a jacket."

"I won't need no jacket. It ain't cold," the girl said.

"Yeah, but my breeze may leave you chilly."

"Ooh," all the kids answered.

They gave Francine high fives as we walked off the bus to the school. She hadn't even stepped foot in the hallway and already she was the girl to know. And Joanna's friend, Jean, introduced her to three more girls who were pregnant, and they hung around each other all day.

That just left me walking up and down the hallway, alone as usual. At least with me and Joanna in the same school there was more to keep me entertained. The high school students weren't so far removed from us, maybe just more curvy and sassy, like they had more years of grown-up TV in their back pockets.

The surprise of the day, though, was walking into the lunchroom and finding Grandma behind the hot-lunch line with a hairnet and wearing a white cotton coat. She was laughing with the kids and dolin' out the grub with a big dipping spoon. They had chicken n' dumplings with corn bread today. Peach cobbler for dessert.

"Grandma, what are you doing here?" I asked in shock.

"I work here, chile. This how I make a livin'. Now go eat your lunch and get some meat on your bones. Don't be shy, these kids ain't gonna hurt you."

None of the cliques in the room seemed to fit me. I took a deep breath and just kind of stood next to Grandma, watching her talk to the kids. She called them *baby* and *honey bunch* and *sugar* and *darling*—all names we'd never ever heard. She asked some of the kids how their folks were doing and what their grandparents been up to. I couldn't believe the woman Grandma had turned into since she'd come back from Chicago.

I looked into my bag to see what was in there and found a turkey sandwich with lettuce and tomatoes, some pork skins, chocolate chip cookies, and an apple. I pulled out the apple and leaned against the wall.

Grandma stopped and looked at me. "Chile, don't stand up under me, get somewhere and sit down." She looked around the room at all the different tables and then pointed to one with a girl sitting by herself reading a book. "Go sit next to Printess over there. Lord knows she needs a friend."

I looked at Grandma, who raised her eyebrows.

"Go on, I said. Git!"

I pushed myself off the wall and plopped down in the seat opposite the girl.

"What's up?" I said.

"Hey," she said, never looking up.

"My name's Gracey. Mind if I sit here?"

She looked up. "Oh yeah. You're that new girl from Chicago."

"Yeah, me and my sisters started our first day today."

"My name's Printess."

"My grandma told me." I nodded in the direction of the food. "What're you reading?"

She closed the book and showed me the cover, a map of the world with a plane in the sky.

"A travel book?"

"Yeah." She got this dreamy look on her face. "I'm going to travel all over one day."

"Hmm." I wasn't really interested. I was still trying to understand *my* world. "Where'd you get your name from?" I asked.

"From my mama, of course."

I sucked my teeth. "Duh, I know that. I mean, what's it mean? Why are you named Printess?"

"My mama wanted to name me Princess, 'cause I was so beautiful, but she thought life might give me too hard a time, so she replaced the *c* with a *t*. I think she should have just went with her first thought, 'cause folks still call me Princess by accident, and sure enough, the world still gives me a hard time. So what's the point? I decided when I turn eighteen, I'm gonna change my name."

"To Princess?"

"No, Natalie. Don't you think I look like a Natalie?" She made a plain face.

"Uh . . . I guess?" I shook my head to get my thoughts straight.

The bell rang not too much later. I told Printess it was nice meeting her, and she invited me to come watch her in an audition for a play after school, *Little Shop of Horrors*. I started to say yes, but then remembered I had to watch Francine race that girl with the shiny fake ponytail. So she said she'd catch me later, and I thought, *Much later.*

The worst part of the day came after school, when all the kids lined up on the sidewalk to see Francine and Lorna-Anne race. That was the girl's name, Lorna-Anne. Francine showed up on time, right after school, but Lorna-Anne was about ten minutes late. And the day had done her no justice. Her hair looked whack. Her ponytail looked like it was just hanging on, and her short hair needed some gel to slick it back down.

She had some young groupie hold the flag, and she told Francine just how far they were supposed to go, stopping right at the end of the gate. Lorna-Anne walked around like she owned the school, with her nose in the air and flinging her ponytail over her shoulder every five minutes.

Stupid girl. My sister was going to smoke her. Frankie just started stretching while Lorna-Anne was going around making everyone chant her name. Then they lined up, toes at the starting point, arms at ninety-degree angles, one up, one down.

"On your marks, get set, *go!*" the little kid said and dropped the flag.

They were off. Lorna-Anne was kicking her butt and tightening her jaw. She was in the lead, until out of nowhere Francine ran up next to her, said something, and then smoked her to the finish line.

The kids went from chanting "Lorna-Anne, Lorna-Anne" to "Go, Frankie! Go Frankie! Yeahhh!" They all cheered when she won. Then they ran down the sidewalk and gathered around her like she was a champ. And yeah, in their eyes she was more of a Frankie than a Francine. For me and Joanna, it depended on the amount of attitude she dished out.

Lorna-Anne was furious. Her eyes got real red and she started huffing and puffing like she was hyping herself up to do something.

Then, like a bull, she charged after Francine. "I'll teach you to show me up. Chicago ain't got squat on us!"

"Oh, I'll show you what Chicago's got . . . South Side!"

Next thing you know, Francine was on top of Lorna-Anne and whalin' on her. Then the whole lot jumped in, and I jumped in to find my sister, and we had a massive fight.

Grandma and Hank showed up then, and Hank started pulling kids off each other. "Get up, I said. Get off her. Get off him. Go get your behinds on the bus. Bad enough I got to explain why y'all's late."

Grandma was leaning on her cane, trying to catch her breath. Joanna was standing far enough behind her to not get hurt.

"What y'all trying to do?" Grandma hollered. "You trying to get kicked out the school before you get your foot in good? I ain't going to waste my time trying to help you."

We shuffled on the bus with our heads down, and nobody said a word. We were all sore and beat up, with the exception of the pregnant girls. All of a sudden, they looked like angels. Grandma and Hank were extra special nice to them too, making sure they were all comfortable and whatnot. I looked at them and rolled my eyes.

Grandma made Francine and me write one hundred times on lined paper, "I will not cause a ruckus at school and embarrass my family." Our hands were cramping so bad afterward that Frankie said she was sure she had "arthur-itus or whatever old people call it." I just laughed at her.

CHAPTER 28

Charlotte
January 1988

I AIN'T GONNA LIE, IT took time to muster up the courage to face my family. My friend Sheila's childhood home was still standing and empty, so I found the spare key hidden on a hook under the bark of the ol' Hickory tree and settled for a day or two, long enough to si-phon the waters of my soul from my head to my heart where the river flowed free. Finally, I stood outside my mother's front door. Seemed like roots were coming out of my feet and burrowing into the cement beneath me. Lead laced my arm as I lifted it to ring the bell. Tilting my face to the air, I could feel the cool breeze of waiting, waiting for my change to come. I would never know what could be until I rang that bell. "Oh, Lord, help me, please," I whispered.

"I'm leaving now. Bye!" a little girl's voice hollered.

I watched as a memory replayed before me.

"You stay out of trouble at that picnic," Mama's voice warned. "I'll be watching out for you now! Don't think just 'cause I'm cookin' I can't see you."

"Yes, Mama," I whispered.

A little girl opened the door and ran out with leather strap sandals and a cross-your-back, below-the-knees forest green dress. But that was me. I looked on as my innocence walked out the door and ran through the fields.

"Girl, don't you leave this house without a jacket." Mama's voice wasn't in the memory, though. It was right there. "And you better be back in two and a half hours, hear? It don't take that long to run a few laps around a track!"

"All right, Grandma!" Francine flung open the door and ran right into me.

Her mouth dropped open as she stared at me. And then, as if someone had flashed a sign with my name in front of her, she screamed, "Mommy!"

She dropped her bags and wrapped her arms around my ribs. I bent over and cried into her neck. It felt so good to hug my little girl, like home on a warm day with the windows open.

"Frankie, why you screaming?" Mama peered her neck out the kitchen and stopped still when she saw me. She was still drying her hands on her apron when she picked up her cane and hobbled to the door.

I stood up and bowed my head. "It's good to see you, Mama."

She gave me a tight squeeze but didn't speak. Then Gracey and Joanna came down the stairs.

Joanna was first. She stood back a ways and held her belly like a young mother who covers to comfort herself, let alone the baby. *Oh.* I covered my chest and thought about what Gracey said in her journal. *My baby's really pregnant.*

"Come here," I said, tears running down my face. "Come here."

She came forward, and I hugged her, taking her face into my hands. "It's all right, you hear me?"

"You're not mad, Mom?" Beautiful Joanna looked up with such innocent eyes.

"No, darlin'. How could I?" I held her hand tight. "How could I be mad?"

And then I looked up and still standing by the stairs was my Gracey, just staring at me. Her hair was parted down the middle and French-braided in two. She had on her favorite pink color and some khakis with a drawstring bow at the bottom. I let go of Joanna and started to move toward her before I realized I hadn't even stepped beyond the entryway of my mother's house.

I looked at my mama. "May I come in?" I asked.

"'Course, child. Who you think you are, Audrey Hepburn, comin' up in here like some superstar? Get on in here and take a load off."

I rolled my eyes and put my mind back on Gracey. As I stepped in, the house groaned contentedly, like things were established . . . comfortable and set in their ways. But then as I took off my shoes and walked onto the cream shag carpet, the air parted around me, and a sweet inward melody filled my space. Something in me said, *It'll be okay.*

Gracey sat down on the stairs and slid up a step as I came closer. Why was she afraid of me? She felt her way up the stairs ever so slowly, and I stopped and looked back at Mama and the girls.

"What's happening?" I asked.

They all shrugged their shoulders as they waited to see what was to come next.

"Gracey, honey, honey. I'm so sorry for leaving, but if you give me a chance, I can make it better."

She didn't say anything.

I heard the same something in me say, *Just be still.*

"Gracey, Gracey, talk to me."

She stopped and looked into my eyes. "You cheated on Dad," she said softly.

No, I'm not ready to deal with this yet. I tried to keep a smile on my face, but I wasn't doing a good job. Sweat gathered in my hairline. "What'd you say, honey?"

"You cheated on Dad," she said, with a look of cradled fear. I knew that look well. It was that kind of fear that came with a shield that kept all the good things out and the bad things in.

"I heard you and Grandma when you were trying to stop her from leaving." Her eyes were wide but dry. "And my dad isn't even my dad. My dad is probably that Micah dude."

I turned to my mama. "You told her?"

"Nope. I didn't tell her anything," Mama said, leaning against the wall.

"Yes, you did. How could you? I was going to tell them, Mama. I was going to tell them everything. You're always trying to ruin my life."

"No, Charlotte, you did that all by yourself."

"No, I didn't. You *know* I said no. You *know* I'm not the person you been making me out to be. And if you don't know, I know enough for the both of us. I am not carrying the guilt of that man's action one second longer." I didn't want to have this conversation in front of the girls.

"Mom, is that true?" Joanna asked, taking a seat in the chair by the dragon tree.

Francine looked horrified.

I sighed. My heart was hurting.

"Yes," I said. "It's true. It's why I left . . . because I felt so awful. I couldn't take care of you girls and live a lie."

Gracey started sobbing and ran to the top of the stairs. "I hate you! You're such a liar! All these years, I thought I was one of the family. I was looking for parts of me that looked like Dad, and there was nothing, nothing at all."

"Yes, you were conceived that way, but I loved you from the moment I knew you were there. And Moses—your daddy—loved you so much. You might not see physical resemblance to him, but I see him every day in who you are, Gracey. You have his wide-open smile, his spirit, his ability to connect with the world around him. You took on so much of his joyful personality. You are Moses's daughter just as much as Joanna and Frankie.

"How you came to be wasn't anything I would have chosen, baby girl, but you know what, God meant for you to be here, and I'm so glad he chose me to be your mother because you and your sisters have always given me reason to keep trying at this thing called life no matter how many times I fail, because I want you all to grow up to be strong and wise and good people who know how to fight for love."

I started up the stairs toward her, but she turned and ran down the hallway. "Stay away from me," she wailed and slammed a door behind her.

I collapsed on the top step, unable to go any further, my breath struggling to regulate. She'd heard nothing I said about the rape, or if she did, it still wasn't a permissible defense. All she heard was who she wasn't.

Still, I understood. Micah just kept violating my mind and my soul the same way he did my body years earlier, even though now I was clear about what had happened. To Gracey, this was all new. I was okay whatever she dealt me. Her revelation of identity didn't take away from my own revelation of innocence. We, as mother and daughter, needed time to process and heal.

I bowed my head, and in the stillness I let things settle. I took deep breaths and made a two-second plea for wisdom.

Then I turned to that closed door, lifted my chin, and spoke loud enough for her to hear me clearly. "Listen, Gracey, I screwed up bigtime, okay? I had a problem so big that I tried to fix it the only way I knew how, and the more I tried, the more I messed up. It took God to set me right. And little by little, day by day, I'm untangling my life."

I moved closer to her door. "I'm sorry, baby. I made a lot of bad decisions, but I'm here now to be the mother you deserve. I didn't know how to love before or what to do. All I knew was that I was always sad and angry and ashamed. But I know how to move forward now. I'm just gonna trust my gut and love you whichever way it naturally bubbles up. I won't suppress anything anymore—not the hugs or the smiles or the compliments . . . I'll just love you. All of you. If I'd trusted myself from the beginning, I would have been a great mom. I knew exactly what to do. I was just scared that I didn't deserve you because you were so good and so perfect, and I felt so dirty inside.

"But I had it all wrong. I was clean. I *am* good enough to have you and care for you and love you. I know that, because God gave you to me, and God doesn't lie. People lie and push their fears on you, but God doesn't lie."

A sound behind me made me turn. At some point Mama, Francine, and Joanna had quietly made their way into the hallway. They felt like fire blankets around me, my comfort. Francine's hands were buried in her pockets. Her eyes were wide, and her lips trembled. Tears were streaming down Joanna's face. She wrapped her arms around herself and slid to the bottom of the wall. A sob broke through, and my mother knelt beside her. In that moment, I saw Joanna's pain, and that broke me. What had she gone through with this boy who didn't treat her right? What did he do to her precious heart?

I reached across the hall and grabbed her hand. Francine stepped closer, and I wrapped an arm around her legs. It took only a minute for her to drop to the floor next to me and lean against my chest. Looking at my oldest, holding my youngest, and talking through the door to Gracey, I said, "If you could just give me a chance to show you, I know we can get to better days. You see, I finally realized, I can't change how people see me or other folks who go through what I went through, but I can change the way I see myself, and I will not let it steal another sweet moment from my life. Your daddy, Moses, who was there for you from the second you were born, was right. We are beautiful women. All of us. We are worthy of love, and we all deserve to live a happy and full life."

In the quiet that followed, Mama cleared her throat and shifted her weight. She must have been uncomfortable sitting on the floor like that, but I was glad she was there. It meant a lot—maybe to both of us—for her to be present.

After a minute, she stirred again. "Charlotte," she said. "I think the girls might need a little time to let things soak in."

Francine mumbled, "Yeah," and Joanna nodded, her head still lowered.

It suddenly felt like we were actors, frozen at the end of a scene, waiting for our next cue, but there was no one there to lower the lights or change the props. *Oh, Lord, where do we go from here? What do I do?*

"Maybe I should stay somewhere else," I said finally. "Till everything's settled."

"You just said you would trust your gut. Stay," Mama whispered. She looked to the wall to support her as she stood up. I came to her side and let her lean on me.

But Gracey's voice came through the door, low and unyielding. "Things will never be settled, Mother. You cheated and lied and ran away."

"That's enough out of you, Gracey," Mama spouted off. "In my house, we respect our elders, so you better watch your mouth before I give it a good washin'—"

"It's okay, Mama. Stop," I interrupted.

But still, Gracey answered, "Yes, ma'am." Then she opened the door, looked at me cautiously, and stepped past. I touched her head and let her braid fall through my hand. She didn't pull away, but she didn't stop either.

Mama nodded briskly. "Charlotte, you ain't got to go nowhere but to the couch to put your bags down. You can sleep there." She looked at the girls. "Girls, I believe you have some dinner to make. Miss Frankie, you going to this track practice or not?"

"No, ma'am. I just can't today."

One by one, they dragged themselves into the kitchen and started clanking pans around. I could hear them talking softly, but Mama interrupted my listening.

She pulled me to the side and said, "What's the meaning of you showing up here without talking to me first? I could have prepared them."

"Prepared them for what, Mama? Let's face it, it's hard to tell whether you're for me or against me. I did call, but I couldn't get to you, and then I thought, you'd just mess up any chance I had of getting back into their lives."

"I'm for the girls."

I waited, but that was all she said.

"That's all you have to say to me—'I'm for the girls'?"

"And I didn't tell Gracey anything."

"Oh, please, Mama. How in the world did she know then?"

"She already told you, she heard us talking."

"Yeah, but that wasn't enough."

"I guess maybe it is when God gives you intuition."

I put my face in my hands and shook my head. "What am I going to do?"

"None of this would have happened if you'd just told the truth all them years ago."

"Yeah, but Mama, I didn't."

"Well, now you're paying for it," Mama said, looking everywhere but at me.

"I know that, Mama."

"I know you know. I just needed to say I told you so."

"You're impossible. You haven't changed a bit."

"Not for you, no."

I slapped my thighs. "Why not for me, Mama?"

"Because you've always been a selfish little thing who thought everything breathing was supposed to bow down to you. You didn't care about me or your brothers."

My mouth fell open, and I stood there in shock. Where was she getting this from?

"All you ever cared about was how *you* felt, what *you* wanted, and how you could *get* what you wanted. Didn't care who you hurt, you just went after it, including that boy, Micah." She waved her hand up in disgust.

"You want to do this right now?" It was too soon for me, but I jumped in anyway. "All right, let's go. I never saw myself as selfish, Mama. I was starving for love. Everybody had their own life, and I didn't fit in nowhere. You didn't hug me. You didn't kiss me. You never said 'good job' on nothin'. And I didn't have a daddy to say, 'You look good today, baby girl.' So yeah, maybe I was a little bit selfish. But it was for my survival.

"Back then I would have taken any kind of love I could get. It just so happened that I was in the desert of my life, and somebody offered me a glass of lemon juice with a little bit of sugar. I was so thirsty I drank it all down before I could taste the bitterness of it. And then you turned a moment of innocence into a town hangin'. I was sixteen, and you destroyed me. At church, in town, at school. You almost destroyed my relationship with God. You sure as heck messed it up, for a lotta years. And the rape—"

She flinched, but I kept going. "Yeah, let's call it what it was, Mama. He raped me, and you knew that's what happened. Yet you have never, *ever* acknowledged the fact that I said no. The fact that I didn't want to do what he did." I shook my head. "What 'happened' to me? *He* happened to me, and you've done nothing but blame me for his actions. How do you think that makes me feel?"

Mama stared at me. She opened her mouth, then closed it. She reached up to massage the nape of her neck with her right hand. She looked at me, and I saw a sudden softness in her that I'd never seen before. Then she closed her eyes and carefully maneuvered her body to drop into a chair.

"Yes, I saw what happened to you, Charlotte." Her voice was quiet, strained. "And I was scared and ashamed for both of us, not to mention angry as hell. When stuff like that happened back then, they blamed it on the woman. No matter what you said, the world would see it as your fault and slap the crazy label on you. So I was trying to protect you. Trying to say, don't even fix your mouth to complain; don't even let the thought form in your mind. Just keep going and act like it never happened because this world—they'll strip you of every ounce of dignity you got. And you need some modicum of self-respect to keep you here, keep you sane, keep you walking above the ground. But then Gracey came, and she was so gorgeous. None of this was her fault. I kept thinking, 'Why couldn't we just get things out in the open so this little girl could get the unconditional love she deserved?' And yet . . . I felt so bad for what I saw that day."

She continued to caress her collarbone. "I didn't want to have anything to do with such an awful thing. I tried so hard, your whole life, to make sure you stayed out of trouble. Yes, I got that man-child sent away, and it ended up reflectin' badly on you. I was powerless against his whole family, but at least he was gone. And then he was back, and he still got his grimy hands on you. Seemed there weren't nothing I could say or do to protect you."

She flopped her arms in defeat. "Next thing you know, I was blaming you for everything and . . . I'm sorry, Charlotte. For some reason that gave me enough peace to sleep at night. Oh, chile . . ." Tears rimmed her eyes, but not one dropped as she whispered, "I'm so sorry."

I sat still, unable to feel this . . . whatever it was. My soul was unable to comprehend it; numbness stood within me like a bodyguard. I thought the moment was over, but then her voice came again.

"What I finally came to understand—just in these last few months—is that silence has the power to poison every aspect of your life. And you should never have had to suffer so over this . . . this one horrible moment. Home was the one place you shoulda been able to call safe. That's what I wanted for you. And I failed."

The dam broke inside me. Tears poured from my eyes, from my heart, and I was the one trembling. My mother got up from her chair, walked to my side, and pulled me to her. Maybe for the first time, my arms went around her. And she let her tear-stained, doughy cheek rest on my forehead for as long as I needed it.

Finally, I took a deep breath and slowly let it go. "So what do we do now?"

"We take it one day at a time and try to heal layer by layer. We have years to go."

❙ ❙ ❙

Dinner was real quiet that night. Nobody hardly said anything. Every time I asked the girls a question, they gave *yes*, *no*, and *I don't know* answers. Mama tried to help by talking about some of the things they'd done at school that day—like how Francine, even though she'd missed practice, was the fastest runner in the school and how Gracey was thinking about going out for the drama club because her new friend, Printess, was in it, but she really wanted to take up debating because she kind of wanted to be a lawyer when she grew up.

But when I smiled and said, "Is that right?" they all just answered, "Yes" and kept eating.

Finally, Mama told them to go to bed. As soon as they left, I screeched my chair back, leaned forward, and put my forehead on the table.

"Be patient, Charlotte," Mama said. "What d'they say, Rome wasn't built in a day? Help me wash these dishes."

We cleaned up the kitchen, then I dragged myself to the couch. I felt sick to my stomach. I knew it was nerves, and I just needed to relax. Mama brought me a cup of chamomile tea after a while and told me to drink it.

"I can't believe she found out."

"You took too long."

"But I thought—"

"See that Bible?"

Of course I saw it. Mama'd had that big, white, leather-bound Bible on her coffee table as long as I could remember.

"That Bible says that whatever is done in the dark shall come to light. We should have known they would find out sooner or later."

"Oh, Mama, I know, I know. Never mind. I can't keep going over and over it again."

We were silent for a while. "How many months is Joanna?" I asked.

"She's about four months or so."

"Do you know the father?"

"No, the girls were on their own when it happened. Gracey said Joanna started skipping school and hanging out with some boy called Chill, and the next thing they knew, she was pregnant."

"Is he still around?"

"Nope. He dumped her soon as he found out. She was crushed. She couldn't understand what she did wrong."

"Oh, my poor sweetie."

I didn't want to discuss it with my mama, but my heart melted for Joanna. I knew at least some of what she must be feeling inside. A ball of love growing in a body of shame and fear. I got up to go say good night to the kids.

"Where you going?" Mama stiffened up and turned toward me.

"I'm going upstairs to say good night to my girls."

"Leave them be and let them rest. They've had enough for one night."

"What are you saying, Mama? Those are my girls up there. I carried them all for nine months. I may have been gone for a time, but I was there for most of their lives."

"Charlotte, you know that ain't true. You were in the same house, but you were never there. You lived in your sorrows."

"I'm going to say good night." But then I spun around to say one more thing. "No. You know what, Mama? Have you forgotten how mean and hateful you were with my girls? Spankin' them, pinchin' them, calling them everything but their names and cuttin' every happy moment. Have you forgotten?"

Not a muscle moved in Mama's face as she looked at me, but I could tell her mind was running a mile a minute. The silence grew thick. Then she rubbed her hand across her jaw and sighed.

"Go on, then," she finally said. I started up the stairs, and she cleared her throat. "Maybe you could talk to Joanna."

"About what?"

"There's something strange going on with her."

"Like what?"

"She never talks about the baby. I try talking to her, and she just gets this sad, faraway look and changes the subject to something else."

My mind went back to the tears she'd shed in the hallway. This boy had made her feel like a fool. But the baby wasn't the boy. The baby was a blessing.

Trudging to the top of the stairs and into the dark tunnel that held my girls, I was thankful for the light glowing from beneath their doors. Soft singing lifted from within me. *"There's not a friend like the lowly Jesus . . ."* I stood still with my back to the wall outside their rooms. Nothing was said, nothing was thought, but I knew my soul was praying. And in the depths of the darkness in that hallway, my heart was encouraged.

With strength, I knocked on the door and went in before the girls could answer. Francine was nearly asleep, but Gracey frowned at me, eyes wide open as if I were a betrayer. All I could do was return her accusations with love, 'cause that was all I had in me. One side of her mouth turned up, showing a disappointed dimple.

I sat on the edge of Francine's bed and rubbed the soft of her arms as she slipped into a deeper sleep. Restful breathing here, but sniffling from the bed across the way. So I turned my point of view and sat on Gracey's bed. My hand hovered over her back awhile before I put it down and began to rub. I spoke softly, my voice low as a whisper, quiet like real love.

"We taught Sunday school together when we was young . . ." And I told her the whole story—his name, where he was from, what kind of parents he had, what he looked like; I told it all. By the time I finished talking, Francine was sound asleep, tangled up in her covers, and Gracey lay on her back, still listening. I could tell she was beginning to understand; her eyes looked different, like wisdom had joined our conversation.

"I want to meet him," she said, sitting up in her bed.

"Oh, Lord, help me." I covered my mouth, not meaning to have said that out loud. "Well, um, you can't. I mean, I don't know where he is now."

"Come on, Mama, I'm sure you can find him. Didn't you say his father was a bishop?"

I kissed her forehead. "Let me think about it. We'll talk later."

I left the room. I'd planned to stop and take time with Joanna, but I was so tired, I had no energy left. I just went in and kissed her good night and then fell on the couch in deep sleep.

Me and the Lord, we'd start again in the morning.

CHAPTER 29

Gracey
January 1988

FEW YEARS BACK, I HEARD Grandma call me an "outside child" one day when she was on the phone with Miss Nelda, but I thought it meant I spent a lot of time on the playground. It never made any sense until lately. And then I thought, *Well, maybe . . . nah.* I always said *nah* 'cause I didn't think my mother would ever do anything like that. Turns out she didn't really, but she did go see him. I didn't understand why she went, but . . . on the real, if Bastian called, I might have gone to him too, maybe. Just to see what was up, you know.

After we talked, I could see myself forgiving her completely one day, like when I'm old and in my twenties. I'd be an auntie by then; I'd have to have it all together.

Anyway, I also found out from this lady I met in the Piggly Wiggly when we first arrived. I was buying my snack—Doritos, Coca-Cola, and a Twix—when the lady behind the counter asks me to go to the bakery section and get a pecan pie for the old lady in front of me. So I left my stuff there and went looking for the pie. I looked and looked for that thing, but I couldn't find it. I wasn't even sure of what it was supposed to look like. I went to the side counter and asked this lady with a hairnet who was frosting a cake if she'd seen the pecan pies.

"Wait a minute, baby, I'm just puttin' on the finishing touches to this birthday cake." When she finished, she wiped her hands on her apron and looked at me. "Lawd a'mighty, girl, you look just like somebody I had a crush on when I used to go to church. What was his name?"

"Moses Downing?" I asked, thinking I found a family friend.

"Moses, no! That's Charlotte's husband. You don't look nothing like him. No, you look the spitting image of a Micah somebody. Now, why can't I remember his name? You even have the dimple just like him. What's his name, girl? You know."

I cleared my throat. "My daddy's name is Moses Downing," I said with a serious look.

"No, you're kidding. Moses . . ." She hesitated and then crossed her arms under her armpits. "So that's your daddy, huh?"

"Yes."

She looked around the room, then started picking at the cake. "Well, that's nice, honey. How's Moses doing anyway?"

"He's dead. Where's the pecan pie?"

The cake lady pointed to the pie and didn't say nothin' else. But she had already said enough.

The last straw came that same day when I went to the record shop to see what kind of music they sold there, and the first thing I saw was two brothers wrestling behind the corner and one of them had the other one in a headlock, talking about "Who's your daddy now?" Those words felt like a dart targeted right at my heart. Then I remembered the Micah dude Grandma talked about when she was leaving. She seemed so angry about him. Maybe he was my dad. Maybe he's the reason I'd never felt quite settled.

I couldn't really say when I knew for sure. Maybe it was the dream, maybe it was Grandma. Maybe it was the lady in the bakery section or the boys in the record store. Could have been a bad piece of Bazooka gum. All I knew was that by the time I saw the look of guilt on Mom's face at Grandma's door, I knew the truth for sure. All of this mess had somethin' to do with me.

The morning after Mom showed up, I hid in the closet and called Bastian. I needed to touch normal life for a second. Just the ringing of the phone in his house made me feel better. I begged the Lord to let Bastian pick up instead of Rosa.

"Yo."

Thank God.

"Bastian, it's me, Gracey."

"Gracey! Looking great in 1988! What is up with you, girl!" he hollered.

I had forgotten that slogan that came out for the year. Everybody talking about how their dreams were gonna be the bomb diggity and actually come true. To me it hadn't been much more than a rhyme to match the year, like "come alive in '85"—so much for that.

I pulled the phone toward me and lowered my voice. "Everything is fine, I guess."

"Really . . . you sound kind of funny. Come on, tell your homey what's up."

"You won't believe this."

"Well, try me. Ain't that why you callin'?"

"All right, here goes. Joanna and Francine are my half sisters, and my dad is somebody I never met."

"What? You trippin'!"

"Nah, Bastian, it's for real."

"Dog, what you gonna do?"

"What can I do? I already told my mom I want to see my real dad, but I don't know what she's going to do about it."

"Man, Gracey, you should hire a detective or something."

"With what money?"

Bastian was silent for a second, then he said, "I know what you could do. Go to one of them libraries that shows you your family tree. Did you get his last name?"

"Yeah, my mom said it's Richards."

"All right. Go ask the librarian to tell you where they keep the archives and look him up. Have you called information yet?"

"I didn't even think of that."

"Don't worry; that's what you have me for."

"Right."

"But straight up, Gracey. That's messed up. But maybe it'll end up working out. You lost one dad, maybe now you'll get another one."

"I don't want him. Not with what he did to my mom. I just want to see what he looks like. After that, I'll probably just turn around and walk away."

"I can't stand my dad, either, not really. But if I'd never met him, I'd want to know a whole lot more than what he looked like."

"Yeah, maybe." I scratched my head and opened the door to get some more light into the stuffy closet. "I wish you were here, Bastian."

"Well, I'm not, but I'll give you a big old hug through the phone. Hold on." He started making all these grunting noises like he was trying to get his arms through the phone, and then he yelled, "You ready?"

I said yes, and he said, "From me to you, *ahhhh, ohhh, hmm, hubba hubba.*"

"Sebastian!" I yelled.

"Just joking, Gracey. Just jokes. Listen, you take care, and I'll be thinking of ya."

"Me too. Oh, Bastian . . ."

"Yeah?"

"Try to keep your juicy lips from leaking. I do plan to visit Chicago again someday."

"Cool, I can do that. Peace, baby!"

"Bye." I stayed on the phone until he hung up and sat in the room until the glow of the conversation left the closet.

Bastian always had a way of making things feel better. Last night I felt like crap. And Francine didn't help. She was just so happy to see our mom. She kept saying, "Can you believe she's here, Gracey?" And before I could say anything, she said, "I can't. I didn't think we'd ever see her again. And now here she is in the same house as us." Then she'd tell me to wait a minute, and she'd sneak out to the hallway and look at her and Grandma from the top of the stairs. She gave me a headache. Finally, I had to pull her in and make her go to bed.

"What were they talking about?" I asked.

"They're working on mother-daughter stuff."

"Waa, I didn't have love." I mimicked a whining voice. "Ugh. Why is that everybody's reason for messin' up?"

"Uh . . . maybe 'cause everybody needs love just like they need food and water and air to breathe."

"Fine time to be poetic." I smirked.

"Forget poetry, it's the truth. If you don't have food, you starve; don't got water, you dehydrate; don't have love, you shrivel up on the inside. You think she'll stay?"

"She better. If she doesn't, she can forget ever seeing me again, 'cause she'll really be invisible then, like I never saw her."

"You can't do that. I could never do that. Your heart would be crying." Francine looked confused.

"I could do it if I had to. Isn't that what Joanna's doing with the baby, actin' like it's not there?"

Frankie pulled the blankets up to her chin. "You've noticed that too? Except for her little belly bump when she wears a tight-fitting shirt around the house and a couple rubs every once in a while, you wouldn't know she was pregnant."

"Of course I noticed. Even the pregnant clique has noticed. They said while they're talking about baby clothes and what kind of diapers they're going to use, she's talking about what college she wants to go to."

Francine sat up and plunked the covers down, hitting the bed. "Please! There's no way she's getting into college with a baby. 'Specially since she skipped so much school this year. She better quit dreamin' and take care of that baby."

"Whatever. We'll see."

We heard a door close. "Hold on." Francine climbed out of her bed and snuck into the hallway again. Then she came back, quicker this time in her bare feet. "It was the bathroom."

"What are they talking about now?"

"They're talking about how Grandma used to treat us."

"Oh, she was cruel," I said, just in case Francine had forgotten.

"No doubt. I don't know what's gotten into her, but—"

"I know what's gotten into her. It's Hank, the bus driver. Men, they can make your world stop or go, I'm telling you. If we didn't have him, she'd be wick-ed."

"Hmm," Francine said. I could see her getting sleepy as she talked through her yawns and her eyes reddened. "Maybe. I'm never going to let some man decide whether I'm happy or sad. I don't care how much I love him."

"We'll see when you get older."

"*You'll* see. If a man makes me sad, I'll kick him out and get a dog."

CHAPTER 30

Gracey
January 1988

THE NEXT MORNING WAS JUST as awkward as ever. Mom was up doing the same thing she used to do, reading the paper and drinking coffee, 'cept she had the paper flat on the table. She used to keep it up like an executive so she didn't have to look at anybody. Maybe she *had* changed. Breakfast was already on the table, oatmeal and buttered toast, orange juice on the side.

Joanna was sitting at the table, scraping the bottom of her bowl with her spoon. Funny, I didn't hear her get up.

Me and Francine were running late, and we had only ten minutes before Grandma whisked us off to Hank's bus.

"We'll see you, Charlotte. You gonna be all right?"

"Yes, I'll be fine. You all go on."

We all kissed her goodbye, and Mom stood at the door as we left. She had this longing look like she wished she were Grandma coming with us. Honestly, my mother had never looked so vulnerable to me. I turned my head and switched to life at school.

Printess looked up from her book and waved me over as soon as she saw me.

"Over here, Gracey."

Oh, great. She saved a seat for me. I smiled. "Hey."

"Hey, how's it going?"

"Good. I was thinking about joining the debate club. It involves a lot of talking and arguing, and that's what I need to do right now."

"The debate club?" Her face scrunched up. "I never pegged you for the popular type or the sports type, so I thought you'd fit with me, the drama type. But now I see you for who you really are . . . the geek type. No wonder you haven't made any friends except for me."

"Whatever," I said and shrugged. "Where's the local library?"

"The library? What you need that for?"

"I kinda need to find some information. Just leave it at that."

"Okay, we can go after school."

I I I

At lunch, I stood on the edge of the line and talked to Grandma while she served the students. With Printess off practicing for her performance, I had no one to sit with and Grandma knew I wasn't leaving her side. She jumped into a serious conversation and told me that I should try forgiving my mom, 'cause bitterness will eat you up inside.

"Ask me how I know," she said.

"How do you know, Grandma?"

"'Cause I spent three-quarters of my life being mad at someone who couldn't care less if I was alive or not. They was just going about their business, happy as could be. I got mad at that, made me mad at the world. But I finally got the picture when I moved back here—you can't put your happiness in people, 'cause they'll never act the way you want them to all the time."

"You talking about the Grandpa I never met, your ex-husband, right? I saw him in a photo."

"How could you have seen him unless you were—"

"What's with all this deep stuff, Grandma? I just want to blend in until lunch is over."

"You talking back to me?"

"Is everything I say talking back? The second I express my opinion, I'm talking back. Don't I get a say about anything I'm feeling?"

"No. You don't get a voice until you're grown and paying bills." She went back to the subject. "All I'm saying is that God can help you forgive. It doesn't have to happen overnight, but sooner or later, you have to do it. Ya hear?"

"Yes." I walked away. The debate team was practicing soon.

"And stay out my room!" I heard over my shoulder.

I went and sat in the back of the auditorium so they couldn't see me. The topic was vouchers versus public schools.

First came the introduction of the vouchers-for-private-school team. A really skinny girl with long, neatly lined cornrows got up and walked to the podium.

"We are going to explain the importance of vouchers and why we believe every child has the right to quality education. In our argument, you will hear statistics about retention rates of public schools and the numerous advantages to private education."

Then a member of the opposing team got up. He was without a doubt the finest boy in the school—tall, light-skinned, with a high-top fade and green eyes. The girls thought he was the next best thing to Al B. Sure!, and the boys thought he was possessed because to them, green eyes and brown skin didn't go together.

"Look at him, man. If he starts growling, I'm outta here."

Then another boy would pass by and make the sign of the cross with his index fingers.

They were so silly. He seemed like a nice dude, he just didn't have any friends. The only ugly thing about him was his voice; it was high and crackly. I touched my ear when he first started speaking. Okay, and maybe his braces; those weren't always so nice to look at either.

"We are the opponents, arguing for public schools," the boy began. "We believe public schools are imperative for quality education for all. In our argument, we will give statistics about the advantages of public education and the importance of diversity. We'll also point out the ways in which we can cultivate better education for our students when we work together."

After he sat down, the games began. Each person had two minutes to make their points, and then came the defense. I really came in just to watch, but I ended up feeling all twisted inside when I heard the arguments. I made comments out loud like a heckler at a comedy show. When the coach stopped the practice to let me say my piece, he was surprised by my response.

"If you allow vouchers in your part of town," I said, "how will the public schools improve? Busing the smart kids to the other side of the city will only cause the public schools to suffer."

Fine Boy just looked at me, stunned, and the kids started clapping.

The teacher, Mr. Bingham, yelled from the stage, "Hey! You're pretty good, kid. You want to join the team? I mean, you, like everybody else, got a lot to learn about life, might as well start here."

"Well, yeah. That'd be cool."

"We practice every Tuesday during lunch."

"Thank you, sir."

The bell rang and I gathered my things to leave. For a split second I wondered what Mr. Bingham meant with the life comment, but then Fine Boy came up to me.

"Hey, nice arguing," he squeaked.

"Thanks," I said. With that smirk in his smile, he looked like he could tell I was still riled up a bit.

"You can't take this stuff personal. We're just stating the facts."

"I know—it's just hard to come back down. My brain is racing through all the things I could have said."

"That's what we do in debate. They give you a topic, and you defend or oppose depending on your assignment. It doesn't matter whether you agree or not."

"Oh." I wasn't expecting that. "How can you defend something you don't feel passionate about?"

"How does a lawyer defend the guilty party?"

"I could never do that."

"Never say never." Fine Boy wagged his finger at me. "Name's Dakota, by the way."

"Like the state?"

"Yeah, my mom was a hippie. Fell in love with a Black Panther, and here I am."

"Ooh." I laughed. "My name's Gracey. Nothing special."

"That remains to be seen, doesn't it?" He smiled and walked away, leaving me with that tingly feeling.

▮ ▮ ▮

The library in this town is a trip, or maybe a joke is a better word for it. I walked into an old, decrepit-looking building that smelled like damp paper. At one time it was probably awesome with its stone stairs and thick Roman columns, its marble walls and golden plaques about the city's history all over the place. But now it just looked beat down, with damp coming up from the corners between the wall and the floors and cracks in the ceiling that ran across the lighting. I was not thrilled.

"Where's all the books?" I asked.

"Are you kidding?" Printess said. "We just got a whole truckload of books from some rich guy in Jackson. This library looks better than it ever has."

"Right," I said smugly. "Can you point me to the archives?"

"Come on." She took my hand and pulled me to the desk. "Can you tell us where the archives are? My friend here is trying to find something, or someone. Uh, which is it, Gracey?"

"Someone," I said.

"Yeah, she's trying to find somebody. Must be important too, 'cause we have a pretty good library in our school."

"Well, now, I just wonder if your friend can't speak for herself," said the lady behind the desk. "How far back you want to go, honey? You ain't looking to see where you come from in Africa or nothing, are you? 'Cause we don't have the records for that kind of information."

Racist lady, I thought. "No, ma'am," I said. "I only want to go back about twenty, thirty years."

"All right then, come with me."

She swung open her little half door and led us around the corner with her dainty right hand resting in the air as if she were holding a short-strapped handbag. Then she opened the door to a very cold glass room.

"I reckon you'll find what you need in here, honey."

"Thanks," I said. I started to step in, but I noticed that Printess wasn't moving.

She hesitated. "I'm just going to go over here and study my lines. You deserve your privacy."

I shrugged. "Okay." I hoped I hadn't pushed her away. A safe distance was all I really wanted.

It wasn't hard to find Bishop Michael Richards. The catalog had him on microfilm from 1969 and up. The problem was finding his son. Bishop Richards was some big politician type, known throughout the state. One of those community preachers that watched over the whole neighborhood and made sure every child had a backpack for school, a present for Christmas, and free lunch during the summer months. Whenever there was a problem, he was right there on the scene trying to help and find resources.

I found a clip where the Black people went on strike because they were getting paid 20 percent less than the white people for the exact same job. He and the church and the Black folks in the factory marched for three weeks until finally their wages were raised. He was an activist too. Who would have thought it?

He was married to a woman named Lola, but they got a divorce after he was caught cheating on her with his press secretary. I read that in the paper too. He and Lola looked so beautiful, like they should be in *Ebony* magazine. Lola's and my eyes were similar, like tears were forever on standby.

I took that roll out of the machine and found a more current one. Scrolling through, I didn't find anything on Micah Richards. I went back to the catalogs and looked under local churches—still nothing. Obviously he decided not to follow in his father's footsteps. Well, I'd just have to go through Grandpa. I wrote down the address of Bethel AME Church, 7719 Hinsdale Drive. "Hope he doesn't mind," I whispered.

Coming out of the room, I had a feeling of accomplishment. I went over to the table where Printess was practicing her lines dramatically and swooping her hands through the air.

"How'd that look?" she asked.

"Great," I lied. "You really looked like you were into it." That was the truth.

"Did you get what you were looking for?"

"Well, sort of. I'm going to church on Sunday to get the rest."

"Church? What do you mean?"

I breathed deep. "I'll have to explain it to you another time. My grandma . . . and my mom are expecting me home."

I started walking home. I didn't have time for the bus. It took forever, moving slow like we had all day.

Mississippi wasn't as lame as it seemed. It was a warm day, and I didn't need my jacket, and other people must have liked the warm air too, 'cause the parks were full of kids, and people sat in rocking chairs outside their stores. In the barbershop, the men were playing chess and smoking pipes with the doors wide open. I could hear people yelling at the TVs in the diner as they ate. I could hear bells ringing as customers walked through doors.

I checked my watch to see how late I was. I decided to stop for a burger and then catch the bus the rest of the way home. Their fries were homemade and drinking from those classic Coca-Cola bottles made me feel grown-up, like my life was slammin'.

I pulled out my journal and mapped out Operation Meet My Dad. I really wanted to go to the church next week, but it was all too soon. Just thinking about it made me want to take a long nap. I'd need to wait for the right timing, and I assumed I'd know it when I felt it. Hopping off the barstool, I made my way home.

"Where have you been?" Grandma asked. Then she leaned forward and sniffed my shoulder. "You smell like greasy food."

"I was at the library with a friend, and then I was sitting next to someone on the bus who was eating McDonald's." I didn't want her to think I skipped dinner for fast food.

"Uh-huh. You lie just like your mama," she said under her breath.

CHAPTER 31

Charlotte
March 1988

MY NOSE WOULD BE LONG as a stick on a mop if I said things just got easier and easier as we went along.

They didn't.

Francine kept waking up in the middle of the night and laying on the couch in the opposite direction to make sure I didn't leave. Mama kept bugging me every day about getting out and getting a job. Joanna was in denial about the coming of her new baby, and Gracey was on some wild-goose chase trying to find her real daddy. If I didn't know any better, I'd have yelled for Calgon to take me away, but I was on a mission, and I wasn't leaving until I had my family back.

My biggest worry was Joanna. There was such a big distance between us, much further than byways and highways. I didn't know how to close the gap. And she was so nice and polite to me, like I was a guest. But I'm her mama, and I wanted more.

Every morning I'd wake up, send Francine back to her room, and drop to my knees asking God for understanding on how to bring these girls closer and not push them away. And I'd pray for strength too, to show them love in ways they weren't expecting.

One night I waited until Joanna turned down the lights, then I tapped on her door and quickly did the Catholic cross thing. After she told me to come in, I tiptoed in and sat on the bed. She was lotioning her belly, so I just took the cocoa butter from her hand and told her to lay back. She sank right into her big pillow. She was six months along and growing nicely.

I hummed as I rubbed the cream along her rounding mound. She was radiant under the light of her lamp. I wished she could see how pretty she was. I could feel the baby's legs all bundled up as I gently rubbed the side. His head was well rounded at the top, poking his mommy's ribs. And then he kicked me.

"Oh, did you feel that?" I asked.

"Yes, it's gas. Sorry." Joanna straightened her body to sit up better to let the gas flow.

"No, sweetie, that was your baby. He's kicking. Didn't you know that?"

"I don't know. I hear all the other girls talking about it, but I didn't think my baby would move inside of me."

"Why not?"

"'Cause, I don't know . . . it seems strange. My own baby moving inside of me . . . it's just weird . . . that."

"Joanna, this child is yours. In three months, he's going to be outside your tummy, right here next to you, and you're going to have to love him."

"But what if it doesn't love me? I mean, why would it even want to love me, Mom? I'm a horrible person; he'll never get to know his dad. I don't even think God is going to let me have this baby. I keep expecting him to take it away any minute."

"What? You mean *die*? You think this baby's going to die?"

Joanna was sniffling now and wiping away her tears. "Yeah."

"Oh, dear God, no, Joanna. Don't do that. Don't think that way. I've been there. It's no way to live." I moved in closer to her. "Listen— if there's one thing I know about God, it's that God loves children. And God wouldn't take them away to punish a parent. Children are gifts from God to the world. Be thankful, baby. And all you have to do is love him, let God do the rest."

I didn't have the words that night to convince her. All I could do was hug her where it hurt. Another time I'd talk, maybe even explain what I'd learned about the kind of love that walks with us through our mistakes. But right then, we just needed each other's shoulders.

We were sleeping in each other's arms when my eyes popped open. The room was quiet, but the air felt different, like somebody in the house was awake.

"Mom? Mommy!"

Oh my goodness, Francine.

"Mommy, where are you? Mom!" She was screaming at the top of her lungs.

All the lights went on, and in seconds, Mama and Gracey appeared in the living room. Mama came out with her housecoat loosely covering her full-length frock, her headscarf tied snug around her head. Gracey stood still in her *Fat Albert* pajamas. I ran down the stairs, and Francine slammed into me as soon as she saw me.

"Mom, I thought you left again."

"No, baby. I fell asleep in Joanna's room is all. Listen, I told you, I will not leave you again. Remember? I meant it."

Mama came and kissed Francine on her head and went back to her room to sleep, and Gracey called her little sister a big baby before returning to their room.

Francine took my hand and pulled me to the couch. She was ready to sleep in my arms for another night. If it weren't for Gracey's journal, none of this would have made sense to me. What she wrote made it seem like not having a mother was devastating, but when I was in the house, I'd never felt like anybody cared. These girls, my girls, had made me feel invisible and unimportant. I had a mother in the house, yes, but most times I wished I didn't. And I wasn't mean like my mother, but apparently I wasn't much better. So I had to read Gracey's journal every night before sleeping. It had to soak in that I mattered to these girls, and as much as I got it, there were pockets and holes in me that didn't.

"Francine, look at me," I said.

"Yeah."

"Honey, I promised you I wasn't going anywhere, and I meant it. Please trust me. You're such a big girl, how about sleeping in your own bed tonight, huh?"

"I don't think—"

"Come on," I interrupted her. "I'll tuck you in. Honey, the only way you're going to learn to trust me is to let go little by little. And every time you look round the corner or pop your head downstairs, and you still see me, then you can breathe easy. After a while you won't even have to check, you'll just know from here on out, I'm here for you."

❙ ❙ ❙

It was two o'clock in the morning before I put the journal down and went to sleep. The line that echoed in my heart was where Gracey said, *Mom was a quiet presence, like love that doesn't say I love you, but you know 'cause you can feel it.*

I had to get up early the next day to make the girls breakfast for school. I had talked Mama into letting me do that much for them. She was running them like a little army: Cook your meals. Wash your clothes. Keep your room spotless. They even had to dust and polish and vacuum the whole house every Saturday before they set foot outside. She and I bleached the bathrooms and took care of the kitchen after they cooked. That was our conference time, I suppose, 'cause she asked me everything under the sun about the girls and our relationship, and I beat around every bush I could to find out how they behaved in the lunchroom.

If anything needed fixing, Hank came over with his toolbox and had a home-cooked meal as thanks. I kind of liked this guy Mama was hangin' with. He was sweet and gentle, and he treated my girls like his own granddaughters. It felt good to know they had a special pair of eyes looking over them at school. Hank wasn't just the bus driver. During school hours, he was the keeper, sweeping floors and cleaning up after half-raised kids.

Anyway, I thought Mama was gonna have a hard time letting me in to have my children back, but she said Hank was what made things easy on her. He told her, "Now, Iona, you done raisin' your children. Let your daughter do her job." I'm sure he probably said more than that to convince her, but she'll never tell what it was. At times I seen her watching us from the kitchen, trying her best not to step in. There's even been times when the girls wouldn't do what I told them to, and then Mama would clear her throat and they'd go on and do it. It tickled me to no end.

By the time spring rolled around, we were really starting to settle. One day I told Francine to wear a light scarf when she went outside, and she threw the biggest fit, like a scarf can ruin your popularity at school. Mama got wind of the conversation, and the next thing I heard was a belt buckle jingling from the kitchen. That child grabbed her scarf and put it on so fast, you'd think a blizzard was coming into the house. I had to laugh when she left. I don't know what I would've done if Mama wasn't around, probably let Francine go out there and catch a cold. I wasn't up for no fightin' just yet.

There were many things I hadn't thought about when I came here, like getting a job.

But first thing Mama said to me one morning was, "Well, you gonna get a job, or you gonna sit up in my house and eat up all my little money?"

"Get a job?" Here we go again. "Mama, you know I've been looking. It's a lot right now. I just came here to get my girls. I never even intended to stay this long. But seems like they're shell-shocked from a war. They need so much help and love, I'm afraid to move them."

"They were in a war, Charlotte." Mama sat down at the kitchen table in front of me. "How in the world you think they paid the bills?"

"Oh, Lord, have mercy." I felt so sick. "I thought everything was all taken care of. I left money from Moses's insurance policy."

"Who are you, Alice in Wonderland? Ain't nobody goin' give no child money just like that. They worked odd jobs on the weekends, sometimes after school, mostly Gracey. You know, that girl is industrious. Little by little folks in the neighborhood started finding out, you know, rumors spread, and people started slipping envelopes of money through the door. Folks left clothes on their doorstep and even brought them meals every now and again. I tell ya, Charlotte, those are some tough girls you got there." Mama shook her fist in a tight ball to show just how tough my girls were. "And they might have made it too, if the school hadn't found out about Joanna. But once the sun rose on the deed done, it was over."

The earth should have opened up and swallowed me whole.

Mama sat back in her chair and wrapped her hand around her coffee mug. "I think that . . . uh . . . I had a hand in all this too." She looked at me. "I left you in the most difficult time of your life, when you needed me."

We both sat in a thick silence, then she finally said, "I'm sorry." The word dropped out of her mouth like a drip given up.

I leaned forward. "Tell me why you left, Mama. Was I that bad?"

"Oh, girl, it wasn't just you and the reminder of what I'd done or hadn't done. I was that bad too. Moses was our buffer. He kept everything nice and light and steady. I couldn't imagine what life would be like without him around. And everyone was so sad, and you looked like you were on the verge of a breakdown. And I said to myself, 'I can't handle this.' So I left. But, girl, I swear if I'd a known you were going to run, I never would have left."

"I didn't run, Mama. I—"

"Oh yes you did. You were scared for your life, and you left your kids in that big old rickety house."

"It was a nice house."

"Charlotte!"

"Sorry. I guess . . ."

"Look, don't you start lying to cover things up. We both messed up, and you know good an' well that house was . . . let's call it different. Unexplained sounds and shaking." Mama narrowed her eyes and leaned in close to me. "I heard Nelda went in there and prayed that stuff, whatever it was, out of there. And God only knows what else they went through. They don't tell us everything. It'll take a lifetime to get over the damage come to them in the time we was gone. I'm still trying to get over my childhood, and I suspect you are too."

"Oh, Mama." I covered my eyes with my hands.

Mama took a deep breath and changed the subject. "All I want to know, Charlotte, is what are you going to do now? Are you going to stay? 'Cause if you are, I already told you, you need to get a job and help out. Or are you going to take the girls and go—and if so, where you going? Here? Savannah? Back to Chicago?"

I scratched my head. "What do you want me to do, Mama?"

"I don't see why y'all can't stay here." She waved her arm like a model showcasing a car.

"Because, Mama, there's going to be a little baby soon, and there won't be enough space for us all."

"Oh, nonsense, there's plenty of room."

"What about me, Mama? I'm a grown woman. I can't keep sleeping on the couch. I need my privacy."

"I wonder if Hank could get some fellas together to add two more rooms onto the house?" Grandma grabbed a pad, licked the lead of her pencil, and started writing.

"Would you . . . would you really do that for us?"

"If you got a job, yes."

"But, Mama, I just don't know for sure."

"Please don't take those girls away." She put her pencil down and looked earnestly at me. "Hard as I am on them, I love those kids, and they love me."

I covered my neck with the palm of my hand. Protection from what, I didn't know.

She went on. "I been wantin' to put some common sense into them girls for years, and now I finally got a chance. I love helping them, and I'm not willing to see them go. Besides, right now I have legal custody."

"Oh no, Mama, please, there's no need to go there. These are my children, and I'll do what's best for them, whether that's staying here or leaving."

Mama put her hands up as if to surrender. "I don't want to fight. I'm just saying . . . I'd like it if you and the girls and my little great-grandchild stayed here. Me and Hank will figure out how to put an addition on the house and everything, but you got to get a job and help out."

"Mama, if I'm here, of course I'll get a job. What you think I'm gonna do, sit around and watch TV all day?"

She looked at me flat-faced. "I don't know. I don't think I ever seen you work, Charlotte."

I wasn't even going to pretend that didn't hurt. And I wasn't in the mood to defend myself. I just got up and walked away. No better time to get out and take in the town. I showered, washed my hair, and put on straight-legged slacks and a long pastel sweater with a tie around the waist. I slipped on some pumps and was out the door.

Walking down the street, I stuck my nose into all kinds of businesses. I didn't really want to do the B and B thing again, so I was looking into places I could imagine myself working, like the little dress shop downtown. It was called Better Than Ever, but when I took the Help Wanted sign inside, they said they had just hired someone that morning. I looked into selling insurance, but the thought of shuffling papers in a wood-paneled office with one fan made me feel a little faint. Not that I had decided to stay, but it didn't hurt to look into things.

I bought a paper and went to the ice-cream parlor. Inside, a nice young man was ready to take my order. "What can I get you, miss?"

"I'll have a tall hot fudge sundae."

"Comin' right up."

While I waited, I took a seat by the window and opened up to the classifieds. There had to be fifty secretarial jobs and two of everything else: teachers, nurses, maids, nannies. Well, I might as well be a secretary at a company I liked. I skimmed through all the listings and came to a hotel looking for a receptionist. That wouldn't be so bad. I'd get to meet all kinds of people. I circled the listing and put the paper down to eat my sundae.

The sound of my spoon scraping against my bowl echoed through the shop as I savored the taste of vanilla bean and chocolate together.

I was just about to lick my fingers when a middle-aged man sitting on a bench outside the shop caught my attention. He was far away, drinking a cola, but I could swear he looked like someone I knew. Not long afterward a young woman in knee-high boots and a flowing skirt came his way and gave him a big hug. He seemed really happy to see her, but then he looked up and gazed directly at me.

My heart sank. It was Micah. Quickly I turned my head and put my empty dish on the table. I ran out of the shop and turned down a street I hadn't been on since I'd skipped Sunday school. There was a big department store there now, Marshall Fields. I had to take my mind off Micah, so I just started grabbing clothes off the rack to try on.

What was he doing in town, and why was I sweating? *Lord, tell me what to do.* How was I going to handle seeing him and talking to him? *Please don't let me ever have to see him again.* I prayed Gracey wouldn't find him ever, ever—*God, please, I beg you. I can't take it.*

I finally convinced myself to leave the dressing room and scuttle home. At home, I got some stationery and a pen and sat down at the kitchen table. Maybe Gracey inspired me with her writing.

> *Dear Candi,*
> *How you doin', girl? I was thinking about you today. How's Ebony, she still hanging on? What about Mr. Goodin, what's he up to? How's life at the B and B?*

Forget it. I called the B and B and asked for Candi.

"Hey, hey, how can I help you?"

"Candi?"

"Charlotte, girl, what you doing callin' here? You was just on my mind."

"Well, that's why I called you, you were on my mind. What's been going on?"

"Well, you know, I'm thinkin' of leaving." Candi's voice was careful like she was testing the waters. "Things are changing around here. There's new construction going on, younger people coming in. I just ain't happy anymore." She sighed. "So how're things with you? You get your girls back? Y'all going back to Chicago soon?"

"Well, yes and no. I got my girls back, but Mama's waving legal custody over my head."

"You're kidding. That ain't right."

"Well, that don't really matter. I was thinking about staying anyway."

"Really? Why?"

"I don't know. It just seems like I fit in better here. Life is slower, friendlier, and the girls are beginning to dig in a bit."

"Wow, that is so strange. I was thinkin' of movin' to Chicago."

"What? Why?"

"Well, after you left, I cleaned Miss Nelda's place from top to bottom, and I had such a good time talking to her. She told me about all the children she's watched over the years and how she knows the mothers of all the famous politicians what come out of Chicago. Did you know she worked at Roosevelt University when Harold Washington and Lorraine Hansberry went to school there? She told me all about them. The woman needs better respect than what she's getting. She's obsessed with dying, though. I told her I thought she had plenty years left on this earth. Then, as I was about to leave, she offered me a job."

"No way."

"Uh-huh, girl, sho' did. Said she ain't been taken care of so well in years, and she'd love it if I would come and stay with her and be her caregiver. Nursing was my first career, so it shouldn't be a problem. She just needed to clear it with Medicaid."

"She's not guaranteed to be around much longer. She is in her eighties."

"Yeah, I know, but I'll cross that bridge when I get there."

"Amazing." I couldn't believe it. "So you going?"

"I'll see. Listen, girl, you know I'm on company time, let me get off this phone. I love you now. Talk to you later."

I hung up the phone with a whine. I wanted to talk more because I had more to say. I needed someone to talk to about seeing Micah.

Keys were jingling in the door, and my family walked in talking, singing, and complaining.

"Francine, stop! You are so tone-deaf," Gracey said.

"Am not."

"Are too."

"Both of y'all cut it out. You gettin' on my nerves now," Mama said, hobbling in with her cane.

"I have a question." Gracey spoke up.

"What's that, honey?" I asked.

"How come we don't go to church on Sundays?"

I looked at Mama, who looked at me, but neither of us had an answer.

"Uh, well. Maybe we should," Mama said.

"Yeah, I think we should." Gracey plunked her backpack on a kitchen chair. "I mean, as much as you two pray and talk about God this and God that, why don't we go to church?"

"Gracey, going to church is no big deal. We weren't trying to avoid it. We just haven't found the right one. You can't just start going to any old church."

"Yeah, but how do we find one, if we never go?"

"True. You have any particular church in mind?"

"My friend told me about this church a couple months ago." Gracey pulled out a piece of paper with some writing scribbled on it.

"You mean the one who made you come home so late you missed dinner?"

"Grandma, I told you. I was at the library," Gracey said.

Mama rolled her eyes, then took the piece of paper from Gracey's hand. Holding it just past her nose, she said, "Bethel AME? Yeah, we can go there. I heard that's a good church."

"Who's the pastor over there?" I asked.

"I can't remember, but he's highfalutin, that's all I know," Mama said. "You know, Gracey?"

"I don't know. They just said it was a good church."

"We'll give it a try, then," I said.

"Just not this Sunday," Mama added. "It's the first Sunday in April and I can't be bothered with Communion—take too long, and my chicken will dry out in the oven."

Anyway, since when did Gracey get interested in going to church?

CHAPTER 32

Gracey
April 1988

YES! I GOT THEM TO agree to go to church with me. It was going to be perfect. I couldn't wait to see my grandfather. And if I could get him alone for five, maybe ten minutes, it'd be like seeing his face through a magnifying glass, my features against his, and maybe I could ask him about his children. I didn't think Mom would mind, 'specially if she had no idea what I was doing.

I was so excited; I went to the closet and called Bastian.

"Oh hi, Miss Rosa, is Sebastian home?"

"Gracey, honey, how are you? I was just asking Sebastian about you."

"Oh, um . . . I'm fine." I didn't want to talk to Rosa.

She lowered her voice to a talking whisper. "He told me about your dad." She took a deep breath. *"Ai yi yi,* you must be devastated. Bastian told me how you were trying to find your real dad and he told you to look in the archives. Did you find him, honey?"

My heart must have really been in my throat because I was finding it hard to breathe.

"Gracey? You there?"

"Yeah, yes, Miss Rosa," I finally said. "I'm here."

"Well, talk to me, honey."

"Sorry. No, I haven't, uh . . . found my dad yet."

"Well, me and the girls at the salon, we're rooting for you. That mama of yours, shame on her. Shame on her, honey."

"Well, I have to go now." I was fuming. She had no right to talk about my mom like that. She didn't even know what happened. Mom didn't do anything to be ashamed of, and I knew I was not my mother's shame.

"No, wait. Didn't you want to talk to Seb—"

"No! I don't need to talk to him anymore. It's okay, really."

"It's not because—"

Click.

I didn't know what else she said, but I didn't want to hear it. I felt like a complete fool; a dumb, birdbrained, gullible, goofy, airheaded Valley girl. I smacked my forehead a couple of times to make the embarrassment fade, but nothing worked save sitting in the closet and letting my heart go back to a steady beat. *What an idiot.*

What did I think—that telling Bastian my innermost feelings would make him like me more? Really, what was I thinking? I knew. I knew he'd tell his mom. I knew he'd tell the world. There was only a 10 percent chance that he wouldn't, and stupid me, I bet on it. But that was his last opportunity to prove that he was a trustworthy friend, and he'd ruined it in front of everybody.

I imagined myself riding on the "L" and seeing a billboard of myself with big, bold, yellow letters that read CONFUSED across the top. I was embarrassed for myself and my family and especially my mom. Yeah, she messed up, but at least she was trying, and her name didn't deserve to be dragged through the streets of Chicago.

I was the only one who had the right to talk trash about her—me and my sisters. Nobody else.

As for Bastian, I was through with him. I understood now. If you had a secret and you wanted to keep it safe, shouldn't share it to keep your friends close. They'd just take that information and treat it like a cream pie on a game show—*splat!*—right in your face. Not that my secret was all that, but it was special to me. It held the answers to my questions, to who and how I was. Now I was exposed, naked from the inside out.

And for the first time, I looked around me and I was glad to be in Mississippi. Glad to be away from the drama. It almost felt like home again but maybe a little better because we had more peace. I wanted to meet my dad because finding out that Moses wasn't my real dad meant a piece of me was missing, and I wanted to feel like a whole person. I didn't want any lingering questions sneaking around inside of me about who I was. I had to find my dad, and I didn't care if Mom or Grandma got upset. I might be a teenager, but my voice was just as important as the adults' around me.

I   I   I

That night Francine came into the room and pounced on the bed. "Gracey, telephone. It's for you, and it's a booooy."

"Who is it?" If it was Bastian, I was hanging up on him.

Francine shrugged. "I don't know who it is."

I grabbed the phone from the hall and pulled the line to my bed. "Hello?"

"Uh, hi. Is this Gracey?"

"Yeah, who's this?"

"This is Dakota."

Dakota? Why in the world was he calling me?

"I was just wondering if you'd like to go to a movie sometime. Say maybe this weekend?"

"Well, that's cool. I mean, I have to ask my grandma . . . and my mom."

"Okay."

There was silence. I had to think of something quick.

Then he said, "How 'bout we talk after practice?"

"Cool."

"Alrighty, then. See ya tomorrow."

I flew down the stairs and landed with a question. "Dakota asked me out on a date to the movies, can I go?"

"Shoot, no!"

That was the first thing that came out of Grandma's mouth, and those words were like a washrag wiping the smile off my face. I looked at Mom.

"Mom, what do you say?"

She looked at Grandma and swallowed hard. Grandma gave her some kind of threatening look.

"Well, you know, you're a teenager. I don't see why you shouldn't be allowed to go out."

Grandma took some strength to cross her legs and cracked some pecans with the nutcracker as she spoke. "Reason number one: Joanna."

"Yeah, but Gracey isn't Joanna. She wouldn't do anything like that. It's just not in her."

"Honey, you always think you know your children until they go and do something off the wall. You never know what's going on in their little minds." Grandma threw back her head and tossed the nuts into her mouth with the palm of her hand.

"I know Joanna wouldn't have gone and gotten pregnant if I were around."

Grandma grunted. "Maybe. Maybe not. I don't see how it would have made no difference."

"Grandma . . ." There was a threat in my voice. She had crossed the line.

"Now hold on, Mama, we've been through all this before," Mom said. "Ain't no sense in going around the same mountain again."

"That's right, so it's all settled. Gracey, you tell that boy the answer's no. Yo' Grandmama said so."

"Gracey, tell him yes. You be back by ten o'clock and call me if you're going to be late."

Grandma stood to her feet and shouted, "If you think I'ma have a house full of outside children runnin' around, you got another thought comin'!"

"What? Outside children?" I said. "Grandma . . . are you talking about me or the baby?"

Grandma looked at me like she'd just come to herself. She relaxed her shoulders, breathed easy, and shook her head. "I'm sorry, baby, I didn't mean it that way. What I meant was—"

"It ain't too many ways you can take what you said, Mama. What was in your heart came out of your mouth. You didn't mean to say it, is all. We forgive you for that." Mom put her arms on my shoulders and leveled her eyes to mine. "You bring that boy to the house and let me get a good look at him. Then y'all can go on to a nice, wholesome, PG movie."

She pinched my cheek while Grandma glared at me from behind her back.

"Okay, Mom." I gave her a big hug and tiptoed past Grandma before I ran upstairs and did a break-dance move.

Francine busted in full of questions. "What'd they say? I couldn't hear everything from the vents. Do you get to go? Is he cute? I don't remember seeing nobody named Dakota."

I only answered the questions I felt like answering, and the rest I left hanging. She didn't care. She just wanted to know what he looked like: light-skinned/dark-skinned, pizza face/baby face, musty/ deodorant/cologne . . . the essentials in boy ranking. According to her *Teen* magazine, he was a seven, and that was good enough for her.

I I I

I couldn't believe how nervous I was before lunch. I kept telling myself, *Calm down, calm down, he's not all that, Gracey.* But my goodness, he was all that and a bowl of grits. And to top it all off, he asked me on a date!

I went to the most secluded bathroom I could find and stood at the mirror taking slow, deep breaths. To me, I looked kind of beautiful for a change. But I didn't know what he'd think. I squeezed a few zits and fixed my hair.

As it was, Dakota was on the stage flipping through some pages when he looked up and smiled with his braces shining. The way he nodded reminded me of Bastian. I wiped my forehead, checking for oily skin with my hand, and waved back.

He came to the edge of the stage and kneeled down while the coach was talking to the other side. "So what's the verdict?"

"She said I could go."

"Yes." Dakota pulled his fist toward him as if it were a truck horn and then reached out to help me climb onto the stage.

"Little late, aren't we, Downing?" the coach said, ticking my name on the attendance list. "We on the debate team take our club very seriously. You do well enough, you could get a scholarship into college one day. So please, don't be late again."

"Yes, sir," I said.

I paged through the notes and found some facts that helped to support my points. I have to say, though, that I still got pretty emotional. During the rebuttal, I called Dakota a couple of rude names.

"Every school should have an arts program because it is through the arts we are able to express ourselves and find emotional healing that may not avail itself otherwise. People always like to cut the arts first, but really it shouldn't even be on the table for consideration. If kids who aren't athletic or into computers or maths and sciences are able to create and design in the school, then rest assured they will find an outlet outside the school, and we may not like how that looks."

"Come on, Dakota. Look at the future—it's all about math, science, and computers. Ask any school to choose which program to cut and they're all going to cut the arts program. Why? Because you can't make any money drawing a picture. You'd know that if you grew up in the hood where you're taught to do something that'll put food on the table, not give you warm fuzzies about coloring within the lines."

The coach blew his whistle and pulled me to the side. For a second, I thought I was on the basketball court.

"Listen, Downing, a good debater doesn't get emotional or personal.

She uses passion, she delivers her point with gusto and gumption, but she never gets to rolling her neck and throwing jabs, like what you just did up there—got that?"

"Yes, sir."

"And stop calling me sir. My name is Mr. Bingham."

"Sorry, sir. Uh, Mr. Bingham, sir . . . Mr. Bingham."

Oh boy, I was making a fool of myself. Everyone was laughing.

"Don't make me regret putting you on the team."

I had no answer. I just stood there until he dismissed me.

After practice, I was so embarrassed, I just left. Forget the date. Dakota probably thought I was some kind of dweeb queen anyway. The walls of the hallway held me up as I slunk to my locker. I opened it and looked at my calendar . . . how many days till spring break?

I slammed my locker shut, turned, and screamed at the sight of Dakota standing right next to me.

"So are we still on for the movies?" he asked, shifting his backpack to the other shoulder.

"Yeah, I guess so. I'm sorry about what I said."

"It's fine. You were good till, you know. Meet you there around six?"

"Yes. I mean no. You have to come and meet my mom. She won't let me go if I don't introduce you to her."

Dakota's forehead wrinkled like he was thinking hard. I thought he was going to say forget the whole thing, but instead he said, "Okay, then I guess I'll be by to pick you up around five-thirty. Then we can take the bus or something, depending on where you live."

"It's 233 Melody Lane," I blurted out.

He looked a little startled that I had spoken so fast, but then he recovered. "Oh yeah, I know where that is. By that old-fashioned burger shop."

"Old-fashioned? I thought it was up-to-date for around here."

"Nah, we got a place called Sonic. That's where it's at. We can sit outside on the pavement and listen to the music."

"So much better. So I'll see you tonight then?" I waved awkwardly. He walked away, and I was so excited I shut my eyes and squeezed my books to my chest. "Yesss!"

▮ ▮ ▮

The rest of the day was so lame, I slept with my eyes open in class. Things livened up in science class when two boys started shooting little wads of toilet paper at each other with their straws. When Ms. Ornot turned her head, she got hit right between the eyes. My ribs hurt from laughing so hard. But we all straightened up when she started handing out detentions for students making fun of her. I didn't want to do anything to turn my mom sour against me.

But I didn't think anything I could have done would have made her upset. That afternoon she was smiling and dancing around like she'd just come out of a party, and all she was doing was dusting the coffee table with a big, feathered stick. I felt like I'd wandered into a sitcom and the producer had just yelled, "Action!"

"What's got you so happy?"

"I don't know. It's just a beautiful day, the sun's shinin', the birds are singin', and things, you know, they ain't half bad."

"That's all?"

"Mm-hmm." Mom clapped her hands and rubbed them together. "So you ready for your big date?"

"Yup, and I know exactly what I'm going to wear—that's a lie."

"I can help you. Come on, let's go through your clothes."

Great. Who wants their mom helping them pick out clothes? "That's okay," I said real quick. "I think I can work it out."

"What? You don't want your old mama helping you pick out your clothes? I tell you what, why don't you give me a chance, and if you don't like it, you can choose something else?"

I followed her to our room, and the first thing she did was spray the Glade air freshener. I guess she didn't like the stuffy gym-shoe smell.

Then she went to the closet and started scraping the hangers across the rod. She pulled out some jeans and a fluorescent pink sweater that I could gather on the side and clip together, but I closed my eyes and turned my head as a refusal.

She pulled out another pant and blouse set less tacky in color.

"Nah. I don't like that outfit either."

Mom shrugged and pulled out another pair of jeans with a peach, fluorescent T-shirt and my stone-washed Jordache jean jacket.

"Yeah, I like that, but I was thinking maybe . . ." I went to the closet and pulled out my blue-jean miniskirt. "This."

Mom tilted her head to the side for a minute. "You know, that's a really cute skirt. But I don't want you wearing a skirt today, let alone a miniskirt." She went to the closet again and pulled out some tie-dye jeans I used to love, but the bottoms were too wide.

"I guess I could wear those. I just have to tight-roll them—you know, fold the bottoms to the side and then roll them up. But why can't I just wear the skirt? It looks so cool on me."

"Because you don't want him thinking he can do things he shouldn't be doing while the movie's playing."

"Oh, Mom, please. Dakota wouldn't do that. He's nice."

"Nice or whatever, he's a boy, and boys have hormones. Now, if you want to go on this date, you'll be wearing pants."

She left the room for me to get dressed. It was okay, I didn't mind wearing jeans. Those ones were funky, and Dakota would like them. I'd pegged him for one of those people that liked anything slightly outside of normal.

Maybe that was why he liked me. I was from Chi-town, not some backward, slue-footed town that made up their own dances 'cause they couldn't catch ours.

Or maybe he liked me because he thought I was pretty. I looked in the mirror. My eyes had one too many red lines, and a blackhead was forming on my right cheek.

Joanna came in and sat on my bed while I was getting ready.

I looked at her like she was crazy. She hadn't been in our room for weeks now, and she hardly ever held a conversation for longer than two minutes.

"Why you in here?"

"Great language skills." She shifted her weight on the bed.

She was getting big now, waddling like a duck everywhere she went, and it took her a long time to muscle her way out of the easy chair. Francine was always there, racing to hold her elbow. I usually helped her with her shoes, since she seemed to find that a chore.

"Heard you have a date tonight."

"Yup, with Dakota."

"Yeah, I seen him around. He seems nice enough."

Then she just sat there like she wanted me to ask her something. But what? And why? I had nothing to talk about with her. She watched my reflection in the glass as I was trying to comb out my hair. She got up and took the comb out my hand. "Let me do it."

She grabbed the TCB grease and pink moisturizer on my desk and rubbed some into her hands, spreading it evenly between both palms. Then she massaged it through my hair until it was easier to comb. Then she parted a line around the middle like the equator and put the top half into a ponytail while letting the bottom half hang loose. As a finishing touch, she pulled a few strands of hair from my forehead and curled them with the electric hot comb. Then, with the help of a brush, every hair was in perfect position.

"I can't remember too many times when you've voluntarily combed my hair," I said. "Why now?"

"I don't know." She shrugged her shoulders and kept smoothing my hair with her hand, admiring her work.

"Well, I liked you much better before you 'fell in love.' Now you act like a zombie, like you can't feel anything. What happened to you?"

"I don't know..." She went quiet on me. All we could hear was a bird outside and the light clanging of someone rinsing dishes in the sink. Then she went to the window. "You hear that whooping bird outside?"

"Yeah, so what. I—"

"Shh." She opened the window. Nature came into our room like it had been waiting for an invitation.

"Now you hear the crickets and the cicadas, the bluebirds, and the robins. You hear the dogs barking and the cats sneaking through the grass?"

I had to admit the sound was beautiful, like its own music, but what was her point? "Yeah, so . . ."

"So . . . it's like a jungle out there, is all I'm sayin'."

There was something more to her words, and she wanted me to ask her something, but I didn't know what. I sat for a while in thought.

"What's it like?" I finally asked.

"What's what like?"

"Sex or love . . . whatever."

"There's a big difference between sex and love."

"Well, what's the difference then?" I was trying to hurry her up because I didn't feel like playing this game, and I already knew the difference. Sex was an action, and love was a feeling, normally going before the action but oftentimes not.

Joanna sat back on my bed and put one foot under her leg. "Sex is like scratchin' a mosquito bite that itches really bad. And when you hit that point where you don't need to scratch anymore because it feels so good you could just coast along, that's the climax. But then afterward you feel kind of bad, like it wasn't even all that serious.

"And love, I guess you could say that's like a journey two souls take together, like down one of these dirt roads out here. The longer they walk, the more they fall in love, and the easier it is to walk without falling out of sync. At least, that's what I think should happen. But what I come to know is that in the beginning, you can walk miles before you ever touch and still be in love."

"Hmm . . . and when'd you learn all this?"

"When I wasn't in school."

"So, you think the jungle has love in it?" I asked, trying to lighten up the room.

She stayed serious but soft. "I think the jungle has animals. And animals . . . they don't know love like we know love."

"I guess not."

The doorbell rang, and I hugged Joanna and quickly checked myself in the mirror before running down the stairs.

Grandma caught me at the bottom. "Girl, what you doin' runnin' down the stairs like you desperate? Get yo' behind back up there and wait till we call you."

"Shh, Grandma, he'll hear you." Still, I turned and walked up the stairs gingerly, like a lady, and waited at the top while Mom answered the door.

"Why, hello there, Dakota. I'm Gracey's mother. It's nice to meet you. Come on in and have a seat."

"It's nice to meet you, Mrs. Downing." He was nervous, I could tell, 'cause his voice was shaking.

Joanna came and stood with me on the stairs. "He sounds nice," she said.

"He is, Joanna. He's really sweet."

Mom continued. "Why don't you have a seat, and I'll bring you out some sweet tea. Gracey! Your friend is here."

Me and Joanna covered our mouths in laughter.

"Okay, Mom, I'll be right down."

I came down lookin' fly in my outfit, and Dakota's eyes lit up when he saw me. He even forced his lips into his mouth to keep from cheesing. He stuck out his hand and then pulled it back like he didn't know what to do.

"Wow, Gracey, you look . . . really nice." He obviously didn't know what to say either. "I really like your hair. Did you do something to it?"

"No, my sister did."

"Oh." He looked around, and his eyes landed on the pictures over the fireplace.

He walked over to the mantel and looked at the Kodak Kmart special we took about five years back. Dad was smiling next to Mom, and we were all standing in front of them. I remember being happy that

Grandma had decided not to be a part of the portrait. She said she didn't feel comfortable with it. *Good*, we all thought.

"Is this your dad? Is he coming home soon?"

"No, he died."

"Oh, my bad. I didn't know."

"It's okay."

There was an awkward silence until we heard the key in the door turning. It was Francine, coming in from a track meet.

"Hey, you're Dakota. Nice to meet you."

"And you're Frankie. Number one track star in the school, came in second at the regionals, and about to go to state."

"Yeah, how'd you know?"

"On the debate team, you got to know what's what and who's who. You never know what your next topic is going to be."

"Yeah, like sports versus education," Francine said.

"Right, and education is my position, because if you get hurt, you'll have something to fall back on."

"Nah, I'd take the sports. You only live once, know what I'm sayin'?" She reached out to slap me five, but I didn't return the love.

"I agree with Dakota, Francine. You have to have a fallback, and besides, what are you going to do after you retire?"

"Oh, that's easy. Broadcasting. 'Hello, this is Francine Downing. Today we're covering the 2012 Olympics. Let's see who our favorites are to win.'"

"Yeah, well, you have to go to college to be a broadcaster."

"Don't worry, I will . . . on a scholarship. Anyway, nice to meet you, Dakota."

"Yeah, you too."

Mom came out with the iced tea, and Grandma was right behind her with a big bowl of sour cream potato chips and onion dip. The smell took over the room as soon as she put the bowl on the table.

"So you're Dakota," Grandma said.

"Yes, ma'am."

"Why they name you after a state?"

"My mom said she lived in South Dakota when she was little and she loved it so much she named me after it."

"Uh-huh, she must be the white one."

"Yes, ma'am."

"Good thing she didn't stay in Idaho." Grandma took a big, uninterested breath and pushed the chips his way. "Here, have some chips."

He hesitated. "No, I'm not too hungry."

"Oh, go on, boy, I insist. Have some." She waved her hand his way.

He reached into the bowl and pulled out one chip, biting it in half. Then Grandma pushed it my way and nudged her head for me to have one. I did, but I made an ugly face to let her know that her way of hospitality was whack. She just wanted to make our breath smell so we wouldn't be kissing. That was just cold-blooded, if you asked me. Like sabotaging a party with classical music.

"Hey, haven't I seen you before?" Dakota wrinkled his forehead to try to figure out from where.

"My grandma's a lunch lady at school."

"Oh yeah, now I recognize you. I didn't know you two were related. You don't look anything alike. You don't even look like your parents, Gracey. I guess your DNA pulled from a different generation, huh?"

Dakota laughed at his joke, but we all just sat there with frozen smiles.

"Well, y'all better get going," Mom said. "Time is moving, and we don't want you coming back late."

Dakota and I jumped at the chance to leave, but he reached down and drank his whole glass of tea before we walked out the door. He shook hands with Mom and Grandma, and I just smiled and turned my back.

We exhaled when we got around the corner.

"I am so sorry," I said. "I knew they were going to trip, but I didn't know how hard."

"It's all right. No biggie."

We caught the bus to the movies and decided to watch *Hairspray*, since so much of our lives was about race anyway. And who knew what the new president would do once in office to ease tensions, if anything. Just sitting in the dark with Dakota made waves of comfort hit my body. There were moments when I was totally into the movie, and all the wigs and all the kissing, but I never forgot the fact that I was on a date. Afterward, sitting across from him at Pizza Hut was so embarrassing, I could hardly eat. It was like my brain kept screaming, *Don't do anything to make a fool out of yourself* . . . like choking on the cheese or dripping sauce on my shirt.

Dakota cut his slices into thinner pieces; he said it gave him more control. I thought that was kind of silly, but I didn't say anything.

We talked about capital punishment, vouchers versus public schools, and even Democrats versus Republicans. In the end, I put my fingers in my water and splashed a few drops his way. "Hey!" he yelled. "A good debater never loses her cool."

"Yeah, well, maybe I'm not a good debater. Maybe I'm an activist: I stand up for what's right instead of trying to force somebody to see a point I don't believe in. That's stupid."

Dakota took his napkin and wiped the water off his face. He shook his head with a *tsk, tsk, tsk.* "You'll never be a lawyer this way. Didn't you learn anything from the movie? There's a dream in your future."

"Who in the world said I wanted to be a lawyer?" I demanded, standing. But really there was no energy behind my anger. I was like an old helium balloon, slowing drifting to the ground. *Please sit me down*, I thought.

His hand shot out and caught me. "It's elementary, my dear."

I took a breath of happy defeat and sank down in my chair.

"What do you mean?"

Dakota wasn't even paying attention. He folded his napkin neatly. I cleared my throat and he looked up as if surprised to see me still there.

"What do you mean, 'it's elementary'?"

"I don't know. From the first time I saw you, I saw a lawyer. You look like a lawyer; you act like one. You even have that confident walk like you're going straight into the courtroom to win your case."

That was the nicest thing anyone ever said to me. And yeah, deep, deep down, in the faintest whisper of a thought not in my mind or even my heart, but in my belly, I really wanted to be a lawyer. But I never in a million years thought it could ever happen.

"Do you really see that?"

"Yeah, I see."

"You mean like a psychic?"

"No, I mean some people can just see stuff or imagine it. They don't see them where they are now, they see them ten, twenty years from now. I see like that. And I'm not the only one. Dr. King, Benjamin Franklin, Harriet Tubman, Thomas Edison—shoot, our teachers should be seers, they just don't pay attention."

"So, you believe in God?"

"I don't know what that has to do with what I said, but yeah." He frowned. "I believe in God more than I believe in my parents. When they get stuck in their own worlds doing whatever they do, God stays right by me. I think it's safe to say we have an understanding."

Yeah, I could relate, but I didn't have the space to go there out loud.

I put my hand on the table. "Hey, listen, I really am sorry for going off on you like that."

"It's all right. I'm used to it. You got to fight for what you believe in, right? Where you got all that passion from, though, that's what I want to know."

"I don't know. I been through a lot, I guess."

"Oh yeah, like your dad . . . if it's okay to ask, how'd he die?" He sat back and crossed his foot over his knee.

"Heart attack."

"Oh, wow. That's the number one killer in the United States for a Black man."

But my dad wasn't some stupid shadowy statistic. He'd been chopped down right when we needed him most. I stared out the window, waiting for the hopeless moment to pass.

I I I

Dakota got me back home five minutes to ten, and my mom was right there looking out the window, waiting for us. He walked me to the step and reached out to shake my hand, and then he pulled me closer and kissed my cheek.

"I had a nice time," I said. That was what they always said in the movies.

"Me too."

Someone was unlocking the door from the other side, and Dakota turned to go.

I gathered my feelings into my heart with my hands and turned the key to lock them there.

Grandma and Mom were both waiting to jump.

"How was it?"

"Did you have a good time?"

"He didn't try nothin', did he?"

"You were a good girl, weren't you, honey?"

Did they think I was like them?

"You know what?" I said. "The problems that you and Grandma and Jo have, those are not my problems, so leave me alone." I threw my purse on the floor and went upstairs.

CHAPTER 33

Charlotte
April 1988

"I TOLD YOU NOT TO go looking out the window! You're too doggone anxious. You should have just sat down like I told you to. At least I learned that much about raising kids. They can't stand to have you breathing down their back." Mama lifted her cane and shook its bottom at me.

"Me? What about you askin' all them questions before she even got in the door good? 'He didn't try nothing, did he?'" I mocked Mama.

"Well, you the one who asked if she was a good girl, patronizing her like she was some reformed hussy."

"Big words from such a small woman!"

Mama's eyes got big, and she put her hands on her hips. "All your life you've had that snooty attitude, like you're better than me. You think 'cause you got more education and you made so slim, you have a right to walk around here like some princess on a high horse? Well, you don't. Yo' daddy may have had good looks and good hair, but that didn't make him no good man. He was horrible, and you ought not be so proud to be who you are."

My hands held my head to keep from losing it.

"Yeah, that's right, I said it. You ain't never had a reason to think you're so much better than me, yet you take every opportunity to throw it in my face."

"What? Mama! Where's all this coming from? I never thought I was better than you. I just wanted a better life. That's all."

"That's what I'm talkin' about. If it was good enough for me and the boys, then it shoulda been good enough for you."

"It wasn't good enough for you, Mama, that's why you wanted to move up north. And it wasn't good enough for the boys, that's why they haven't spoken to you or me in ten years. Our lives were miserable, and you know it. You just did a good job pretending. What you really mean is misery loves company."

Mama took hold of her cane to support herself and waved her hand. "I'm through with this conversation. The girl is home, and that's good. She had a good time."

"Yeah, that's right, Mama, walk away. Act like nothing never happened. The words in this argument were never spoken."

"Don't you preach to me about walking away. You done more walking than anybody in this house. I just don't have the energy tonight. Maybe another day, chile. Another day."

I I I

The next day, I hit the streets again to look for help-wanted signs. I was enjoying being an at-home mom, and for a while, Mama actually let me rest by not saying anything, but she was right. I needed something to do.

A maternity shop was hiring, but it just seemed too hypocritical for me. One of the salesladies was in there knitting some booties in order to pass time. She looked to be about six months pregnant herself. I never did that for my girls when I was pregnant; I always thought knitting was too prissy. It was enough that I went down to the local Woolworth's and picked out some baby clothes. And we never did get to do a room with all the baby decorations; we just put the crib in the spare room and decorated it with pink blankets and teddy bears.

I remember Moses came in one day when I was pregnant with Francine with this mobile hanging from his hands. It was blue with footballs, basketballs, and baseballs hanging from the strings.

"Moses, remember, the doctor reckoned it was a girl because I'm carrying high."

"Yeah, I know," he said with a smile on his face. "That doesn't mean he's right, and even if he is, she can be an athlete. I got a good feeling about this one. She might even get a full scholarship."

"Look at you, already worrying about college tuition."

"Every time you have a baby, you have to think about it. We want our girls to know they can be anything they want to be. This is the seventies!"

So we put the mobile above Francine's bed, and sure enough, here she was playing ball and running track.

Moses seemed to have some extra sense when it came to his girls. I remember one day the house got suddenly quiet, and it was him who jumped out his seat and ran upstairs. "Girls, what're you doing up here?" he called. "What's all this quiet going on?" True to his senses, Joanna and Gracey and Francine had their bottle of paste and some watercolor pictures in hand, trying to put wallpaper on the walls.

Oh, you should have heard him that day. First he yelled and made the girls cry, and then he laughed and made the girls giggle, and then I think he pretended to cry and the girls came and crowded on top of him, patting his back like a baby to make him feel better.

Now here I was, about to be a grandma. Who would have imagined it? I was just getting hold of being a mother, and here come another baby. Maybe this time I could get it right from beginning to end.

Lately, everywhere I went, I saw mothers . . . pushing strollers with their groceries stuffed in the pocket at the bottom or sitting in McDonald's dipping french fries in the little ketchup cup for their toddlers. There were mothers on elevators pulling frisky hands back before they pressed all the buttons, mothers on the bus talking about life with their teenagers—the latest singer, the latest miniskirt, is a French kiss really from France. I'd burst out laughing when I heard that one.

I stopped off at a lady's boutique, Elegance by Design, and filled out an application to be a salesperson. The manager wasn't too impressed when she found out I didn't have any experience, but when I complimented a customer on a dress she'd tried on and suggested a nice little silk scarf to wear across the shoulders, she hired me on the spot. I had filled out other applications earlier too—the library, the school office, the local Walgreens. None of them were places I had a mind to work at.

A young girl in a pink camouflage outfit flashed by me, chasing a boy down the street in laughter. When she caught up to him, they wrestled back and forth until he tickled her to the ground.

I had to say, Gracey shocked me when she came home from her date, telling me the problems I had she don't have. Every woman had these problems if they really liked a guy, unless they were so hand in hand with God that nothing moved them and even then, it was some real swaying going on. And I was sorry, but I didn't think that was the case with Gracey.

I stopped off at the ice-cream parlor on the way home. I had a taste for some butter pecan.

The thirty-something manager wiped down the table by the window and pulled out a chair for me to sit down. "Where you been?" he asked with a welcoming smile. "I've missed you. Chocolate sundae again?"

"No, just a scoop of butter pecan today. Keep it simple." I turned my head to the window and looked straight at the bench where I had seen Micah. I wondered if he would show up again today with his young girlfriend.

My friend handed me the cone and went back behind the counter. He looked my way and cleared his throat. "So you, uh . . . you seein' anybody?"

"No, not right now. I'm still trying to get my life in order."

"Oh yeah," he said. "I feel ya there. Me too. I mean, look at me. I work in an ice-cream parlor, and I still live with my mother."

I dug into my ice cream. That was more information than I needed to know. The first bite made me grin. It didn't take much to make me happy.

When I got up to leave, the manager came out to say goodbye. "Hey, you wouldn't want to go out sometime, would you?"

I shook my head politely. "No."

I could see him thinking, trying to come up with a reason to convince me to say yes.

"You're just not my type," I finally said.

He backed away, hands out, retreat-style. "Well . . . come back soon."

I waved goodbye and stood outside, looking toward the bench. Waiting. I gave myself ten seconds. Ten . . . nine . . . eight . . .

I turned to walk away and gave myself a little slap. What was I doing, anyway? Was I sick? Looking for the man who took advantage of me, got me pregnant? After all I'd been through, how could I still be looking for him?

Maybe I needed professional help, or maybe I needed Micah rehabilitation treatment. Since I didn't know how to get hold of either, I stepped into a Catholic church for the first time in my life. The church was a royal building with great big murals spread across the walls and half-naked wilting people posing as angels. Statues of saints stood in front of different stations where I just knew people lit candles as prayers for their loved ones.

I lit one for Moses, even though I knew he was in heaven safe and sound. Maybe the Lord would sprinkle a little more blessing on him. Eventually a man came up and led me down a long, narrow, dark hall to a little room. I sat there looking forward, a window on the right side of my head.

I cleared my throat. "I've sinned," I said.

The little door slid open, and I jumped.

"You are not Catholic?"

"No." How'd he know?

"Yes. Go on."

"Um, well, I found myself looking for the man who took advantage of me and got me pregnant while I was still married to my husband."

"Did you want to hurt him?"

"No, I didn't want to hurt him. I just wanted to see him. I thought I saw him with another woman, and I felt, I don't know, jealous, angry, or something."

There was silence between our walls.

"Do you love him?"

"No, but I used to. But it wasn't right. He wasn't the one for me. I just got caught up on what could have been, and that's how I ended up pregnant."

"So now you know that what could have been was never meant to be."

"Yes."

"Then you must never look for him again."

"But what if I do?"

The priest raised his voice. "Then pray. Deny yourself. Remember 2 Timothy 1:7, God has not given you a spirit of fear, but of power, love, and a sound mind."

"Oh, help, Lord." I lowered my head.

"I absolve you from your sins in the name of the Father and of the Son and of the Holy Spirit."

The door closed.

I had to get Micah off my mind once and for all. Maybe going to church Sunday would help wipe away the whispers of what happened under that tree. The priest was right—I should never have looked for him, and if I couldn't control my feelings, then I'd just have to bury them and act like they weren't there. Maybe I would have to pray and fast too—either that or beat my heart with a stick.

▮ ▮ ▮

At four o'clock, I went to Francine's track meet. With a bag of popcorn and a Diet Pepsi in hand, I was standing in the aisle trying to find my child in a field of children jumping over hurdles, plunging themselves into the sand, and sending long sticks with pointy ends sailing through the air.

"Charlotte, over here! Over here, Charlotte!" It was Mama, waving.

I waved back with a smile, but inside I was thinking, *What's she doin' here?* Trying to win my children over so they'll never love me like a mother, no doubt.

I made my way over to her and sat down. "I didn't expect to see you here."

"Yeah, ol' Grandma gets around every once in a while." Mama clapped her hands and yelled out, "Leave 'em in the dust, Frankie! You can do it!"

My eyes were squinting hard, trying to find Francine on the field with all those kids, but I didn't want to ask Mama. *Lord, show me where she is.*

I looked again, and there was Francine, stretching her legs on the sidelines. She looked up at the sound of Mama's voice and waved. When she saw me, she widened her smile and waved even wilder. I blew her kisses, and she went back to stretching and jogging in place. She looked so cute in her little jogging suit.

I cleared my throat to mess with Mama. I had to make sure she stayed off my turf. "So how many meets you been to?"

"I don't know, maybe five, six."

"How come you never invited me to come?"

"Don't know. Seems kind of strange, asking your daughter to go to her own daughter's meet with you. I figured you the one should be asking me to come. Besides, you got your own little world going on, what with all the job hunting you been doing. I figured you too busy to come."

She'd said it like she thought looking for a job was selfish. But I shrugged off the jab. Somebody had to be the adult. "I found a job, at a boutique. I don't work on Friday nights or Saturdays, so I should be able to come."

"Well, congratulations," Mama said dryly. "Don't make me no mind, s'long as you bringing in some money and you ain't doing nothing crazy."

I took a mental shovel and threw her words out like she never spoke them and kept to the subject. "You didn't tell me about the meets because you wanted to keep Francine all to yourself."

Mama raised an eyebrow and snorted. "Oh, come on! Frankie always says, 'Mom, I have a meet today' or 'Mom, I have a game today.' And all you ever do is pat her on the shoulder and tell her to have a good time. When she comes back, you don't ask her how she did, did they win, nothing."

"Well, that's because I never thought to. It just didn't cross my mind. She's never said, 'Mom, will you come and watch?'"

"And you call yourself a mother." Mama shook her head. "What kind of brain do you have where showing up to your own child's meet doesn't cross your mind?"

Oh, Lord, I thought, *I can't take this.* I opened the flap in my purse and looked at what I'd scribbled down on a piece of paper from the Scripture I heard earlier. "Power, love, sound mind." Focusing on Francine, I said those three words over and over. "Power, love . . ."

Mama must have heard me, because she got this guilty look on her profile and changed her tune. "Listen, I'm sorry about all what I said. I didn't mean nothin' by it."

"I forgive you," I said. But I didn't turn to look at her. Soon as I let my guard down, she'd punch me again anyway, so I just stayed tight.

Francine was up next. She stripped off her jogging suit down to some mini shorts and a T-shirt with no sleeves.

The girls lined up at their numbers. Frankie was in the middle lane, staggered behind three other girls. They knelt down with their behinds up and their hands on the ground, still as the air around them. And then *pow* went the gun, and the girls were off. Everybody was standing up screaming, including me.

"Come on, Frankie! Come on! You can do it! Kick their butts, girl, go, go, go!"

I screamed and screamed until she crossed that finish line. When she won, I let out the loudest "That's my baby" ever yelled.

All the parents turned and looked at me till Mama pulled the back of my sweater and made me sit down. "Don't embarrass the girl."

Francine looked up and gave us the *Rocky* victory wave and then jumped right into the arms of a boy in a gray jogging suit, who picked her up and swung her around. They walked together to where the coach stood waiting to give her a high five.

"Who's that boy?"

"I guess that's her friend. I don't know." Mama sighed, annoyed.

"Well, maybe we should find out."

"I'm tellin' you, Charlotte, you think Gracey gave you a mouthful, you better leave that one alone. Frankie's a firecracker if ever there was one."

"Oh no, Francine wouldn't treat me like that. We have a special relationship. She just started sleeping in her own room not too long ago. Before that, she was right with me every night."

"All right, but don't say I didn't warn you . . . Ms. Mama."

She thought I didn't know my own girls? I knew Francine was a firecracker. I'd known that from the time she put Gracey's Barbie doll in the oven and turned it up to 300 degrees when she wouldn't let her play with it. But she's always shown respect for me.

I went down to the field to talk to her. She was so happy. She ran and gave me a big hug.

"Did you see me, Mom? Did you see how fast I was? I was this close to breaking my own record!" She made an inch with her fingers.

"Yeah, I saw you out there, honey. You did real good. Who's that boy who hugged you?"

"Oh, that's just my friend, Liam."

"He looked like more than a friend to me."

"Oh, Mom, come on! This is the twentieth century. Girls and boys are much friendlier than they were back in your day, when you couldn't touch each other ever. We hug when we see each other. We show our support. Girls too. Nobody thinks anything of it. Hey, thanks for coming."

Francine was looking toward the exit, where I could see Mama walking out.

"Grandma's already gone. She knows I always go with the team to BK after a meet."

"Oh, well, I'll see you later then."

"Yeah."

Mama was waiting for me outside, nosy as ever. "What she say?"

"Nothing."

"Oh yes she did. I can tell by the look on your face. What she say?"

"She's so grown. I feel like I've missed ten years instead of months."

"Take it from me, honey, some days you can't get back. Days that seem to change your children overnight, days you just wish you had been there to witness a moment and maybe even mold it before it hardened like a rock."

I stopped in my tracks. "You go on and take the bus, Mama. I'll be home soon."

"Suit yourself."

CHAPTER 34

Gracey
April 1988

MY INSIDES WERE TINGLING WHEN I woke up on the morning we were supposed to go to church, and there was a crackling in the air like the day already knew how it was going to go. I was scared, straight up. My heart pounded, and for a minute I didn't even have the guts to put my feet on the floor. And for good reason too. This day could change my life forever. I planned to join the church at the end of service and walk up to my grandfather in front of everybody and tell him that he was my long-lost grandpa. And then he'd have this shocked look on his face and the whole congregation would start cheering as he hugged me tight, engulfing me with his robe. He'd say something like, "Welcome to the family, baby girl." And I'd be like, "Thank you so much. I already love you, Grandpa." And if for some reason that didn't work, I'd treat him like a pop star after a concert and try to find him backstage. I hadn't figured out yet how I could ditch Grandma and them, but I knew I'd think of something.

Come on, come on. Get up, you can do it. Just get up. I tried to help myself by propping myself up with my pillow, but all I did was pull my knees to me and hide behind them.

"What's with you?" Francine stared at me like I'd fallen off my rocker.

"Nothing. I was just trying to get myself psyched up for church."

"What's the big deal? We'll go, pass notes, doodle on the program, take a catnap, and come home."

"Yeah, I guess."

"This whole thing was your idea, wasn't it?"

"Well, yeah, but now I wish I hadn't said anything."

"Whatever. Don't be indecisive. It's not becoming."

We got there a little late because we got off at the wrong stop. Hinsdale was our stop, not De La Soul Street. And we knew that, but everyone just kept arguing like dry leaves in a windstorm, and we weren't paying attention. It took Grandma's big mouth to make us be quiet once we started walking. She turned right around and said, "All y'all stop this bickering. You gettin' on my last nerve."

And so we did, not because she said anything so powerful, but because we knew if we didn't stop, she was going to snap in front of all the other folks walking, dressed in their Sunday best, and we didn't want to get embarrassed.

Bethel AME church was huge; the choir loft alone could have filled the average church. I'd never seen so many Black people in one place at one time. All the seats were packed, and everyone was rockin' to "Goin' up Yonder" and clapping their hands. Francine started bouncing as soon as she heard the beat.

The usher gave us a once-over and led us all the way to the fourth row. He made everyone move their belongings and scooch closer together.

"Thank you," I told the man. Because I really needed to be able to see. And I made sure I sat at the end in case I needed to make a quick entry to the pulpit for an introduction.

I wouldn't have a problem standing in front of the church today: my hair was together because I'd gotten it done earlier in the week, my clothes were nice, and I'd put on foundation for the first time to cover up my pimples. Joanna said it was a bit too dark for my skin, but when I looked in the mirror, I liked what I saw. Smooth flawless skin, just like a fashion model.

After all the prayers and announcements and the Scripture reading, out came this regal old man in a big, flowing, white robe. His hair was more salt than pepper, his walk was like a lion's prowl, and his voice was deep and raspy. Seemed like he had that grandpa care about him, the way he looked at everyone as he spoke.

Every time he glanced my way, I put on a big smile and straightened my back to let him know I was listening. I loved this church. I didn't even pass notes with Francine and them, and I didn't take a stick of Juicy Fruit gum or butterscotch candy when it was passed down the aisle.

I tried to get Bishop Richards to notice how much of me was just like him. But I don't think he saw me any different from the boy in front of me. He was adorable and kept yelling, "Amen, Pastor, amen!" And his mother kept elbowing him to be quiet, but it just made him laugh.

Great. How was the preacher going to notice me? I had to think about this one real hard. I wish I remembered what he preached about, but I didn't really listen until the music started at the end, and that was 'cause it moved me from within.

The pastor walked down from the pulpit and spoke to us like we were his friends. "I tell you what, there's something to seeing a person all the way through a thing." He put his finger on his chin. "Sarai stayed with Abram, Noah's wife stayed with him, Adam stayed with Eve, Rachel stayed with Jacob . . . Makes you think God expects us to stay together through thick and thin."

By the time he finished, the organ stopped, and the piano drifted in between the silences of people's sighs and groans of agreement. I looked around at the women tracing their bottom lids with the tips of their fingers, and I forced myself to stay focused, still trying to figure out how to get noticed. A woman screamed in the back of the church, and the ushers ran to her side to console her. God knows I wasn't about to pretend to get the Holy Ghost like that.

Then I decided to stick to the Operation Meet My Dad plan, as embarrassing as it may come to be. The music changed from a somber melody, like a chisel lightly chipping away at the crust around the soul, to a pretty, escalating song filled with hope, like a dry brook filling with water.

"Now is the time to give your life to the Lord. Do you want the rewards of Mary? Do you want to be rewarded for your dedication to Jesus? Come on, give your life to him and let him take care of you like he did his mama. Let him deliver you like he did Mary Magdalene. Won't you come?" The bishop walked to the other side of the pulpit and looked out. "Won't you come?"

I smoothed my skirt and took a deep breath to get up and give my life to Jesus, and wouldn't you know it—Joanna gets up with tears streaming down her face and walks to the front.

I couldn't believe it. She ruined the whole thing.

The choir started singing "I Surrender All," and the pastor put his arms around Joanna as if he wanted to show her off.

"Look at this girl, look at her. If she can stand up in front of all these people, you can too. Ain't no shame in her game. It's not too late, come on."

The ushers came up and stood beside Joanna. I inspected my nails for chips in my nail polish while deciding what I was going to do, and the next thing you know, Grandma had stood up and hop-sticked herself on up there. The whole congregation started clapping. I looked over to my mom, who was standing there with hands clasped over her heart, and to Francine, who was blowing tiny bubbles with her Juicy Fruit and watching like she was knee-deep in a movie.

Then the best thing in the world happened to me. The bishop, my grandpa, looked at our row and called us all up to the pulpit to stand next to him.

He sees me! He sees me! It's a miracle!

"This is what it's all about, y'all. Praise the Lord! This is what Jesus called us to do. What difference does it make if somebody comes up to you in the desert and asks for a drink of water, and you say, 'Jesus loves you'? No, you got to give that man, that woman some water and *then* say Jesus loves you. Amen?"

"Amen," the congregation answered.

"We're giving out drinks of water today." He turned to us and said, "Repeat after me, 'Jesus.'"

"Jesus," the whole congregation answered. I almost fell over. He took the whole church through the sinner's prayer, whether they were already saved or not. I found myself going through the motions of repeating the words, and then I thought about what they meant. Like did I really need salvation? Wasn't I already in good with God? I felt whole most days, sort of.

Then I thought about it. No, I was like a body trapped in a broken mirror. Nothing fit together, and I was constantly trying to figure me out. *Make me whole, Jesus.* I said it again, and I meant it.

Bishop Grandpa interrupted the song for the benediction. He raised one hand in the air to bless the people, and Mom kept hold of Joanna's hand.

"May God bless you and keep you. May God lift your spirits and sustain you. May God help you to go about each day with peace and love permeating your heart for the good of all. Amen. Go in peace, my brothers and sisters."

At the end of the service, all kinds of people came up to us, hugging and kissing on us. I kept looking back to see if the bishop was free, but there were so many people around him, like he was a superstar. I thought he'd at least go to the back and shake everybody's hand as they left, but he never did. After a while, he just disappeared out the back.

I panicked. "Think quick, Gracey, come on!"

"S'cuse me?" someone asked.

"Uh, nothing." I didn't know I'd spoken out loud. I ran back to my seat and put into action part two of the plan—I stuck my purse under the pew.

We trickled out of the church like a flowing river into different facets and streams. Everyone was talking and laughing, shielding the sun from their eyes. Kids were chasing each other in their Sunday bests made up of colorful dresses with bobby socks or slacks and V-neck vests . . . but I was in another world.

"Gracey, you all right? You look like you're a million miles away." That was my mom.

"Yeah, I'm fine," I said. "So do you think we can come back some-time, like next week or something?"

We were standing at the bus stop waiting when I yelled the word *action* in my head. I looked around bewildered, like *The Cosby Show*'s Vanessa on a very bad day. "I think I left my purse," I said.

Mom and Grandma gave each other funny looks.

"Well, go on back in the church and look for it then. And hurry up!" Grandma said.

I didn't want anything to ruin the day, but I had to do this thing, and I didn't care to make everybody wait a little longer for my peace of mind. At first, hesitation kept me. I hated that feeling you get when you walk into an empty classroom that was once full of all your friends playin' and hangin' out. Or when you go to a slammin' party and then you have to run back in to make a phone call because your ride is late and all the adult people have started throwing away paper plates and Styrofoam cups. I braced myself and went in.

There were a few people standing around in little clusters. Ushers collected the programs from the pews. My heart dropped as I just tried to keep the good of the service in my mind. I ran to where I'd been seated and knelt down to look under the chair. Nothing. The plan was working. I asked an usher if she'd seen my purse, and she pointed me in the direction of the secretary's office.

I went to the back of the church and came to a glass window with a lady behind it, talking on the phone. "Excuse me, is this the secre-tary's office?" I knocked on the glass.

The lady looked up from the phone with an attitude, and then it turned into a smile. "Oh, hi, you the new girl with the family. How you doin'?"

"I'm fine."

"It was such a blessing to have y'all here today. How can I help you?"

"Um, they told me my purse might be back here?"

The lady turned and spoke to me like I was a little girl. "Uh-huh. We found a purse. You want to tell me what it looks like?"

I heard a loud laugh behind her, and then the raspy, booming voice of the bishop came through. He was on the phone. "Man, I tell you what, you bring that golf game to Mississippi, I'll teach you a thing or two." Then after a pause, he laughed so hard he started coughing.

"Is that the bishop?" I asked, knowing darn well it was.

"Yup, that's my father. Now, you goin' tell me about that purse, or should I just leave it for somebody else?"

"Oh, um, it's small and black with a long strap so I can carry it sideways, like this." I made a horizontal line from my right shoulder to my left hip.

"Very good. There you go, honey." She handed me the purse.

"Thanks," I said. I started to leave, but my feet kind of just stuck to the ground. "So you're the bishop's daughter?"

"Yes." She looked a little annoyed now, but I just kept going.

"Um, well, do you know Micah Richards?"

"That's my stepbrother. How d'you know him?"

Oh, God, I never practiced this part. What should I say? I put my head down and outlined the linoleum with my toe.

She studied my face closely and sat back in her chair. "Let me guess. You think he's your daddy?"

"Well, yeah, that's what my mom told me." I answered her stare.

"Daddy," she called calmly. "Daddy, you'd better get off the phone and come here."

He hung up the phone and came out looking concerned, wrinkles deep around his eyes, disheveled eyebrows—we didn't have as much in common as I thought.

"What is it? What is it, baby girl?" he asked.

She pointed to me. "Here's another one."

"What?" He leaned toward me and looked closely. "You're my son's daughter."

"Yes, sir."

He took his reading glasses off and tried to focus. "Come on in the office."

Closing the door, he motioned for me to sit on the opposite side of him at his desk. "You ever meet him?"

"No, sir."

He relaxed his stance. "You want to meet him, don't you?"

"Yes, sir."

"So you can have a relationship with him and know what it's like to have a real father?"

"Well, no. I mean, yes. I mean, I know what it's like to have a real father, and he was great. It's just that he died. And then I found out—"

"Uh-huh. Listen, darlin'. I'd be glad to let you meet your father, but I'll tell you—it might not make you feel any better. You're the third child that's come through here in the last five years. We've had lawsuits and out-of-court settlements, and to tell you the truth, I'm real tired of defending him. I'm seventy-four years old. I done got too old for this. You want a grandfather, I can be that for ya. I got a great big old family and plenty of love to go around. You're welcome any time you want to come over. You can meet the whole family and even your other half brothers and sister. Y'all favor each other."

"Oh." I looked around the room to keep from crying. The moment wasn't going or feeling as great as I'd expected. I didn't really know what to do next. Part of me was like, I have brothers, like boys who might be nice to me and watch out for me cause they want to and we share DNA? The other part of me was like, what if the people in the family don't like me? That receptionist auntie had an attitude problem. Who had time for that mess?

Bishop Grandpa leaned forward in his chair with his eyes looking into my soul. "You all right, darlin'?"

I had to move past the pain in my throat to speak. "Yes, sir." I sniffed. "I'm fine. Well, thanks. Maybe I'll see ya around." I stood abruptly and he stood to walk me out.

"You should come back to church, let us get to know you."

"Maybe," I said, knowing he just saw me as another member to add to his congregation.

And with that, I was out of there. I knew I didn't want to come back into the church. I was so dumb to leave my purse. I slapped myself on the way out.

"Hey there, granddaughter?" Bishop Grandpa called. "What's your name?"

"Gracey." I turned around, annoyed.

"Gracey. It's nice to meet you." He bowed his head. "I meant what I said about coming back. This ain't no promised land, that's for sure, but it'll do."

"Yeah," I said, but I meant no. "I'll think about it" trickled out.

And then I walked on. If he really cared, the first thing he would have asked me was my name, and how old I was, and who my mother was, and where I was from, and how I came to be there. Over and over this man proved that he didn't care anything about me. Promised land or not, I would take a pass on that.

When I got back to the bus stop, everybody was still buzzing from the service, waiting patiently, except Grandma.

"Girl, where you been? We had to let two buses pass us by. And I'm as hungry as a lioness. I got a big meal waiting in the oven."

"Sorry, I was just talking to some of the people."

Mom and Grandma exchanged looks again.

"About what?"

"Um, about the history of the church, you know, how things used to be and how they are now. This church sure has grown a lot over the last couple of years."

"Yeah, that's what I hear," Grandma said.

The bus finally came, and we all went home to a big meal. Hank met us there. He believed in God, but he didn't go to church. He had the usual excuse—too many hypocrites.

For dinner we had baked chicken steeped in gravy, mashed potatoes, green beans, corn on the cob, and rolls. Grandma said Hank had high cholesterol, so she didn't want to feed him anything too salty or greasy.

"Y'all have a good day at church?"

"We did. You shoulda been there," Grandma said, shaking a healthy portion of salt on her chicken. "We had ourselves a good old time, didn't we?" She smiled around the table and gave us a look. She was up to something.

"Yes . . . Mm-hmm. . . Real nice," we all answered, raising our eyebrows and nodding our heads.

Hank put down his fork. "What?"

We shrugged our shoulders.

"What? Somethin' happen today?"

"No," we said together.

"Yes, it did. What, y'all went and got saved, didn't you?" Hank was waiting to hear, slowly shaking his head back and forth.

"Uh, excuse me. Some of us were already saved. We just needed to get right with the Lord," Grandma said in a flirty tone.

"Uh-huh." Hank picked his fork back up and started eating again. He looked thoughtful.

"So I was thinking, Hank," Grandma said. "We ought to just go ahead and make ourselves legit in the eyes of God."

Hank's fork fell into his plate again, but this time we had our noses all up in the conversation. My problems went out the window real quick. Francine's mouth was wide open, her eyes expectant. I couldn't tell if Mom was breathing or not. Nothing on her was moving.

Hank looked around at all our faces. "Iona, I don't think now is the time to talk about this."

"Why not?"

"'Cause—"

"'Cause what?"

"Doggone it, woman! I asked you to marry me long time ago, and you said no. So I got used to the idea of living this way, and I have to say I like it right well. We got a nice groove going."

There was a gasp at the table, and all of us covered our mouths. Francine let out a big "Oh, gross," but the rest of us were cool. Although I did kind of lose my appetite.

Grandma put her napkin down and kindly said, "You ain't getting no more milk without buying the cow. I told you I was gettin' right with God."

"Oh, all right, Ona. Don't start boiling over. I ain't got no problems marrying you."

"Then propose."

"What?"

"You heard me, Hank. Propose to me, now."

"Ona, you must have gone and lost your mind. Can't we talk about this in private?" Hank had both his hands midway in the air, begging for mercy.

"Nope," she said, both hands flat on the table. "This is one wrong I want to right in front of my family and God, now!"

Mom stared at the clock behind Grandma's head. I wondered what she was thinking.

Hank pushed himself out of his chair and stood up, slamming his napkin on the table. "You know what, lady, you think you can tell me what to do, treat me like your little servant. All I want to know is"—he walked around the table and got in her face—"do you want to marry me or not?"

Then he got on one knee and pulled a ring out of his navy blue pants pocket. "'Cause, Iona, I'd be honored if we could spend the rest of our years on this earth together."

"Oh, snap, he had the ring in his pocket the whole time!" Francine yelled out.

"Of course I did." Hank never took his eyes off Grandma. "Iona, when I wake up in the morning, I get excited to face the day 'cause I know me and you goin' to work together. And when the weekend come, I feel bad 'cause I got to wait till six o'clock bingo 'fore I see you again. And I'm tired of just acting like your best friend to keep your family in the dark. I love you, woman, and I want all of you."

"Ah, Hank, you know I ain't sentimental." Grandma had her head turned away from his face, and then she swatted him on the head with her napkin. "Get up and give me a kiss. 'Course I'll marry you."

He got up and kissed her, and we were clapping up a storm. Even Mom had to fight back a tear or two.

That night Hank didn't leave till about nine o'clock. It was hard to see him in our house for so long. Maybe he figured engagement gave him a license to hang, but to me it was nerve-racking. I spent most of my time in the kitchen with the radio off, just trying to think things through.

Maybe the Lord did me a big favor by giving me Moses as a dad. At least he cared about me and spent time with me. That Micah dude never even came looking for me, and who knows how many babies he didn't stick around for. There was something wrong with him. God must have known I didn't need nobody like him in my life, and Mom didn't neither. *Shoot.*

I gave the cabinet a big kick and yelled "Ouch!" Then I covered my mouth. I didn't want to have any heart-to-hearts with anyone right now. I felt like I wanted to cry but I couldn't, and I wanted to scream but I didn't want folks thinking I was crazy.

Other thoughts started crowding my mind: Did Daddy really love me? He always did treat me kind of different. Maybe nobody in the family loved me, that was how come I could be in the kitchen for so long without anybody noticing.

But then I thought about the way Daddy put the word beautiful before our names on them ugly days, and the ocean of love in his eyes that we could swim in without drowning, and I thought, *God loves everybody, even me.* So I just kept saying it over and over, "I am loved, I am loved, like a rose on a slammin' day, I am loved," until finally all them crazy thoughts went away. I didn't come through this much to lose it now. I got out my notebook and wrote.

Dear God,
I'm Gracey, the one who gave my life to you today. I'm sure
you remember me. Anyway, I made a big fool of myself. I went
and schemed behind my mom's back trying to find my real
dad. It didn't work. It's not like I read the Bible all that much,
but in the red letters when the strong women get in trouble,

*they always come and find you and then you kinda patch
things up for them. So I thought I'd give it a try. I'm sorry for
what I did, and so now please smooth things over, like nothing
ever happened?*
    Thanks,
    Gracey

Francine came flying through the door just when I was beginning
to find some peace.

"I been looking all over for you. You seen my pen?"

I looked at the pen I was using. "Yeah, here."

"Thanks." She was about to leave but stopped. "How come it's so
quiet in here?"

"Just wanted some silence, I guess."

She tilted her head to the side like she was listening. "I always need
noise or music. I can't imagine life without it. I might crack or something."

"Yeah, I know what you mean," I said. Then a question popped into
my head. "Did you really get saved today when you were up there?"

"Um." Francine went to the fridge and pulled out a diet cola. "I
don't know. I said the words, but I didn't feel anything."

"I think I had a delayed reaction."

"Yeah," she said. "I can see that."

I sat there and looked at her. I didn't have anything to say, and I
didn't feel like fishing. My little sister looked so mature in that moment and yet so lost. She scratched her ear.

"So, like, how do you know if you're saved if you said the words,
and you believe like they say to, and nothing happens?" she asked.
"What are you supposed to do?"

I shrugged my shoulders. "Keep on livin', I guess."

"Yeah, you know, that's exactly what I plan to do." Then she pointed
to the ceiling. "You might not love me, God, but I love you."

"I'm sure God loves you, Francine."

"Yeah?" She took a big gulp of her cola. "Time will tell."

CHAPTER 35

Charlotte
April 1988

LORD, HAVE MERCY. THIS WASN'T the worst weekend of my life, but it sho' went down in the record books for the scariest. When I got to the church and read the sign on the sidewalk that said Bishop Michael Richards, I almost choked on my gum. It took Mama to keep me from reachin' up and snatchin' that child's hair right out her head. Gracey talked about God like he was the car she needed to get from one destination to another. It was the way we lived our lives for so long that led her to believe that way, to act like God was the social thing to do on Sundays and use him like a vehicle to get to her biological father.

That was what I thought before the sermon, anyway. Before the sermon, I was planning to take Gracey, lock her in a room, throw some pork chops in there every once in a while, and never let her out. But after the sermon, I was a little more civilized. I could see things a little easier from her side. Maybe I didn't agree with her, but then again, I wasn't fourteen going on thirty-eight.

Mama was real good to me that day. She told the girls to walk on ahead, then she lowered her voice and gave me the plan.

She said, "Girl, don't you let your daughter get the upper hand on you. You make a big deal out of this, and she liable to make a fool out of all of us in the middle of the service. You know what teenagers are like, selfish as a two-year-old baby reachin' for his mama's breast in the middle of a crowd. They don't care." She used her hands to lay out the plan like I was in a boxing match. "Now, all you got to do is act like you don't know a thing, and then it's all on her. You understand?"

I wiped my forehead with my white pressed handkerchief. "I guess so."

She was right too. It turned out to be one of those days you never want to forget. When I saw Joanna go up there, baby and all, giving her life back to Jesus, well, let's just say, I could have danced awhile.

That night I sat in the chair next to her bed.

"I seen you in the Elegance boutique the other day," Joanna started in. She was lying in her bed, looking away toward the window. "You looked real pretty."

"Thanks, I was trying to get a job. They hired me."

"Yeah?"

"Yeah. Sometimes you just got to show them."

"Probably didn't hurt that you look so nice."

"Looks ain't everything, honey."

"If I was as pretty as you, I never would have gotten pregnant."

"Why you say that?"

"'Cause I would have believed that more than one person could love me."

"Oh, girl, if you really knew how pretty you were, you'd have to get a calendar for all the dates you'd have. You got to know yourself and love yourself. Men love confidence, honey. They can't get enough of it."

"I ain't got nothing to be confident about. My life has been a living hell. You don't know the half of it, Mom. My grades fell, I smoked weed, I passed a few brown envelopes so Gracey would shut up." She paused, expecting me to say something. "And then I fell in love with a jerk and got pregnant."

I suspect I was the only person she told that to, and I wasn't going to judge her for it, not one bit. "You know what?" I said, feeling the space to share. "When I was real little, I had a dream about angels in my room, talking."

Joanna rolled over and looked at me. "Really? What were they talking about?"

"Well, they talked about children and how they saved this one from getting electrocuted or that one from falling off the roof. One time I accidentally whispered *whoa* to one of their stories, and they all stopped. One of them looked at me and smiled. And I tell ya, I'll never forget that smile. It lit up the whole room with a golden glow. And then one spoke right to me, but I couldn't hear a thing.

"I tried to motion to him that I couldn't hear him. I told him I wanted to hear. He smiled again and nodded his head. And within seconds they all disappeared. But the room was crackling, so I knew they were still there, and there came this soft voice, 'We'll be here for your children too.'"

Joanna chewed on her lip, stewing on the thought.

"I couldn't believe it. I couldn't even imagine myself with children. I was just a little girl. But I never forgot that day. I really do believe the angels were there watching over me, but that was the only time I ever dreamed about them."

"Maybe God sent angels to watch over us in that house."

I nodded. "I'm almost sure they were there. Even on the scariest nights."

"It's good to know we weren't alone."

"I left you, Joanna, and I wish to God I hadn't, but you were never alone."

❙ ❙ ❙

The next morning when I woke, I said a prayer for Gracey and her search for where she belonged and found a way to hang my anger on a coatrack.

I headed downstairs for a cup of coffee to ward off the leftover bits of frustration hanging on. As I lifted the pot, the phone rang. I almost didn't answer it, but I figured I needed somebody to interrupt my thinking.

"Charlotte, how you doin', girl?"

"Candi! I was just thinkin' about you."

"Listen, honey, I'm calling to tell you something. I been keeping an eye on your house for you, going to collect your mail and all. You know you haven't paid your taxes in months."

"I know. I been saving up. I was going to pay it soon as I could."

"Well, there's more. Somebody broke into it and stole the furniture. I don't even know how they got that piano out of there with the neighborhood watch."

"Oh my. It's been all I could handle to get my life together here. I should have thought to put an alarm on the house."

"Well, I been wondering. Since the place me and Miss Nelda are in is pretty small, I was thinking maybe I could buy the house off you. Me and her, we could go in on it together, me payin' the lion's share, of course."

"Candi, I don't know. This is all so sudden. I need to think about it."

"Charlotte, listen to me. That house is falling apart. It's an eyesore on the block, and neighbors are complaining. This is actually the third time it's been broken into, and Miss Nelda's nephew said it's getting harder and harder to keep the squatters away."

"How much you thinking of giving me for it?"

"I can only give you ten thousand, 'cause it'll take another fifteen grand to refurbish it. And then I have to install a mechanical stair lift to the stairs, another couple thousand."

I was silent on the phone. I had to think. *What do I do?*

The void was sweet. I didn't want to hang up without giving her an answer.

I shut my eyes tight and gritted my teeth. "Okay, I'll sell it."

"Oh, thank you, Charlotte! I'm tellin' you, you won't regret it! When you come to visit, you won't even recognize it. I'll get my Realtor to draw up the papers first thing tomorrow and send 'em to you."

"All right."

"Oh, bless you, girl, you don't know what this means to me!"

A few more words, and we hung up. I wanted to talk about my life and what was going on, but it still didn't seem like the right time.

Everything was so upside-down. It was bad enough that I had a daughter who almost embarrassed the daylights out of me, but my own mama was about to get married at the age of . . . of . . . I didn't know how old she was. Sixty something.

She deserved to be happy. To be honest, I'd never really seen her happy. She was always heavy and moody, trying to protect what was hers. She worked, she cleaned, she went to church. And I never seen her bat her eyes at no man, ever. It was like she flicked the love light off the day my father left, shut the windows, and closed the door. And then came Hank.

Truth be told, when I saw how much Hank loved her, I felt a little jealous pang in my gut. I was glad nobody could see it on my face. Thank God for my brown skin. Made me want to holler, what about me? What about what I wanted . . . to love a man with peace of mind and to be loved back as if I were made just for him, like the last two pieces of a jigsaw puzzle.

If Mama could cause all the mess she had and still find love, then why couldn't I? I mean, Moses, God rest his soul . . .

I wouldn't never say it out loud, but sometimes I wondered if we ever did fit.

"Charlotte, what you doin' in here?"

I near leaped outta my skin at Mama standing in the doorway like my jealousy had summoned her.

"Just cleaning up a little." I snatched a cloth and started dusting. "So what kind of wedding you havin'?" I cut my thoughts off before they could run to judgment.

"A small, private church wedding, with a few folks from the school and my family."

"You invitin' the boys?"

"Honey, let me tell you somethin'. Them out-of-sight-out-of-mind people, they ain't family."

"It takes two, you know?"

"That's right, and I did my part. I raised them. Lot of thanks I get."

I let it go. That was a mountain with roots, and my pitchfork wasn't no match to handle it.

"You know, as long as I'm gettin' things right with the Lord," Mama said, "I need to tell you somethin'."

"Oh no." I covered my forehead.

"A couple of years after Gracey was born, I told Moses he wasn't the father."

"You *what*?" A flush of embarrassment poured over me. "Why didn't you tell me?"

"I'm sorry. I just felt like the man ought to know." She shrugged.

"What'd he say?"

"Well, he didn't believe me at first. Then I showed him a picture of you and Micah together in Sunday school, and he saw how much Gracey looked like him, even the dimple."

"Oh, Lord, Mama. How'd he take it? Was he angry? Did he hate me?"

"More than anything, Charlotte, he was hurt. He said he thought you all were close enough to get through anything, and then come to find out you didn't trust him enough to tell the truth."

"Why didn't he say anything to me?"

"Well, I told him to confront you and get it all hashed out, but he said no. Said he respected your decision, and it would just make things worse between you and me."

My mind went back to the time when Moses was acting strange, and then he stopped laughing and joking and he could hardly look at me.

"I can't believe he knew all that and never cheated on me."

"Well, I wouldn't say all that."

My heart sank and fear almost drowned me.

"Rumors are that Moses was going around with one of the women from the school nearby. The girls call her Miss Mabel. You know who I'm talkin' about. One night she took him back to her house. They had the candles goin', the music playin', drinkin' champagne . . . and then he got an achin' in his heart and a burnin' in his arm so bad, he had to go home. And it's a good thing too, 'cause, well, no tellin' what would've happened if they kept goin'."

"And where do you get your sources from, Mama?"

"Miss Nelda."

"What? Why didn't she tell me? Hold on, how'd she know?" I knew Miss Nelda was a gossip, but she had to know somebody that knew somebody to get that kind of information.

"Remember the night her husband, Jack, died?" Mama said lowering her chin and raising a brow. "Word is, the woman—um, Mabel—and Moses was there in the bar all cuddled up."

"Oh, so he saw and . . . no wait, he couldn't have come back and said anything, 'cause he died."

"Right. So what happened was when he saw Moses and Mabel together, honey, he had a stone-cold fit. Came charging after Moses like a bull to a red cape. But you know Moses ain't no fightin' man, some of them other men in there got to piling up on Jack so good, they couldn't tell who killed him with what blow."

"Oh, God, have mercy." I covered my temples with my fingers.

"Hmm, it all came down to who had the most respect. Wasn't about right and wrong that night. The strong won over the weak. Or vice versa, dependin'."

"And nobody told me nothin'? And I was at Miss Nelda's before I left, and she had the nerve to make me go see Mabel and say thank you. Thank you for trying to steal my girls. And no wonder Mabel didn't let me in her house. She must a been feelin' some kind of way."

"Funny thing about our neighbors in Chicago, Charlotte. Everybody thought you were a frail little flower that couldn't take too much sun or too much rain. I used to tell them you was stronger than you looked, but they wouldn't believe me. Maybe 'cause I told them a lot of other things about you that didn't quite line up. Anyway, Miss Nelda said she didn't want to be the one to make you wilt. And neither did I."

"You know what, you all are ridiculous. You should have told me. Things might have turned out different."

"Aww, Charlotte. Folks make their own decisions. And sometimes the consequences are deadly. We didn't want no more trouble. Didn't matter no way, 'cause after that, Moses didn't go see Mabel no more. Said the Lord was trying to tell him to be faithful to the woman of his youth, and that was you."

"Well . . ."

"Well, it worked out in the end. She the one who took your children in when DCFS said they couldn't stay in the house no more."

"I heard the girls talking about her. She was kind to them."

"Mm-hmm. Miss Nelda said they was making phone calls left and right, trying to figure out what to do, then Miss Nelda told Mabel to call me and I'd figure somethin' out. Anyway, that heffa called me, and you know I started to hang up on her and show her I didn't want to have nothin' to do with her and her dirty ways, uh-uh. But instead I told her I was busy and I'd have to call her back, but you know I never did. Finally, Miss Nelda called, told me what was going on, and I said yes, I'd take them. They was my grandchildren. I told her she should have just called me in the first place, but she said she thought it'd be good for me to talk to Mabel. Never did say nothin' to her, even though I knew I owed her. Anyway, I knew I would need some money, so I asked and the government people gave it, and I didn't take no shame for it neither."

"Why was she so kind to my girls?"

"I don't know, Charlotte. Love shows itself different ways. Maybe she knew that was as close as she was ever goin' to get to Moses. Maybe she just loves kids."

"Maybe God found a way to squeeze some good out of a bad situation."

Mama shrugged.

"I can't believe Moses knew."

I I I

In the middle of the night, lying on the couch, I still couldn't believe Moses knew. It was beyond my understanding. To know so much and say so little and to have loved so hard . . . what kind of man was Moses

Downing? Maybe I didn't know him at all. God was trying to show me what true love was all about, and I was so blind, I couldn't see anything but my own little world. One conversation could have changed our entire destiny.

CHAPTER 36

Gracey
May 1988

BEFORE WE KNEW IT, LIFE brought us to the end of spring. One evening, peace followed me into the night as I lay on my bed, naming every noise that ticked my ear: my sister breathing, the couch springs creaking as my mother turned over in the living room, and cards being shuffled and passed out as Grandma and Hank played Old Maid together. To help the baby sleep inside the womb, Miles Davis lightly floated out from under Joanna's door. Then a mockingbird warbled outside my window, and I turned toward it.

"It's been a while," I said, "since you sang outside my window. I suppose you didn't follow me from Chicago."

The bird just kept singing, confident he was loved. I opened my window slowly and sat on the edge, singing his song back as best I could. And soon he started talking back. He would sing and then wait for me to answer. So I'd whistle back and wait. Sometimes a different bird would answer when the one lost focus. We must have talked for a good long while, because the moon moved from where it started, and the shadows in my room grew darker.

I could have slept right there in my window with nature as my lullaby, drifted off and let the warm air fill my lungs without my chest ever lifting, my heart beating with the pulse of the earth. I could have sat there forever, dreaming of lying on hot sand under the boiling sun and the sound of seagulls, when a big wave came and washed over me.

"Y'all, my water broke!" Joanna cried. "The baby's coming!"

CHAPTER 37

Charlotte
May 1988

I WAS HAVING THE MOST restless night. Something was different, and I couldn't figure out what. It was like I was in another realm, another dimension or something. *What is it, Lord?* I prayed. *What's going on?*

I closed my eyes and saw a woman from earlier in the day struggling to get up from the bench at the bus stop. She was bulging with pregnancy, one hand resting on her belly, the other supporting her lower back. The purse on her shoulder brushed up against me. "Excuse me," she said. I should have helped her, made small talk or something.

My spirit wouldn't let me sleep as I thought about that woman. I repented to the Lord and closed my eyes. They popped back open. That wasn't it.

A little lullaby ran through my mind, so I sang it out loud, "Hush, little baby—"

"The baby!" I yelled.

"The baby's coming!" Joanna yelled.

"Jo's in labor." Mama hightailed it up the stairs right behind me. In the rush that followed, Mama took charge. She sent Gracey to fetch hot water and towels, then she quickly washed her hands and tore some sheets into strips, tying them to the bed for Jo to hold on to.

"What are you doing?" I stumbled into Joanna's room. "Mama, we got to call a taxi or an ambulance! She can't give birth here. She's almost a month early." I picked up the phone and dialed 911.

"Oh yes she can," Mama said. She lifted up Joanna's gown and checked to see if she was dilated. "The ambulance can come, but we ain't got no time to be riskin' transportation. Don't want this baby born on the street, do we? Besides, I used to be a midwife. I got plenty of experience."

"You were never a midwife, Mama. I never seen you help nobody, especially a woman in labor."

"I was a midwife, Charlotte. Before your daddy left us. Couldn't handle leavin' y'all for days at a time after he left. Now, you gonna argue with me over this, or you gonna get over here and help your daughter give birth to her baby?"

Joanna let out a big scream. "Please help me!"

I washed my hands and came back to her side. She was panting and sweating—she looked so scared.

Pulling up a chair, I sat right beside her and smoothed the wet strands of hair away from her face. Then I took one of her hands away from the straps and held it in mine with a tight grip.

With every contraction, I was there, bearing her strength and praying that it would be over soon. When she relaxed, I was there to stroke her head and wipe the nape of her neck with a cool towel. I would have given anything to have traded places with her. I would have gladly taken on her pain, would have gladly said, "Here's my whisper for your holler. Here's my ease for your push, my peace for your pain."

A couple of hours later, with the help of a medic team, the baby was born. They whisked him off in an ambulance to the hospital where he stayed for three weeks, continuing to grow. Joanna said she wanted to name him Charlie—that was the only name he answered to when she called him by the ones she had written in her notebook.

He was such a cute little baby, the spitting image of his grandpa Moses, 'cept for the light brown eyes. Those were Chill's, just in case he ever wondered. The girls oohed and aahed over the baby every time they leaned over his incubator. His little body was the size of my wrist and hand together, his skin leaving room for the weight that would soon come. Tubes were taped with wafer-like stickers all over his body, a monitor to his heart.

My little grandson was fighting for his life, and I couldn't help but stick my hands through the little holes and gently rub his precious chocolate marshmallow feet.

Mama was quite proud of her handiwork. She kept saying, "I'm surprised I still remembered everything," and "I can't believe I still knew how to do that." Even the doctor shook her hand and told her she did well.

That newborn nostalgia was all over me. I counted his toes and his fingers, I checked his ears and cuticles to see what his natural color would be, and I lightly touched the soft spot on top of his head, just to see if it still felt like the indent of an overripe peach. He smelled so lovely, I could have held him all night. But I knew him and his mother needed bonding time.

"There's two things you didn't tell me, Mom," Joanna said as she stared into his face. "How much it would hurt, and how much love I'd have for him."

I rubbed her arm gently. "Sweetie, those are two things you can't explain no matter how hard you try."

CHAPTER 38

Gracey
August 1988

MONTHS AFTER THE BABY WAS born, Joanna started night school. We all thought she was crazy, but her goal was to graduate high school in August of the next year. That way she could start college in the fall with all her friends. I didn't know if it was fair that Joanna got to have a baby and not miss a beat, but maybe that was what families were for. I was proud of her.

I had to say, life with a new baby around wasn't nothing like what I had expected. Charlie was up all night long crying and screaming. We had to take turns feeding and walking him just so Joanna could get a little bit of rest. The kid was impossible sometimes. I didn't know how mothers did it on their own. I couldn't take it.

Mom was great with Charlie, though. He could be crying his lungs out, and soon as she got hold of him, he'd lay his little head down on her shoulder. The first time she laid eyes on him, she melted into butter and started talking all that baby talk.

"Ohh, he's so cute. Look at my little sugar plum. Isn't he adorable? You look just like your granddaddy, yes, you do." She wiggled his little toes and fingers and tickled his nose with hers, and then she rocked him and rocked him until he fell asleep in her arms. I didn't think I'd ever seen her look so blessed. Angels smiled down on her, I was sure.

Francine was different. When she found out the baby couldn't talk or crawl, she basically left him alone, except to pinch his cheeks every once in a while, and that made him scream. Every time it was her turn to feed him, she passed him off to someone else, like me.

The only thing I liked doing was rapping lullabies off the top of my head, like, "There's a smile in Charlie and he wants to get it out. But there's a tie in his tummy that's making him pout. So I'll pat and I'll pat and I'll rub his back till all the air in his tummy goes—*pop!*" And then I'd make a popping sound with my lips, and he'd laugh and laugh.

Grandma took the cake, though. One day I walked into the kitchen and found her and Hank trying to teach Charlie gin rummy. They got to arguing over whether or not Hank had cheated, and the baby started crying. No baby talk came from Grandma's mouth—she spoke to him like an adult.

"Oh, stop all that crying, boy. Somebody's got to teach you to be a man growin' up in this house with all these women. And let me tell you something. You got less than one year to get out of them diapers, you hear me?" Then she reached down and kissed his little toes and picked up her cards again.

Hank gave me one of those I'll-never-understand-women looks and shook his head.

Most of all, I loved watching Joanna growing into a great mom. One night after everyone had gone to sleep, I sneaked out and sat right outside her door. She was still playing that Mozart music, but I could hear her talking quietly. I kneeled down to see under the door, and there was Joanna, reading bedtime stories to Charlie under the lamp. She looked at him as if he were the most amazing thing God ever created, as if she couldn't believe he came from her.

Other times I'd listen in when she came home late from school and hadn't had a chance to call. As soon as she burst through the door, she'd run upstairs to check on Charlie and squeeze and hug him till he couldn't hardly catch his breath. If he was sleeping, she'd stand right over his crib and watch the air in his little chest ebb and flow just like the tide on the beach. She loved him in ways I'd never seen a mother love.

And I loved him too. I promised him that, when he got old enough,

I'd teach him how to change a light bulb and unstop a sink. All the things Daddy taught me, I was going to teach him. It was the least I could do. Let Francine teach him all the crazy stuff like how to dig for worms and climb trees to the highest branch without falling out.

I I I

Here in the South, there's been times when it rained while the sun was still shining. There's been all kinds of tales as to why this was so, but I thought it was pretty simple. The Lord was raining down blessings. At least that was what happened last Sunday.

We had five minutes of sunny rain. It was one of those days you just wanted to put in your Most Important Days book. Everyone had gone to the church picnic but me and Mom. We just decided we didn't want to go. We kicked it around the house for a while, but the outside just kept callin' us, what with kids riding up and down the street, little lemonade stands, and the trees clapping so loudly. Finally, we got to the point where we couldn't take looking at another wall.

"Hey, Mom, why don't we go get some ice cream?"

"Sounds good to me, honey."

We went to the parlor and sat in the window eating our identical hot fudge sundaes with sprinkles and whipped cream. A nice view of the park was to the right of us.

I sat there for a while looking at my mom. She was so different from the woman I'd known a year ago. She was like a whole person now. And people loved her. Even sitting in the shop, people kept coming over to talk to her. Something about her made them feel free to chat and share about their lives. But truthfully, I didn't mind. I was proud of her.

I asked her what her favorite color was, and she said, "Peach."

"Mine too," I answered back. "What's your favorite food?"

"Well," she said, turning her body to the side and crossing her legs. "I used to love me some soul food, but lately, I like Italian."

"I like Italian too. I love pizza."

"Yeah, but I was thinking more like shrimp scampi, lasagna, and linguine alfredo."

"I don't know what shrimp scampi is," I said.

Mom took a deep breath. "It's the way they cook it in certain spices, garlic, butter, wine . . ."

My stomach rumbled in appreciation, and Mom laughed. "We'll have to try it sometime."

"What's your favorite song?"

"Hmm. That's hard to say. The songs I like kind of change with my mood. Does that make sense to you?"

"Yeah," I said. It made a lot of sense. "How about TV shows?"

"I'll always love *Fame*."

"Yeah, me too," I said, "for the dancers."

"Not *The Cosby Show*?"

"Not so much these days," I said, kind of happy that my mom wasn't Clair Huxtable. "Okay, one more question," I said, waving my hands like Printess so often did.

Mom sat back and looked at me with a smile. "Go ahead, shoot."

"Do you believe in miracles?"

Mom got all teary-eyed.

"I'm sorry," I said. I grabbed a napkin and gave it to her. "I didn't mean to make you cry."

"It's okay," she managed to say. "Yes. I believe in God and angels"— she stopped and blew her nose before continuing—"and miracles."

I took a breath and sneaked a look around to see if anyone was watching. But my mom, she was unashamed.

"What about you, Gracey? Do you believe in miracles?"

"Yeah." I looked out the window. "Yeah, I do."

There was a man sitting on a bench across the street reading a paper. He was handsome, my complexion, not too hip. He put the paper down and stared right into the window, as if he was trying to figure something out. Then he zeroed in on me.

I looked away.

"You see that man across the street?" Mom pointed.

"Yes."

She waited. "That's your father."

"Oh." That was my answer. *Oh.* All this time, I'd waited for this moment, and I felt nothing inside. Like he was just another man on the street. I looked at him and looked at him. And he stared back at me. Still there was nothing, not in my heart or my mind or my inner, inner parts.

A look. It was the most of a father-daughter talk we'd ever have, and I was cool with that.

After a while he folded his paper, put it under his arm, and walked away.

A couple of steps into the sidewalk, he turned around and looked back. He was looking at Mom.

She took one of those mature-woman breaths and rubbed the goose bumps down on her arms. I looked at her and then at him. There was something in their eyes. A peaceful goodbye maybe, like a tiny sailboat drifting off to sea.

Finally, Mom looked at me. "So, you still want to talk to him?"

I shook my head. "No, it's all good. I'm not ready for him to be a part of my life, and he doesn't want to anyway. Otherwise, he would have walked toward us and not away."

I didn't tell my mom what I saw between them that day. That little bit was none of my business, and the older I got, the more I understood why people kept secrets. I even understood why it was so hard to let them go.

When we left the parlor, Mom started humming "What a Friend," and Miss Nelda came to mind. Suddenly, I felt like a champion . . . like I'd been in a long fight, and finally I got to take home the prize.

ACKNOWLEDGMENTS

SPECIAL THANKS TO MY SON and daughter who always believed I could and never doubted me. Your unconditional love kept me going. Thank you to my mother and her sisters who were also my angels, always around to fill me with love and laughter even in the tough times. Thank you to my father and his brothers for being towers of protection.

Thank you, Phyllis, for being Harriet Tubman and parting the Red Sea; George and Regina, for helping me to see clearly when I made it to the other side.

To Jacob Ross, who pulled the story out of my soul while I sat in his writers' workshop, thank you. To my editor, Janyre Tromp, thanks for being strong enough to push me past the point of stuck. To my agent, Amanda Leudeke, thanks for the faith and patience to journey all this way. To all the women writers and storytellers who inspired me from childhood till now, thank you. It's a learning way.

Finally, thank you, Lucretia Strong, for the moments you suspended your disbelief and trusted your gut.